W9-CNO-633

EPISODE I

THE PHANTOM MENACE™

EPISODE I
THE PHANTOM MENACE™

TERRY BROOKS

BASED ON THE STORY AND SCREENPLAY
BY GEORGE LUCAS

THE BALLANTINE PUBLISHING GROUP
NEW YORK

A Del Rey Book®
Published by The Ballantine Publishing Group

Copyright © 1999 Lucasfilm Ltd. & ™.
All Rights Reserved. Used Under Authorization.

All rights reserved under International and Pan-American Copyright
Conventions. Published in the United States by The Ballantine
Publishing Group, a division of Random House, Inc., New York, and
simultaneously in Canada by Random House of Canada Limited,
Toronto.

Del Rey and colophon are registered trademarks of
The Ballantine Publishing Group, a division of Random House, Inc.

www.randomhouse.com/delrey/
www.starwars.com

Library of Congress Catalog Card Number: 98-96827

ISBN 0-345-42765-3

Interior design by Michaelis/Carpelis Design Assoc. Inc.

First Edition: May 1999

10 9 8 7 6 5 4 3 2 1

To Lisa, Jill, Amanda, & Alex,
the kids who grew up with the story
&
to Hunter,
the first of the next generation

A LONG TIME AGO IN A GALAXY FAR, FAR AWAY....

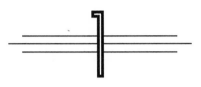

Tatooine.

The suns burned down out of a cloudless blue sky, washing the vast desert wastes of the planet in brilliant white light. The resultant glare rose off the flat, sandy surface in a wet shimmer of blistering heat to fill the gaps between the massive cliff faces and solitary outcroppings of the mountains that were the planet's sole distinguishing feature. Sharply etched, the monoliths stood like sentinels keeping watch in a watery haze.

When the Podracers streaked past, engines roaring with ferocious hunger and relentless drive, the heat and the light seemed to shatter and the mountains themselves to tremble.

Anakin Skywalker leaned into the curve of the raceway that took him past the stone arch marking the entry into Beggar's Canyon on the first lap of the run, easing the thruster bars forward, giving the engines a little more juice. The wedge-shaped rockets exploded with power, the right a tad harder than the left, banking the Pod in which Anakin sat sharply left to clear the turn. Swiftly, he adjusted the steering to straighten the racer, boosted power further, and shot through the arch. Loose sand whiplashed in the wake of his passing, filling the air with a gritty sheen, whirling and dancing through the heat. He ripped into the canyon, fingers playing across the controls, hands steady on the steering.

It was all so quick, so instantaneous. One mistake, one misjudgment, and he would be out of the race and lucky if he weren't dead. That was the thrill of it. All that power, all that speed, just at his fingertips, and no margin for error. Two huge turbines dragged a fragile Pod over sandy flats, around jagged-edged mountains, down shadowed draws, and over heart-wrenching drops in a series of twisting, winding curves and jumps at the greatest speed a driver could manage. Control cables ran from the Pod to the engines, and energy binders locked the engines to each other. If any part of the three struck something solid, the whole of the assembly would collapse in a splintering of metal and a fiery wash of rocket fuel. If any part broke free, it was all over.

A grin split Anakin's young face as he injected a bit more power into the thrusters.

Ahead, the canyon narrowed and the shadows deepened. Anakin bore down on the slit of brightness that opened back onto the flats, keeping low to the ground where passage was widest. If he stayed high, he risked brushing the cliff faces on either side. That had happened to Regga in a race last month, and they were still looking for the pieces.

It would not happen to him.

He shoved the thruster bars forward and exploded through the gap onto the flats, engines screaming.

Sitting in the Pod with his hands on the controls, Anakin could feel the vibration of the engines travel up the control cables and fill him with their music. Wrapped in his rough-made jumpsuit, his racing helmet, his goggles, and his gloves, he was wedged so closely in his seat that he could feel the rush of the wind across the Pod's skin beneath him. When he raced like this, he was never simply the driver of a Podracer, never just an additional part. Rather, he was at one with the whole, and engines, Pod, and he were bound together in a way he could not entirely explain. Each shimmy, each small throb, each tug and twist of strut and tie were apparent to him, and he could sense at any given moment exactly what was happening throughout the length and breadth of his racer. It spoke to him in its own language, a mix of sounds and feelings, and though it did not use words, he could understand everything it said.

Sometimes, he thought dreamily, he could sense what it would say before it even spoke.

A flash of gleaming orange metal shot past him on his right, and he watched the distinctive split-X of Sebulba's engines flare out before him, taking away the lead he had seized through an unusually quick start. His brow wrinkled in disgust at himself for his momentary lapse of concentration and his dislike of the other racer. All gangly and crook-legged, Sebulba was as twisted inside as out, a dangerous adversary who won often and took delight in doing so at the expense of others. The Dug had caused more than a dozen crashes of other Podracers in the past year alone, and his eyes glinted with wicked pleasure when he recounted the tales to others on the dusty streets of Mos Espa. Anakin knew Sebulba well—and knew better than to take chances with him.

He rode the thruster bars forward, fed fresh power to the engines, and rocketed ahead.

It didn't help, he supposed as he watched the distance between them narrow, that he was human or, much worse, that he was the only human ever to drive in the Podraces. The ultimate test of skill and daring on Tatooine and the favorite spectator sport of the citizens of Mos Espa, it was supposed to be beyond the skill and capability of any human. Multiple arms and multi-hinged joints, stalk eyes, heads that swiveled 180 degrees, and bodies that twisted as if boneless gave advantages to other creatures that humans could not begin to overcome. The most famous racers, the best of a rare breed, were strangely shaped, complexly formed beings with a penchant for taking risks that bordered on insanity.

But Anakin Skywalker, while nothing like these, was so intuitive in his understanding of the skills required by his sport and so comfortable with its demands that his lack of these other attributes seemed to matter not at all. It was a source of some mystery to everyone, and a source of disgust and growing irritation to Sebulba in particular.

Last month, in another race, the wily Dug had tried to run Anakin into a cliff face. He had failed only because Anakin sensed him coming up from behind and underneath, an illegal razor saw extended to sever Anakin's right Steelton control cable, and Anakin lifted away to safety before the saw could do its damage. His escape cost him the race, but allowed him to keep his life. It was a trade he was still angry at having been forced to make.

The racers whipped through columns of ancient statuary and across the floor of the arena erected on the edge of Mos Espa. They swept under the winner's arch, past row upon row of seats crammed with spectators cheering them on, past pit droids, repair stations, and the boxes where the Hutts watched in isolated splendor above the commoners. From an overlook in a tower centered on the arch, the two-headed Troig who served as announcer would be shouting out their names and positions to the crowd. Anakin allowed himself a momentary glimpse of blurred figures that were left behind so fast they might have been nothing more than a mirage. His mother, Shmi, would be among them, worrying as she always did. She hated watching him drive in the Podraces, but she couldn't help herself. She never said so, but he thought she believed that simply by being there she could keep him from coming to harm. It had worked so far. He had crashed twice and failed to finish even once, but after more than half a dozen races he was unharmed. And he liked having her there. It gave him a strange sort of confidence in himself he didn't like to think about too closely.

Besides, what choice did they have in the matter? He raced because he was good at it, Watto knew he was good at it, and whatever Watto wanted of him he would do. That was the price you paid when you were a slave, and Anakin Skywalker had been a slave all his life.

Arch Canyon rose broad and deep before him, an expanse of rock leading into Jag Crag Gorge, a twisting channel the racers were required to navigate on their way to the high flats beyond. Sebulba was just ahead, rocketing low and tight across the ground, trying to put some distance between Anakin and himself. Behind Anakin, close now, were three other racers spread out against the horizon. A quick glance revealed Mawhonic, Gasgano, and Rimkar trailing in his strange bubble pod. All three were gaining. Anakin started to engage his thrusters, then drew back. They were too close to the gorge. Too much power there, and he would be in trouble. Response time in the channel was compacted down to almost nothing. It was better to wait.

Mawhonic and Gasgano seemed to agree, settling their Pods into place behind his as they approached the split in the rock. But

Rimkar was not content to wait and roared past Anakin split seconds before they entered the cleft and disappeared into darkness.

Anakin leveled out his Pod, lifting slightly from the rockstrewn floor of the channel, letting his memory and his instincts take him down the winding cut. When he raced, everything around him slowed down rather than sped up. It was different than you'd expect. Rock and sand and shadows flew past in a wild mix of patterns and shapes, and still he could see so clearly. All the details seemed to jump out at him, as if illuminated by exactly what should make them so difficult to distinguish. He could almost close his eyes and drive, he thought. He was that much in tune with everything around him, that much aware of where he was.

He eased swiftly down the channel, catching glimpses of Rimkar's engine exhausts as they flashed crimson in the shadows. Far, far overhead, the sky was a brilliant blue streak down the center of the mountain, sending a frail streamer of light into the gap that lost brilliance with every meter it dropped so that by the time it reached Anakin and his fellow racers, it barely cut the dark. Yet Anakin was at peace, lost deep within himself as he drove his Pod, bonded with his engines, given over to the throb and hum of his racer and the soft, velvet dark that folded about.

When they emerged into the light once more, Anakin jammed the thruster bars forward and streaked after Sebulba. Mawhonic and Gasgano were right behind. Ahead, Rimkar had caught Sebulba and was trying to edge past. The lanky Dug lifted his split-X engines slightly to scrape against Rimkar's Pod. But Rimkar's rounded shell eased smoothly away, unaffected. Side by side the racers tore across the high flats, headed for Metta Drop. Anakin closed on them, drawing away from Mawhonic and

Gasgano. People said what they wanted about Watto—and there was plenty to say that wasn't good—but he had an eye for Podracers. The big engines jumped obediently as Anakin fed fuel into the thrusters, and in seconds he was drawing alongside Sebulba's split-X.

They were even when they reached Metta Drop and rocketed over and tumbled straight down.

The trick with drops, as every racer knew, was to gather enough speed going down to gain time over your opponents, but not so much speed that the racer couldn't pull out of the drop and level out again before it nose-dived into the rocks below. So when Sebulba pulled out early, Anakin was momentarily surprised. Then he felt the backwash of the split-X engines hammer into his Pod. The treacherous Dug had only looked as if he would pull out and instead had lifted away and then deliberately fishtailed atop both Anakin and Rimkar, using his exhaust to slam them against the cliff face.

Rimkar, caught completely by surprise, jammed his thruster bars forward in an automatic response that took him right into the mountain. Metal fragments of Pod and engines careened away from the rock wall in a fiery shower, leaving a long black scar along the ravaged surface.

Anakin might have gone the same way but for his instincts. Almost before he knew what he was doing, at the same instant he felt the backwash of Sebulba's engines slam into him, he lifted out of his own descent and away from the mountain, almost colliding with a surprised Sebulba, who veered off wildly to save himself. Anakin's sudden wrenching of his Pod's steering took him spinning away into the midday, off course and out of control. He pulled back on the steering, eased off on the thrusters, cut the fuel supply to the big engines, and watched the ground rise up to meet him in a rush of sand and reflected light.

He struck the ground in a bone-wrenching skid that severed both control cables, the big engines flying off in two directions while the Pod careened first left, then right, and then began to roll. Anakin could only brace himself inside, spinning and twisting in a roil of sand and heat, praying that he didn't wind up against an outcropping of rock. Metal shrieked in protest and dust filled the Pod's interior. Somewhere off to his right, an engine exploded in a ground-shaking roar. Anakin's arms were stretched out to either side, keeping him squarely placed through the pummeling the Pod experienced as it continued to roll and then roll some more.

Finally, it stopped, tilted wildly to one side. Anakin waited a moment, then loosened his restraining belt and crawled out. The heat of the desert rose to meet him, and the blinding sunlight bore down through his goggles. Overhead, the last of the Podracers streaked away into the blue horizon, engines whining and booming. Silence followed, deep and profound.

Anakin glanced left and right at what remained of his engines, taking in the damage, assessing the work they would need to operate again. He looked finally at his Pod and grimaced. Watto would not be happy.

But then Watto seldom was.

Anakin Skywalker sat down with his back against the ruined Pod, gaining what small relief he could from its shadow in the glare of Tatooine's twin suns. A landspeeder would be along in a few minutes to pick him up. Watto would be there to chew him out. His mother would be there to give him a hug and take him home. He wasn't satisfied with how things had turned out, but he wasn't discouraged either. He could have won the race if Sebulba had played fair. He could have won easily.

He sighed and tipped back his helmet.

One day soon he would win a lot of races. Maybe even next year, when he reached the age of ten.

Do you have any idea what this is going to cost me, boy? Do you have any idea at all? *Oba chee ka!*"

Watto hovered before him, launching into Huttese without even thinking about it, choosing a language that offered a vast array of insulting adjectives he could draw upon. Anakin stood stoically in place, his young face expressionless, his eyes fastened on the pudgy blue Toydarian hovering before him. Watto's wings were a blur of motion, beating with such ferocity it seemed as if they must surely fly off his lumpy little body. Anakin stifled an urge to laugh as he imagined this happening. It would not do to laugh just now.

When Watto paused for breath, Anakin said quietly, "It wasn't my fault. Sebulba flashed me with his port vents and nearly smashed me into Metta Drop. He cheated."

Watto's mouth worked as if chewing something, his snout wrinkling over his protruding teeth. "Of course he cheated, boy! He always cheats! That's how he wins! Maybe you should cheat just a little now and then! Maybe then you wouldn't crash your Pod time after time and cost me so much money!"

They were standing in Watto's shop in the merchants' district of Mos Espa, a dingy mud-and-sand hut fronting an enclosure packed with rocket and engine parts salvaged from scrapped and junked wrecks. It was cool and shadowy inside, the planet's heat shut out by the thick walls, but even here dust hung in the air in hazy streamers caught by the ambient light cast by glow lamps. The race had long since ended and the planet's twin suns had dropped toward the horizon with evening's slow approach. The wrecked Podracer and its engines had been transported by mechanic droids from the flats back to the shop. Anakin had been transported back as well, though with somewhat less enthusiasm.

"Rassa dwee cuppa, peedunkel!" Watto screamed, starting in again on Anakin in a fresh burst of Huttese.

The pudgy body lurched forward a few centimeters with each epithet, causing Anakin to step back in spite of his resolve. Watto's bony arms and legs gestured with the movements of his head and body, giving him a comical appearance. He was angry, but Anakin had seen him angry before and knew what to expect. He did not cringe or bow his head in submission; he stood his ground and took his scolding unflinchingly. He was a slave and Watto was his master. Scoldings were part of life. Besides, Watto would wind down shortly now, his anger released in a manner that would satisfy his need to cast blame in a direction other than his own, and things would go back to normal.

All three fingers of Watto's right hand pointed at the boy. "I shouldn't let you drive for me anymore! That's what I should do! I should find another driver!"

"I think that is a very good idea," Shmi agreed.

Anakin's mother had been standing to one side, not saying anything during the whole of Watto's diatribe, but now she was quick to take advantage of a suggestion she would have made herself, if asked.

Watto wheeled on her, spinning violently, wings whirring, and flew to confront her. But her calm, steady gaze brought him up short, pinning him in the air midway between mother and son.

"It's too dangerous in any case," she continued reasonably. "He's only a boy."

Watto was immediately defensive. "He's my boy, my property, and he'll do what I want him to do!"

"Exactly." Shmi's dark eyes stared out of her worn, lined face with resolution. "Which is why he won't race anymore if you don't want him to. Isn't that what you just said?"

Watto seemed confused by this. He worked his mouth and trunklike nose in a rooting manner, but no words would come out. Anakin watched his mother appreciatively. Her lank, dark hair was beginning to gray, and her once graceful movements had slowed. But he thought she was beautiful and brave. He thought she was perfect.

Watto advanced on her another few centimeters, then stopped once more. Shmi held herself erect in the same way that Anakin did, refusing to concede anything to her condition. Watto regarded her sourly for a moment more, then spun around and flew at the boy.

"You will fix everything you ruined, boy!" he snapped, shaking his finger at Anakin. "You will repair the engines and the Pod and make them as good as new! Better than new, in fact! And you'll start right now! Right this instant. Get out there and get to work!"

He spun back toward Shmi defiantly. "Still plenty of daylight for a boy to work! Time is money!" He gestured at first mother and then son. "Get on with it, the both of you! Back to work, back to work!"

Shmi gave Anakin a warm smile. "Go on, Anakin," she said softly. "Dinner will be waiting."

She turned and went out the door. Watto, after giving Anakin a final withering glance, followed after her. Anakin stood in the shadowed room for a moment, staring at nothing. He was thinking that he shouldn't have lost the race. Next time—and there would be a next time, if he knew Watto—he wouldn't.

Sighing in frustration, he turned and went out the back of the shop into the yard. He was a small boy, even at nine years of age, rather compactly built, with a mop of sandy hair, blue eyes, a pug nose, and an inquisitive stare. He was quick and strong for his age, and he was gifted in ways that constantly surprised those around him. He was already an accomplished driver in the Podraces, something no human of any age had ever been before. He was gifted with building skills that allowed him to put together almost anything. He was useful to Watto in both areas, and Watto was not one to waste a slave's talent.

But what no one knew about him except his mother was the way he sensed things. Frequently he sensed them before anyone even knew they would happen. It was like a stirring in the air, a whisper of warning or suggestion that no one else could feel. It had served him well in the Podraces, but it was also there at other times. He had an affinity for recognizing how things were or how they ought to be. He was only nine years old and he could already see the world in ways most adults never would.

For all the good it was doing him just at the moment.

He kicked at the sand in the yard as he crossed to the

engines and Pod the droids had dumped there earlier. Already his mind was working on what it would take to make them operable again. The right engine was almost untouched, if he ignored the scrapes and tears in the metal skin. The left was a mess, though. And the Pod was battered and bent, the control panel a shambles.

"Fidget," he muttered softly. "Just fidget!"

Mechanic droids came out at his beckoning and set to work removing the damaged parts of the racer. He was only minutes into sorting through the scrap when he realized there were parts he needed that Watto did not have on hand, including thermal varistats and thruster relays. He would have to trade for them from one of the other shops before he could start on a re-assembly. Watto would not like that. He hated asking for parts from other shops, insisting that anything worth having he already had, unless it came from off world. The fact that he was trading for what he needed didn't seem to take the edge off his rancor at having to deal with the locals. He'd rather win what he needed in a Podrace. Or simply steal it.

Anakin looked skyward, where the last of the day's light was beginning to fade. The first stars were coming out, small pinpricks against the deepening black of the night sky. Worlds he had never seen and could only dream about waited out there, and one day he would visit them. He would not be here forever. Not him.

"Psst! Anakin!"

A voice whispered cautiously to him from the deep shadows at the back of the yard, and a pair of small forms slipped through the narrow gap at the fence corner where the wire had failed. It was Kitster, his best friend, creeping into view with Wald, another friend, following close behind. Kitster was small and dark, his hair cut in a close bowl about his head, his clothing loose and nondescript, designed to preserve moisture and deflect heat and sand. Wald, trailing uncertainly, was a Rodian, an off-worlder who had come to Tatooine only recently. He was several years younger than his friends, but bold enough that they let him hang around with them most of the time.

"Hey, Annie, what're you doing?" Kitster asked, glancing around doubtfully, keeping a wary eye out for Watto.

Anakin shrugged. "Watto says I have to fix the Pod up again, make it like new."

"Yeah, but not today," Kitster advised solemnly. "Today's almost over. C'mon. Tomorrow's soon enough for that. Let's go get a ruby bliel."

It was their favorite drink. Anakin felt his mouth water. "I can't. I have to stay and work on this until . . ."

He stopped. Until dark, he was going to say, but it was nearly dark already, so . . .

"What'll we buy them with?" he asked doubtfully.

Kitster motioned toward Wald. "He's got five druggats he says he found somewhere or other." He gave Wald a sharp look. "He says."

"Got 'em right here, I do." Wald's strange, scaly head nodded assurance, his protruding eyes blinking hard. He pulled on one green ear. "Don't you believe me?" Wald said in Huttese.

"Yeah, yeah, we believe you." Kitster winked at Anakin. "C'mon, let's go before old flapping wings gets back."

They went out through the gap in the fence and down the road behind, turned left, and hurried through the crowded plaza toward the food stores just ahead. The streets were still crowded, but the traffic was all headed homeward or to the Hutt pleasure dens. The boys zipped smoothly through knots of people and carts, past speeders hovering just off surface, down walks beneath awnings in the process of being drawn up, and along stacks of goods being set inside under lock and key.

In moments, they had reached the shop that sold ruby bliels and had worked their way up to the counter.

Wald was as good as his word, and he produced the requisite druggats in exchange for three drinks and handed one to each of his friends. They took them outside, sipping at the gooey mixture through straws, and made their way slowly back down the street, chatting among themselves about racers and speeders and mainline ships, about battle cruisers and starfighters and the pilots who captained them. They would all be pilots one day, they promised each other, a vow they sealed with spit and hand slaps.

They were right in the middle of a heated discussion over the merits of starfighters, when a voice close to them said, "Give me the choice, I'd take a Z-95 Headhunter every time."

The boys turned as one. An old spacer stood leaning on a speeder hitch, watching them. They knew what he was right away from his clothing, weapons, and the small, worn fighter corps insignia he wore stitched to his tunic. It was a Republic insignia. You didn't see many of those on Tatooine.

"Saw you race today," the old spacer said to Anakin. He was tall and lean and corded, his face weatherworn and sun-browned, his eyes an odd color of gray, his hair cut short so that it bristled from his scalp, his smile ironic and warm. "What's your name?"

"Anakin Skywalker," Anakin told him uncertainly. "These are my friends, Kitster and Wald."

The old spacer nodded wordlessly at the other two, keeping his eyes fixed on Anakin. "You fly like your name, Anakin. You walk the sky like you own it. You show promise." He straightened and shifted his weight with practiced ease, glancing from one boy to the next. "You want to fly the big ships someday?"

All three boys nodded as one. The old spacer smiled. "There's nothing like it. Nothing. Flew all the big boys, once upon a time, when I was younger. Flew everything there was to fly, in and out of the corps. You recognize the insignia, boys?"

Again, they nodded, interested now, caught up in the wonder of coming face-to-face with a real pilot—not just of Podracers, but of fighters and cruisers and mainline ships.

"It was a long time ago," the spacer said, his voice suddenly distant. "I left the corps six years back. Too old. Time passes you by, leaves you to find something else to do with what's left of your life." He pursed his lips. "How're those ruby bliels? Still good? Haven't had one in years. Maybe now's a good time. You boys care to join me? Care to drink a ruby bliel with an old pilot of the Republic?"

He didn't have to ask twice. He took them back down the street to the shop they had just left and purchased a second drink for each of them and one for himself. They went back outside to a quiet spot off the plaza and stood sipping at the bliels and staring up at the sky. The light was gone, and stars were sprinkled all over the darkened firmament, a wash of silver specks nestled against the black.

"Flew all my life," the old spacer advised solemnly, eyes fixed on the sky. "Flew everywhere I could manage, and you know what? I couldn't get to a hundredth of what's out there. Couldn't get to a millionth. But it was fun trying. A whole lot of fun."

His gaze shifted to the boys again. "Flew a cruiser filled with Republic soldiers into Makem Te during its rebellion. That was a scary business. Flew Jedi Knights once upon a time, too."

"Jedi!" Kitster exhaled sharply. "Wow!"

"Really? You really flew Jedi?" Anakin pressed, eyes wide.

The spacer laughed at their wonder. "Cross my heart and call me bantha fodder if I'm lying. It was a long time ago, but I flew four of them to a place I'm not supposed to talk about even now. Told you. I've been everywhere a man can get to in one lifetime. Everywhere."

"I want to fly ships to those worlds one day," Anakin said softly.

Wald snorted doubtfully. "You're a slave, Annie. You can't go anywhere."

The old pilot looked down at Anakin. The boy couldn't look at him. "Well," he said softly, "in this life you're often born one thing and die another. You don't have to accept that what you're given when you come in is all you'll have when you leave."

He laughed suddenly. "Reminds me of something. I flew the Kessel Run once, long ago. Not many have done that and lived to tell about it. Lots told me I couldn't do it, told me not to bother trying, to give it up and go on to something else. But I wanted that experience, so I just went ahead and found a way to prove them wrong."

He looked down at Anakin. "Could be that's what you'll have to do, young Skywalker. I've seen how you handle a Podracer. You got the eyes for it, the feel. You're better than I was at twice your age." He nodded solemnly. "You want to fly the big ships, I think maybe you will."

He stared at the boy, and Anakin stared back. The old spacer smiled and nodded slowly. "Yep, Anakin Skywalker, I do think maybe one day you will."

* * *

He arrived home late for dinner and received his second scolding of the day. He might have tried making something up about having to stay late for Watto, but Anakin Skywalker didn't lie to his mother. Not about anything, not ever. He told her the truth, about stealing away with Kitster and Wald, about drinking ruby bliels, and about sharing stories with the old spacer. Shmi wasn't impressed. She didn't like her son spending time with people she didn't know, even though she understood how boys were and how capable Anakin was of looking after himself.

"If you feel the need to avoid the work you've been given by Watto, come see me about the work that needs doing here at home," she advised him sternly.

Anakin didn't argue with her, smart enough by now to realize that arguing in these situations seldom got him anywhere. He sat quietly, eating with his head down, nodding when nodding was called for, thinking that his mother loved him and was worried for him and that made her anger and frustration with him all right.

Afterward, they sat outside on stools in front of their home in the cool night air and looked up at the stars. Anakin liked sitting outside at night before bed. It wasn't so close and confined as it was inside. He could breathe out here. His home was small and shabby and packed tight against dozens of others, its thick walls comprised of a mixture of mud and sand. It was typical of quarters provided for slaves in this part of Mos Espa, a hut with a central room and one or two bumpouts for sleeping. But his mother kept it neat and clean, and Anakin had his own room, which was rather larger than most and where he kept his stuff. A large workbench and tools took up most of the available space. Right now he was engaged in building a protocol droid to help his mom. He was adding the needed parts a piece at a time, scavenging them from wherever he could, slowly restoring the whole. Already it could talk and move about and do a few things. He would have it up and running soon.

"Are you tired, Annie?" his mother asked after a long silence.

He shook his head. "Not really."

"Still thinking about the race?"

"Yes."

And he was, but mostly he was thinking about the old spacer and his tales of flying mainline ships to distant worlds, of going into battle for the Republic, and of rubbing shoulders with Jedi Knights.

"I don't want you racing Pods anymore, Annie," his mother said softly. "I don't want you to ask Watto to let you. Promise me you won't."

He nodded reluctantly. "I promise." He thought about it a moment. "But what if Watto tells me I have to, Mom? What am I supposed to do then? I have to do what he tells me. So if he asks, I have to race."

She reached over and put a hand on his arm, patting him gently. "I think maybe after today he won't ask again. He'll find someone else."

Anakin didn't say so, but he knew his mother was wrong. There wasn't anyone better than he was at Podracing. Not even Sebulba, if he couldn't cheat. Besides, Watto would never pay to have someone else drive when he could have Anakin do it for free. Watto would stay mad another day or two and then begin to think about winning again. Anakin would be back in the Podraces before the month was out.

He gazed skyward, his mother's hand resting lightly on his arm, and thought about what it would be like to be out there, flying battle cruisers and fighters, traveling to far worlds and strange places. He didn't care what Wald said, he wouldn't be a slave all his life. Just as he wouldn't always be a boy. He would find a way to leave Tatooine. He would find a way to take his mother with him. His dreams whirled through his head as he watched the stars, a kaleidoscope of bright images. He imagined how it would be. He saw it clearly in his mind, and it made him smile.

One day, he thought, seeing the old spacer's face in the darkness before him, the wry smile and strange gray eyes, I'll do everything you've done. Everything.

He took a deep breath and held it.

I'll even fly with Jedi Knights.

Slowly he exhaled, the promise sealed.

The small Republic space cruiser, its red color the symbol of ambassadorial neutrality, knifed through starry blackness toward the emerald bright planet of Naboo and the cluster of Trade Federation fleet ships that encircled it. The ships were huge, blocky fortresses, tubular in shape, split at one end and encircling an orb that sheltered the bridge, communications center, and hyperdrive. Armaments bristled from every port and bay, and Trade Federation fighters circled the big beasts like gnats. The more traditionally shaped Republic cruiser, with its tri-engines, flat body, and squared-off cockpit, looked insignificant in the shadow of the Trade Federation battleships, but it continued toward them, undeterred.

The cruiser's captain and copilot sat side by side at the forward console, hands moving swiftly over the controls as they steered closer to the ship with the Trade Federation viceroy insignia emblazoned on its bridge. There was a nervous energy to their movements that was unmistakable. From time to time, they would glance uneasily at each other—and over their shoulders at the figure who stood in the shadows behind.

On the viewscreen in front of them, captured from his position on the bridge of the battleship toward which they were headed, was Trade Federation Viceroy Nute Gunray, his reddish orange eyes staring out at them expectantly. The Neimoidian wore his perpetually sour expression, mouth downturned, bony brow emphasizing his discontent. His green-gray skin reflected the ambient lighting of the ship, all pale and cold in contrast to his dark robes, collar, and tricornered headdress.

"Captain."

The cruiser captain turned slightly in her seat to acknowledge the figure concealed in the shadows behind her. "Yes, sir?"

"Tell them we wish to board at once."

The voice was deep and smooth, but the measure of resolution it contained was unmistakable.

"Yes, sir," the captain said, giving the copilot a covert glance, which the copilot returned. The captain faced Nute Gunray on the screen. "With all due respect, Viceroy, the ambassadors for the supreme chancellor have requested that they be allowed to board immediately."

The Neimoidian nodded quickly. "Yes, yes, Captain, of course. We would be happy to receive the ambassadors at their convenience. Happy to, Captain."

The screen went dark. The captain hesitated, glancing back at the figure behind her. "Sir?"

"Proceed, Captain," Qui-Gon Jinn said.

The Jedi Master watched silently as the Trade Federation battleship loomed before them, filling the viewport with its gleaming bulk. Qui-Gon was a tall, powerfully built man with prominent, leonine features. His beard and mustache were close-cropped and his hair was worn long and tied back. Tunic, pants, and hooded robe were typically loose-fitting and comfortable, a sash binding them at his waist where his lightsaber hung just out of view, but within easy reach.

Qui-Gon's sharp blue eyes fixed on the battleship as if to see what waited within. The Republic's taxation of the trade routes between the star systems had been in dispute since its inception, but until now all the Trade Federation had done in response was to complain. The blockade of Naboo was the first act of outright defiance, and while the Federation was a powerful body, equipped with its own battle fleet and army of droids, its action here was atypical. The Neimoidians were entrepreneurs, not fighters. They lacked the backbone necessary to undertake a challenge to the Republic. Somehow they had found that backbone. It bothered Qui-Gon that he could not explain how.

He shifted his weight as the cruiser moved slowly into the gap in the Trade Federation flagship's outer wheel toward the hangar bay. Tractor beams took hold, guiding the cruiser inside where magnetic clamps locked the ship in place. The blockade had been in effect now for almost a month. The Republic Senate continued to debate the action, searching for an amicable way to resolve the dispute. But no progress had been made, and at last the supreme chancellor had secretly notified the Jedi Council that he had sent two Jedi directly to the ostensible initiators of the blockade, the Neimoidians, in an effort to resolve the matter more directly. It was a bold move. In theory, the Jedi Knights served the supreme chancellor, responding on his direction to life-threatening situations. But any interference in the internal politics of the Senate's member bodies, particularly where an armed conflict between worlds was involved, required Senate approval. The supreme chancellor was skirting the edges of his authority in this case. At best, this was a covert action and would spark heated debate in the Senate at a later date.

The Jedi Master sighed. While none of this was his concern, he could not ignore the implications of what it meant if he failed. The Jedi Knights were peacemakers; that was the nature of their order and the dictate of their creed. For thousands of years they had served the Republic, a constant source of stability and order in a changing universe. Founded as a theological and philosophical study group so far back that its origins were the stuff of myth, the Jedi had only gradually become aware of the presence of the Force. Years had been spent in its study, in contemplation of its meaning, in mastery of its power. Slowly the order had evolved, abandoning its practice of and belief in a life of isolated meditation in favor of a more outward-looking commitment to social responsibility. Understanding the Force sufficiently to master its power required more than private study. It required service to the greater community and implementation of a system of laws that would guarantee equal justice for all. That battle was not yet won. It probably never would be. But the Jedi Knights would not see it lost for lack of their trying.

In the time of Qui-Gon Jinn, ten thousand Jedi Knights in service to the Republic carried on the struggle each day of their lives in a hundred thousand different worlds spread across a galaxy so vast it could barely be comprehended.

He turned slightly as his companion in this present enterprise arrived on the bridge and came up to stand beside him. "Are we to board?" Obi-Wan Kenobi asked softly.

Qui-Gon nodded. "The viceroy will meet with us."

He glanced momentarily at his protégé, taking his measure. Obi-Wan, in his mid-twenties, was more than thirty years younger and still learning his craft. He was not yet a full Jedi, but he was close to being ready. Obi-Wan was shorter than Qui-Gon, but compact and very quick. His smooth, boyish face suggested an immaturity that had been long since shed. He wore the same type of clothes as Qui-Gon, but his hair was cut in the style of a Padawan learner, short and even, save for the tightly braided pigtail that hung over his right shoulder.

Qui-Gon was staring out the viewport at the interior of the Trade Federation battleship when he spoke again. "Why Naboo, do you think, my young apprentice? Why blockade this particular planet, when there are so many to choose from, most larger and more likely to feel the effects of such an action?"

Obi-Wan said nothing. Naboo was indeed an odd choice for an action of this sort, a planet at the edge of the galaxy, not particularly important in the scheme of things. Its ruler, Amidala, was something of an unknown. New to the throne, she had only been Queen a few months before the blockade had begun. She was young, but it was rumored she was prodigiously talented and extremely well trained. It was said she could hold her own with anyone in a political arena. It was said she could be circumspect or bold when necessary, and was wise beyond her years.

The Jedi had been shown a hologram of Amidala before they left Coruscant. The Queen favored theatrical paint and ornate dress, cloaking herself in trappings and makeup that disguised her true appearance while lending her an aura of both splendor and beauty. She was a chameleon of sorts, masking herself to the world at large and finding companionship almost exclusively with a cadre of handmaidens who were always with her.

Qui-Gon hesitated a moment longer, thinking the matter through, then said to Obi-Wan, "Come, let's be off."

They passed downward through the bowels of the ship to the

main hatch, waited for the light to turn green, and released the locking bar so that the ramp could lower. Raising their hoods to help conceal their faces, they stepped out into the light.

A protocol droid named TC-14 was waiting to escort them to their meeting. The droid took them from the bay down a series of hallways to an empty conference room and motioned them inside.

"I hope your honored sirs will be comfortable here." The tinny voice reverberated inside the metal shell. "My master will be with you shortly."

The droid turned and went out, closing the door softly behind. Qui-Gon watched it go, glanced briefly at the exotic, bird-like creatures caged near the door, then moved to join Obi-Wan at a broad window that looked out through the maze of Federation battleships to where the lush green sphere of Naboo hung resplendent against the dark sky.

"I have a bad feeling about this," Obi-Wan said after a moment's contemplation of the planet.

Qui-Gon shook his head. "I don't sense anything."

Obi-Wan nodded. "It's not about here, Master. It's not about this mission. It's something . . . elsewhere. Something elusive . . ."

The older Jedi put his hand on the other's shoulder. "Don't center on your anxiety, Obi-Wan. Keep your concentration on the here and now, where it belongs."

"Master Yoda says I should be mindful of the future—"

"But not at the expense of the present." Qui-Gon waited until his young apprentice was looking at him. "Be mindful of the living Force, my young Padawan."

To his credit, Obi-Wan managed a small smile. "Yes, Master." He looked out the viewport again, eyes distant. "How do you think the viceroy will deal with the supreme chancellor's demands?"

Qui-Gon gave an easy shrug. "These people are cowards. They will not be hard to persuade. The negotiations will be short."

On the bridge of the Trade Federation battleship, Neimoidian Viceroy Nute Gunray and his lieutenant, Daultay Dofine, stood staring in shock at the protocol droid they had sent to look after the supreme chancellor's ambassadors.

"What did you say?" Gunray hissed furiously.

TC-14 was impervious to the look the Neimoidian gave it. "The ambassadors are Jedi Knights. One of them is a Jedi Master. I am quite certain of it."

Dofine, a flat-faced, restless sort, wheeled on his companion in dismay. "I knew it! They were sent to force a settlement! The game's up! Blind me, we're done for!"

Gunray made a placating gesture. "Stay calm! I'll wager the Senate is completely unaware of the supreme chancellor's moves in this matter. Go. Distract them while I contact Lord Sidious."

The other Neimoidian gaped at him. "Are you brain-dead? I'm not going in there with two Jedi Knights! Send the droid!"

He waved hurriedly at TC-14, who bowed, made a small squeaky sound in response, and went out.

When the protocol droid was gone, Dofine summoned Rune Haako, the third member of their delegation, drew both his compatriots to a closed, separate space on the bridge where they could be neither seen nor heard by anyone else, and triggered a holographic communication.

It took a few moments for the hologram to appear. As it did so, a stoop-shouldered, dark-robed shape appeared, cloaked and hooded so that nothing of its face could be seen.

"What is it?" an impatient voice demanded.

Nute Gunray found his throat so dry that for a moment he could not speak. "The Republic ambassadors are Jedi Knights."

"Jedi?" Darth Sidious breathed the word softly, almost reverently. There was a measure of calm about his acceptance of the news. "Are you sure?"

Nute Gunray found what little courage he had been able to muster for this moment quickly evaporating. He stared at the black form of the Sith Lord in mesmerized terror. "They have been identified, my lord."

As if unable to endure the silence that followed, Daultay Dofine charged into the gap, wild-eyed. "This scheme of yours has failed, Lord Sidious! The blockade is finished! We dare not go up against Jedi Knights!"

The dark figure in the hologram turned slightly. "Are you saying you would rather go up against me, Dofine? I am amused." The hood shifted toward Gunray. "Viceroy!"

Nute stepped forward quickly. "Yes, my lord?"

Darth Sidious's voice turned slow and sibilant. "I don't want this stunted piece of slime to pass within my sight again. Do you understand?"

Nute's hands were shaking, and he clasped them together to still them. "Yes, my lord."

He wheeled on Dofine, but the other was already making his way from the bridge, his face filled with terror, his robes trailing behind him like a shroud.

When he was gone, Darth Sidious said, "This turn of events is unfortunate, but not fatal. We must accelerate our plans, Viceroy. Begin landing your troops. At once."

Nute glanced quickly at Rune Haako, who was trying his best to disappear into the ether. "Ah, my lord, of course, but . . . is that action legal?"

"I will make it legal, Viceroy."

"Yes, of course." Nute took a quick breath. "And the Jedi?"

Darth Sidious seemed to grow darker within his robes, his face lowering further into shadow. "The supreme chancellor should never have brought the Jedi into this. Kill them now. Immediately."

"Yes, my lord," Nute Gunray answered, but the hologram of the Sith Lord had already vanished. He stared at the space it had left behind for a moment, then turned to Haako. "Blow up their ship. I will send a squad of battle droids to finish them."

In the conference room in which they had been left, Qui-Gon and Obi-Wan stared at each other across a long table.

"Is it customary for Neimoidians to make their guests wait this long?" the younger Jedi asked.

Before Qui-Gon could respond, the door opened to admit the protocol droid bearing a tray of drinks and food. TC-14 crossed to their table, placed the tray before them, and handed each a drink. It stepped back then, waiting. Qui-Gon motioned to his young companion, and they lifted the drinks and tasted them.

Qui-Gon nodded at the droid, then looked at Obi-Wan. "I sense an unusual amount of maneuvering for something as trivial as this trade dispute. I sense fear as well."

Obi-Wan placed his drink back on the table. "Perhaps—"

An explosion rocked the room, spilling the drinks, sending the tray with its food skidding toward the edge. The Jedi leapt to their feet in response, lightsabers drawn and activated. The protocol droid backpedaled quickly, arms lifting, muttering its apologies, looking every which way at once.

"What's happened?" Obi-Wan asked quickly.

Qui-Gon hesitated, closed his eyes, and retreated deep within himself. His eyes snapped open. "They've destroyed our ship."

He glanced around swiftly. It took only a moment for him to detect a faint hissing sound from the vents near the doorway.

"Gas," he said to Obi-Wan in warning.

In the cage beside the door, the birdlike creatures began to drop like stones.

On the bridge, Nute Gunray and Rune Haako watched through a viewscreen as a squad of battle droids marched into the hallway just outside the conference room in which the Jedi were trapped. On crooked metal legs, they approached the doorway, blasters held at the ready, a hologram of Nute directing them from behind.

"They must be dead by now, but make certain," he directed the battle droids, and switched off the hologram.

The Neimoidians watched closely as the foremost of the battle droids opened the door and stepped back. A cloud of noxious green gas poured from the room, and a solitary figure stumbled into view, arms waving.

"Excuse me, sirs, I'm so sorry," TC-14 babbled as it maneuvered through the battle droids, holding aloft its tray of scattered food and spilled drinks.

In the next instant the Jedi appeared, charging from the room with lightsabers flashing. Qui-Gon's weapon sent a pair of the battle droids flying in a shower of sparks and metal parts that scattered everywhere. Obi-Wan's saber deflected blaster fire into several more. He raised his hand, palm outward, and another of the droids went crashing into the wall.

On the bridge viewscreen, smoke and lingering clouds of

green gas obscured everything. Alarms began to sound throughout the battleship, reverberating off its metal skin.

"What in blazes is going on down there?" Nute Gunray demanded of his associate, eyes wide.

Rune Haako shook his head doubtfully. There was fear in his orange-red eyes. "You've never encountered Jedi Knights before, have you?"

"Well, no, not exactly, but I don't see . . ." The alarms continued to blare, and suddenly Nute Gunray was unabashedly afraid. "Seal off the bridge!" he shouted frantically.

Rune Haako backed away as the doors to the bridge began to close. His voice was small and went unheard as he whispered to himself, "That won't be enough."

In seconds, the Jedi were standing in the hallway outside the bridge, dispatching the last of the battle droids that stood in their way. An unstoppable force, the two men worked in unison against their adversaries, seemingly able to anticipate every form of attack. Lightsabers flashed and stabbed in brilliant bursts of color. Droids and blasters fell away in broken pieces.

"I want destroyer droids up here at once!" Nute Gunray screamed, watching as one of the Jedi began cutting through the bridge door with his lightsaber. He felt his throat tighten and his skin begin to crawl. "Close the blast doors! Now!"

One after another, the blast doors began to shut and seal with hissing sounds. The crew stood transfixed as on the viewscreen the Jedi continued their attack, lightsabers cutting at the massive doors, melting away the steelcrete like soft butter. Mutters of disbelief were heard, and Nute screamed at them to be silent. Sparks showered off the blast door under attack by the Jedi, and a red spot appeared at its center where the larger man plunged his lightsaber into the metal almost up to its hilt.

The viewscreen suddenly went blank. At the center of the door, the metal began to turn molten and drop away.

"They're still coming," Rune Haako whispered, gathering his robes as he backed away further.

Viceroy Nute Gunray said nothing in response. *Impossible!* he was thinking. *Impossible!*

Qui-Gon was hammering at the blast door with every ounce of strength he possessed, determined to break through to the treacherous Neimoidians, when his instincts warned him of danger from another quarter.

"Obi-Wan!" he shouted to his companion, who wheeled toward him at once. "Destroyer droids!"

The younger Jedi nodded, smiling. "Offhand, I'd say this mission is past the negotiation stage."

In the hallway just beyond the area in which the Jedi fought, ten destroyer droids rolled into view. They resembled gleaming metal wheels as they rounded a corner, smooth and silent in their approach. One by one they began to unfold, releasing tripods of spidery legs and stunted arms into which laser guns had been built. Crooked spines unlimbered, and the droids rose to a standing position, armored heads cocked forward. They were wicked-looking and deadly, and they were built for one purpose only.

Skittering around the final corner to the bridge entry, they triggered their laser guns, filling the open area with a deadly crossfire. When the lasers went still, the destroyer droids advanced, searching for their prey.

But the anteway was empty, and the Jedi Knights were gone.

On the bridge, Nute Gunray and Rune Haako watched the viewscreen flicker back to life. The destroyer droids were

reverting to their wheeled forms, spinning away across the entry
and down the hallway, clearly in pursuit of the Jedi.

"We have them on the run," Rune Haako breathed, scarcely
able to believe their good fortune.

Nute Gunray said nothing, thinking that their escape had
been entirely too close. It was ridiculous that they should be
fighting Jedi Knights in any event. This was a matter of commerce, not of politics. The Trade Federation was fully justified in
resisting the Republic Senate's foolish decision to impose a tax
on trade routes when there was no basis in law for doing so. That
the Neimoidians had found an ally to stand with them in this
matter, to advise them on imposing a blockade and forcing a
withdrawal of sanctions, was no cause for calling in the Jedi.

He hunched his shoulders and made a fuss over straightening
his robes to disguise his shaking.

He was distracted suddenly by a call from the communications center behind him. "Sir, a transmission from the city of
Theed on Naboo."

The viewscreen to the planet flickered to life, and a woman's
face appeared. She was young, beautiful, and serene. An applied
beauty mark of deepest crimson split her lower lip, and a golden
headdress framed her powdery-white face. She stared out at the
Neimoidians from the screen as if she were so far above and beyond them as to be unapproachable.

"It's Queen Amidala herself," Rune Haako whispered, just
out of holocam view.

Nute Gunray nodded, moving closer. "At last we're getting
results," he whispered back.

He moved to where he could be seen by the Queen. Cloaked
in her ceremonial robes, Amidala sat on her throne, an ornate
chair on a raised dais fronted by a low, flat-surfaced divider. The

Queen was surrounded by five handmaidens, all of them cloaked and hooded in crimson. Her gaze was steady and direct as it took in the viceroy's leathery countenance.

"The Trade Federation is pleased you have chosen to come before us, Your Highness," he began smoothly.

"You will not be so pleased when you hear what I have to say, Viceroy," she said flatly, cutting him short. "Your trade boycott is ended."

Nute fought down his shock, regained his composure, and smirked at Rune. "Really, Your Highness? I was not aware—"

"I have word that the Senate is finally voting on the matter," she continued, ignoring him.

"I take it you know the outcome already, then." Nute felt a measure of uncertainty take hold. "I wonder why they bother to vote at all."

Amidala leaned forward slightly, and the Neimoidian could see the fire in her brown eyes. "I have had enough of pretense, Viceroy. I am aware that the supreme chancellor's ambassadors are with you now, and that you have been commanded to reach a settlement. What is it to be?"

Nute Gunray felt a deep hole open in his waning confidence. "I know nothing about any ambassadors. You must be mistaken."

There was a flicker of surprise on the Queen's face as she studied the viceroy carefully. "Beware, Viceroy," she said softly. "The Federation has gone too far this time."

Nute shook his head quickly, drawing himself up in a defensive posture. "Your Highness, we would never do anything in defiance of the Senate's will. You assume too much."

Amidala sat motionless, brown eyes fixed on him—as if she could see the truth he was trying to hide, as if he were made of glass. "We shall see," she said softly.

The viewscreen went blank. Nute Gunray drew a long breath and exhaled slowly, not caring much for how this woman made him feel.

"She's right," Rune Haako said at his elbow. "The Senate will never let—"

Nute lifted one hand to cut him short. "It's too late now. The invasion is under way."

Rune Haako was silent for a moment. "Do you think she suspects an attack?"

The viceroy wheeled away. "I don't know, but I don't want to take any chances. We must move quickly to disrupt all communications down there until we're finished!"

In the main hangar bay of the ship, Qui-Gon Jinn and Obi-Wan Kenobi crouched silently in the opening of a large circulation vent that overlooked six massive double-winged Federation landing ships surrounded by a vast array of transports. The transports were large boot-shaped vehicles with bulbous noses. The doors that formed those noses gaped open, racks were extended, and thousands of sleek silvery shapes were marching inside in perfect formation to be secured.

"Battle droids," Qui-Gon said softly. There was surprise and dismay in his deep voice.

"It's an invasion army," Obi-Wan said.

They continued to watch for a time, taking in the scene, counting transports and droids as they filled the half-dozen landing craft, taking measure of the size of the army.

"It's an odd play for the Federation," Qui-Gon observed. "We've got to warn the Naboo and contact Chancellor Valorum."

Obi-Wan nodded. "We'd best do it somewhere besides here."

His mentor glanced at him. "Maybe we can hitch a ride with our friends down there."

"It's the least they can do after the way they've treated us so far." Obi-Wan pursed his lips. "You were right about one thing, Master. The negotiations were short."

Qui-Gon Jinn smiled and beckoned him ahead.

A twilight that was misty and seemed perpetual lay in silvery gray layers over the green lushness of Naboo as the Federation landing ships descended out of the black infinity of space to settle slowly planetward. One set of three moved away from the others, dropping silently through clouds that hung still and endless across the world's emerald surface. Ghostlike as they passed through the haze, double wings shaped like a giant *I*, they materialized one by one near a vast, murky swamp. As they gently landed next to the dark waters and clumps of trees and grasses, their metal bodies parted to allow the bulbous-nosed transports to offload onto the surface and begin forming up.

Some distance away from the closest of the landing craft, Obi-Wan Kenobi's head broke the swamp's still waters. A quick breath, and he was gone again. He surfaced once more, farther away, and this time took a moment to look back at the invasion force. Dozens of transports filled with battle droids and tanks were moving into place in front of the landing craft. Some hovered above the swamp's waters. Some had found purchase on dry ground.

Far to his left, he caught sight of a shadowy form running through the mist and trees. Qui-Gon. Obi-Wan took another deep breath, submerged swiftly, and began to swim.

Qui-Gon Jinn slipped wraithlike through the swamp, listening to the sounds of heavy rustling and snapping branches behind him as the Trade Federation transports began to advance. Mixed with the deeper, heavier whine of the transport engines was the higher pitched buzzing of STAPs—single trooper aerial platforms—small, individually piloted mobile gun units used to transport battle droids as scouts for the main army. The STAPs whipped above the watery terrain of Naboo, fleeting shadows as they surged in front of the larger transports.

Animals of all shapes and sizes began to scatter from their places of concealment, racing past Qui-Gon in search of safety. Ikopi, fulumpasets, motts, peko pekos—the names recalled themselves instantly to the Jedi Master from his preparation for this journey. Dodging the frightened creatures stampeding around him, he cast about for Obi-Wan, then picked up his pace as the dark shadow of a transport appeared out of the mist directly behind him.

He was running out of firm ground and searching for a way past a large lake when he saw a strange froglike creature before him. It was squatting in the water, its rubbery body crouched over a shell it had just pried open, its long tongue licking out the insides with a quick whipping movement, its throat swallowing. Casting aside the empty shell, it rose to face Qui-Gon, its long, flat ears dangling from its amphibious head in broad flaps, its ducklike snout working thoughtfully around whatever delicacy it had removed from the shell. Eyes that protruded from the top of its head blinked in confusion, taking in Qui-Gon and the animals about him, then seeing clearly for the first time the massive shadow from which they fled.

"Oh, oh," the creature muttered, the syllables clouded, but recognizable.

Qui-Gon broke left past the strange creature, anxious to get out of the path of the approaching transport. The creature dropped the shell, eyes wide and frantic, and grabbed onto Qui-Gon's robes.

"Hep me, hep me!" it cried plaintively, rubbery face contorting in shock and desperation.

"Let go!" Qui-Gon snapped, trying in vain to break free.

The transport thundered toward them, skimming the surface of the swamp, flattening grasses and stirring up water spouts in the wake of its passing. It bore down on Qui-Gon as he fought to break free of the creature that clung to him, dragging it sideways in a futile effort to escape.

Finally, with the transport only meters away and looming over him like a building about to topple, the Jedi Master pushed the creature into the shallow water and sprawled facedown on top of it. The Trade Federation transport passed over them in a wash of sound and shocked air, the vibrations hammering into their prone forms, flattening them into the mire.

When it was safely past, Qui-Gon pulled himself out of the mud and took a deep, welcome breath. The strange creature rose with him, still clinging to his arm, cloudy water dripping from its flat-billed face. It gave a quick glance after the departing transport, then threw itself on Qui-Gon, hugging him ecstatically.

"Oh boi, oh boi!" it gasped with a high-pitched, warbled sound. "I love yous, love yous forever!"

The creature began kissing him.

"Let go!" Qui-Gon huffed. "Are you brainless? You almost got us killed!"

The creature looked offended. "Brainless? I speak!"

"The ability to speak does not make you intelligent!" Qui-Gon was having none of it. "Now let go of me and get out of here!"

He freed himself from the creature and began to move off, glancing around uneasily as the high-pitched buzz of STAPs sounded in the distance.

The creature hesitated, then began trailing after him. "No, no, me stay wit you! Me stay! Jar Jar be loyal, humble Gungan servant. Be yous friend, me."

The Jedi Master barely glanced at him, watching the shadows, searching now for Obi-Wan. "Thanks, but that won't be necessary. Better be off with you."

Jar Jar the Gungan splashed after him, billed mouth working, arms waving. "Oh, bot tis necessary! Tis demanded by da Guds. Tis life debt. Me know dis, sure as name be Jar Jar Binks!"

The swamp reverberated with the sound of STAP engines, and now two of the gun platforms burst from the mist, bearing down on a fleeing Obi-Wan Kenobi, battle droid drivers wheeling their speeders to the attack.

Qui-Gon pulled free his lightsaber, motioning Jar Jar away. "I have no time for this now—"

"But must take me wit yous, keep me—" Jar Jar stopped, hearing the STAPs, turning to see them bearing down, eyes going wide all over again. "Oh, oh, we gonna—"

Qui-Gon grabbed the Gungan and threw him facedown in the swamp water once more. "Stay put." He flicked on the lightsaber, bracing himself as Obi-Wan and the pursuing STAPs approached.

Jar Jar's head popped up. "We gonna die!" he screamed.

The battle droids opened fire with laser cannons from their gun platforms just as Obi-Wan reached his friend. Qui-Gon blocked the bolts with his lightsaber and deflected them back into the attack craft. The STAPs exploded in shards of hot metal and fell into the swamp.

An exhausted Obi-Wan wiped his muddied brow, gasping for breath. "Sorry, Master. The swamp fried my lightsaber."

He pulled out his weapon. The business end was blackened and burned. Qui-Gon took it from him and gave it a cursory inspection. Behind him, Jar Jar Binks pulled himself out of the muddy swamp water and blinked curiously at the newly arrived Jedi.

"You forgot to turn off your power again, didn't you, Obi-Wan?" his friend asked pointedly.

Obi-Wan nodded sheepishly. "It appears so, Master."

"It won't take long to recharge, but it will take some time to clean it up. I trust you have finally learned your lesson, my young Padawan."

"Yes, Master." Obi-Wan accepted the proffered lightsaber with a chagrined look.

Jar Jar pushed forward, amphibious feet flopping, ears flapping, long limbs looking as if they might take him in almost any direction. "Yous save me again, hey?" he asked Qui-Gon rhetorically.

Obi-Wan stared. "What's this?"

"A Gungan. One of the locals. His name's Jar Jar Binks." Qui-Gon's attention was directed out at the swamp. "Let's go, before more of those STAPs show up."

"More?" Jar Jar gasped worriedly. "Yous say more?"

Qui-Gon was already moving, shifting into a steady trot through the mire. Obi-Wan was only a step behind, and it took a moment for Jar Jar to catch up to them, his long legs working frantically, his eyes rolling.

"Exsqueeze me, but da most grand safest place is in Otoh Gunga," he gasped at them, trying to catch their attention. All about, lost somewhere in the mists, STAPs sounded their high-pitched whine. "Otoh Gunga," Jar Jar repeated. "Tis where I grew. Tis safe city!"

Qui-Gon brought them to a halt, staring fixedly now at the Gungan. "What did you say? A city?" Jar Jar nodded eagerly. "Can you take us there?"

The Gungan seemed suddenly distraught. "Ah, oh, oh . . . mebbe me not rilly take yous . . . not rilly, no."

Qui-Gon leaned close, his eyes dark. "No?"

Jar Jar looked as if he wished he could disappear into the swamp completely. His throat worked and his billed mouth opened and closed like a fish's. "Tis embarrassment, but . . . me afraid me be banished. Sent oot. Me forget Boss Nass do terrible hurt to me if go back dere. Terrible bad hurt."

A low, deep, pulsating sound penetrated the whine of the STAPs, rising up through mist and gloom, growing steadily louder. Jar Jar glanced around uneasily. "Oh, oh."

"You hear that?" Qui-Gon asked softly, placing a finger on the Gungan's skinny chest. Jar Jar nodded reluctantly. "There's a thousand terrible things heading this way, my Gungan friend . . ."

"And when they find you, they will crush you into dust, grind you into little pieces, and then blast you into oblivion," Obi-Wan added with more than a little glee.

Jar Jar rolled his eyes and gulped. "Oh, oh. Yous point very good one." He gestured frantically. "Dis way! Dis way! Hurry quick!"

In a rush, they raced away into the twilight mist.

Sometime later, the Jedi and the Gungan emerged from a deep stand of swamp grass and thick rushes at the edge of a lake so murky that it was impossible to see anything in the reflection of twilight off the surface. Jar Jar bent double, three-fingered hands resting on bony knees as he fought to catch his breath. His rubbery form twisted this way and that as he looked back in the direction from which they had come, long ears flapping with the movement. Obi-Wan shook his head at Qui-Gon Jinn in faint reproval. He was not happy with the Jedi Master's decision to link up with this foolish-looking creature.

Somewhere in the distance, they could hear the steady, deep thrum of Federation transport engines.

"How much farther?" Qui-Gon pressed their reluctant guide.

The Gungan pointed at the lake. "We go underwater, okeday?"

The Jedi looked at each other, then extracted small containers from their clothing, releasing portable breathing devices the size of the palms of their hands.

"Me warning yous." Jar Jar's eyes shifted from one to the other. "Gungans no like yous outlanders. Yous not gonna get warm welcome."

Obi-Wan shrugged. "Don't worry. This hasn't been our day for warm welcomes."

"Get going," Qui-Gon motioned, fitting the device between his teeth.

The Gungan shrugged, as if to disclaim all responsibility for what would follow, turned back to the lake, performed a wild double somersault, and disappeared into the gloom.

The Jedi waded after him.

Downward into the murkiness they swam, the Jedi following the slender form of the Gungan, who seemed far more at home in the water than on land. He swam smoothly and gracefully, long limbs extended, body undulating with practiced ease. They swam for a long time, angling steadily deeper, the light from the surface fading slowly away behind them. What light there was came from sources beneath the surface, not all of them visible. The minutes slipped away, and Obi-Wan began to have second thoughts about what they were doing.

Then suddenly there was a new light, this one a steady glow that came from ahead. Slowly Otoh Gunga came into view. The city was comprised of a cluster of bubbles that connected to one another like balloons and were anchored to several huge rock pillars. One by one, the bubbles grew more distinct, and it became possible to make out the particulars of the structures within and the features of the Gungans as they moved about their business.

Jar Jar swam directly toward one of the larger bubbles, the Jedi close on his heels. When he reached the bubble, he pushed at it with his hands and it gave way to him, accepting first his arms, then his head and body, and finally his legs, swallowing him whole and closing behind him without rupturing. Amazed, the Jedi followed, moving through the strange membrane, entering the bubble without resistance.

Once inside, they found themselves on a platform that led down to a square surrounded by buildings. Light emanated from the bubble's walls in a steady glow, brightening the space inside. The Jedi found the air breathable. As they descended to the square below, water dripping from their clothing, Gungans began to catch sight of them and to scatter with small cries of alarm.

In short order a squad of uniformed Gungan soldiers appeared, riding two-legged mounts with billed faces not entirely dissimilar to their own. Kaadu, Qui-Gon recalled—swamp runners with powerful legs, great endurance, and keen senses. The Gungans carried long, deadly-looking electropoles, which they used to motion back the distraught populace at the same time they advanced on the intruders.

"Heyday ho, Cap'n Tarpals," Jar Jar greeted the leader of the squad cheerfully. "Me back!"

"Notta gain, Jar Jar Binks!" the other snapped, clearly irritated. "Yous goen ta Boss Nass. See what he say. Yous mebbe in big trubble dis time."

Ignoring the Jedi, he gave Jar Jar a quick poke with his electropole, sending a shock through the hapless Gungan that lifted him a half meter off the ground. Jar Jar rubbed his backside ruefully, muttering.

The Gungan soldiers took them through the buildings of the city, down several connecting passages, and into what, Jar Jar whispered to his companions, was the High Tower Boardroom. The room was transparent on all sides, and small glowing fish swam about the outside of the membrane, tiny stars against a darker backdrop. A long, circular bench dominated one end of the room with one section set higher than the rest. All the seats were occupied by Gungan officials in their robes of office, and a way was quickly made for the newcomers through Gungans already present to conduct other business.

The Gungan occupying the highest seat was a heavyset, squat fellow so compressed by age and weight that it was impossible to imagine he had ever been as slender as Jar Jar Binks. Folds of skin draped from his body in loose layers, his neck was compressed into his shoulders, and his face bore such a sour look that even

Jar Jar seemed more than a little cowed as they were motioned forward.

The Gungan officials stared, muttering among themselves as the Jedi approached. "What yous want, outlanders?" Boss Nass rumbled at them, after identifying himself.

Qui-Gon Jinn told him, relating what had brought the Jedi to Naboo, warning of the invasion taking place above, asking the Gungans to give them help. The Gungan council listened patiently, saying nothing until Qui-Gon was finished.

Boss Nass shook his head, the flesh of his thick neck jiggling with the movement. "Yous can't be here. Dis army of maccaneks up dere tis not our problem."

Qui-Gon held his ground. "That army of battle droids is about to attack the Naboo. We must warn them."

"We no like da Naboo!" Boss Nass growled irritably. "And dey no like da Gungans. Da Naboo think dey more smart den us. Dey think dey brains so big. Dey have nutten ta do wit us cause we live in da swamp and dey live up dere. Long time no have nutten ta do wit each other. Dis not gonna change because of maccaneks."

"After that army takes control of the Naboo, they will come here and take control of you," Obi-Wan said quietly.

Boss Nass chuckled. "No, me think not. Me talk mebbe one, two times wit Naboo in whole life, and no talk ever wit maccaneks. Maccaneks no come here! Dey not even know Gungans exist!"

The remaining members of the council nodded in agreement, muttering their verbal approval of Boss Nass's wisdom.

"You and the Naboo are connected," Obi-Wan insisted, his youthful face intent, not ready to concede the matter. "What happens to one will affect the other. You must understand this."

Boss Nass dismissed him with a wave of one thick hand. "We know nutten of yous, outlander, and we no care about da Naboo."

Before Obi-Wan could continue his argument, Qui-Gon stepped forward. "Then speed us on our way," he demanded, bringing up one hand in a casual motion, passing it smoothly before the Gungan chief's eyes in a quick invocation of Jedi mind power.

Boss Nass stared at him, then nodded. "We speed yous far away."

Qui-Gon held his gaze. "We need transport to Theed."

"Okeday." Boss Nass nodded some more. "We give yous bongo. Da speedest way tada Naboo is goen through da core. Yous go now."

Qui-Gon stepped back. "Thank you for your help. We go in peace."

As the Jedi turned to leave, Obi-Wan whispered, "Master, what is a bongo?"

Qui-Gon glanced at him and cocked one eyebrow thoughtfully. "A ship of some sort, I hope."

They were moving away from Boss Nass and the other Gungan officials when they caught sight of Jar Jar Binks standing forlornly to one side, wearing wrist binders and awaiting his fate. Qui-Gon slowed and made eye contact with the unfortunate creature.

"Master," Obi-Wan said softly in warning. He knew Qui-Gon too well not to see what was coming.

The tall Jedi moved over to Jar Jar and stood looking at him.

"Dey setten yous up for bad fall!" the Gungan declared sullenly, glancing around to see if anyone else might be listening. "Goen through da core is bad danger."

Qui-Gon nodded. "Thank you, my friend."

Jar Jar Binks shrugged and looked sad. "Ahhh, tis okay." Then he gave the Jedi Master a slow, sheepish grin and a hopeful look. "Hey, any hep here would be hot."

Qui-Gon hesitated.

"We are short of time, Master," Obi-Wan advised quietly, moving to his side.

The Jedi Master turned to face his protégé, eyes distant. "Time spent here may help us later. Jar Jar might be of some use."

Obi-Wan shook his head in frustration. His mentor was too eager to involve himself when it was not necessary. He was too quick to adopt causes that were not his own. It had cost him time and time again with the Jedi Council. One day it would be his undoing.

He bent close. "I sense a loss of focus."

Qui-Gon's eyes fixed on him. "Be mindful, young Obi-Wan," he chastised gently. "Your sensitivity to the living Force is not your strength."

The younger Jedi held his gaze only a moment, then looked away, stung by the criticism. Qui-Gon turned from him and walked back to Boss Nass. "What is to become of Jar Jar Binks?" he asked.

Boss Nass, who was engaged in conversation with another of the Gungan officials, turned to him in annoyance, his heavy jowls puffing. "Binks breaks nocomeback law. Breaks exile. He be punished."

"Not too severely, I trust?" the Jedi Master pressed. "He has been of great help to us."

A slow laugh rumbled out of Boss Nass. "Pounded unto death, dis one."

Somewhere in the background, Jar Jar Binks moaned loudly. There were mutterings about the room. Even Obi-Wan, who was back at his Master's side, looked shocked.

Qui-Gon was thinking fast. "We need a navigator to get us through the core to Theed. I saved Jar Jar's life on the surface. He owes me for that. I claim a life debt on him."

Boss Nass stared at the Jedi in silence, a deep frown furrowing his brow and twisting his mouth. His head seemed to sink deeper into his shoulders, into the wattles of skin that obscured his neck.

Then his small eyes sought the unfortunate Jar Jar, and he gestured. "Binks?"

Jar Jar moved forward obediently to stand beside the Jedi.

"Yous haf life debt wit dis outlander?" Boss Nass demanded darkly.

Jar Jar nodded, head and ears hanging, but a flicker of hope springing into his eyes.

"Your gods demand he satisfy that debt," Qui-Gon insisted, passing his hand in front of Boss Nass's eyes, invoking his Jedi power once more. "His life belongs to me now."

The head Gungan considered the matter only a moment before nodding in agreement. "His life tis yous. Worthless, anywhat. Beggone wit him."

A guard came forward and removed Jar Jar's wrist binders.

"Come, Jar Jar," Qui-Gon Jinn advised, turning him away.

"Through da core?" Jar Jar gasped, realizing suddenly what had happened. "Count me outta dis! Better dead here den dead in da core! Me not go . . ."

But by then the Jedi were dragging him out of the room and all sight and sound of Boss Nass.

* * *

On the bridge of the Trade Federation's lead battleship, Nute Gunray and Rune Haako stood alone before a hologram of Darth Sidious. Neither of the Neimoidians was looking at the other, and both were hoping the Sith Lord could not sense what they were thinking.

"The invasion is on schedule, my lord," the viceroy was saying, robes and headdress hiding the occasional twitching of his limbs as he faced the cloaked and hooded form before him. "Our army nears Theed."

"Good. Very good." Darth Sidious spoke in a soft, calm voice. "I have the Senate bogged down in procedures. By the time this incident comes up for a vote, they will have no choice but to accept that your blockade has been successful."

Nute Gunray glanced quickly at his compatriot. "The Queen has great faith that the Senate will side with her."

"Queen Amidala is young and naive. You will find controlling her will not be difficult." The hologram shimmered. "You have done well, Viceroy."

"Thank you, my lord," the other acknowledged as the hologram faded away.

In the ensuing silence, the Neimoidians turned to each other with knowing looks. "You didn't tell him," Rune Haako said accusingly.

"Of the missing Jedi?" Nute Gunray made a dismissive gesture. "No need to tell him that. No need to tell him anything until we know for certain what has happened."

Rune Haako studied him a long time before turning away. "No, no need," he said softly, and walked from the room.

Obi-Wan Kenobi sat hunched over the controls of the bongo, familiarizing himself with their functions as Jar Jar Binks, positioned next to him, rambled on and on about nothing. Qui-Gon sat in the shadows behind them, silent and watchful.

"Dis is nutsen!" Jar Jar moaned as the bongo motored steadily away from the shimmering lighted bubbles of Otoh Gunga and deeper into the waters of Naboo.

The bongo was an ungainly little underwater craft that consisted mostly of an electrical power plant, guidance system, and passenger seating. It looked somewhat like a species of squid, having flat, swept-back fins and aft tentacles that rotated to propel the craft. Three bubble-canopied passenger compartments were arranged symmetrically, one on each wing and the third forward on the nose.

The Jedi and the Gungan occupied the nose compartment, where Obi-Wan had assumed command of the controls and Jar Jar had been instructed to start directing them through the core. It seemed that there were underwater passageways all through the planet, and if you were able to locate the right one, you could cut travel time considerably.

Or in the alternative, Obi-Wan thought darkly, you could cut your own throat.

"We doomed," Jar Jar muttered plaintively. His flat-billed face lifted away from the directional guidance system toward the Jedi, his long ears swaying like ridiculous flaps. "Heydey ho? Where we goen, Cap'n Quiggon?"

"You're the navigator," Qui-Gon observed.

Jar Jar shook his head. "Me? Yous dreaming. Don't know nutten 'bout dis, me."

Qui-Gon placed a hand on the Gungan's shoulder. "Just relax, my friend. The Force will guide us."

"Da Force? What tis da Force?" Jar Jar did not look impressed. "Maxibig thing, dis Force, yous betcha. Gonna save me, yous, all us, huh?"

Obi-Wan closed his eyes in dismay. This was a disaster waiting to happen. But it was Qui-Gon's disaster to manage. It was not his place to interfere. Qui-Gon had made the decision to bring Jar Jar Binks along, after all. Not because he was a skilled navigator or had displayed even the slightest evidence of talent in any other regard, but because he was another project that Qui-Gon, with his persistent disregard for the dictates of the Council, had determined had value and could be reclaimed.

It was a preoccupation that both mystified and frustrated Obi-Wan. His mentor was perhaps the greatest Jedi alive, a commanding presence at Council, a strong and brave warrior who refused to be intimidated by even the most daunting challenge, and a good and kind man. Maybe it was the latter that had gotten him into so much trouble. He repeatedly defied the Council in matters that Obi-Wan thought barely worthy of championing. He was possessed of his own peculiar vision of a Jedi's purpose, of the nature of his service, and of the causes he should undertake, and he followed that vision with unwavering single-mindedness.

Obi-Wan was young and impatient, headstrong and not yet at one with the Force in the way that Qui-Gon was, but he understood better, he thought, the dangers of overreaching, of taking on too many tasks. Qui-Gon would dare anything when he found a challenge that interested him, even if he risked himself in the undertaking.

So it was here. Jar Jar Binks was a risk of the greatest magnitude, and there was no reason to think that embracing such a risk would reap even the smallest reward.

The Gungan muttered some more, all the while casting about through the viewport as if seeking a road sign that would allow him to at least pretend he knew what he was doing. Obi-Wan gritted his teeth. Stay out of it, he told himself sternly. Stay out of it.

"Here, take over," he snapped at Jar Jar.

He moved out of his seat to kneel close to Qui-Gon. "Master," he said, unable to help himself, "why do you keep dragging these pathetic life-forms along with us when they are of so little use?"

Qui-Gon Jinn smiled faintly. "He seems that way now perhaps, but you must look deeper, Obi-Wan."

"I've looked deep enough, and there is nothing to see!" Obi-Wan flushed with irritation. "He is an unneeded distraction!"

"Maybe for the moment. But that may change with time." Obi-Wan started to say something more, but the Jedi Master cut him short. "Listen to me, my young Padawan. There are secrets hidden in the Force that are not easily discovered. The Force is vast and pervasive, and all living things are a part of it. It is not always apparent what their purpose is, however. Sometimes that purpose must be sensed first in order that it may be revealed later."

Obi-Wan's young face clouded. "Some secrets are best left concealed, Master." He shook his head. "Besides, why must you always be the one to do the uncovering? You know how the Council feels about these . . . detours. Perhaps, just once, the un-covering should be left to someone else."

Qui-Gon looked suddenly sad. "No, Obi-Wan. Secrets must be exposed when found. Detours must be taken when encoun-tered. And if you are the one who stands at the crossroads or the place of concealment, you must never leave it to another to act in your place."

The last of the lights from Otoh Gunga disappeared in a wash of murkiness, and the waters closed around them in a dark cloud. Jar Jar Binks was taking the craft ahead at a slow, steady speed, no longer muttering or squirming, his hands fixed on the controls. He flipped on the lights as darkness closed about, and the broad yellow beams revealed vast stretches of multicolored coral weaving and twisting away through the black.

"I respect your judgment in this, Master," Obi Wan said fi-nally. "But it doesn't stop me from worrying."

Like all of the Jedi Knights, Obi-Wan Kenobi had been iden-tified and claimed early in his life from his birth parents. He no longer remembered anything of them now; the Jedi Knights had become his family. Of those, he was closest to Qui-Gon, his men-tor for more than a dozen years, who had become his most trusted friend.

Qui-Gon understood his attachment and shared it. Obi-Wan was the son he would never have. He was the future he would leave behind when he died. His hopes for Obi-Wan were enormous, but he did not always share his student's beliefs.

"Be patient with me, Obi-Wan," he replied softly. "A little faith sometimes goes a long way."

The bongo navigated a coral tunnel, the bridge work revealed in deep fissures of crimson and mauve in the glow of the little craft's lights. All about, brightly colored fish swam in schools through the craggy rock.

"Are the Gungans and the Naboo at war with each other?" Qui-Gon asked Jar Jar thoughtfully.

The Gungan shook his head. "No war. Naboo and Gungans don't fight. Long time ago, mebbe. Now, Naboo keep outta swamp, Gungans keep outta plains. Dey don't even see each other."

"But they don't like each other?" the Jedi Master pressed.

Jar Jar snorted. "Da Naboo gotta big heads, alla time think dey so much better den da Gungans! Big nuttens!"

Obi-Wan bent over Jar Jar Binks, his eyes directed out the viewport. "Why were you banished, Jar Jar?" he asked.

The Gungan made a series of small smacking sounds with his billed lips. "Tis kinda long story, but keeping dis short, me . . . oh, oh, ahhh . . . kinda clumsy."

"You were banished because you're clumsy?" Obi-Wan exclaimed in disbelief.

The bongo turned down through an open stretch of water between two huge coral shelves. Neither the Jedi nor the Gungan saw the dark shape that detached itself from the larger outcropping and began to track them.

Jar Jar squirmed. "Me cause mebbe one or two little bitty axaudents. Boom da gasser, crash der Bosses' heyblibber. Den dey banish me."

Obi-Wan was not entirely sure what Jar Jar was telling him. But before he could ask for clarification, there was a loud thump as something struck the bongo, causing it to lurch sharply to one side. A huge crustacean with multiple legs and massive jaws ringed with teeth had hooked them with its long tongue and was drawing them steadily toward its widespread maw.

"Opee sea killer!" Jar Jar cried in dismay. "We doomed!"

"Full speed ahead, Jar Jar!" Qui-Gon ordered quickly, watching the jaws open behind them.

But instead of pushing the throttles forward, Jar Jar panicked and jammed them into reverse, causing the little ship to fly directly into the mouth of their attacker. The bongo slammed into the back of the monster's throat with a heavy thump that sent the Jedi reeling over the seats and into the walls. Rows of jagged teeth began to close about them as the lights on the control panel flickered uncertainly.

"Oh, oh," Jar Jar Binks said.

Obi-Wan leapt quickly back into the copilot's seat. "Here, give me the controls!"

He seized the throttles and steering apparatus and shoved everything into forward, full speed ahead. To his surprise, the opee sea killer's mouth opened with a spasmodic jerk, and they shot through its teeth as if from a laser cannon.

"We free! We free!" Jar Jar was jumping about in his seat, ecstatic over their good fortune.

But a quick glance back revealed that they were lucky for a different reason than they thought. The opee sea killer was caught in the jaws of a creature so huge that it dwarfed even the beast it was eating. A long, eel-like hunter with clawed forelegs, rear fins, and a wicked pair of jaws was crunching the sea killer into tiny bits and swallowing it down eagerly.

"Sando aqua monster, oh, oh!" Jar Jar Binks moaned, burying his face in his hands.

Obi-Wan increased power, trying to put more distance between themselves and this newest threat. The sando aqua monster disappeared behind them, but the lights of the bongo were flickering ominously. The little craft dived deeper, penetrating the planet's core. Suddenly something exploded inside a control panel behind them, showering the cabin with sparks. Seams split overhead, and water began leaking through the bongo's outer skin.

"Master," Obi-Wan said as the power-drive whine took a sudden dive, "we're losing power."

Qui-Gon was working over the troubled control panel, head lowered. "Stay calm. We're not in trouble yet."

"Not yet!" Jar Jar had lost all pretense of calm and was flailing about in his seat. "Monstairs out dere! Leakin in here. We sinkin with no power! Yous nuts! When yous think we in trubble?"

With that, the lights inside the bongo went completely black. Jar Jar Binks had his answer.

In the conference room of the lead battleship of the Trade Federation fleet, a hologram of Darth Sidious towered over Nute Gunray and Rune Haako. The Neimoidian viceroy and his lieutenant stood motionless before it, reddish orange eyes fixed and staring, reptilian faces betraying every bit of the fear that held them paralyzed.

The black-cloaked figure of Darth Sidious regarded them silently. There was no hint of expression on his shadowed countenance, which was mostly hidden within the folds of the cloak's hood. But the rigid posture of the Sith Lord's body spoke volumes.

"You disappoint me, Viceroy," he hissed at Nute Gunray.

"My lord, I am certain that all—" The subject of his anger tried futilely to explain.

"Worse, you defy me!"

The Neimoidian's face underwent a terrifying transformation. "No, my lord! Never! These Jedi are . . . resourceful, that's all. Not easily destroyed—"

"Alive, then, Viceroy?"

"No, no, I'm sure they're dead. They must be. We—we just haven't been able to confirm it . . . yet."

Darth Sidious ignored him. "If they are alive, they will show themselves. When they do, Viceroy, I want to know immediately. I will deal with them myself."

Nute Gunray looked as if he might collapse under the weight of the Sith Lord's penetrating stare. "Yes, my lord," he managed as the hologram vanished.

Inside the troubled bongo, Obi-Wan fought to keep control as the little craft began to drift aimlessly.

Abruptly the whine of the power drive came alive and the aft drive fins began to turn. "Power's back," Obi-Wan breathed gratefully.

The lights on the control panels blinked on, flickered, and steadied. The exterior directional lights followed, momentarily blinding them as they reflected off rock walls and jagged out-croppings. Then Jar Jar screamed. A new monster was sitting right in front of them, all spines and scales and teeth, crooked clawed forelegs raised defensively.

"Colo claw fish!" the Gungan shrieked. "Yous Jedi do something! Where da Force now, you think?"

"Relax," Qui-Gon Jinn said softly, placing his hand on Jar

Jar's twitching shoulder. The Gungan jerked and promptly fainted.

"You overdid it," Obi-Wan observed, wheeling the bongo about and jetting away through the darkness.

Even without looking, he knew the colo claw fish was in pursuit. They were inside a tunnel that probably served as the creature's lair. They were lucky to have caught it by surprise. He angled the bongo toward the cave entrance and a series of overhangs that might provide them with a little protection on their way out. Something slammed into the bongo, held it fast momentarily, then released it. Obi-Wan increased power to the drive fins.

"Come on, come on!" he breathed softly.

They shot out of the cave directly into the jaws of the waiting sando aqua monster. The creature jerked back at the unexpected invasion, giving Obi-Wan just an instant to bank their craft hard to the right. The jaws of the aqua monster were still open as they sped between teeth the size of buildings.

Jar Jar's eyes flickered open. He caught sight of the teeth and promptly fainted again.

Out through a gap in the sando aqua monster's fangs they sped, the bongo shaking with the thrust of its power drive. But the colo claw fish, still in pursuit, did not veer aside quickly enough and flew right into the larger hunter's maw. The jaws came down, engulfing it.

Obi-Wan increased power to the drive fins as bits of the colo claw fish reemerged briefly through the sando aqua monster's grinding teeth, only to be sucked quickly from sight again.

"Let's hope that's all the snack he requires," the Jedi observed with a quick glance back.

Apparently it was, because it did not come after them. It took a while to revive Jar Jar and a good deal longer to complete their voyage through the core, but with the Gungan's somewhat questionable help, they finally emerged from the darkness of the deeper waters toward a blaze of sunlight. The bongo popped to the surface of an azure body of water, green hills and trees rising about them, clouds and blue sky overhead. Obi-Wan steered the little craft to the nearest shore, shut down the engines, and released the nose hatch. Qui-Gon rose and looked around.

"We safe now," Jar Jar observed with a grateful sigh, leaning back in his seat. "Tis okeday, hey?"

"That remains to be seen," the Jedi Master said. "Let's be off."

He climbed from the bongo onto the shore and started away. Obi-Wan glanced meaningfully at Jar Jar and followed.

The Gungan stared doubtfully after the departing Jedi. "Me comen, me comen," he muttered, and hurried after.

It was a little more than a week after the Podrace and the encounter with the old spacer that Watto summoned Anakin into the musty confines of the junk shop and told him he was to take a speeder out to the Dune Sea to do some trading with the Jawas. The Jawas, scavengers, were offering a number of droids for sale or trade, some of them mechanics, and while Watto wasn't about to part with usable currency, he didn't want to pass up a bargain if it could be had for a favorable barter. Anakin had traded on Watto's behalf before, and the Toydarian knew that the boy was good at this, too.

The blue face hovered close to Anakin's own, tiny wings beating madly. "Bring me what I need, boy! And don't mess up!"

Anakin was entrusted with a variety of difficult-to-obtain engine and guidance systems parts that the Jawas would covet and Watto could afford to give up for the right set of droids. The boy was to take the speeder out into the Dune Sea for a midday meeting with the Jawas, make his trade, and be back by sunset. No detours and no fooling around. Watto hadn't forgiven him yet for

losing the Podrace and smashing his best racer, and he was letting the boy know it.

"March the droids back if you can't barter for a float sled."
Watto flitted about, issuing orders, a blue blur. "If they can't
walk this far, they aren't of any use to me. *Peedunkel!* Make sure
you don't get taken! My reputation is at stake!"

Anakin listened attentively and nodded at all the right places,
the way he had learned to do over the years. It was only a little
past midmorning and there was plenty of time to do what was
needed. He had traded with the Jawas many times, and he knew
how to make certain they did not get the best of him.

There was a great deal Watto didn't know about Anakin Skywalker, the boy thought to himself as he went out the door to
claim his speeder and begin his journey. One of the tricks to being a successful slave was to know things your master didn't
know and to take advantage of that knowledge when it would do
you some good. Anakin had a gift for Podracing and a gift for
taking things apart and putting them back together and making
them work better than they had before. But it was his strange
ability to sense things, to gain insights through changes in
temperament, reactions, and words, that served him best. He
could tune in to other creatures, bond with them so closely he
could sense what they were thinking and what they would do almost before they did. It had served him well in dealing with the
Jawas, among others, and it gave him a distinct edge in bartering
on Watto's behalf.

Anakin had a couple of important secrets he kept from Watto
as well. The first was the protocol droid he was reconstructing in
his bedroom work area. It was far enough along that even though
it was missing its skin and an eye, it could stand and move
around, and its intelligence and communications processors were

up and running. Good enough to do the job he required of it, he concluded, which was to accompany him on his bartering mission. The droid could listen in on the Jawas in their own peculiar language, which Anakin did not understand or speak particularly well. By doing so, it could let Anakin know if they were trying to slip anything by him. Watto didn't know how far he had gotten with the droid, and there wasn't much danger Watto could find out while they were out in the Dune Sea.

The second and more important secret concerned the Podracer the boy was building. He had been working on it for almost two years, salvaging bits and pieces as he went, assembling it under cover of an old tarp in an area of the common refuse dump in back of the slave housing. His mother had indulged him, mindful of his interest in taking things apart and putting them back together. She didn't see the harm in allowing him to have this project to work on in his spare time, and Watto knew nothing of the Pod.

That was an inspired bit of subterfuge on Anakin's part. He knew, just as with the droid, that if it appeared to have any value at all, Watto would claim it. So he deliberately kept it looking as if it were a complete piece of junk, disguising its worth in a variety of clever ways. To all intents and purposes, it would never run. It was just another childish project. It was just a little boy's dream.

But for Anakin Skywalker, it was the first step in his life plan. He would build the fastest Podracer ever, and he would win every race in which it was entered. He would build a starfighter next, and he would pilot it off Tatooine to other worlds. He would take his mother with him, and they would find a new home. He would become the greatest pilot ever, flying all the ships of the mainline, and his mother would be so proud of him.

And one day, when he had done all this, they would be slaves no longer. They would be free.

He thought about this often, not because his mother encouraged him in any way or because he was given any reason to think it might happen, but simply because he believed, deep down inside where it mattered, that it must.

He thought about it now as he guided his speeder through the streets of Mos Espa, the protocol droid sitting in the rear passenger compartment, skeletal-like without its skin and motionless because he had deactivated it for the ride out. He thought about all the things he would do and places he would go, the adventures he would have and the successes he would enjoy, and the dreams he would see come true. He drove the speeder out from the city under Tatooine's suns, the heat rising off the desert sands in a shimmering wave, the light reflecting off the metal surface of the speeder like white fire.

He proceeded east for about two standard hours until he reached the edge of the Dune Sea. The meeting with the Jawas was already in place, arranged by Watto the day before by transmitter. The Jawas would be waiting by Mochot Steep, a singular rock formation about halfway across the sea. Goggles, gloves, and helmet firmly in place, the boy cranked up the power on the speeder and hastened ahead through the midday heat.

He found the Jawas waiting for him, their monstrous sandcrawler parked in the shadow of the Steep, the droids they wished to trade lined up at the end of the crawler's ramp. Anakin parked his speeder close to where the little robed figures waited, yellow eyes gleaming watchfully in the shadows of their hoods, and climbed out. He activated the protocol droid and ordered him to follow. With the droid trailing obediently, he walked slowly down the line of mechanicals, making a show of carefully studying each.

When he was finished, he drew his droid aside. "Which ones are best, See-Threepio?" he asked. He'd given it a number the night before, choosing *three* because the droid made the third member of his little family after his mother and himself.

"Oh, well, Master Anakin, I'm flattered that you would ask, but I would never presume to infringe on your expertise, my own being so meager, although I do have knowledge of some fifty-one hundred different varieties of droids and over five thousand different internal processors and ten times that many chips and—"

"Just tell me which ones are best!" Anakin hissed under his breath. He had forgotten that C-3PO was first and foremost a protocol droid and, while possessed of extensive knowledge, tended to defer to the humans he served. "Which ones, Three-pio?" he repeated. "Left to right. Number them off to me."

C-3PO did so. "Do you wish me to enumerate their capabilities and design specialties, Master Anakin?" he asked solicitously, cocking his head.

Anakin silenced him with a wave of his hand as the head Jawa approached. They bartered back and forth for a time, Anakin getting a sense of how far the Jawas could be pushed, how much subterfuge was taking place with regard to their droids, and how badly they wanted the goods he was offering in exchange. He was able to determine that several of the best droids were still inside the crawler, a fact that C-3PO picked up from an unguarded comment made by a Jawa off to one side. The head Jawa squeaked at him furiously, of course, but the damage was done.

Three more droids were brought out, and again Anakin took a few moments to inspect them, C-3PO at his side. They were good models, and the Jawas were not particularly eager to part with them for anything less than a combination of currency and goods. Anakin and the head Jawa, who were of about the same height and weight, stood nose to nose arguing the matter for a long time.

When the bartering was completed, Anakin had traded a little more than half of what he had brought as barter for two mechanic droids in excellent condition, three more multipurpose droids that were serviceable, and a damaged hyperdrive converter that he could put back into service in no time. He could have traded for another two or three droids, but the quality of those that remained wasn't sufficiently high to part with any more of Watto's goods, and Watto would be quick to see that.

There was no float sled to be had, so Anakin lined up the newly purchased droids behind the speeder, placed C-3PO in the rear passenger compartment to keep an eye on them, and set off for Mos Espa. It was just after midday. The little procession was a curious sight, the speeder leading, hovering just off the sand, thrusters on dead slow, the droids trailing behind, jointed limbs working steadily to keep pace.

"That was an excellent trade, Master Anakin," C-3PO advised cheerfully, keeping his one good eye on their purchases. "You are to be congratulated! I think those Jawas learned a hard lesson today! You really did show them a thing or two about hard bargaining! Why, that pit droid alone is worth much more than . . ."

The droid rattled on incessantly, but Anakin let him alone, ignoring most of what he said, content to let his mind wander for a bit now that the hard part was done. Even with the droids slowing them down, they should reach the edge of the Dune Sea before midafternoon and Mos Espa before dark. He would have

time to sneak C-3PO back into his bedroom and deliver the purchased droids and the balance of the trade goods to Watto.
Maybe that would get him back in the Toydarian's good graces.
Certainly Watto would be pleased with the converter. They were
hard to come by out here, and if it could be made to work—
which Anakin was certain it could—it would be worth more than
all the rest of the purchases combined.

They crossed the central flats and climbed the slow rise to
Xelric Draw, a shallow, widemouthed canyon that split the Mospic High Range just inside the lip of the Dune Sea. The speeder
eased inside the canyon, droids strung out in a gleaming mechanical line behind, passing out of sunlight into shadow. The
temperature dropped a few degrees, and the silence changed
pitch in the lee of the cliffs. Anakin glanced about warily, knowing the dangers of the desert as well as any who were from Mos
Espa, although he was inclined to think from time to time that it
was safer out here than in the city.

"... a four-to-one ratio of Rodians to Hutts when the settlement began to take on the look and feel of a trading center, although even then it was clear the Hutts were the dominant
species, and the Rodians might just as well have stayed home
rather than chance a long and somewhat purposeless flight . . ."

C-3PO rambled on, changing subjects without urging, asking nothing in return for his nonstop narrative but to be allowed
to continue. Anakin wondered if he was suffering some sort of
sensory vocal deprivation from being deactivated for so long.
These protocol droids were known to be temperamental.

His gaze shifted suddenly to the right, to something that
seemed strange and out of place. At first it was just a shape
and coloring amid the desert sand and rock, almost lost in the
shadows. But as he stared harder, it took on fresh meaning. He

banked the speeder sharply, bringing the line of droids around with him.

"Master Anakin, whatever are you doing?" C-3PO protested peevishly. His one eye fixed on Anakin. "Mos Espa is down the canyon draw, not through the side of the—Oh, my! Is that what I think it is? Master, there is every reason to turn right around—"

"I know." Anakin cut the droid short. "I just want a look."

C-3PO's arms fluttered anxiously. "I must protest, Master Anakin. This is most unwise. If I am correct, and I must tell you that I have calculated that degree of probability at ninety-nine point seven, then we are headed directly toward . . ."

But Anakin didn't need to be told what lay ahead, having already determined exactly what it was. A Tusken Raider lay crumpled on the ground, half-buried by a pile of rocks close against the cliff face. The look and garb of the Sand People were unmistakable, even at this distance. Loose, tan-colored clothing, heavy leather gloves and boots, bandolier and belt, cloth-wrapped head with goggles and breath mask, and a long, dual-handled blaster rifle lying a meter away from an outstretched arm. A fresh scar slicing down from the cliff face bore evidence of a slide. The Raider had probably been hiding above when the rock gave way beneath his feet and buried him in the fall.

Anakin stopped the speeder and climbed down.

"Master Anakin, I don't think this is a good idea at all!" C-3PO declared in a sharp tone of admonishment.

"I just want a look, that's all," the boy repeated.

He was wary and a little scared of doing this, but he had never seen a Tusken Raider up close, although he had heard stories about them all his life. The Tuskens were a reclusive, fierce, nomadic people who claimed the desert as their own and lived

off those foolish enough to venture into their territory unprepared. On foot or astride the wild banthas they had claimed from
the wastelands, they traveled where they chose, pillaging outlying homes and way stations, waylaying caravans, stealing goods
and equipment, and terrorizing everyone in general. They had
even gone after the Hutts on occasion. The residents of Mos
Espa, themselves a less than respectable citizenry, hated the Sand
People with a passion.

Anakin had not yet made up his mind about them. The stories were chilling, but he knew enough of life to know there were
two sides to every story and mostly only one being told. He was
intrigued by the wild, free nature of the Tuskens, of a life without
responsibility or boundaries, of a community in which everyone
was considered equal.

He left the speeder and walked toward the fallen Raider.
Threepio continued to admonish him, to warn him he was making a mistake. In truth, he wasn't all that sure the droid was
wrong. But his trepidation was overcome by his curiosity. What
could it hurt to have just the briefest of looks? His boyish nature
surfaced and took control. He would be able to tell his friends he
had seen one of the Sand People close up. He would be able to
tell them what one really looked like.

The Tusken Raider lay sprawled facedown, arms akimbo, head
turned to one side. Rocks and debris buried most of the lower
part of his body. One leg lay pinned beneath a massive boulder.
Anakin edged closer to where the blaster rifle lay, then reached
down and picked it up. It was heavy and unwieldy. A man would
have to be strong and skilled to handle one, he thought. He
noted the strange carvings on the stock—tribal markings perhaps. He had heard the Tuskens were a tribal people.

Suddenly the fallen Raider stirred, drawing back one arm,

bracing himself, and lifting his wrapped head. Opaque goggles stared directly at Anakin. The boy backed away automatically. But the Tusken just stared at him for a moment, taking in who he was and what he was doing, then laid his head down again.

Anakin Skywalker waited, wondering what he should do. He knew what Watto would say. He knew what almost everyone would say. Get out of there! Now! He put the blaster rifle down again. This was no business of his. He took a step back, then another.

The Tusken Raider lifted his head once more and stared at him. Anakin stared back. He could sense the pain in the other's gaze. He could feel his desperation, trapped and helpless beneath that boulder, stripped of his weapon and his freedom both.

Anakin's brow furrowed. Would his mother tell him to get out of there, too? What would she say, if she were there?

"Threepio," he called back to the droid. "Bring everybody over here."

Protesting vehemently with every step, C-3PO gathered up the newly purchased droids and herded them to where the boy stood staring at the fallen Tusken. Anakin put the droids to work clearing away the smaller rocks and stones, then rigged a lever and used the speeder's weight to tilt the rock just enough that they could pull the pinned man free. The Tusken was awake briefly, but then lapsed back into unconsciousness. Anakin had the droids check for other weapons and kept the blaster rifle safely out of reach.

While the Tusken Raider was unconscious, the droids laid him on his back so he could be checked for injuries. The leg pinned by the boulder was smashed, the bones broken in several places. Anakin could see the damage through the torn cloth. But he wasn't familiar with Tusken physiology, and he didn't know exactly what to do to repair the damage. So he applied a quick-seal splint from the medical kit in the speeder to freeze the leg in place and left it alone.

He sat down then and thought about what he should do next. The light was beginning to fail. He had spent too much time freeing the Tusken to reach Mos Espa before nightfall. He could make the edge of the Dune Sea by dark, but only by leaving the Tusken behind, untended and alone. Anakin frowned. Given the things that roamed the desert when it got dark, he might as well bury the man and have done with it.

So he had the droids pull a small glow unit out of the landspeeder. When twilight descended, he powered up the glow unit and attached an extender fuel pack to assure it would burn all night. He broke out an old dried food pack and munched absently as he stared at the sleeping Tusken. His mother would be worried. Watto would be mad. But they knew him to be capable and reliable, and they would wait until daybreak to do anything about his absence. By then, he hoped, he would be well on his way home.

"Do you think he'll be all right?" he asked C-3PO.

He had placed the speeder and the other droids under the lee of a cliff face behind the glow unit, safely tucked from view, but had kept C-3PO with him for company. Boy and droid sat huddled close together on one side of the glow unit while the Tusken Raider continued to sleep on the other.

"I am afraid I lack the necessary medical training and information to make that determination, Master Anakin," C-3PO advised, cocking his head. "I certainly think you have done everything you possibly could."

The boy nodded thoughtfully.

"Master Anakin, we really shouldn't be out here at night,"

the droid observed after a moment. "This country is quite dangerous."

"But we couldn't leave him, could we?"

"Oh, well, that's a very difficult determination to make." C-3PO pondered the matter.

"We couldn't take him with us either."

"Certainly not!"

The boy sat in silence for a time, watching the Tusken sleep. He watched him for so long, in fact, that it came as something of a surprise when the Tusken finally stirred awake. It happened all at once, and it caught the boy off guard. The Tusken Raider shifted his weight with a lurching movement, exhaled sharply, propped himself up on one arm, looked at himself, then looked at the boy. The boy made no move or sound. The Tusken regarded him intently for a long minute, then slowly eased into a sitting position, his wounded leg stretched out in front of him.

"Uh, hello," Anakin said, trying out a smile.

The Tusken Raider made no response.

"Are you thirsty?" the boy asked.

No response.

"I don't think he likes us very much," C-3PO observed.

Anakin tried a dozen different approaches at conversation, but the Tusken Raider ignored them all. His gaze shifted only once, to where his blaster rifle lay propped against the rocks behind the boy.

"Say something to him in Tusken," he ordered C-3PO finally.

The droid did. He spoke at length to the Tusken in his own language, but the man refused to respond. He just kept staring at the boy. Finally, after C-3PO had gone on for some time, the Tusken glanced at him and barked a single word in response.

"Gracious!" the droid exclaimed.

"What did he say?" the boy asked, excited.

"Why he—he told me to shut up!"

That was pretty much the end of any attempt at conversation. The boy and the Tusken sat facing each other in silence, their faces caught by the glow of the fire, the desert's darkness all around. Anakin found himself wondering what he would do if the Tusken tried to attack him. It was unlikely, but the man was large and fierce and strong, and if he reached the boy, he could easily overpower him. He could take back his blaster rifle and do with the boy as he chose.

But somehow Anakin didn't sense that to be the Tusken's intent. The Tusken made no effort to move and gave no indication he had any intention of trying to do so. He just sat there, wrapped in his desert garb, faceless beneath his coverings, locked away with his own thoughts.

Finally he spoke again. The boy looked quickly at C-3PO. "He wants to know what you are going to do with him, Master Anakin," the droid translated.

Anakin looked back at the Tusken, confused. "Tell him I'm not going to do anything with him," he said. "I'm just trying to help him get well."

C-3PO spoke the words in Tusken. The man listened. He made no response. He did not say anything more.

Anakin realized suddenly that the Tusken was afraid. He could sense it in the way the other spoke, in the way he sat waiting. He was crippled and weaponless. He was at Anakin's mercy. The boy understood the Tusken's fear, but it surprised him anyway. It seemed out of character. The Sand People were supposed to be fearless. Besides, he wasn't afraid of the Tusken. Maybe he should have been, but he wasn't.

Anakin Skywalker wasn't afraid of anything.

Was he?

Staring into the opaque lenses of the goggles that hid the Tusken Raider's eyes, he contemplated the matter. Most times he thought there was nothing that could frighten him. Most times he thought he was brave enough that he would never be afraid.

But in that most secret part of himself where he hid the things he would reveal to no one, he knew he was cheating on the truth. He might not ever be afraid for himself, but he was sometimes very afraid for his mother.

What if something were to happen to her? What if something awful were to happen to her, something he could do nothing to prevent?

He felt a shiver go down his spine.

What if he were to lose her?

How brave would he be then, if the person he was closest to in the whole, endless universe was suddenly taken away from him? It would never happen, of course. It couldn't possibly happen.

But what if it did?

He stared at the Tusken Raider, and in the deep silence of the night he felt his confidence tremble like a leaf caught in the wind.

He fell asleep finally, and he dreamed of strange things. The dreams shifted and changed without warning and took on different story lines and meanings as they did so. He was several things in the course of his dreams. Once he was a Jedi Knight, fighting against things so dark and insubstantial he could not identify them. Once he was a pilot of a star cruiser, taking the ship into hyperspace, spanning whole star systems on his voyage. Once he was a great and feared commander of an army, and he came back to Tatooine with ships and troops at his command to free the planet's slaves. His mother was waiting for him, smiling, arms outstretched. But when he tried to embrace her, she vanished.

There were Sand People in his dreams, too. They appeared near the end, a handful of them, standing before him with their blaster rifles and long gaffi sticks lifted and held ready. They regarded him in silence, as if wondering what they should do with him.

He awoke then, jarred from his sleep by an unmistakable sense of danger. He jerked upright and stared about in confusion and fear. The glow unit had burned down to nothing. In the faint, silvery brightening of predawn, he found himself confronted by the dark, faceless shapes of the Sand People of his dreams.

Anakin swallowed hard. Motionless figures against the horizon's dim glow, the Tusken Raiders encircled him completely. The boy thought to break and run, but realized at once how foolish that would be. He was helpless. All he could do was wait and see what they intended.

A guttural muttering rose from their midst, and heads turned to look. Through a gap in the ranks, Anakin could just make out a figure being lifted and carried away. It was the Raider he had rescued, speaking to his people. The other Raiders hesitated, then slowly backed away.

In seconds, they were gone.

Sunlight began to crest the dark bulk of the Mospic, and C-3PO was speaking to him in a rush of words that tumbled over one another, the skeletal metal arms jerking this way and that.

"Master Anakin, they've gone! Oh, we're lucky to be alive! Thank goodness they didn't hurt you!"

Anakin climbed to his feet. There were Tusken Raider footprints everywhere. He glanced about quickly. The speeder and the droids obtained from the Jawas sat undisturbed beneath the overhang. The Tusken blaster rifle was gone.

"Master Anakin, what should we do?" C-3PO wailed in dismay.

Anakin looked around at the empty canyon floor, at the high ragged walls of the cliff face, and at the brightening sky where the stars were fading away. He listened to the deep silence and felt impossibly alone and vulnerable.

"We should go home," he whispered, and moved swiftly to make it happen.

Nute Gunray stood in silence at the center of the palace
throne room in the Naboo capital city of Theed and listened patiently as Governor Sio Bibble protested the Trade Federation
presence. Rune Haako stood at his side. Both wore their Federation robes of office and inscrutable expressions. Two dozen
battle droids held the Naboo occupants of the room at gunpoint.
The city had fallen shortly after sunrise. There had been little
resistance; the Naboo were a peaceful people. The Trade Federation invasion had come as a surprise, and the droid army was inside the gates of the city before any substantial defense could
be mounted. What few weapons there were had been confis-
cated and the Naboo removed to detention camps. Battle droids
were combing the city even now to put an end to any lingering
resistance.

Gunray resisted a smile. Apparently the Queen had believed
right up to the end that negotiations would prevail and the Senate would provide the people of Naboo with protection.

"It is bad enough, Viceroy, that you dare to disrupt transmis-

sions between the Queen and Senator Palpatine while he is attempting to argue our cause before the Republic Senate, bad
enough that you pretend that this blockade is a lawful action, but
landing an entire army on our planet and occupying our cities is
too outrageous for words."

Sio Bibble was a tall, balding man with a sharply pointed
beard and an even sharper tongue. He held the floor just at the
moment, but Gunray was getting tired of listening to him.

He glanced at the other captives. Captain Panaka, the Queen's
head of security, and four of the Queen's personal guards stood
to one side, stripped of their weapons and helpless. Panaka was
stone-faced and hard-eyed as he watched the Neimoidians. He
was a big, powerfully built man with a dark, smooth face and
quick eyes. The Neimoidian did not like the way those eyes were
fixed on him.

The Queen sat upon her throne, surrounded by her handmaidens. She was serene and aloof, detached from everything,
as if what was taking place had no effect on her, could not touch
her in any way. She wore black, her white-painted face in sharp
contrast to the black feathered headdress that wrapped and framed
it. A gold chain lay across her regal brow and the red beauty mark
split her lower lip. She was considered beautiful, Gunray had been
told, but he had no sense of human beauty and by Neimoidian
standards she was simply colorless and small-featured.

What interested him was her youth. She was barely out of
girlhood, certainly not a full-grown woman, and yet the people
of Naboo had chosen her as their Queen. This wasn't one of
those monarchies where blood determined right of rule and dy-
nasties prevailed. The Naboo chose the wisest among them as
their ruler by popular acclaim, and Queen Amidala governed at
the sufferance of her people. Why they would choose someone

so young and naive was a mystery to him. From his point of view it certainly hadn't served them well in this instance.

Governor Sio Bibble's voice echoed through the cavernous chamber, rising to the high, vaulted ceiling, bouncing off the smooth, sunlit walls. Theed was an opulent, prosperous city and the throne room reflected its history of success.

"Viceroy, I ask you point-blank." Sio Bibble was concluding his oration. "How do you intend to explain this invasion to the Senate?"

The Neimoidian's flat, reptilian countenance managed a small flicker of humor. "The Naboo and the Trade Federation will forge a treaty that will legitimize our occupation of Theed. I have been assured that such a treaty, once produced, will be quickly ratified by the Senate."

"A treaty?" the governor exclaimed in astonishment. "In the face of this completely unlawful action?"

Amidala rose from her throne and stepped forward, surrounded by her cloaked and hooded handmaidens. Her eyes were sharp with anger. "I will not cooperate."

Nute Gunray exchanged a quick glance with Rune Haako. "Now, now, Your Highness," he purred. "Don't be too hasty with your pronouncements. You are not going to like what we have in store for your people. In time, their suffering will persuade you to see our point of view."

He turned away. "Enough talk." He beckoned. "Commander?" Battle droid OOM-9 stepped forward, narrow metal snout lowering slightly in response. "Process them," the viceroy ordered.

OOM-9 signaled for one of his sergeants to take over, metallic voice directing that the prisoners be taken to Camp Four. The battle droids herded the Queen, her handmaidens, Governor Bibble, Captain Panaka, and the Naboo guards from the room.

Nute Gunray's slit reddish orange eyes followed them out, then shifted back to Haako and the room. He felt a deep sense of satisfaction take hold. Everything was going exactly as it should.

The sergeant and a dozen battle droids moved the prisoners along the polished stone halls of the Theed palace and outside to where a series of terraced steps led downward through statuary and buttress work to a broad plaza. The plaza was filled with Federation tanks and battle droids and was empty of Naboo citizens. The tanks were squat, shovel-nosed vehicles with their main cannon mounted on a turret above and behind the cockpit and smaller blasters set low and to either side. They had the look of foraging beetles as they edged about the plaza's perimeter.

Beyond, the buildings of Theed stretched away toward the horizon, a vast sprawl of high stone walls, gilded domes, peaked towers, and sculpted archways. Sunlight bathed the gleaming edifices, their architecture in counterpoint to the lush greenness of the planet. The rush of waterfalls and bubble of fountains formed a soft, distant backdrop to the strange silence created by the absence of the populace.

The prisoners were taken across the plaza past the Trade Federation machines of war. No one spoke. Even Governor Bibble had gone silent, his gray-bearded head lowered in dark contemplation. They departed the plaza and turned down a broad avenue that led to the outskirts of the city and the newly constructed Trade Federation detention camps. STAPs hummed overhead, shadows flitting off the walls of the buildings, metal shells gleaming as they darted away.

The droids had just turned their prisoners down a quiet byway when their sergeant, who was leading the procession, brought them to an abrupt halt.

Two men stood directly in their way, both wearing loose robes over belted tunics, the taller with his hair worn long, the shorter with his cut to a thin braided pigtail. Their arms hung loosely at their sides, but they did not have the look of men who were unprepared.

For a moment, each group stared at the other in silence. Then the narrow face of a Gungan peeked out from behind the two robed figures, eyes wide and frightened.

Qui-Gon Jinn stepped forward. "Are you Queen Amidala of the Naboo?" he asked the young woman in the feathered headdress.

The Queen hesitated. "Who are you?"

"Ambassadors from the supreme chancellor." The Jedi Master inclined his head slightly. "We seek an audience with you, Your Highness."

The droid sergeant suddenly seemed to remember where he was and what he was doing. He gestured to his soldiers. "Clear them away!"

Four of the battle droids moved to obey. They were just shifting their weapons into firing position when the Jedi activated their lightsabers and cut them apart. As the shattered droids collapsed, the Jedi moved quickly to dispatch the others. Laser bolts were blocked, weapons were knocked aside, and the remaining droids were reduced to scrap metal.

The sergeant turned to flee, but Qui-Gon brought up his hand, holding the droid fast with the power of the Force. In seconds, the sergeant lay in a ruined heap with his command.

Quickly, the Naboo soldiers moved to recover the fallen weapons. The Jedi Knights flicked off their lightsabers and motioned everyone out of the open street and into the shelter of an alley between two buildings. Jar Jar Binks followed, muttering in wonder at the cold efficiency with which the Jedi had dispatched their enemies.

Qui-Gon faced the Queen. "Your Highness, I am Qui-Gon Jinn and my companion is Obi-Wan Kenobi. We are Jedi Knights as well as ambassadors for the supreme chancellor."

"Your negotiations seem to have failed, Ambassador," Sio Bibble observed with a snort.

"The negotiations never took place." Qui-Gon kept his eyes directed toward the Queen. Her painted face showed nothing. "Your Highness," he continued, "we must make contact with the Republic."

"We can't," Captain Panaka volunteered, stepping forward. "They've knocked out all our communications."

An alarm was being given from somewhere close, and there was the sound of running. Qui-Gon glanced toward the street where the battle droids lay. "Do you have transports?"

The Naboo captain nodded, quick to see what the Jedi intended. "In the main hangar. This way."

He led the little group to the end of the alleyway, where they crossed to other passageways and backstreets, encountering no one. They moved quickly and silently through the growing sound of alarms and the wicked buzz of STAPs. To their credit, the Naboo did not resist Qui-Gon's leadership nor question his appearance. With Panaka and his men newly armed, the Naboo Queen and her companions had a sense of being in control of their own destiny once more and seemed more than ready to take a chance on their rescuers.

It did not take them long to reach their destination. A series of connected buildings dominated one end of a broad causeway, each one domed and cavernous, the central structures warded by arched entrances and low, flat-walled outbuildings. Battle droids were stationed everywhere, weapons held at the ready, but Captain Panaka was able to find an unguarded approach down a narrow corridor between adjoining buildings.

At a side door to the main hangar, Panaka brought the group to a halt. After a quick glance over his shoulder for droids, he unlocked and nudged open the hangar door. With Qui-Gon Jinn pressed close, he peered inside. A handful of Naboo ships were grouped at the center of the hangar, sleek gleaming transports, their noses pointed toward a wide opening in the far wall. Battle droids guarded each, positioned across the entire floor of the hangar to cut off any unseen approach.

Panaka pointed to a long, low ship on the far side of the hangar with swept-back wings and powerful Headon-5 engines. "The Queen's personal transport," he whispered to the Jedi Master.

Qui-Gon nodded. A J-type 327 Nubian. In the distance, the alarms continued to sound their steady wail. "That one will do," he said.

Panaka scanned the hangar interior. "The battle droids. There are too many of them."

The Jedi eased back from the door. "That won't be a problem." He faced the Queen. "Your Highness. Under the circumstances, I suggest you come to Coruscant with us."

The young woman shook her head, the feathers on her headdress rustling softly. Her white-painted face was calm and her gaze steady. "Thank you, Ambassador, but my place is here with my people."

"I don't think so," Qui-Gon responded, locking eyes. "The Trade Federation has other plans. They will kill you if you stay."

Sio Bibble pushed to the Queen's side. "They wouldn't dare!"

"They need her to sign a treaty to make this invasion of theirs legal!" Captain Panaka pointed out. "They can't afford to kill her!"

The Queen looked from face to face, the barest flicker of uncertainty showing in her eyes.

"The situation here is not what it seems," Qui-Gon pressed. "There is something else going on, Your Highness. There is no logic to the Federation's actions. My instincts tell me they will destroy you."

A shadow of real alarm crossed Sio Bibble's face as the Jedi Master finished. His strong features melted slightly. "Your Highness," he said slowly. "Perhaps you should reconsider. Our only hope is for the Senate to take our side in this matter. Senator Palpatine will need your help."

Captain Panaka was having none of it. "Getting past their blockade is impossible, Your Highness—even if we were to get off the planet! An escape attempt is too dangerous—"

"Your Highness, I will stay here and do what I can," Sio Bibble interrupted, shaking his head at Panaka. "They will have to retain the Council of Governors in order to maintain some semblance of order. But you must leave—"

Queen Amidala brought up her hand sharply to silence the debate. Turning from her governor and head of security and the Jedi as well, she looked suddenly to her handmaidens, who were pressed close about her. "Either choice presents great risk to all of us. . . ," she said softly, looking from face to face.

Qui-Gon watched the exchange, puzzled. What was the Queen seeking?

The handmaidens glanced at one another, faces barely visible within the confines of red and gold hooded robes. All were silent.

Finally, one spoke. "We are brave, Your Highness," Padmé said firmly.

Alarms continued to sound. "If you are to leave, Your Highness, it must be now," Qui-Gon urged.

Queen Amidala straightened and nodded. "So be it. I will plead our case before the Senate." She glanced at Sio Bibble. "Be careful, Governor."

She took the governor's hand briefly, then beckoned to three of her handmaidens. Those not chosen began to cry softly. Amidala embraced them and whispered words of encouragement. Captain Panaka selected two of the four guards to stay behind with the handmaidens and Sio Bibble.

The Jedi Knights moved through the side door and into the hangar, leading the way for Jar Jar and the Naboo. "Stay close," Qui-Gon admonished softly over his shoulder.

Captain Panaka moved next to him, dark face intense. "We need a pilot for the vessel." He pointed to where a group of Naboo were being held captive in a corner of the hangar by a squad of battle droids. The insignia on their uniforms indicated a mix of guards, mechanics, and pilots. "There."

"I'll take care of it," Obi-Wan declared, and veered toward the Naboo captives.

Qui-Gon and the rest continued on, striding boldly across the hangar floor, moving directly toward the Queen's vessel, ignoring the battle droids who moved to intercept them. Qui-Gon took note of the fact that the boarding ramp to the transport was lowered. More battle droids were closing on them, curious without yet being alarmed.

"Don't stop for anything," he said to the Queen, and he reached beneath his cloak for the lightsaber.

They were barely twenty meters from the Queen's transport

when the nearest of the battle droids challenged them. "Where are you going?" it asked in its blank, metallic voice.

"Get out of the way," Qui-Gon ordered. "I am an ambassador for the supreme chancellor, and I am taking these people to Coruscant."

The droid brought up his weapon quickly, blocking the Jedi Master's passage. "You are under arrest!"

It was scrap metal within seconds, dissected by Qui-Gon's lightsaber. More of the battle droids rushed to stop the Jedi, who stood alone against them as his charges boarded the Nubian vessel. Captain Panaka and the Naboo guards formed a protective screen for the Queen and her handmaidens as they hurried up the ramp. Jar Jar Binks clambered after, holding on to his head with his long arms. Laser bolts lanced through the hangar from all directions, and new alarms blared wildly.

On the far side of the hangar, Obi-Wan Kenobi launched himself at the battle droids holding the Naboo pilots hostage, cutting into them with ferocious determination. Qui-Gon watched his progress, long hair flying out as he withstood yet another rush from the battle droids attempting to reclaim the Queen's transport, blocking their laser bolts as he fought to hold the boarding ramp. Obi-Wan was running toward him now, a handful of the Naboo in tow. Explosions rose all around them, deadly laser fire burning into metal and flesh. Several of the Naboo went down, but the battle droids were unable to slow the Jedi.

Qui-Gon called sharply to Obi-Wan as he went past, telling him to get the ship in the air. More battle droids were appearing at the hangar doors, weapons firing. Qui-Gon backed quickly up the loading ramp and into the transport's dimly lit interior. The ramp rose behind him and closed with a soft whoosh.

The Headon-5 engines were firing even before the Jedi

Master reached the main cabin and flung himself into a chair. Laser fire hammered at the sides of the sleek craft, but it was already beginning to move forward. The pilot sat hunched forward over the controls, his weathered face intense, a sheen of sweat beading his forehead, hands steady on the controls. "Hold on," he said.

The Nubian shot through the hangar doors, ripping past battle droids and laser fire, lifting away from the city of Theed into the blue, sunlit sky. The planet of Naboo was left behind in seconds, the ship rising into the darkness of space, arcing toward a suddenly visible cluster of Trade Federation battleships blocking its way.

Qui-Gon left his seat and came forward to stand beside the pilot.

"Ric Olié," the other announced with a quick glance up at the Jedi. "Thanks for helping out back there."

Qui-Gon nodded. "Better save your thanks until we deal with what's up here."

The pilot gave him a rakish grin. "Copy that. What do we do about these big boys? Our communications are still jammed."

"We're past the point of talking. Just keep the ship on course." Qui-Gon turned to Obi-Wan. "Make sure everyone is settled safely in place." His eyes moved to where Jar Jar Binks was already up and poking about.

The younger Jedi moved quickly to take the Gungan in hand, propelling him forcibly through the main cabin door and into the anteway beyond. Ignoring Jar Jar's protests, he glanced about for somewhere to stash the bothersome creature. Catching sight of a low, cramped entry with the words ASTROMECH DROIDS lettered above, he released the retaining latch and shoved the Gungan inside.

"Stay here," he directed with a meaningful look. "And keep out of trouble."

Jar Jar Binks watched the door close behind him, then glanced around. A line of five R2 astromech droids stood against one wall, short, dome-topped, all-purpose mechanics painted different colors, their lights off, their engines quiet. Five identical units, each stout body positioned between two sturdy restraint arms, they gave no indication of being aware of him. The Gungan ambled along in front of them, waiting to be noticed. Maybe they weren't activated, he thought. Maybe they weren't even alive.

"Heydey ho, yous," he tried, hands gesturing. "'Tis a long trip somewheres, hey?"

No response. Jar Jar tapped the closest R2 unit, a bright red droid, on the head. The tap made a hollow sound, and the head popped up a notch from the cylindrical body.

"Whoa!" Jar Jar said, surprised. He glanced around, wondering why the Jedi had put him down here when everyone else was up there. Nothing much to do down here, he thought disconsolately. Nothing much happening.

Curious, he gripped the red droid's head and lifted gently. "Dis opens?" he whispered. He lifted some more. Something caught. He yanked hard. "Dis . . . ooops!"

The head lifted right out of its seating. Springs and wires popped out in a tangled mess. Jar Jar quickly jammed the red droid's head back into place, easing his three-fingered hands away cautiously.

"Oh, oh, oh," he murmured, glancing about to make sure no one had seen, hugging himself worriedly.

He moved down the line of droids, still looking for something to occupy his time. He didn't want to be in this room, but he didn't think he should try to leave, either. The younger Jedi, the one who had stuck him in here, didn't like him much as it was. The Jedi would like him a whole lot less if he caught Jar Jar sneaking out of this room.

Explosions sounded close by the transport. Cannon fire. The ship rocked in response to a series of near misses. Jar Jar looked about wildly, suddenly not liking where he was at all. Then the running lights began to flicker, and the transport shook violently. Jar Jar moaned, and crouched down in a corner. More explosions sounded, and the craft was buffeted from side to side.

"We doomed," the frightened Gungan muttered. "Tis bad business, dis."

Abruptly the ship began to spin as if caught in a whirlpool. Jar Jar cried out, fastening his arms about a strut to keep from being thrown against the walls. The lights in the compartment all came on, and the droids were abruptly activated. One by one, they began to whir and beep. Released from their restraints, they rolled out of their racks toward an airlock at one end of the compartment—all but the red R2, who rolled directly into a wall and fell over, more parts tumbling out.

The R2 unit painted blue paused as it motored by its red counterpart, then charged past Jar Jar, giving out a loud screech that caused the Gungan to jerk away in fright.

One after another, the four R2 units entered the airlock lift and were sucked up toward the top of the ship.

Left behind in the storage compartment with the droid he had unwittingly sabotaged, Jar Jar Binks moaned in despair.

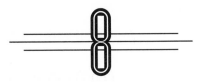

Obi-Wan Kenobi had just reentered the transport's cockpit when explosions began to buffet the ship. He could see a huge Trade Federation battleship looming ahead through the viewport, cannons firing. The Queen's transport was rocked so violently by the blasts that it was thrown from its trajectory. Ric Olié's gloved hands were locked onto the steering grips, fighting to bring the slender craft back into line.

"We should abort, sir!" the pilot shouted at Qui-Gon, who was braced at his side, eyes fixed on the battleship. "Our deflector shields can't withstand much more of this!"

"Stay on course," the Jedi Master ordered calmly. He glanced down at the controls. "Do you have a cloaking device?"

"This is not a warship!" Captain Panaka snapped, looking angry and betrayed. "We have no weapons, Ambassador! We're a nonviolent people, which is why the Trade Federation was brave enough to attack us in the first place!"

A series of explosions jarred the Nubian, and the lights on the control panel flickered weakly. An alarm sounded, shrill and angry. The transport shuddered, its power drive stalling momentarily in a high-pitched whine.

"No weapons," Qui-Gon Jinn breathed. Obi-Wan was next to him, feeling the weight of the other's gaze as it shifted to find him, steady and unwavering. One hand settled on Ric Olié's shoulder. "The Trade Federation uses pulser tracking for its weapons. Spin the ship. It will make it difficult for them to get a reading on us."

The pilot nodded, flipped a series of levers, and put the Nubian into a slow spin. Ahead, the battleship filled the viewport, then lost focus. The Queen's transport accelerated, racing toward the enemy craft, whipping past towers and gunports, bays and stabilizers, speeding down an alleyway of jagged metal protrusions and cannon fire. A laser bolt hammered into them, causing sparks and smoke to explode from one panel, sending the ship reeling. For a brief moment they were tumbling out of control. Then Ric Olié pulled back hard on the controls, and the hull of the battleship receded.

"Something's wrong," the pilot announced quietly, fighting the steering, feeling the ship shudder beneath. "Shields are down!"

They continued to spin, to hug the cavernous shell of the Trade Federation battleship, so close that the larger guns were rendered useless and only the smaller could chance firing at them. But without shields even a glancing hit could be disastrous.

"Sending out the repair crew!" Olié shouted, and flipped a lever.

On the viewscreen, an airlock snapped open, and one by one a series of astromech droids popped out of the hatch and onto the transport's hull. The transport straightened and leveled out, and the spinning stopped. The droids motored swiftly across the hull, seeking out the damage as Ric Olié hugged the battleship's shadow in an effort to protect them.

But now there was a new threat. Unable to bring the weapons of their warship to bear in an effective manner, the Trade Federation command dispatched a squad of starfighters. Small, sleek, robot attack ships, they consisted of twin compartments attached to a rounded, swept-back head. As they roared out of the battleship bays, their compartments opened into long slits that exposed their laser guns. Down the length of the mother ship they tore, seeking out the Queen's transport. Fast and maneuverable, they had no trouble working close to the battleship's hull. In seconds, they were on top of the transport, weapons firing. Ric Olié struggled to find cover and gain speed. Two of the R2 units were blown away, one on a direct hit, the second when its hold on the transport hull was shattered.

On the viewscreen, the blue R2 unit could be seen working furiously to connect a series of wires exposed by a damaged hull plate. Laser fire lanced all around it, but it continued its effort without stopping. The fourth droid, working close by, disappeared in a cloud of shattered metal and brilliant fire.

Now only the blue unit remained, still busy amid the onslaught of Trade Federation starfighters. Something changed on the cockpit display, and Ric Olié gave a shout of approval. "The shields are up! That little droid did it!" He jammed the thrusters all the way forward, and the transport rocketed away from both the battleship and the starfighters, leaving the Trade Federation blockade and the planet of Naboo behind.

The lone R2 unit turned and motored back into the airlock and disappeared from view.

When they were well away from any Trade Federation

presence, Ric Olié made a thorough check of the controls, assessing their damage, trying to determine what was needed. Obi-Wan sat next to him in the copilot's seat, lending help. Qui-Gon and Captain Panaka stood behind them, awaiting their report. The Queen and the rest of the Naboo had been secured in other chambers.

Ric Olié shook his head doubtfully. "We can't go far. The hyperdrive is leaking."

Qui-Gon Jinn nodded. "We'll have to land somewhere to make repairs to the ship. What's out there?"

Ric Olié punched in a star chart, and they hunched over the monitor, studying it.

"Here, Master," Obi-Wan said, his sharp eyes picking out the only choice that made any sense. "Tatooine. It's small, poor, and out of the way. It attracts little attention. The Trade Federation has no presence there."

"How can you be sure?" Captain Panaka asked quickly.

Qui-Gon glanced at him. "It's controlled by the Hutts."

Panaka started in alarm. "The Hutts?"

"It's risky," Obi-Wan agreed, "but there's no reasonable alternative."

Captain Panaka was not convinced. "You can't take Her Royal Highness there! The Hutts are gangsters and slavers! If they discovered who she was—"

"It would be no different than if we landed on a planet in a system controlled by the Trade Federation," Qui-Gon interrupted, "except the Hutts aren't looking for the Queen, which gives us an advantage."

The Queen's head of security started to say something more, then thought better of it. He took a deep breath instead, frustration etched on his smooth, dark face, and turned away.

Qui-Gon Jinn tapped Ric Olié on the shoulder. "Set course for Tatooine."

In a remote conference room on the Trade Federation's flagship, Nute Gunray and Rune Haako sat side by side at a long table, staring nervously at a hologram of Darth Sidious positioned at the table's head. The hologram shimmered with the movements of the Sith Lord's dark cloak, a patchwork of small nuances that the Neimoidians found themselves unable to read.

The Sith Lord had not been summoned. The Neimoidians would have been happy if he had chosen not to communicate with them at all this day. But in keeping with the way he always seemed to sense when things were not going right, he had appeared on his own. Demanding a report on the progress of the invasion, he had settled back to listen to Nute Gunray's narrative and had said nothing since.

"We control all the cities in the northern and western part of the Naboo territory," the viceroy was relating, "and we are searching for any other settlements where resistance—"

"Yes, yes," Darth Sidious interrupted suddenly, his soft voice vaguely impatient. "You've done well. Now, then. Destroy all their high-ranking officials. Do so quietly, but be thorough." He paused. "What of Queen Amidala? Has she signed the treaty?"

Nute Gunray took a deep breath and let it out slowly. "She has disappeared, my lord. There was an escape—"

"An escape?" The Sith Lord spoke the words in a low hiss.

"One Naboo cruiser got past the blockade—"

"How did she escape, Viceroy?"

Nute Gunray looked at Rune Haako for help, but his counterpart was paralyzed with fear. "The Jedi, my lord. They found their way to her, overpowered her guards . . ."

Darth Sidious stirred within his robes like a big cat, shadows glimmering within the confines of his concealing hood. "Viceroy, find her! I want that treaty signed!"

"My lord, we have been unable to locate the ship she escaped on," the Neimoidian admitted, wishing he could sink into the floor right then and there.

"Viceroy!"

"Once it got by us, we tried to give pursuit, but it managed to elude us! Now it's out of our range—"

A wave of one robed arm cut him short. "Not for a Sith, it isn't," the other whispered.

Something shimmered in the background of the hologram, and a figure emerged from the darkness behind Darth Sidious. Nute Gunray froze. It was a second Sith Lord. But whereas Darth Sidious was a vague and shadowy presence, this new Sith was truly terrifying to look upon. His face was a mask of jagged red and black patterns, the design etched into his skin, and his skull was hairless and studded with a crown of short, hooked horns. Gleaming yellow eyes fixed on the Neimoidians, breaking past their defenses, stripping them bare and dismissing them as insignificant and foolish.

"Viceroy," Darth Sidious spoke softly in the sudden silence, "this is my apprentice, Lord Maul. He will find your lost ship."

Nute Gunray inclined his head slightly in acknowledgment, averting his eyes from the frightening presence. "Yes, my lord."

The hologram shimmered and disappeared, leaving the conference room empty of sound. The Neimoidians sat without moving, without even looking at each other, reptilian eyes fixed on the space the hologram had occupied.

"This is getting out of hand," Nute Gunray ventured finally, his voice high and tight, thinking that their plans for sabotaging the trade-routes tax did not contemplate risking their lives in the process.

Rune Haako managed a quick nod. "We should not have made this bargain. What will happen when the Jedi become aware that we are doing business with these Sith Lords?"

Nute Gunray, his hands clasped tightly before him, did not care to venture an answer.

Aboard the Queen's transport, the Jedi stood with Captain Panaka and the remaining R2 unit as the captain gave his report to the Queen on the events surrounding their escape through the Trade Federation blockade. Amidala sat surrounded by her three handmaidens, white face framed by the black headdress, dark eyes steady, listening as the captain concluded.

"We are lucky to have this one in our service, Your Highness." Panaka glanced down at the blue-domed astromech droid. "It is an extremely well put together little droid. Without a doubt, it saved the ship back there, not to mention our lives."

Amidala nodded, eyes shifting to the droid. "It is to be commended. What is its number?"

The little blue droid, lights blinking on and off as it processed the conversation, gave a series of small beeps and tweets. Captain Panaka reached down and scraped a large smudge off the droid's metal shell, then straightened.

"Artoo-Detoo, Your Highness."

Queen Amidala leaned forward, and a slender white hand came out to touch the droid's domed casing. "Thank you, Artoo-Detoo. You have proven both loyal and brave." She glanced over her shoulder. "Padmé."

One of her handmaidens came forward. Qui-Gon Jinn, listening to the exchange with half an ear as he considered the problems that lay ahead on Tatooine, noticed it was the young woman who had supported the Queen's decision to escape from Naboo. He frowned. Except, it hadn't been exactly like that . . .

"See to the cleaning up of this little droid." The Queen was speaking to the girl. "Artoo-Detoo deserves our gratitude." She turned back to Panaka. "Please continue with your report, Captain."

Panaka glanced uncomfortably at the Jedi Knights. "Your Highness, we are heading for a remote planet called Tatooine." He paused, unwilling to speak further on the matter.

"It is a system far beyond the reach of the Trade Federation." Qui-Gon stepped into the gap smoothly. "Once there, we will be able to make needed repairs to the ship, then to travel on to Coruscant and complete our journey."

"Your Highness," Captain Panaka said quickly, regaining his thoughts on the matter. "Tatooine is very dangerous. It's controlled by the Hutts. The Hutts are gangsters and slavers. I do not agree with the Jedi on their decision to land there."

The Queen looked at Qui-Gon. The Jedi did not waver. "You must trust my judgment, Your Highness."

"Must I?" Amidala asked quietly. She shifted her gaze to her handmaidens, ending with Padmé. The girl had not moved from the Queen's side, but seemed to remember suddenly she had been given a task to complete. She nodded briefly to the Queen, and moved to take R2-D2 in hand.

Amidala looked back at Qui-Gon Jinn. "We are in your hands," she advised, and the matter was settled.

Jar Jar Binks had been left in the droid storage hold until after the lone R2 unit returned through the airlock and the

Naboo came to retrieve it. They didn't seem to have any orders regarding the Gungan, so they simply left him to his own devices. At first Jar Jar was reluctant to venture out, still thinking of the younger Jedi's admonishment to stay put and out of trouble. He'd managed one out of two, and he wasn't sure he wanted to tempt fate.

But in the end his curiosity and restlessness got the better of him. The transport had stopped spinning, the Trade Federation attack had ceased, and the warning alarms had been silenced. Everything was peaceful, and the Gungan saw no reason why he should have to stay shut away in this tiny room for one more minute.

So he cracked the door, stuck his billed face out for a look around, eyestalks swiveling guardedly, saw no one, and made his decision. He left the storage room and wandered along the ship's corridors—choosing a path that took him away from the cockpit, where the Jedi were likely to be found. He waited for someone to tell him to go back to where he had come from, but no one did, so he began to poke into things, careful what he touched, but unable to help himself sufficiently to forgo all investigation.

He was following a narrow corridor that led up from the lower levels of the transport to the main cabin when he poked his head through an airlock to find one of the Queen's handmaidens hard at work with an old cloth cleaning the R2 astromech droid.

"Heydey ho!" he called out.

The handmaiden and the R2 unit both started, the girl with a small cry and the droid with a loud beep. Jar Jar jumped in turn, then slowly eased himself through the opening, embarrassed that he had frightened them so badly.

"Me sorry," he apologized. "Me not mean to scare yous. Okeday?"

The girl smiled. "That's all right. Come over here."

Jar Jar came forward a few steps, studying the condition of the droid. "Me find oilcan back dere. Yous need it?"

The girl nodded. "It would help. This little guy is quite a mess."

Jar Jar scrambled back through the opening, groped about a bit, found the oilcan he had remembered, and brought it to the girl. "This helps?"

"Thank you," she said, accepting the can. She flipped up the cap and poured some of the oil onto the cloth, then began rubbing the R2 unit's dome.

"Me Jar Jar Binks," Jar Jar said after a few moments, taking a chance on trying to continue the conversation. He liked this Naboo girl.

"I'm Padmé," the girl answered. "I attend Her Highness, Queen Amidala. This is Artoo-Detoo." She rubbed a black smudge from the droid's strut. "You're a Gungan, aren't you?" Jar Jar nodded, long ears flapping against his neck. "How did you end up here with us?"

Jar Jar thought about it a minute. "Me not know exactly. Da day start okeday wit da sunnup. Me munchen clams. Den, boom! Maccaneks every which way, dey flyen, dey scooten . . . Me get very scared. Den Jedi runnen, and me grab Quiggon, den maccaneks rollen over, den go down under da lake to Otoh Gunga ta da Boss Nass . . ."

He stopped, not knowing where else to go. Padmé was nodding encouragingly. R2-D2 beeped. "Tis 'bout it. Before me know what, pow! Me here!"

He sat back on his haunches and shrugged. "Get very, very scared."

He looked from the girl to the droid. Padmé smiled some more. R2-D2 beeped again. Jar Jar felt pretty good.

In the cockpit, Ric Olié was directing the transport toward a large yellowish planet that was steadily filling up the viewport as they approached its surface. The Jedi and Captain Panaka stood behind him, peering over his shoulder at the ground maps he had punched up on the monitors.

"Tatooine," Obi-Wan Kenobi confirmed, speaking to no one in particular.

Ric Olié pointed to one of the maps on the scopes. "There's a settlement that should have what we need . . . a spaceport, it looks like. Mos Espa." He glanced up at the Jedi.

"Land near the city's outskirts," Qui-Gon Jinn ordered. "We don't want to attract attention."

The pilot nodded and began to guide the transport in. It took only moments to direct it down through the planet's atmosphere to a patch of desert just in sight of the city. The Nubian landed in a swirl of dust, settling comfortably in place atop its landing struts. In the distance, Mos Espa glimmered faintly through the shimmer of the midday heat.

Qui-Gon sent his protégé to uncouple the hyperdrive and Captain Panaka to advise the Queen of their landing. He was settled on going into the spaceport alone as he left the cockpit to find other clothing and came upon Jar Jar Binks, the Queen's hand-maiden Padmé, and the little R2 unit.

He slowed, considering the possibility that going into the city alone would make him more noticeable. "Jar Jar," he said finally. "Get ready. You're going with me. The droid as well."

He continued on without looking back. The Gungan stared

after him in disbelief, then in horror. By the time he regained his
wits, the Jedi was out of view. Wailing in dismay, he chased after
him and came upon Obi-Wan in the main cabin hoisting the
hyperdrive out of the bowels of the ship.

"Obi-One, sire!" he gasped, throwing himself to his knees in
front of the younger Jedi. "Pleeese, me no go wit Quiggon!"

Obi-Wan was inclined to agree, but knew better than to say
so. "Sorry, but Qui-Gon is right. This is a multinational spaceport, a trading center. You'll make him appear less obvious by
going along." His brow furrowed as he turned back to the
hyperdrive. "I hope," he muttered to himself.

Jar Jar climbed to his feet and trudged disconsolately toward
R2-D2, his mouth set in a grimace of forbearance. The astromech droid beeped in sympathy, then made a series of encouraging clicks.

Qui-Gon reappeared, dressed now as a farmer in tunic,
leggings, and a poncho. He walked past them to where Obi-Wan
was studying the hyperdrive. "What have you found?"

Obi-Wan's young face clouded. "The generator is shot. We'll
need a new one."

"I thought as much." The Jedi Master knelt next to his
protégé. "Well, we can't risk a communication with Coruscant
this far out on the edge of the galaxy. It might be intercepted and
our position revealed. We'll have to get by on our own." He lowered his voice to a near whisper. "Don't let anyone send a transmission while I'm gone. Be wary, Obi-Wan. I sense a disturbance
in the Force."

Obi-Wan's eyes lifted to find his. "I feel it also, Master. I will
be careful."

Qui-Gon rose, gathered up Jar Jar and the R2 unit, and

headed down the loading ramp to the planet's floor. An empty carpet of sand stretched away in all directions, broken only by massive rock formations and the distant skyline of Mos Espa. The suns that gave the planet life beat down with such ferocity that it seemed as if they were determined to steal that life back again. Heat rose off the sand in a shimmering wave, and the air was so dry it sucked the moisture from their throat and nose passages.

Jar Jar glanced skyward, eyestalks craning, billed amphibious face wrinkling in dismay. "Dis sun gonna do murder ta da skin of dis Gungan," he muttered.

At a signal from Qui-Gon, they began to walk—or, in the case of the R2 unit, to roll. A strange caravan of animals and riders, carts and sleds appeared against the distant skyline like a shadowy mirage, all misshapen and threatening to evaporate in the blink of an eye. Jar Jar muttered some more, but no one was paying attention.

They had not gotten far when a shout brought them around. Two figures were running toward them from the transport. As they neared, Qui-Gon was able to make out Captain Panaka and a girl dressed in rough peasant's garb. He stopped and waited until they caught up, a frown creasing his leonine features.

Panaka was sweating. "Her Highness commands you to take her handmaiden with you. She wishes for Padmé to give her own report of what you might—"

"No more commands from Her Highness today, Captain," Qui-Gon interrupted quickly, shaking his head in refusal. "Mos Espa is not going to be a pleasant place for—"

"The Queen wishes it," Panaka interrupted him right back, his face angry and set. "She is emphatic. She wishes to know more about this planet."

The girl took a step forward. Her dark eyes found Qui-Gon's. "I've been trained in self-defense. I speak a number of languages. I am not afraid. I can take care of myself."

Captain Panaka sighed, looking over his shoulder toward the ship. "Don't make me go back and tell her you refuse."

Qui-Gon hesitated, prepared to do exactly that. Then he looked at Padmé again, saw strength in her eyes, and changed his mind. She might be useful. Traveling with a girl, they might suggest a family in transit and present a less aggressive look.

He nodded. "I don't have time to argue the matter, Captain. I still think this is a bad idea, but she may come." He gave Padmé a look of warning. "Stay close to me."

He started away again, the others trailing. Captain Panaka stood watching with undisguised relief as the strange little procession of Jedi Master, handmaiden, Gungan, and astromech droid moved off into the sweltering landscape toward Mos Espa.

It was not yet midafternoon by the time the members of the little company under Qui-Gon Jinn's command reached Mos Espa and made their way toward the spaceport's center. Mos Espa was large and sprawling and had the look of a gnarled serpent hunkered down in the sand to escape the heat. The buildings were domed and thick-walled and curved to protect against the sun, and the stalls and shops were fronted by awnings and verandas that provided a measure of shade to their vendors. Streets were broad and packed with beings of every shape and size, most from off planet. Some rode the desert-seasoned eopies. Domesticated banthas, massive and horned, and lumbering dewbacks hauled carts, sleds, and wagons that ran on wheels and mechanical tracks by turn, a mishmash of commerce trafficking between Tatooine's smaller ports and the planets of star systems beyond.

Qui-Gon kept a close watch for trouble. There were Rodians and Dugs and others whose purpose was always suspect. Most of those they passed paid them no notice. One or two turned to glance at Jar Jar, but dismissed the Gungan almost out of hand once they got a good look at him. As a group, they blended in nicely. There were so many combinations of creatures of every species that the appearance of one more meant almost nothing.

"Tatooine is home to Jabba the Hutt, who controls the bulk of the trafficking in illegal goods, piracy, and slavery that generates most of the planet's wealth," Qui-Gon was explaining to Padmé. He had been on Tatooine before, though it had been some years ago. "Jabba controls the spaceports and settlements, all of the populated areas. The desert belongs to the Jawas, who scavenge whatever they can find to sell or trade, and to the Tuskens, who live a nomadic life and feel free to steal from everyone."

The Jedi kept his voice low and conversational. The girl walked silently at his elbow, her sharp eyes taking in everything. Speeders nosed by them, and droids of every size toiled in the service of desert-garbed aliens.

"There are a number of farms as well, outlying operations that take advantage of the climate—moisture farms for the most part, operated by off-worlders not a part of the indigenous tribes and scavengers, not connected directly to the Hutts." His eyes swept the street ahead. "This is a rough and dangerous place. Most avoid it. Its few spaceports have become havens for those who do not wish to be found."

Padmé glanced up at him. "Like us," she said.

A pair of domesticated banthas rumbled down the broad avenue, hairy bulks clearing a path for a sled train of quarry blocks and metal struts, horned heads nodding sleepily, padded feet stirring sand and dust in thick clouds with each lumbering step. Their driver dozed atop the foremost sled in the train, small and insignificant in their shadow.

Jar Jar Binks stayed as close as he could manage to the Jedi and the girl, his eyes darting left and right, head swiveling as if it might twist right off his shoulders. Nothing he saw was familiar or welcome. Hard looks followed after him. Sharp eyes measured him for things he would just as soon not think about. Stares were at best challenging and at worst unfriendly. He did not like this place. He wished he were almost anywhere else.

"Tis very bad, dis." He swallowed against a dryness in his throat that was caused by more than the heat. "Nutten good 'bout dis place!" He took a careless step and found himself ankle deep in a foul-smelling ooze. "Oh, oh. Tis icky!"

R2-D2 rolled cheerfully along at his side, beeping and chirping in a futile effort at reassuring the Gungan that all was well.

They traveled the main street of the spaceport to its far end and turned down a side street that led to a small plaza ringed with salvage dealers and junk shops. Qui-Gon glanced at the mounds of engine parts, control panels, and communication chips recovered from starships and speeders.

"We'll try one of these smaller dealers first," he advised, nodding toward one in which a vast pile of old transports and parts was heaped within an attached compound.

They walked through the shop's low entry and were greeted by a pudgy blue creature who flew into their faces like a crazed probe, tiny wings buzzing so fast they could barely be seen. *"Hi chubba da nago?"* it snapped in a frizzy, guttural voice, demanding to know their business.

A Toydarian, Qui-Gon thought. He knew enough to recognize one, but not much else. "I need parts for a J-type 327 Nubian," he advised the other.

The Toydarian fairly beamed with delight, his reticular snout curling over his toothy mouth and making odd smacking noises. "Ah, yes! Nubian! We have lots of that." The sharp, bulbous eyes flicked from one face to the other, ending with the Gungan. "What's this?"

Jar Jar shrank behind Qui-Gon fearfully. "Never mind that." The Jedi brushed the Toydarian's question aside. "Can you help us or not?"

"Can you pay me or not—that's the question!" The skinny blue arms crossed defiantly over the rounded torso as the Toydarian regarded them with disdain. "What kinda junk you after, farmer?"

"My droid has a readout of what I need," Qui-Gon advised the other with a glance down at the R2 unit.

Still hanging midair in front of Qui-Gon's nose, the Toydarian glanced over one shoulder. *"Peedunkel! Naba dee unko!"*

A small, disheveled boy raced in from the salvage yard, coming to an uncertain stop in front of them. His clothes were ragged and thick with grime, and he had the look of someone about to be given a beating. He flinched as the Toydarian wheeled back and lifted a hand in admonishment.

"What took you so long?"

"Mel tass cho-pas kee," the boy responded quickly, blue eyes taking in the newcomers with a quick glance. "I was cleaning out the bin like you—"

"Chut-chut!" The Toydarian threw up his hands angrily. "Never mind the bin! Watch the store! I've got some selling to do!"

He flitted back around to face his customers. "So, let me take you out back. You'll soon find what you need."

He darted toward the salvage yard, beckoning Qui-Gon ea-

gerly. The Jedi followed, with R2-D2 trundling after. Jar Jar moved
to a shelf and picked up an odd-looking bit of metal, intrigued by
its shape, wondering what it was.

"Don't touch anything," Qui-Gon called over his shoulder,
his tone of voice sharp.

Jar Jar put the item down and made a face at Qui-Gon's departing back, sticking out his long tongue in defiance. When the
Jedi was out of sight, he picked up the part again.

Anakin Skywalker could not take his eyes off the girl. He noticed her the moment he entered Watto's shop, even before
Watto said anything, and he hadn't been able to stop looking at
her since. He barely heard what Watto said to him about watching the shop. He barely noticed the strange-looking creature that
had come in with her and was poking around in the shelves and
bins. Even after she noticed he was staring at her, he could not
help himself.

He moved now to an open space on the counter, hoisted
himself up, and sat watching her while pretending to clean a
transmitter cell. She was looking back at him now, embarrassment turning to curiosity. She was small and slender with long,
braided brown hair, brown eyes, and a face he found so beautiful that he had nothing to which he could compare it. She
was dressed in rough peasant's clothing, but she seemed very
self-possessed.

She gave him an amused smile, and he felt himself melting
in confusion and wonder. He took a deep breath. "Are you an
angel?" he asked quietly.

The girl stared. "What?"

"An angel." Anakin straightened a bit. "They live on the

moons of Iego, I think. They are the most beautiful creatures in the universe. They are good and kind, and so pretty they make even the most hardened space pirates cry like small children."

She gave him a confused look. "I've never heard of angels," she said.

"You must be one of them," Anakin insisted. "Maybe you just don't know it."

"You're a funny little boy." The amused smile returned. "How do you know so much?"

Anakin smiled back and shrugged. "I listen to all the traders and pilots who come through here." He glanced toward the salvage yard. "I'm a pilot, you know. Someday, I'm going to fly away from this place."

The girl wandered to one end of the counter, looked away, then back again. "Have you been here long?"

"Since I was very little—three, I think. My mom and I were sold to Gardulla the Hutt, but she lost us to Watto, betting on the pod races. Watto's a lot better master, I think."

She stared at him in shock. "You're a slave?"

The way she said it made Anakin feel ashamed and angry. He glared at her defiantly. "I am a person!"

"I'm sorry," she said quickly, looking upset and embarrassed. "I don't fully understand, I guess. This is a strange world to me."

He studied her intently for a moment, thinking of other things, wanting to tell her of them. "You are a strange girl to me," he said instead. He swung his legs out from the counter. "My name is Anakin Skywalker."

She brushed at her hair. "Padmé Naberrie."

The strange creature she had come in with wandered back to the front of the shop and bent over a stout little droid body with a bulbous nose. Reaching up curiously, it pushed at the nose with one finger. Instantly armatures popped out from every direction, metal limbs swinging into place. The droid's motors whizzed and whirred, and it jerked to life and began moving forward. Padmé's odd companion went after it with a moan of dismay, grabbing on in an effort to slow it down, but the droid continued marching through the shop, knocking over everything it came in contact with.

"Hit the nose!" Anakin called out, unable to keep himself from laughing.

The creature did as it was told, pounding the droid's nose wildly. The droid stopped at once, the arms and legs retracted, the motors shut down, and the droid went still. Both Anakin and Padmé were laughing now, and their laughter increased as they saw the look on the unfortunate creature's long-billed face.

Anakin looked at Padmé and the girl at him. Their laughter died away. The girl reached up to touch her hair self-consciously, but she did not divert her gaze.

"I'm going to marry you," the boy said suddenly.

There was a moment of silence, and she began laughing again, a sweet musical sound he didn't mind at all. The creature who accompanied her rolled his eyes.

"I mean it," he insisted.

"You are an odd one," she said, her laughter dying away. "Why do you say that?"

He hesitated. "I guess because it's what I believe . . ."

Her smile was dazzling. "Well, I'm afraid I can't marry you . . ." She paused, searching her memory for his name.

"Anakin," he said.

"Anakin." She cocked her head. "You're just a little boy."

His gaze was intense as he faced her. "I won't always be," he said quietly.

* * *

In the salvage yard, Watto was studying the screen of a portable memory bank he held in one hand, tracing through his inventory record. Qui-Gon, arms folded into his farmer's poncho, stood waiting patiently, the R2 unit at his side.

"Ah, here it is. A T-14 hyperdrive generator!" The Toydarian's wings beat wildly as he hovered before the Jedi, his gnarled finger jabbing at the viewscreen. "You're in luck. I'm the only one hereabouts who has one. But you might as well buy a new ship. It would be cheaper. Speaking of which, how're you going to pay for all this, farmer?"

Qui-Gon considered. "I have twenty thousand Republic dataries to put toward—"

"Republic credits?" Watto exploded in disgust. "Republic credits are no good out here! I need something better than that, something of value . . ."

The Jedi Master shook his head. "I don't have anything else." One hand came up, passing casually in front of the Toydarian's face. "But credits will do fine."

"No, they won't!" Watto snapped, buzzing angrily.

Qui-Gon frowned, then passed his hand in front of the pudgy blue alien again, bringing the full force of his Jedi suggestive power to bear. "Credits will do fine," he repeated.

Watto sneered. "No, they won't!" he repeated. "What do you think you're doing, waving your hand around like that? You think you're some kinda Jedi? Hah! I'm a Toydarian! Mind tricks don't work on me—only money! No money, no parts, no deal! And no one else has a T-14 hyperdrive generator, I can promise you that!"

Chagrined, Qui-Gon wheeled back for the shop, the R2 unit

following at his heels. The Toydarian shouted after them to come back when they had something worthwhile to trade, still scolding the Jedi Master for trying to foist Republic credits on him. Qui-Gon reentered the shop just as Jar Jar pulled a part from a large stack and sent the entire arrangement tumbling to the floor. His efforts at correcting the problem brought a second display crashing down as well.

The boy and the Queen's handmaiden were deep in discussion, paying no attention to the Gungan.

"We're leaving," Qui-Gon announced to the girl, moving toward the shop's entry, the R2 unit trundling along behind.

Jar Jar was quick to follow, anxious to escape his latest mess. Padmé gave the boy a warm smile. "I'm glad I met you, Anakin," she said, turning after them.

"I'm glad I met you, too," he called after, a reluctance evident in his voice.

Watto flew in from the salvage yard, shaking his head in disgust. "Outlanders! They think because we live so far from everything, we know nothing!"

Anakin was still staring longingly after Padmé, his gaze fixed on the empty doorway. "They seemed nice enough to me."

Watto snorted and flew into his face. "Clean up this mess, then you can go home!"

Anakin brightened, gave a small cheer, and went quickly to work.

Qui-Gon led his companions back through the little plaza of salvage shops toward the main avenue. At a place where two buildings divided to form a shadowed niche, the Jedi Master moved everyone from view and brought out his comlink from beneath his poncho. Padmé and the R2 unit stood waiting patiently, but Jar Jar prowled the space as if trapped, eyes fixed nervously on the busy street.

When Obi-Wan responded to the comlink's pulse, Qui-Gon quickly filled him in on the situation. "Are you sure there isn't anything of value left on board?" he concluded.

There was a pause at the other end. "A few containers of supplies, the Queen's wardrobe, some jewelry maybe. Not enough for you to barter with. Not in the amounts you're talking about."

"All right," Qui-Gon responded with a frown. "Another solution will present itself. I'll check back."

He tucked the comlink beneath his poncho and signaled to the others. He was moving toward the street again when Jar Jar grabbed his arm.

"Noah gain, sire," the Gungan pleaded. "Da beings hereabouts crazy nuts. We goen be robbed and crunched!"

"Not likely," Qui-Gon replied with a sigh, freeing himself. "We have nothing of value. That's our problem."

They started back down the street, Qui-Gon trying to think what to do next. Padmé and R2-D2 stayed close as they made their way through the crowds, but Jar Jar began to lag behind, distracted by all the strange sights and smells. They were passing an outdoor café, its tables occupied by a rough-looking bunch of aliens, among them a Dug who was holding forth on the merits of Podracing. Jar Jar hurried to catch up to his companions, but then caught sight of a string of frogs hanging from a wire in front of a nearby stall. The Gungan slowed, his mouth watering. He had not eaten in some time. He glanced around to see if anyone was looking, then unfurled his long tongue and snapped up one of the frogs. The frog disappeared into Jar Jar's mouth in the blink of an eye.

Unfortunately, the frog was still securely tied to the wire. Jar Jar stood there, the wire hanging out of his mouth, unable to move.

The vendor in charge of the stall rushed out. "Hey, that will be seven truguts!"

Jar Jar glanced frantically down the street for his companions, but they were already out of sight. In desperation, he let go of the frog. The frog popped out of his mouth as if catapulted, winging away at the end of the taut wire. It ricocheted this way and that, breaking free at last to land directly in the Dug's soup, splashing gooey liquid all over him.

The gangly Dug leapt to his feet in fury, catching sight of the hapless Jar Jar as he tried to move away from the frog vendor. Springing across the table on all fours, he was on top of the Gungan in an instant, grabbing him by the throat.

"*Chubba!* You!" the Dug snarled through its corded snout. Feelers and mandibles writhed. "Is this yours?"

The Dug shoved the frog in the Gungan's face threateningly. Jar Jar could not get any words out, gasping for breath, fighting to break free. His eyes rolled wildly as he looked for help that wasn't there. Other creatures pushed forward to surround him, Rodians among them. The Dug threw Jar Jar to the ground, shouting at him, hovering over him in a crouch. Desperately, the Gungan tried to scramble to safety.

"No, no," he moaned plaintively as he sought an avenue of escape. "Why me always da one?"

"Because you're afraid," a voice answered calmly.

Anakin Skywalker pushed his way through the crowd, coming

up to stand next to the Dug. The boy seemed unafraid of the creature, undeterred by the hard-eyed crowd, his bearing self-assured. He gave the Dug an appraising look. "*Chess ko*, Sebulba," he said. "Careful. This one's very well connected."

Sebulba turned to face the boy, cruel face twisting with disdain as he caught sight of the newcomer. *"Tooney rana dunko, shag?"* he snapped, demanding to know what the boy meant.

Anakin shrugged. "Connected—as in Hutt." The blue eyes fixed the Dug and saw a hint of fear in the other's face. "Big-time connected, this one, Sebulba. I'd hate to see you diced before we had a chance to race again."

The Dug spit in fury. "*Neek me chawa!* Next time we race, *wermo*, it will be the end of you!" He gestured violently. "*Uto notu wo shag!* If you weren't a slave, I'd squash you here and now!"

With a final glare at the cringing Jar Jar, Sebulba wheeled away, taking his companions with him, back to their tables and their food and drink. Anakin stared after the Dug. "Yeah, it'd be a pity if you had to pay for me," he said softly.

He was helping Jar Jar back to his feet when Qui-Gon, Padmé, and R2-D2, having finally missed the Gungan, reappeared hurriedly through the crowd.

"Hi!" he greeted cheerfully, happy to see Padmé again so soon. "Your buddy here was about to be turned into orange goo. He picked a fight with a Dug. An especially dangerous Dug."

"Nossir, nossir!" the chagrined Gungan insisted, brushing off dust and sand. "Me hate crunchen. Tis da last thing me want!"

Qui-Gon gave Jar Jar a careful once-over, glanced around at the crowd, and took the Gungan by the arm. "Nevertheless, the boy saved you from a beating. You have a penchant for finding trouble, Jar Jar." He gave Anakin a short nod. "Thank you, my young friend."

Padmé gave Anakin a warm smile as well, and the boy felt himself blush with pride.

"Me doen nutten!" Jar Jar insisted, still trying to defend himself, hands gesturing for emphasis.

"You were afraid," the boy told him, looking up at the long-billed face solemnly. "Fear attracts the fearful. Sebulba was trying to overcome his fear by squashing you." He cocked his head at the Gungan. "You can help yourself by being less afraid."

"And that works for you?" Padmé asked skeptically, giving him a wry look.

Anakin smiled and shrugged. "Well . . . up to a point."

Anxious to spend as much time as possible with the girl, he persuaded the group to follow him a short distance down the street to a fruit stand, a ramshackle affair formed by a makeshift ragged awning stretched over a framework of bent poles. Boxes of brightly colored fruit were arranged on a rack tilted toward the street for viewing. A weathered old lady, gray-haired and stooped, her simple clothing patched and worn, rose from a stool to greet them on their approach.

"How are you feeling today, Jira?" Anakin asked her, giving her a quick hug.

The old lady smiled. "The heat's never been kind to me, you know, Annie."

"Guess what?" the boy replied quickly, beaming. "I've found that cooling unit I've been searching for. It's pretty beat up, but I'll have it fixed up for you in no time, I promise. That should help."

Jira reached out to brush his pink cheek with her wrinkled hand, her smile broadening. "You're a fine boy, Annie."

Anakin shrugged off the compliment and began scanning the fruit display. "I'll take four pallies, Jira." He glanced at Padmé eagerly. "You'll like these."

He reached into his pocket for the truguts he had been saving, but when he brought them out to pay Jira, he dropped one. The farmer, standing next to him, bent to retrieve it. As he did, his poncho opened just far enough that the boy caught sight of the lightsaber hanging from the belt about his waist.

The boy's eyes went wide, but he masked his surprise by focusing on the coins. He only had three, he found. "Whoops, I thought I had more," he said quickly, not looking up. "Make that three pallies, Jira. I'm not that hungry anyway."

The old woman gave Qui-Gon, Padmé, and Jar Jar their pallies and took the coins from Anakin. A gust of wind whipped down the street, rattling the framework of poles and causing the awning to billow. A second gust sent dust swirling in all directions.

Jira rubbed her arms with her gnarled hands. "Gracious, my bones are aching. There's a storm coming, Annie. You'd better get home quick."

The wind gusted in a series of sharp blasts that sent sand and loose debris flying. Anakin glanced at the sky, then at Qui-Gon. "Do you have shelter?" he asked.

The Jedi Master nodded. "We'll head back to our ship. Thank you again, my young friend, for—"

"Is your ship far?" the boy interrupted hurriedly. All around them, shopkeepers and vendors were closing and shuttering windows and doors, carrying goods and wares inside, wrapping coverings over displays and boxes.

"It's on the city's outskirts," Padmé answered, turning away from the stinging gusts of sand.

Anakin took her hand quickly, tugging on it. "You'll never reach the outskirts in time. Sandstorms are very, very dangerous. Come with me. You can wait it out at my home. It's not far. My mom won't mind. Hurry!"

With the wind howling all about them and the air clouded with sand, Anakin Skywalker shouted good-bye to Jira and led his newly adopted charges down the street in a rush.

On the outskirts of Mos Espa, Obi-Wan Kenobi stood near the nose of the Nubian as the wind gathered force, whipping at his robe, tearing across the broad expanse of the Tatooine desert. His troubled eyes looked off into the distance where Mos Espa was beginning to disappear behind a curtain of sand. He turned as Captain Panaka came down the ramp of the transport to join him.

"This storm's going to slow them down," the Jedi observed worriedly.

Panaka nodded. "It looks pretty bad. We'd better seal up the ship before it gets any worse."

There was a beep from the soldier's comlink. Panaka retrieved the communicator from his belt. "Yes?"

Ric Olié's voice rose from the speaker. "We're receiving a message from home."

Panaka and Obi-Wan exchanged glances. "We'll be right there," the captain advised.

They went up the ramp quickly, sealing it behind them. The transmission had been received in the Queen's chambers. At Ric Olié's direction, they found Amidala and her handmaidens Eirtaé and Rabé viewing a hologram of Sio Bibble that was shimmering weakly at one end of the room, the governor's voice breaking up in transmission.

". . . cut off all our food supplies until you return . . . death toll rising, catastrophic . . . must bow to their wishes, Your Highness . . ." Sio Bibble's image and voice faded and returned, garbled still. "Please, I beg of you, tell us what to do! If you can hear me, Your Highness, you must contact me . . ."

The transmission flickered and disappeared. The governor's voice faded into silence. Queen Amidala sat staring at the empty space it left behind, her smooth face troubled. Her hands worked quietly in her lap, betraying a nervousness she could not quite manage to hide.

Her gaze shifted to Obi-Wan. The Jedi shook his head quickly. "It is a trick. Send no reply, Your Highness. Send no transmission of any kind."

The Queen stared at him uncertainly for a moment, then nodded in acquiescence. Obi-Wan left her chambers without further comment, hoping fervently he had made the right decision.

The sandstorm raged through the streets of Mos Espa in a blinding, choking whirlwind that tore at clothes and exposed skin with relentless force. Anakin held Padmé's hand so as not to lose her, the farmer, the amphibious creature, and the R2 unit trailing behind, fighting to reach his home in the city's slave quarters while there was still time. Other residents and visitors struggled past, engaged in a similar pursuit, heads lowered, faces covered, bodies bent over as if weighted by age. Somewhere in the distance, an eopie bawled in fright. The light turned an odd yellowish gray, obscured by sand and grit, and the buildings of the city disappeared in a deep, impenetrable haze.

Even as he fought his way through the storm, Anakin's thoughts were directed elsewhere. He was thinking of Padmé, of having the chance to take her home to meet his mother, of being able to show her his projects, of holding her hand some more. It sent a flush through him that was both warm and kind of scary. It made him feel good about himself. He was thinking of the farmer, too—if that's what he was, which Anakin was pretty sure he wasn't. He carried a lightsaber, and only Jedi carried light-sabers. It was almost too much to hope for, that a real Jedi might be going to his home, to visit him. But Anakin's instincts told him he was not mistaken, and that something mysterious and exciting had brought this little group to him.

He was thinking, finally, of his dreams and his hopes for himself and his mother, thinking that maybe something wonderful would come out of this unexpected encounter, something that would change his life forever.

They reached the slave quarters, a jumbled collection of hovels stacked one on top of the other so that they resembled anthills, each complex linked by common walls and switchback stairways, the plaza fronting them almost empty as the sandstorm chased everyone under cover. Anakin led his charges through the gritty gloom to his front door and pushed his way inside.

"Mom! Mom! I'm home!" he called excitedly.

Adobe walls, whitewashed and scrubbed, glimmered softly in a mix of storm-clouded sunlight admitted through small, arched windows and a diffuse electric glow from ceiling fixtures. They stood in the main room, a smallish space dominated by a table and chairs. A kitchen occupied one wall and a work space another. Openings led to smaller nooks and sleeping rooms.

Outside, the wind howled past the doors and windows, shaving a fresh layer of skin from the exterior of the walls.

Jar Jar Binks looked around with a mix of curiosity and relief. "Tis cozy," he murmured.

Anakin's mother entered from a work area off to one side, brushing her hands on her dress. She was a woman of forty, her long brown hair tied back from her worn face, her clothing rough and simple. She had been pretty once, and Anakin would say she was pretty still, but time and the demands of her life were catching up with her. Her smile was warm and youthful as she greeted her son, but it faded quickly as she caught sight of the people behind him.

"Oh, my!" she exclaimed softly, glancing uncertainly from face to face. "Annie, what's this?"

Anakin beamed. "These are my friends, Mom." He smiled at Padmé. "This is Padmé Naberrie. And this is—" He stopped. "Gee, I guess I don't know any of your names," he admitted.

Qui-Gon stepped forward. "I'm Qui-Gon Jinn, and this is Jar Jar Binks." He indicated the Gungan, who made a sort of fluttering gesture with his hands.

The R2 unit made a small beep.

"And our droid, Artoo-Detoo," Padmé finished.

"I'm building a droid," Anakin announced quickly, anxious to show Padmé his project. "You wanna see?"

"Anakin!" His mother's voice stopped him in his tracks. Resolve tightened her features. "Anakin, why are they here?"

He looked at her, confused. "There's a sandstorm, Mom. Listen."

She glanced at the door, then out the windows. The wind howled past, a river of sand and grit.

"Your son was kind enough to offer us shelter," Qui-Gon explained. "We met at the shop where he works."

"Come on!" Anakin insisted, grabbing Padmé's hand once more. "Let me show you my droid."

He led Padmé toward his bedroom, already beginning a detailed explanation of what he was doing. The girl followed without arguing, listening attentively. R2-D2 went with them, beeping in response to the boy's words.

Jar Jar stayed where he was, still looking around, appearing to want someone to tell him what to do. Qui-Gon stood facing the boy's mother in awkward silence. Grains of sand beat against the thick glass of the windows with a rapid pocking sound.

"I'm Shmi Skywalker," she said, holding out her hand. "Anakin and I are pleased to have you as our guests."

Qui-Gon had already appraised the situation and determined what was needed. He reached under his poncho and pulled five small capsules from a pouch in his belt. "I know this is unexpected. Take these. There's enough food for a meal."

She accepted the capsules. "Thank you." Her eyes lifted and lowered again. "Thank you very much. I'm sorry if I was abrupt. I'll never get used to Anakin's surprises, I guess."

"He's a very special boy," Qui-Gon offered.

Shmi's eyes lifted again, and the look she gave him suggested they shared an important secret.

"Yes," she said softly, "I know."

In his bedroom, Anakin was showing Padmé C-3PO. The droid lay on his workbench, deactivated at the moment because the boy was in the process of fabricating its metal skin. He had completed the internal wiring, but its torso, arms, and legs were still bare of any covering. One eye was out of its head as well, lying nearby where he had left it after tightening down the visual refractor the night before.

Padmé bent over his shoulder, studying the droid carefully.

"Isn't he great?" Anakin asked eagerly, anxious for her reaction. "He's not finished yet, but he will be soon."

"He's wonderful," the girl answered, genuinely impressed.

The boy flushed with pride. "You really like him? He's a protocol droid . . . to help Mom. Watch!"

He activated C-3PO with a flip of its power switch, and the droid sat up at once. Anakin rushed around hurriedly, searching, then snatched up the missing eye from his workbench and snapped it into its proper socket.

C-3PO looked at them. "How do you do? I am a protocol droid trained in and adept at cyborg relatives . . . customs and humans . . ."

"Ooops," Anakin said quickly. "He's a little confused."

He snatched up a long-handled tool with an electronic designator and fitted it carefully to a port in C-3PO's head, then ratcheted the handle several turns, studying the setting as he did so. When he had it where he wanted, he pushed a button on the handle. C-3PO jerked several times in response. When Anakin removed the designator, the droid stood up from the workbench and faced Padmé.

"How do you do? I am See-Threepio, human-cyborg relations. How may I serve you?"

Anakin shrugged. "I just named him the other day, but I forgot to enter the code in his memory banks so he could tell you himself."

Padmé grinned at Anakin, delighted. "He's perfect!"

R2-D2 sidled up to them and emitted a sharp flurry of beeps and whistles.

C-3PO glanced down curiously. "I beg your pardon . . . what do you mean, I'm naked?"

R2-D2 beeped some more.

"Goodness! How embarrassing!" C-3PO glanced quickly over his skeletal limbs. "My parts are showing? My goodness!"

Anakin pursed his lips. "Sort of. But don't worry, I'll fix that soon enough." He eased the droid back toward the workbench, glancing over his shoulder at Padmé. "When the storm is over, you can see my racer. I'm building a Podracer. But Watto doesn't know about it. It's a secret."

Padmé smiled. "That's okay. I'm very good at keeping secrets."

The storm continued throughout the remainder of the day, engulfing Mos Espa, sand blown in from the desert piling up against the shuttered buildings, forming ramps against doorways and walls, clouding the air, and shutting out the light. Shmi Skywalker used the food capsules Qui-Gon had given her to prepare dinner for them. As she worked on their meal and while Padmé was occupied with Anakin in the other room, Qui-Gon moved off alone into one corner and surreptitiously contacted Obi-Wan on the comlink. The connection was less than perfect, but they were able to communicate sufficiently for the Jedi Master to learn of the transmission from Naboo.

"You made the right choice, Obi-Wan," he assured his young protégé, keeping his voice low.

"The Queen is very upset," the other advised, his response crackling through the storm.

Qui-Gon glanced over to where Shmi was standing at the cook surface, her back turned. "That transmission was bait to establish a trace. I'm certain of it."

"But what if Governor Bibble is telling the truth and the Naboo are dying?"

Qui-Gon sighed. "Either way, we're running out of time," he advised quietly, and ended the transmission.

They sat down to eat Shmi's dinner a short while after, the storm still howling without, an eerie backdrop of sound against the silence within. Qui-Gon and Padmé occupied the ends of the table, while Anakin, Jar Jar, and Shmi sat at its sides. Anakin, in the way of small boys, began talking about life as a slave, in no way embarrassed to be doing so, thinking of it only as a fact of his life and anxious to share himself with his new friends. Shmi, more protective of her son's station, was making an effort to help their guests appreciate the severity of their situation.

"All slaves have transmitters placed inside their bodies," Shmi was explaining.

"I've been working on a scanner to try to locate them, but so far no luck," Anakin said solemnly.

Shmi smiled. "Any attempt at escape . . ."

". . . and they blow you up!" the boy finished. "Poof!"

Jar Jar had been slurping contentedly at his soup, listening with half an ear as he devoured the very tasty broth. He overdid it on hearing this, however, making such a loud noise that he stopped conversation altogether. All eyes turned on him momentarily. He lowered his head in embarrassment and pretended not to see.

Padmé looked back at Shmi. "I can't believe slavery is still permitted in the galaxy. The Republic's antislavery laws should—"

"The Republic doesn't exist out here," Shmi interrupted quickly, her voice hard. "We must survive on our own."

There was an awkward silence as Padmé looked away, not knowing what else to say.

"Have you ever seen a Podrace?" Anakin asked, trying to ease her discomfort.

Padmé shook her head no. She glanced at Shmi, noting the sudden concern on the woman's lined face. Jar Jar launched his tongue at a morsel of food nestled deep in a serving bowl at the far end of the table, deftly plucking it out, drawing it in, swallowing it, and smacking his lips in satisfaction. A disapproving look from Qui-Gon quickly silenced him.

"They have Podracing on Malastare," the Jedi Master observed. "Very fast, very dangerous."

Anakin grinned. "I'm the only human who can do it!" A sharp glance from his mother wiped the grin from his face. "Mom, what? I'm not bragging. It's true! Watto says he's never heard of a human doing it."

Qui-Gon studied him carefully. "You must have Jedi reflexes if you race Pods."

Anakin smiled broadly at the compliment. Jar Jar's tongue snaked toward the serving bowl in an effort to snare another morsel, but this time Qui-Gon was waiting. His hand moved swiftly, and in a heartbeat he had secured the Gungan's tongue between his thumb and forefinger. Jar Jar froze, his mouth open, his tongue held fast, his eyes wide.

"Don't do that again," Qui-Gon advised, an edge to his soft voice.

Jar Jar tried to say something, but it came out an unintelligible mumble. Qui-Gon released the Gungan's tongue, and it snapped back into place. Jar Jar massaged his billed mouth ruefully.

Anakin's young face lifted to the older man's, and his voice was hesitant. "I . . . I was wondering something."

Qui-Gon nodded for him to continue.

The boy cleared his throat, screwing up his courage. "You're a Jedi Knight, aren't you?"

There was a long moment of silence as the man and the boy stared at each other. "What makes you think that?" Qui-Gon asked finally.

Anakin swallowed. "I saw your lightsaber. Only Jedi Knights carry that kind of weapon."

Qui-Gon continued to stare at him, then leaned back slowly in his chair and smiled. "Perhaps I killed a Jedi and stole it from him."

Anakin shook his head quickly. "I don't think so. No one can kill a Jedi."

Qui-Gon's smile faded and there was a hint of sadness in his dark eyes. "I wish that were so . . ."

"I had a dream I was a Jedi," the boy said quickly, anxious to talk about it now. "I came back here and freed all the slaves. I dreamed it just the other night, when I was out in the desert." He paused, his young face expectant. "Have you come to free us?"

Qui-Gon Jinn shook his head. "No, I'm afraid not . . ." He trailed off, hesitating.

"I think you have," the boy insisted, defiance in his eyes. "Why else would you be here?"

Shmi was about to say something, to chastise her son for his impudence perhaps, but Qui-Gon spoke first, leaning forward conspiratorially. "I can see there's no fooling you, Anakin. But you mustn't let anyone know about us. We're on our way to Coruscant, the central system in the Republic, on a very important mission. It must be kept secret."

Anakin's eyes widened. "Coruscant? Wow! How did you end up out here in the Outer Rim?"

"Our ship was damaged," Padmé answered him. "We're stranded here until we can repair it."

"I can help!" the boy announced quickly, anxious to be of service to them. "I can fix anything!"

Qui-Gon smiled at his enthusiasm. "I believe you can, but

our first task, as you know from our visit to Watto's shop, is to acquire the parts we need."

"Wit nutten ta trade," Jar Jar pointed out sourly.

Padmé was looking at Qui-Gon speculatively. "These junk dealers must have a weakness of some kind."

"Gambling," Shmi said at once. She rose and began clearing the table of dishes. "Everything in Mos Espa revolves around betting on those awful Podraces."

Qui-Gon rose, walked to the window, and stared out through the thick, diffuse glass at the clouds of windblown sand. "Podracing," he mused. "Greed can be a powerful ally, if it's used properly."

Anakin leapt to his feet. "I've built a racer!" he declared triumphantly. His boy's face shone with pride. "It's the fastest ever! There's a big race day after tomorrow, on Boonta Eve. You could enter my Pod! It's all but finished—"

"Anakin, settle down!" his mother said sharply, cutting him short. Her eyes were bright with concern. "Watto won't let you race!"

"Watto doesn't have to know the racer is mine!" the boy replied quickly, his mind working through the problem. He turned back to Qui-Gon. "You could make him think it was yours! You could get him to let me pilot it for you!"

The Jedi Master had caught the look in Shmi's eyes. He met her gaze, silently acknowledged her consternation, and waited patiently for her response.

"I don't want you to race, Annie," his mother said quietly. She shook her head to emphasize her words, weariness and concern reflected in her eyes. "It's awful. I die every time Watto makes you do it. Every time."

Anakin bit his lip. "But, Mom, I love it!" He gestured at

Qui-Gon. "And they need my help. They're in trouble. The prize money would more than pay for the parts they need."

Jar Jar Binks nodded in support. "We in kinda bad goo."

Qui-Gon walked over to Anakin and looked down at him. "Your mother's right. Let's drop the matter." He held the boy's gaze for a moment, then turned back to his mother. "Do you know of anyone friendly to the Republic who might be able to help us?"

Shmi stood silent and unmoving as she thought the matter through. She shook her head no.

"We have to help them, Mom," Anakin insisted, knowing he was right about this, that he was meant to help the Jedi and his companions. "Remember what you said? You said the biggest problem in the universe is that no one helps anyone."

Shmi sighed. "Anakin, don't—"

"But you said it, Mom." The boy refused to back down, his eyes locked on hers.

Shmi Skywalker made no response this time, her brow furrowed, her body still.

"I'm sure Qui-Gon doesn't want to put your son in danger," Padmé said suddenly, uncomfortable with the confrontation they had brought about between mother and son, trying to ease the tension. "We will find another way . . ."

Shmi looked over at the girl and shook her head slowly. "No, Annie's right. There is no other way. I may not like it, but he can help you." She paused. "Maybe he was meant to help you."

She said it as if coming to a conclusion that had eluded her until now, as if discovering a truth that, while painful, was obvious.

Anakin's face lit up. "Is that a yes?" He clapped his hands in glee. "That *is* a yes!"

* * *

Night blanketed the vast cityscape of Coruscant, cloaking the endless horizon of gleaming spires in deep velvet layers. Lights blazed from windows, bright pinpricks against the black. As far as the eye could see, as far as a being could travel, the city's buildings jutted from the planet's surface in needles of steel alloy and reflective glass. Long ago, the city had consumed the planet with its bulk, and now there was only the city, the center of the galaxy, the heartbeat of the Republic's rule.

A rule that some were intending to end once and for all. A rule that some despised.

Darth Sidious stood high on a balcony overlooking Coruscant, his concealing black robes making him appear as if he were a creature produced by the night. He stood facing the city, his eyes directed at its lights, at the faint movement of its air traffic, disinterested in his apprentice, Darth Maul, who waited to one side.

His thoughts were of the Sith and of the history of their order.

The Sith had come into being almost two thousand years ago. They were a cult given over to the dark side of the Force, embracing fully the concept that power denied was power wasted. A rogue Jedi Knight had founded the Sith, a singular dissident in an order of harmonious followers, a rebel who understood from the beginning that the real power of the Force lay not in the light, but in the dark. Failing to gain approval for his beliefs from the Council, he had broken with the order, departing with his knowledge and his skills, swearing in secret that he could bring down those who had dismissed him.

He was alone at first, but others from the Jedi order who believed as he did and who had followed him in his study of the dark side soon came over. Others were recruited, and soon the ranks of the Sith swelled to more than fifty in number. Disdaining the concepts of cooperation and consensus, relying on the belief that acquisition of power in any form lends strength and yields control, the Sith began to build their cult in opposition to the Jedi. Theirs was not an order created to serve; theirs was an order created to dominate.

Their war with the Jedi was vengeful and furious and ultimately doomed. The rogue Jedi who had founded the Sith order was its nominal leader, but his ambition excluded any sharing of power. His disciples began to conspire against him and each other almost from the beginning, so that the war they instigated was as much with each other as with the Jedi.

In the end, the Sith destroyed themselves. They destroyed their leader first, then each other. What few survived the initial bloodbath were quickly dispatched by watchful Jedi. In a matter of only weeks, all of them died.

All but one.

Darth Maul shifted impatiently. The younger Sith had not yet learned his Master's patience; that would come with time and training. It was patience that had saved the Sith order in the end. It was patience that would give them their victory now over the Jedi.

The Sith who had survived when all of his fellows had died had understood that. He had adopted patience as a virtue when the others had forsaken it. He had adopted cunning, stealth, and subterfuge as the foundation of his way—old Jedi virtues the others had disdained. He stood aside while the Sith tore at each other like kriks and were destroyed. When the carnage was complete, he went into hiding, biding his time, waiting for his chance.

When it was believed all of the Sith were destroyed, he

emerged from his concealment. At first he worked alone, but he was growing old and he was the last of his kind. Eventually, he went out in search of an apprentice. Finding one, he trained him to be a Master in his turn, then to find his own apprentice, and so to carry on their work. But there would only be two at any one time. There would be no repetition of the mistakes of the old order, no struggle between Siths warring for power within the cult. Their common enemy was the Jedi, not each other. It was for their war with the Jedi they must save themselves.

The Sith who reinvented the order called himself Darth Bane.

A thousand years had passed since the Sith were believed destroyed, and the time they had waited for had come at last.

"Tatooine is sparsely populated." His student's rough voice broke into his thoughts, and Darth Sidious lifted his eyes to the hologram. "The Hutts rule. The Republic has no presence. If the trace was correct, Master, I will find them quickly and without hindrance."

The yellow eyes glimmered with excitement and anticipation in the strange mosaic of Darth Maul's face as he waited impatiently for a response. Darth Sidious was pleased.

"Move against the Jedi first," he advised softly. "You will then have no difficulty taking the Queen back to Naboo, where she will sign the treaty."

Darth Maul exhaled sharply. Satisfaction permeated his voice. "At last we will reveal ourselves to the Jedi. At last we will have our revenge."

"You have been well trained, my young apprentice," Darth Sidious soothed. "The Jedi will be no match for you. It is too late for them to stop us now. Everything is going as planned. The Republic will soon be in my control."

In the silence that followed, the Sith Lord could feel a dark heat rise inside his chest and consume him with a furious pleasure.

In the home of Anakin Skywalker, Qui-Gon Jinn stood silently at the doorway of the boy's bedroom and watched him sleep. His mother and Padmé occupied the other bedroom, and Jar Jar Binks was curled up on the kitchen floor in a fetal position, snoring loudly.

But Qui-Gon could not sleep. It was this boy—this boy! There was something about him. The Jedi Master watched the soft rise and fall of his chest as he lay locked in slumber, unaware of Qui-Gon's presence. The boy was special, he had told Shmi Skywalker, and she had agreed. She knew it, too. She sensed it as he did. Anakin Skywalker was different.

Qui-Gon lifted his gaze to a darkened window. The storm had subsided, the wind abated. It was quiet without, the night soft and welcoming in its peace. The Jedi Master thought for a moment on his own life. He knew what they said about him at Council. He was willful, even reckless in his choices. He was strong, but he dissipated his strength on causes that did not merit his attention. But rules were not created solely to govern behavior. Rules were created to provide a road map to understanding the Force. Was it so wrong for him to bend those rules when his conscience whispered to him that he must?

The Jedi folded his arms over his broad chest. The Force was a complex and difficult concept. The Force was rooted in the balance of all things, and every movement within its flow risked an upsetting of that balance. A Jedi sought to keep the balance in place, to move in concert to its pace and will. But the Force existed on more than one plane, and achieving mastery of its multiple passages was a lifetime's work. Or more. He knew his own weakness. He was too close to the life Force when he should have been more attentive to the unifying Force. He found himself reaching out to the creatures of the present, to those living in the here and now. He had less regard for the past or the future, to the creatures that had or would occupy those times and spaces.

It was the life Force that bound him, that gave him heart and mind and spirit.

So it was he empathized with Anakin Skywalker in ways that other Jedi would discourage, finding in this boy a promise he could not ignore. Obi-Wan would see the boy and Jar Jar in the same light—useless burdens, pointless projects, unnecessary distractions. Obi-Wan was grounded in the need to focus on the larger picture, on the unifying Force. He lacked Qui-Gon's intuitive nature. He lacked his teacher's compassion for and interest in all living things. He did not see the same things Qui-Gon saw.

Qui-Gon sighed. This was not a criticism, only an observation. Who was to say that either of them was the better for how they interpreted the demands of the Force? But it placed them at odds sometimes, and more often than not it was Obi-Wan's position the Council supported, not Qui-Gon's. It would be that way again, he knew. Many times.

But this would not deter him from doing what he believed he must. He would know the truth about Anakin Skywalker. He would discover his place in the Force, both living and unifying. He would learn who this boy was meant to be.

Minutes later, he was stretched out on the floor, asleep.

The new day dawned bright and clear, Tatooine's twin suns blazing down out of a clear blue sky. The sandstorm had moved on to other regions, sweeping the landscape clean of everything but the mountains and rocky outcroppings of the desert and the buildings of Mos Espa. Anakin was up and dressed before his guests stirred awake, eager to get to the shop and advise Watto of his plan for the upcoming Podrace. Qui-Gon warned him not to be too eager in making his suggestion to the Toydarian, but to stay calm and let Qui-Gon handle the bargaining. But Anakin was so excited he barely heard what the other was saying. The Jedi Master knew it would be up to him to employ whatever mix of cunning and diplomacy was required to achieve their ends.

Greed was the operative word in dealing with Watto, of course, the key that would open any door the Toydarian kept locked.

They walked from the slave quarters through the city to Watto's shop, Anakin leading the way, Qui-Gon and Padmé close at his heels, Jar Jar and R2-D2 bringing up the rear. The city was awake and bustling early, the shopkeepers and merchants shoveling and sweeping away drifts of sand, reassembling stalls and awnings, and righting carts and damaged fences. Eopies and rontos performed the heavy labor where sleds and droids lacked sufficient muscle. Wagons were already hauling fresh supplies and merchandise from warehouses and storage bins, and the receiving bays of the spaceport were back to welcoming ships from off planet.

Qui-Gon let Anakin go on ahead to the shop as they drew near, in order to give the boy a chance to approach Watto on the subject of the Podraces first. With the others in tow, the Jedi Master moved to a food stall across the way, persuaded a vendor to part with a handful of gooey dweezels, and bided his time. When the dweezels were consumed, he moved his group across the plaza to the front of Watto's shop. Jar Jar, already unsettled anew by all the activity, took up a position on a crate near the shop entry, his back to the wall, his eyes darting this way and that in anticipation of something awful befalling him. R2-D2 moved over beside him, beeping softly, trying to reassure him that everything was okay.

Qui-Gon told Padmé to keep a wary eye on the Gungan. He didn't want Jar Jar getting into any more trouble. He was starting into the shop when the girl put a hand on his arm.

"Are you sure about this?" she asked, doubt mirrored clearly in her brown eyes. "Trusting our fate to a boy we hardly know?" She wrinkled her smooth brow. "The Queen would not approve."

Qui-Gon met her gaze squarely. "The Queen does not need to know."

Her eyes blazed defiantly. "Well, I don't approve."

He gave her a questioning look, then turned away wordlessly.

Inside the salvage shop, he found Watto and Anakin engaged in a heated discussion, the Toydarian hovering centimeters from the boy's face, blue wings a blur of motion, snout curled inward as he gestured sharply and purposely with both hands.

"Patta go bolla!" he shouted in Huttese, chubby body jerking with the force of his words.

The boy blinked, but held his ground. *"No batta!"*

"Peedunkel!" Watto flitted backward and forward, up and down, everything moving at once.

"Banyo, banyo!" Anakin shouted.

Qui-Gon moved out of the shadowed entry and into the light where they could see him clearly. Watto turned away from Anakin at once, toothy mouth working, and flew into Qui-Gon's face in a frenzy of ill-concealed excitement.

"The boy tells me you want to sponsor him in the race tomorrow!" The words exploded out of him. "You can't afford parts! How can you afford to enter him in the race? Not on Republic credits, I think!"

He broke into raucous laughter, but Qui-Gon did not miss the hint of curiosity that gleamed in his slitted eyes.

"My ship will be the entry fee," the Jedi advised bluntly.

He reached beneath his poncho and brought out a tiny holoprojector. Clicking on the power source, he projected a hologram of the Queen's transport into the air in front of Watto. The Toydarian flitted closer, studying the projection carefully.

"Not bad. Not bad." The wrinkled blue proboscis bobbed. "A Nubian."

"It's in good order, except for the parts we need." Qui-Gon gave him another moment, then flicked off the holoprojector and tucked it back beneath his poncho.

"But what would the boy ride?" Watto demanded irritably. "He smashed up my Pod in the last race. It will take too long to fix it for the Boonta."

Qui-Gon glanced at Anakin, who was clearly embarrassed. "Aw, it wasn't my fault, really. Sebulba flashed me with his port vents. I actually saved the Podracer . . . mostly."

Watto laughed harshly. "That he did! The boy is good, no doubts there!" He shook his head. "But still . . ."

"I have acquired a Pod in a game of chance," Qui-Gon interrupted smoothly, drawing the other's attention back to him. "The fastest ever built."

He did not look at Anakin, but he imagined the expression on the boy's face.

"I hope you didn't kill anyone I know for it!" Watto snapped. He burst into a new round of laughter before bringing himself under control again. "So, you supply the Podracer and the entry fee; I supply the boy. We split the winnings fifty-fifty, I think."

"Fifty-fifty?" Qui-Gon brushed the suggestion aside. "If it's going to be fifty-fifty, I suggest you front the cost of the entry. If we win, you keep all the winnings, minus the cost of the parts I need. If we lose, you keep my ship."

Watto was clearly caught by surprise. He thought the matter through, hand rubbing at his snout, wings beating the air with a buzzing sound. The offer was too good, and he was suspicious. Out of the corner of his eye, Qui-Gon saw Anakin glance over at him nervously.

"Either way, you win," Qui-Gon pointed out softly.

Watto pounded his fist into his open palm. "Deal!" He turned to the boy, chuckling. "Your friend makes a foolish bargain, boy! Better teach him what you know about how to deal for goods!"

He was still laughing as Qui-Gon left the shop.

*   *   *

The Jedi Master collected Padmé, Jar Jar, and R2-D2, and left word for Anakin to join them as soon as Watto would free him up to work on the Podracer. Since Watto was more interested in the upcoming race than in managing the shop, he dismissed the boy at once with instructions to make certain the racer he would be driving was a worthy contender and not some piece of space junk that would cause everyone to laugh at the Toydarian for his foolish decision to enter it in the first place.

As a result, Anakin was home almost before Qui-Gon and the others, eagerly leading them to where his project was concealed in the slave quarter bone yards. The Podracer was shaped like a narrow half cylinder with a rudder-skid attached to its flat bottom, a cockpit carved into its curved top, and steering arms attached at its sides. Sleek Radon-Ulzer fighter engines with scoop-air stabilizers towed the Pod at the end of Steelton cables. The effect was something like seeing a doop bug attached to a pair of banthas.

Working together, the company activated the antigrav lifts and guided the Pod and its enormous engines into the courtyard in back of Anakin's home. With Padmé, Jar Jar, and R2-D2 lending assistance and encouragement, the boy immediately went to work prepping the Pod for the upcoming race.

While Anakin and his helpers were thus engaged, Qui-Gon mounted the back porch of the Skywalker home, glanced around to make certain he was alone, and switched on the comlink to contact Obi-Wan. His protégé answered immediately, anxious for a report, and Qui-Gon filled him in on what was happening.

"If all goes well, we will have our hyperdrive generator by tomorrow afternoon and be on our way," he concluded.

Obi-Wan's silence was telling. "What if this plan fails, Master? We could be stuck here for a long time."

Qui-Gon Jinn looked out over the squalor of the slave quarters and the roofs of the buildings of Mos Espa beyond, the suns a bright glare overhead. "A ship without a power supply will not get us anywhere. We have no choice."

He switched off the comlink and tucked it away. "And there is something about this boy," he whispered to himself, leaving the thought unfinished.

Shmi Skywalker appeared through the back door and moved over to join him. Together they stood watching the activity in the courtyard below.

"You should be proud of your son," Qui-Gon said after a moment. "He gives without any thought of reward."

Shmi nodded, a smile flitting over her worn face. "He knows nothing of greed. Only of dreams. He has . . ."

"Special powers."

The woman glanced at him warily. "Yes."

"He can see things before they happen," the Jedi Master continued. "That's why he appears to have such quick reflexes. It is a Jedi trait."

Her eyes were fixed on him, and he did not miss the glimmer of hope that shone there. "He deserves better than a slave's life," she said quietly.

Qui-Gon kept his gaze directed out at the courtyard. "The Force is unusually strong with him, that much is clear. Who was his father?"

There was a long pause, long enough for the Jedi Master to realize he had asked a question she was not prepared to answer. He gave her time and space to deal with the matter, not pressing her, not making it seem as if it were necessary she answer at all.

"There is no father," she said finally. She shook her head slowly. "I carried him, I gave birth to him. I raised him. I can't tell you any more than that."

She touched his arm, drawing his eyes to meet hers. "Can you help him?"

Qui-Gon was silent for a long time, thinking. He felt an attachment to Anakin Skywalker he could not explain. In the back of his mind, he sensed he was meant to do something for this boy, that it was necessary he try. But all Jedi were identified within the first six months of birth and given over to their training. It was true for him, for Obi-Wan, for everyone he knew or had heard about. There were no exceptions.

Can you help him? He did not know how that was possible.

"I don't know," he told her, keeping his voice gentle, but firm. "I didn't come here to free slaves. Had he been born in the Republic, we would have identified him early, and he might have become a Jedi. He has the way. I'm not sure what I can do for him."

She nodded in resignation, but her face revealed, beneath the mask of her acceptance, a glimmer of hope.

As Anakin tightened the wiring on the thruster relays to the left engine, a group of his friends appeared. The older boys were Kitster and Seek, the younger girl was Amee, and the Rodian was Wald. Anakin broke off his efforts to complete the wiring long enough to introduce them to Padmé, Jar Jar, and R2-D2.

"Wow, a real astromech droid!" Kitster exclaimed, whistling softly. "How'd you get so lucky?"

Anakin shrugged. "That isn't the half of it," he declared, puffing up a bit. "I'm entered in the Boonta tomorrow."

Kitster made a face and pushed back his mop of dark hair. "What? With this?"

"That piece of junk has never even been off the ground," Wald said, nudging Amee. "This is such a joke, Annie."

"You've been working on that thing for years," Amee observed, her small, delicate features twisting in disapproval. She shook her blond head. "It's never going to run."

Anakin started to say something in defense of himself, then decided against it. Better to let them think whatever they wanted for now. He would show them.

"Come on, let's go play ball," Seek suggested, already turning away, a hint of boredom in his voice. "Keep it up, Annie, and you're gonna be bug squash."

Seek, Wald, and Amee hurried off, laughing back at him. But Kitster was his best friend and knew better than to doubt Anakin when he said he was going to do something. So Kitster stayed behind, ignoring the others. "What do they know?" he said quietly.

Anakin gave him a grin of appreciation. Then he noticed Jar Jar fiddling with the left engine's energy binder plate, the power source that locked the engines together and kept them in sync, and the grin disappeared.

"Hey! Jar Jar!" he shouted in warning. "Stay away from those energy binders!"

The Gungan, bent close to the protruding plate, looked up guiltily. "Who, me?"

Anakin put his hands on his hips. "If your hand gets caught in the beam, it will go numb for hours."

Jar Jar screwed up his face, then put his hands behind his back and stuck his billed face back down by the plate. Almost instantly an electric current arced from the plate to his mouth, causing him to yelp and jump back in shocked surprise. Both hands clamped over his mouth as he stood staring at the boy in disbelief.

"Ist numm! Ist numm!" Jar Jar mumbled, his long tongue hanging loosely. "My tongue is fat. Dats my bigo oucho." Anakin shook his head and went back to work on the wiring.

Kitster moved close to him, watching silently, his dark face intense. "You don't even know if this thing will run, Annie," he observed with a frown.

Anakin didn't look up. "It will."

Qui-Gon Jinn appeared at his shoulder. "I think it's about time we found out." He handed the boy a small, bulky cylinder. "Use this power pack. I picked it up earlier in the day. Watto has less need for it than you." One corner of his mouth twitched in a mix of embarrassment and amusement.

Anakin knew the value of a power pack. How the Jedi had managed to secure one from under Watto's nose, he had no idea and no interest in finding out. "Yes, sir!" he beamed.

He jumped into the cockpit, fitted the power pack into its sleeve in the control panel, and set the activator to the ON position. Then he pulled on his old, dented racing helmet and gloves. As he did so, Jar Jar, who had been fiddling around at the back of one of the engines, managed to get his hand caught in the afterburner. The Gungan began leaping up and down in terror, his mouth still numb from the shock he had received from the energy binders, his bill flapping to no discernible purpose. Padmé caught sight of him at the last minute—his arms windmilling frantically—and yanked him free an instant before the engines ignited.

Flame exploded from the afterburners, and a huge roar rose from the Radon-Ulzers, building steadily in pitch until Anakin eased off on the thrusters, then settling back into a throaty rumble. Cheers rose from the spectators, and Anakin waved his hand in response.

On the porch of their home, Shmi Skywalker watched word-lessly, her eyes distant and sad.

Twilight brought a blaze of gold and crimson in the wake of Tatooine's departing suns, a splash of color that filled the hori-zon in a long, graceful sweep. Night climbed after, darkening the sky, bringing out the stars like scattered shards of crystal. In the deepening black, the land was silent and watchful.

A gleam of bright metal caught the last of the fading suns' rays, and a small transport sped out of the Dune Sea toward Mos Espa. Shovel-nosed and knife-edged, its wings swept back and its vertical stabilizers crimped inward top to bottom, it hugged the landscape as it climbed promontories and descended valleys, searching. Dark and immutable, it had the look of a predator, of a hunter at work.

Beyond the Dune Sea, following the failing light, the craft settled swiftly on the broad plateau of a mesa that gave a long-range view of the land in all directions. Wild banthas scattered with its approach, tossing their hairy heads and massive horns, trumpeting their disapproval. The transport came to rest and its engines shut down. It sat there in silence, waiting.

Then the aft hatchway slid open, metal stairs lowered, and Darth Maul appeared. The Sith Lord had discarded his black robes and wore loose-fitting desert garb, a collared coat belted at the waist, his lightsaber hanging within easy reach. His stunted horns, fully exposed now with his hood removed, formed a wicked crown above his strange red-and-black-colored face. Ig-noring the banthas, he walked to the edge of the mesa, produced a pair of low-light electrobinoculars, and began to scan the horizon in all directions.

Desert sand and rocks, he was thinking. Wasteland. But a city there, and another there. And there, a third.

He took the electrobinoculars from his eyes. The lights of the cities were clearly visible against the growing dark. If there were others, they were far on the other side of the Dune Sea where he had already been, or beyond the horizon much farther still where he would later be required to go.

But the Jedi, he believed, were here.

There was no expression on his mosaic face, but his yellow eyes gleamed expectantly. Soon now. Soon.

He lifted his arm to view the control panel strapped to his forearm, picked out the settings he wished to engage, and punched in the calculations required to identify the enemy he was looking for. Jedi Knights would manifest a particularly strong presence in the Force. It took only a minute. He turned back toward his ship. Spherical probe droids floated through the hatchway, one after another. When all were clear, they rocketed away toward the cities he had identified.

Darth Maul watched until they were out of view, the darkness closing quickly now. He smiled faintly. Soon.

Then he walked back to his ship to begin monitoring their response.

Darkness cloaked Mos Espa in deepening layers as night descended. Anakin sat quietly on the balcony rail of his back porch while Qui-Gon studied a deep cut in the boy's arm. Anakin had sustained the cut sometime during the afternoon's prep work on the Podracer, and in typical boy fashion, he hadn't even noticed it until now.

Anakin gave the injury a cursory glance as the Jedi prepared
to clean it, then leaned back to look up at the blanket of stars in
the sky.

"Sit still, Annie," Qui-Gon instructed.

The boy barely heard him. "There are so many! Do they all
have a system of planets?"

"Most of them." Qui-Gon produced a clean piece of cloth.

"Has anyone been to all of them?"

Qui-Gon laughed. "Not likely."

Anakin nodded, still looking up. "I want to be the first one
then, the first to see them all—ouch!"

Qui-Gon wiped a smear of blood from the boy's arm, then
applied some antiseptic. "There, good as new."

"Annie! Bedtime!" Shmi called out from inside.

Qui-Gon produced a comlink chip and wiped a sample of
Anakin's blood onto its surface. The boy leaned forward interest-
edly. "What are you doing?"

The Jedi barely looked up. "Checking your blood for
infections."

Anakin frowned. "I've never seen—"

"Annie!" his mother called again, more insistent this time.
"I'm not going to tell you again!"

"Go on," Qui-Gon urged, gesturing toward the doorway.
"You have a big day tomorrow." He tucked the cloth into his
tunic. "Good night."

Anakin hesitated, his eyes fixed on the Jedi Master, intense
and questioning. Then he turned and darted off into his home.
Qui-Gon waited a moment, making sure he was alone, then
slipped the chip with the boy's blood sample into a relay slot in
the comlink and called Obi-Wan aboard the Queen's transport.

"Yes, Master?" his protégé responded, alert in spite of the lateness of the hour.

"I'm transmitting a blood sample," Qui-Gon advised, glancing about guardedly as he spoke. "Run a midi-chlorian test on it."

He sent the blood readings through the comlink to Obi-Wan and stood waiting in the silence. He could feel the beating of his heart, quick and excited. If he was right about this . . .

"Master," Obi-Wan interrupted his musings. "There must be something wrong with the sample."

Qui-Gon took a slow, deep breath and exhaled softly. "What do the readings say, Obi-Wan?"

"They say the midi-chlorian count is twenty thousand." The younger Jedi's voice tightened. "No one has a count that high. Not even Master Yoda."

No one. Qui-Gon stood staring out into the night, staggered by the immensity of his discovery. Then he let his gaze wander back toward the hovel where the boy was sleeping, and stiffened.

Shmi Skywalker stood just inside the doorway, staring at him. Their eyes met, and for just an instant it felt to the Jedi Master as if the future had been revealed to him in its entirety. Then Shmi turned away, embarrassed, and disappeared back into her home.

Qui-Gon paused a moment, then remembered the open comlink. "Good night, Obi-Wan," he said softly, and clicked the transmitter off.

Midnight approached. Anakin Skywalker, unable to sleep, had slipped out of his bed and gone down into the backyard to complete a final check of the racer, of its controls, its wiring, its relays, its power source—everything he could think of. Now he stood staring at it, trying to determine what he might have missed, what he might have overlooked. He could afford no mistakes. He must make certain he had done all that he could.

So that he would win tomorrow's race.

Because he must.

He must.

He watched R2-D2 scuttle around the racer, applying paint in broad strokes to its polished metal body, aided by a light projecting from a receptacle mounted over his visual sensors and a steady stream of advice from C-3PO. The boy had activated the latter earlier on the advice of Padmé. Many hands make light work, she had intoned solemnly, then grinned. C-3PO wasn't much with his hands, but his vocoder was certainly tireless. In any case, R2-D2 seemed to like having him around, exchanging beeps and chirps with his protocol counterpart as he scuttled about the racer. The little astromech droid worked tirelessly, cheerfully, and willingly. Nothing perturbed him. Anakin envied him. Droids were either well put together or they weren't. Unlike humans, they didn't respond to weariness or disappointment or fear . . .

He chased the thought away quickly and looked up at the starry sky. After a moment, he sat down, his back against a crate of old parts, his goggles and racing helmet at his side. Idly, he fingered the japor carving in his pocket, the one he was working on for Padmé. His thoughts drifted. He couldn't explain it exactly, but he knew that tomorrow would change his life. That strange ability to see what others did not, that sometimes gave him insights into what would happen, told him so. His future was coming up on him in a rush, he sensed. It was closing fast, giving him no time to consider, ascending with the certainty of a sunrise.

What would it bring him? The question teased at the edges of his consciousness, refusing to show itself. Change, but in what form? Qui-Gon and his companions were the bringers of that change, but he did not think even the Jedi Knight knew for certain what the end result would be.

Maybe the freedom he had dreamed about for himself and his mother, he thought hopefully. Maybe an escape to a new life for both of them. Anything was possible if he won the Boonta. Anything at all.

That thought was still foremost in his cluttered, weary mind when his eyes closed and he fell asleep.

Anakin Skywalker dreamed that night, and in his dream he was of a different, but indeterminate age. He was young still, though not so young as now, but old, too. He was cut from stone, and his thoughts were emblazoned with a vision so frightening he could not bring himself to consider it fully, only to leave it just out of reach, simmering over a fire of ambition and hope. He was in a different place and time, in a world he did not recognize, in a landscape he had never seen. It was vague and shadowy in his dream, all flat and rugged at once, changing with the swiftness of a mirage born out of Tatooine's desert flats.

The dream shimmered, and voices reached out to him, soft and distant. He turned toward them, away from a wave of dark movement that suddenly appeared before him, away from the sleep that gave his dream life.

"I hope you're about finished," he heard Padmé say.

But Padmé was at the head of the dark wave of his dream, and the wave was an army, marching toward him . . .

R2-D2 whistled and beeped, and C-3PO chimed in with

hasty assurances, saying everything was done, all was in readiness, and he stirred again.

A hand touched his cheek, brushing it softly, and the dream faded and was gone. Anakin blinked awake, rubbing at his eyes, yawning and turning over on his side. He was no longer stretched out by the parts crate where he had fallen asleep the night before, but was back in his own bed.

The hand lifted away from his cheek, and Anakin stared up at Padmé, at a face he found so beautiful it brought a tightness to his throat. Yet he stared at her in confusion, for she had been the central figure in his dream, different from now, older, sadder . . . and something more.

"You were in my dream," he said, swallowing hard to get the words out. "You were leading a huge army into battle."

The girl stared at him in wonder, then smiled. "I hope not. I hate fighting." Her voice was merry and light, dismissive in a way that bothered him. "Your mother wants you to get up now. We have to leave soon."

Anakin climbed to his feet, fully awake. He walked to the back door and stood looking out at the anthill complex of the slave quarters, at the bustle of slaves going about their daily work, at the clear, bright early morning sky that promised good weather for the Boonta Eve race. The Podracer hung level before him on its antigrav lifts, freshly painted and gleaming in the new day's sunlight. R2-D2 bustled about with a brush and can of paint, completing the final detailing of the craft. C-3PO, still missing most of his outer skin, his working parts clearly visible, followed along, pointing out missed patches, giving unsolicited opinions and bits of advice.

The sharp wheeze of an eopie brought him around to find Kitster riding toward them on the first of two of the beasts he had commandeered to help haul the Podracer to the arena. Kitster's dark face was aglow with expectation, and he waved eagerly at Anakin as he approached.

Anakin waved back, shouting, "Hook 'em up, Kitster!" He turned back to Padmé. "Where's Qui-Gon?"

The girl gestured. "He left with Jar Jar for the arena. They've gone to find Watto."

Anakin sprinted to his bedroom to wash and dress.

Qui-Gon Jinn strolled through the main hangar of the Mos Espa Podracer arena, glancing at the activity about him with seemingly casual interest. The hangar was a cavernous building that housed Podracers and equipment year round and served as a staging area for vehicles and crews on race days. A handful of racers were already in place on the service pads, dozens of aliens who had found their way to Tatooine from every corner of the galaxy crawling all over the Pods and engines as pit bosses and pilots shouted instructions. The clash and shriek of metal on metal echoed in an earsplitting din through the hangar's vast chamber, forcing conversations to be held at something approaching a shout.

Jar Jar hugged one shoulder of the Jedi Master while Watto buzzed close by the other. The former was his normal fretful, nervous self, eyes rolling on their stalks, head twisting this way and that with such frantic concern it seemed certain it must soon twist off altogether. Watto flew with blatant disregard for everything but his own conversation, which rambled on and on, covering the same points endlessly.

"So it must be understood clearly that our bargain is sealed, outlander," he repeated for at least the third time in the last ten minutes. His blue-snouted head bobbed with emphasis. "I'll want to see your spaceship the moment the race is over."

He made no bones about the fact that he believed that gaining lawful possession of the Naboo transport was only a matter of time. He had not once since Qui-Gon had found him at the betting booths suggested that things might work out otherwise.

The Jedi Master demurred with a shrug. "Patience, my blue friend. You'll have your winnings before the suns set, and my companions and I will be far away from here."

"Not if your ship belongs to me, I think!" Watto snorted, and gave a satisfied laugh. Just as quickly, his sharp eyes fixed on the Jedi. "I warn you, no funny business!"

Qui-Gon kept walking, his gaze directed elsewhere, carefully baiting the hook he had set for the Toydarian. "You don't think Anakin will win?"

Watto flew around in front of him and brought them all to a stop. Wings beating furiously, he motioned to a bright orange racer parked close at hand, its engines modified so that when the energy binders were activated and the engines joined, they formed a distinctive X-shape. Sitting to one side of the racer was the Dug who had attacked Jar Jar two days earlier, Sebulba, his wicked eyes fixed on them, his slender limbs drawn up in a vaguely menacing gesture. A pair of lithesome Twi'leks worked diligently massaging the Dug's neck and shoulders. The Twi'leks were humanoid aliens from the planet Ryloth; they had pointed teeth, smooth blue skin, and twin tentacles that draped gracefully from their hairless heads down their silken backs. Their red eyes lifted to Qui-Gon momentarily, interest flickering in their depths, then returned quickly to their master.

Watto snorted. "Don't get me wrong," he announced, shaking his head in an odd cocking motion. "I have great faith in the boy. He's a credit to your species." His snaggletoothed mouth tightened. "But Sebulba there is going to win, I think."

Qui-Gon pretended to study the Dug carefully. "Why?"

"Because he always wins!" The Toydarian broke into a fit of laughter, consumed by his own cleverness. "I'm betting heavily on Sebulba!"

"I'll take that bet," Qui-Gon said at once.

Watto stopped laughing instantly, jerking away as if scalded by hot oil. "What?" He shook his head in astonishment. "What do you mean?"

Qui-Gon advanced a step, backing the Toydarian away. "I'll wager my new racing Pod against . . ." He trailed off thoughtfully, letting Watto hang. "Against, say, the boy and his mother."

Watto was aghast. "A Pod for slaves! I don't think so!" The blue wings were a blur as he flitted this way and that, head cocked. "Well, perhaps. Just one. The mother, maybe. The boy isn't for sale."

Qui-Gon frowned. "The boy is small. He can't be worth much."

Watto shook his head decisively.

"For the fastest Pod ever built?"

Watto shook his head again.

"Both, or no bet."

They were standing near the front entry of the hangar, and the noise of the crew work had lessened. Beyond, the arena stands rose against the desert sky, a vast, curved complex complete with boxes for the Hutts, a race announcer's booth, course monitoring equipment, and food stands. Already the stands were beginning to fill, the population of Mos Espa turning out in full force for the event, shops and stalls closed, the city on holiday. Bright streamers and banners flew, and approaching racers flamed with the reflection of sunlight and polish.

Qui-Gon caught sight of Anakin appearing through the crowds, riding an eopie with Padmé up behind him, towing one of the massive Radon-Ulzer engines. His friend Kitster followed on a second eopie, towing the other engine. The eopies were gangly, long-snouted pack animals with tough, leathery skin and short fur particularly well-suited to resisting the Tatooine desert heat. R2-D2 and C-3PO trailed the little procession with the Pod and Shmi. The Jedi Master deliberately turned to watch their approach, drawing Watto's gaze after his own. The Toydarian's eyes glittered at the sight of the boy and the racer.

He looked back at Qui-Gon and gave an anxious snort. "No Pod's worth two slaves . . . not by a long shot! One slave or nothing!"

Qui-Gon folded his arms over his chest. "The boy, then."

Watto huffed and shook his head. He jerked with the tension his deliberation was generating inside his pudgy blue body. "No, no . . ."

Then abruptly he reached inside his pocket and produced a small cube, which he tossed from one hand to the other as if it were too hot to hold. "We'll let fate decide. Blue, it's the boy. Red, it's the mother."

Watto cast the cube to the hangar floor. As he did, Qui-Gon made a small, surreptitious gesture with one hand, calling on his Jedi power to produce a small inflection in the Force.

The cube bounced, rolled, settled, blue side facing up. Watto threw up his hands angrily, his eyes turning narrow and sharp.

"You won the toss, outlander!" he sneered in dismissal. "But you won't win the race, so it makes little difference, I think."

"We'll see," Qui-Gon replied calmly.

Anakin and the others reached them, entering the hangar with the Pod and engines. Watto wheeled away from Qui-Gon in a huff, pausing long enough to snap irritably at the boy.

"Better stop your friend's betting," he declared with an angry snort, "or I'll end up owning him, too!"

One of the eopies sniffed expectantly at him, and he swore at the beast in Huttese with such ferocity that it backed away. His wings beating madly, Watto gave Qui-Gon a withering glance and flew off into the hangar shadows.

"What did he mean by that?" Anakin asked as he slowed the eopie beside Qui-Gon, glancing after the retreating Toydarian.

Qui-Gon shrugged. "I'll tell you later."

Kitster pulled to a stop beside Anakin, his face alight with excitement as he looked around. "This is so wizard! I'm sure you'll do it this time, Annie!"

Padmé's gaze shifted from one to the other. "Do what?" she asked suspiciously.

Kitster beamed. "Finish the race, of course!"

The girl paled. Her eyes burned into Anakin. "You've never even *finished* a race?" she demanded incredulously.

The boy blushed. "Well . . . not exactly." His mouth tightened with determination. "But Kitster's right. I will this time."

Qui-Gon took the eopie's reins in his hand and patted the boy's leg. "Of course, you will," he agreed.

From atop the eopie, Padmé Naberrie just stared at him wordlessly.

* * *

In the center of Mos Espa the crowds were beginning to thin as the population gravitated in increasing numbers toward the pod racer arena at the edge of the spaceport. Most of the shops and stalls were already closed, and the rest were in the process of doing so. Owners and vendors were completing sales and glancing anxiously in the direction of the traffic's steady flow.

Amid the confusion and bustle, a Sith probe droid slowly floated along, mechanical eye traveling from shop to shop, from face to face, searching.

Over a hundred thousand beings had filled the Podracer arena by midmorning, jamming into the grandstand seats, crowding onto the broad viewing platforms, filling the available space. The arena became a vast sea of color and movement and sound in the emptiness of the surrounding desert. Flags and banners bearing the insignia of the racers and their sponsors waved over the assemblage, signifying favorites and creating impromptu cheering sections. Bands played in support of some racers, and isolated horns and drums beat in wild appreciation for all. Vendors walked the aisles, carrying food and drink from canopied stands below to sell to the crowd. Everywhere, excitement and anticipation was building.

Then a roar erupted as the racers began to emerge from the main hangar on the far side of the start line. One by one the Podracers hove into view, some towed by eopies, some by hand, some by repulsorsled, all part of a long procession of pilots, pit crews, and hangers-on. Standard bearers, each carrying a flag that identified the pilot and sponsor, marched along, forming a colorful line in front of the assembly of Podracers. Overhead, the twin suns of Tatooine shone down with a bright, hungry glare.

As the racers moved onto the track in front of the arena stands, a flurry of movement in the royal box signaled the arrival of Jabba the Hutt and Gardulla, his female friend. Slithering into the cooled interior of the box, the two Hutts oozed their way along the flooring to their designated places amid the bright silks that draped the rough stone. Jabba came foremost, proceeding directly to the arched overlook where he could be seen by the people of Mos Espa. Lifting his pudgy arm in greeting, he basked in the crowd's appreciative roar. Gardulla muttered her approval, nodding her neckless head on the end of a thick, shapeless body, slitted eyes glittering. A coterie of humans and aliens filed in behind the two Hutts, guests of Mos Espa's rulers on race day, a coveted designation. A line of slave girls of varying species came last, chained together, there for the amusement of those who had chosen freely to attend.

Below, the Podracer pilots formed a line facing the royal box and on command bowed deeply in recognition of and to pay homage to their benefactor.

"*Chowbaso!*" Jabba rumbled, his deep voice echoing through the sound enhancers and out across the flats. "*Tam ka chee Boonta rulee ya, kee madd ahdrudda du wundee!* Welcome!"

The crowd roared some more, arms and flags waving madly. Horns sounded as Jabba began his introduction of the racers.

"*Kubba tee.* Sebulba *tuta* Pixelito!"

The Dug, standing immediately next to Anakin, rose on his back legs and waved to the stands. A band played wildly in support, and Sebulba's fans and anxious bettors depending on the odds that favored the Dug cheered and shouted in response.

One by one, Jabba recognized the Podracer pilots. Gasgano. Boles Roor. Ben Quadinaros. Aldar Beedo. Ody Mandrell. Xelbree. Mars Guo. Clegg Holdfast. Bozzie Baranta. Wan Sandage. Anakin listened to the names, shifting anxiously, eager to begin. A glance over his shoulder revealed Kitster at work attaching the Radon-Ulzers to his Pod with the Steelton cables, checking the fastenings with sharp tugs.

". . . Mawhonic *tuta* Hok," Jabba boomed. "Teemto Pagalies *tuta* Moonus Mandel. Anakin Skywalker *tuta* Tatooine . . ."

Applause burst from the crowd, though it was not as enthusiastic as it had been for Sebulba or Gasgano or several of the others. Anakin waved in response, eyes traveling over the thousands gathered, his mind already out in the flats.

When he turned to walk to his racer, his mother was standing in front of him. Her worn face was calm and determined as she bent down to give him a hug and a kiss. Her eyes were steady as she backed him off, her hands gripping his shoulders, and she could not quite mask the worry reflected there.

"Be safe, Annie," she told him.

He nodded, swallowing. "I will, Mom. I promise."

She smiled, warm and reassuring, and moved away. Anakin continued on, watching Kitster and Jar Jar unhitch the eopies so that Kitster could lead them away. R2-D2 rolled up to Anakin and beeped with approval and reassurance. C-3PO solemnly warned against the dangers of driving too fast and wished his master well. All was ready.

Jar Jar patted the boy on the back, his billed face a mask of worry and consternation. "Tis very loony, Annie. May da Guds be kind, me friend."

Out of the corner of his eye Anakin saw Sebulba wander over from his own racer and begin examining the boy's. Hitching along on his spindly legs, he worked his way around the Radon-Ulzers with undisguised interest. Stopping finally at the left engine, he reached up suddenly and banged hard on a stabilizer, glancing around quickly to see if anyone had noticed.

Padmé appeared and bent down to kiss Anakin's cheek. Her dark eyes were intense. "You carry all our hopes," she said quietly.

Anakin's lower lip jutted out. "I won't let you down."

She gave him a long stare, then moved away. As she did so, Sebulba sidled up to him, his wizened, whiskery face angling close.

"You won't walk away from this one, slave scum," he wheezed softly, grinning. "You're bantha poodoo."

Anakin stood his ground, giving the Dug a stony look. "Don't count on it, slime face."

Qui-Gon was approaching, and Sebulba backed away toward his own racer, malevolence mirrored in his flat stare. Horns blared, and a new roar rose from the crowd. Jabba the Hutt oozed to the lip of the royal box, his thick arms lifting.

"Kaa bazza kundee da tam hdrudda!" he growled. "Let the challenge begin!"

The roar of the crowd began to build even further. Qui-Gon helped Anakin climb into his Pod. The boy settled himself in place in the seat, securing his straps, fitting his old, battered racing helmet over his head and bringing down his goggles.

"Are you all set, Annie?" the Jedi Master asked calmly. The boy nodded, eyes intense, steady. Qui-Gon held his gaze. "Remember, concentrate on the moment. Feel, don't think. Trust your instincts."

He put a hand on the boy's shoulder and smiled. "May the Force be with you, Annie."

Then he backed away, and Anakin Skywalker was alone.

* * *

Qui-Gon moved quickly through the crowd to the viewing platform where Shmi, Padmé, and Jar Jar waited. He glanced back only once at Anakin and found the boy calmly fitting his goggles in place. The Jedi Master nodded to himself. The boy would do all right.

He mounted the viewing platform with Jar Jar and the women just as it began to lift into position for the race. Shmi gave him a worried, questioning look.

"He's fine," Qui-Gon assured her, touching her shoulder.

Padmé shook her head doubtfully. "You Jedi are far too reckless," she said quietly. "The Queen—"

"The Queen trusts my judgment, young handmaiden," Qui-Gon interrupted smoothly, directing his words only to her. "Perhaps you should, too."

She glared at him. "You assume too much."

The viewing platform locked into place, and all eyes turned toward the racers. Energy binders were engaged, powerful electromagnetic currents arcing between coaxial plates, locking the twin engines of each Podracer together as a single unit. Now the engines themselves began to turn over, their booming coughs and rumbles mingling with and then overwhelming the roar of the crowd. Flag bearers and pit crews moved hastily aside, clearing the start line beneath the arch that marked the beginning and end of the race. Overhead, a red light held the racers in place. Anticipating the green, the pilots gunned their engines, the massive casings shaking with the force of the power they generated, the cables that bound them to the Pods and their drivers straining to break free.

Standing next to Qui-Gon, Jar Jar Binks covered his eyes in dismay. "Me no watch. Dis gonna be messy!"

Though he could not bring himself to say so, the Jedi Master was inclined to agree. *Steady, Anakin Skywalker,* he thought to himself. *Concentrate.*

Then the light over the starting line flashed bright green, and the race was under way.

When the starting light turned green, Anakin Skywalker jammed the twin thruster bars to the extreme forward position, sending maximum power to the Radon-Ulzers. The big rocket engines bucked, roared like a caged beast, and promptly died.

The boy froze. All around him, racers shot from the start in a cacophony of sound and a flashing of bright metal. Sand fountained in the wake of their passing, clouding the air in a whirlwind of grit. In seconds, the boy was alone, save for Ben Quadinaros's Quadra-Pod, which sat stalled at the starting line in mirror image of his own.

Anakin's mind raced desperately. He'd fed in too much fuel from a dead start. The reworked engines couldn't handle all that power at once if the racer wasn't already moving. He yanked back on the thruster bars, returning them to the neutral position. Ratcheting back the switches to the feeder dump, he cleared the lines, then sealed them anew. Taking a deep breath, he pressed the ignition buttons. The starters cranked over and caught, and the big Radon-Ulzers roared to life with a booming cough. He fed in fuel more cautiously this time, impatience flooding through him, then slid the thruster bars forward smoothly. The engines shot ahead, dragging the Pod and the boy after them, exploding out of the start.

Anakin gave chase with single-minded determination, not bothering with anything but the dots in the distance that marked the location of the other racers. He tore across the flats, the whine of the Pod's engines growing steadily sharper, the land beneath fading to a wash of heat and light. The course was flat and open in the beginning, and he pushed the thruster bars forward some more. He was accelerating so quickly that everything about him turned swiftly to a sun-drenched blur.

Ahead, the first set of rock formations rose up against the horizon. Anakin could see the other Podracers now, bright metal shapes whipping across the flats, engines throwing off fire and smoke. He closed on them quickly, the Radon-Ulzers screaming. In an open stretch, he knew, there were no other engines that could match them.

A flush of white-hot excitement burned through him as he caught the trailing Podracers.

He hauled back on the thruster bars as he came up on them, giving himself space to maneuver. He went by two as if they were standing still, angling his way left and then right, threading the needle of space they had left between them. When he was clear, he fed power to the engines anew, and the g-force slammed him back against his padded seat. He caught multilimbed Gasgano next. Easing up to the Troiken's snub-nosed Podracer, he got ready to pass. Arch Canyon loomed ahead, and he wanted to be clear of the others when he navigated through the ravine. Maneuvering cautiously, he prepared to overtake on the right. But Gasgano saw him, and quickly moved to cut him off. Anakin waited, then angled left for another try. Again, Gasgano cut him off. Back and forth they slid above the desert floor like a krayt dragon chasing a womp rat.

A cliff drop off a low mesa appeared as a ragged line on the horizon. Anakin slowed, giving Gasgano the impression he was preparing for a drop shift. The wiry pilot, glancing back quickly to make certain where the boy was, held his position until he reached the mesa edge, then took the drop first. The moment he did so, Anakin jammed the thruster bars all the way forward, and his racer accelerated with such speed that it rocketed right over the top of Gasgano before the other could do anything to prevent it.

The dark crease of the canyon loomed ahead, and Anakin threaded the eye of its needle opening with a seamstress's skill, racing into the cool shadows beyond. The Radon-Ulzers hummed anxiously, the energy binders keeping them in sync, the Steelton cables drawing on the racing Pod with just the right amount of give through the wicked turns. Anakin worked the thruster bars with small, precise movements, envisioning the course in his mind—each twist, each deviation, each rise and drop. Everything was clear and certain to him. Everything was revealed.

He shot through the canyon and back out onto the open flats. Ahead, beyond a dozen others, Mawhonic and Sebulba fought for the lead. The Dug's distinctive X-shaped engines lifted and rose, maneuvering for position. But Mawhonic's slender racer was slowly gliding away.

Then Sebulba accelerated and swung violently left, careening toward the other pilot. Mawhonic reacted instinctively, swinging left as well—and directly into a massive rock formation. Mawhonic disappeared in a huge ball of flame and black smoke.

Next it was Xelbree challenging, trying to sneak past Sebulba from above, much as Anakin had done with Gasgano. But the Dug sensed his presence and rose to block his passage. Xelbree slid left, drawing alongside, holding fast. Sebulba seemed to lose ground, to give way slightly. But when Xelbree was next to him, the Dug triggered a side vent in his left exhaust. Fire spewed laterally into Xelbree's engine, cutting apart the metal housing as if it were made of flimsiplast. Xelbree tried frantically to move away, but he was too slow. Fuel caught and ignited. The damaged engine exploded, and the remaining engine and its Pod flew off into a cliff face and shattered.

Without slowing, Sebulba sped away from the wreckage, alone at the head of the pack.

In the arena stands and from viewing platforms scattered throughout the course, the crowd watched the progress of the race on handheld viewscreens as pictures of the racers were transmitted from droid observation holocams. From a monitoring tower, a two-headed announcer who bantered incessantly with himself reported on the leaders. Qui-Gon studied a screen with Padmé and Shmi, but there was neither mention nor sight of Anakin. The announcer's twin voices rose and fell in measured cadence, filling the air with their inflection, building in pitch to stir the already frenzied crowd.

Qui-Gon stared out into the flats, searching for movement. On his right, Jar Jar bickered with a skinny, sour-faced alien named Fanta, trying to peer over his shoulder, besieging him with questions, trying to make friends in the mistaken belief that because they looked vaguely alike, the Poldt would reciprocate his overtures. It wasn't working out. Fanta wanted nothing to do with Jar Jar and kept his back turned to the Gungan, deliberately hiding the screen from view. Jar Jar was growing impatient.

Qui-Gon shifted his gaze. In the crew pits, R2-D2, C-3PO, and Kitster waited in solitary isolation.

In a private box somewhat in back of and lower than Jabba's, Watto laughed and joked with his friends. The Toydarian flitted this way and that, catching glimpses of the race on various viewscreens, rubbing his hands together anxiously. He caught sight of Qui-Gon and gestured rudely, his meaning clear.

Below, at the start line, Ben Quadinaros still struggled to ignite the engines of his Quadra-Pod.

Qui-Gon closed his eyes and blocked everything away, sounds and movements alike, becoming one with the Force, disappearing into its flow, searching for Anakin. He stayed lost within himself as the roar of the crowd lifted anew, and the sound of rocket engines rose out of the distance. At the edge of the horizon, a clump of dark specks hove into view.

On the starting line, Ben Quadinaros finally managed to start the engines of his racer, all four bulbous monsters roaring to life, vibrating wildly within their casings. Engines and Pod lurched as Quadinaros locked in the thrusters. But in the next instant the energy binders collapsed under the strain, the connecting cables snapped, and the engines shot off in four separate directions, exploding against stone walls, rock formations, and low dune banks. The crowd gasped in shock, shielding eyes and covering ears as the Pod and Ben Quadinaros collapsed to the racetrack in a useless heap.

Almost simultaneously Sebulba's racer screamed past the arena, shooting under the finish arch, and rocketing off on the start of the second lap. Two other racers followed, their engines roaring loudly as they whipped past, their colorful metal bodies agleam in the midday suns.

There was no sign of Anakin.

Qui-Gon kept his eyes closed, searching within his consciousness. Beside him, Shmi and Padmé exchanged worried glances. Jar Jar still hung on Fanta, pounding him on the back now in excitement as the other grimaced and tried to move away.

Three more racers tore past, the sound of their engines dying into silence as they faded from view. A fourth, Ody Mandrell, turned into the pits, the engines of his Pod shaking and smoking as he screeched to a stop. Pit droids rushed to service the racer, swarming over the engines. Ody stood up in the cockpit, a big, squat, reptilian Er'Kit, arms gesturing. But when the engines ignited anew, DUM-4, a pit droid, was standing at the left intake, and the engine sucked it inside, chewed it up, and spit it out the exhaust in a mangled heap.

The crowd went back to their viewscreens, intent on the race.

Then R2-D2, standing with Kitster and C-3PO at the edge of their station, gave an excited beep.

Qui-Gon's eyes snapped open. "Here he comes!" he exclaimed quickly.

Anakin Skywalker exploded out of the midday glare, the big Radon-Ulzers howling in fury.

Amid the cheers and shouts of his companions and the crowd, Qui-Gon Jinn just smiled. Anakin had begun to overtake the pack.

At the beginning of the second lap, Anakin was in sixth place. As the race progressed, he was slowly disappearing into the workings of his racer, becoming one with its engines, feeling the strain and tug on each rivet and screw. Wind whipped by him in a screaming rush, locking him away in its white noise. There was only himself and the machine, all speed and response. It was the way racing affected him, melding his body with the Pod and engines until he was a part of both. Moment by moment, the symbiosis deepened, joining them, giving him insights and understandings that transcended his senses and knowledge, projecting him past the present and into a place others could not reach.

Approaching Arch Canyon, he bore down on the leaders, young face intense. Skimming the flats, he whipped past Aldar Beedo and sideslipped Clegg Holdfast. To one side, a fast-closing Ody Mandrell banked too hard over a sandy rise and caught his engine in the sand. Ody's racer cartwheeled in a spectacular twisting of engines and Pod and exploded apart.

Anakin was only four racers back from Sebulba and could see the Dug's craft clearly in the distance.

Everything happened quickly after that.

The racers whipped through Arch Canyon and out the other side in a ragged line, with Anakin narrowing the gap between himself and the others. Tusken Raiders, hiding in the rocks of the cliffs that formed the corner of Tusken Turn, got lucky and hit Teemto Pagalies. Teemto's racer simply exploded and was gone. Anakin flew through the vaporized wreckage in pursuit of the others. He passed Elan Mak and Habba Kee in a rush. Ahead, Mars Guo was closing on Sebulba, wary of the Dug, keeping down and away, trying to sneak past. Anakin drew nearer to both, leapfrogging sand dunes in a long depression, easing slowly up on Mars Guo.

Suddenly Sebulba reached out of his Pod's cockpit and released a ragged bit of metal directly into Mars Guo's left engine intake. Metal clashed violently against metal, and the damaged engine began to spew smoke and fire. Mars tried to hold the machine steady, but the failing engine bucked and lost power, causing the Pod to veer sharply into Anakin. The racers collided in a shriek of metal, and a leading edge of Mars Guo's vertical stabilizer snagged the Steelton line to Anakin's left engine and released the binding.

Instantly Anakin's Pod began to swing violently at the end of its single remaining line, whipsawing back and forth. The Radon-Ulzers continued to act in concert, locked together by the energy binders, but the racer was out of control. Anakin worked the stabilizer pedals with his feet, fighting to hold the Pod steady as it swung like a pendulum. The unhooked line snapped viciously in the wake of the engine's exhaust, threatening to tangle or snag on an outcropping and drag the racer down. Anakin groped along the floor of his cockpit, searching for the magnetic retriever. When he found it, he flicked on the power button and extended the retriever out to the left side, trying to make contact with the loose line. The effort forced him to pull back on the thruster bars to cut power, and he fell behind Sebulba once more. Elan Mak, Habba Kee, and now Obitoki as well swept by him, giving chase to the Dug.

Anakin glanced frantically over his shoulder. The bulk of the pack was closing on him once more.

After a dozen tries, he finally focused his concentration sufficiently to snag the loose engine line with the retriever and maneuver it back to its hook. Sweat and grit coated his face, and his jacket sleeve was ripped. Casting down the retriever, he jammed the thruster bars forward once more. Stabilized at the ends of the Steelton lines, the Pod held steady now as the Radon-Ulzers bucked, and the racer accelerated after the leaders.

Anakin caught Elan Mak first and slid around him easily. He was closing on Habba Kee when Obitoki tried to pass Sebulba.

The Dug waited until his rival had pulled alongside, then used the same tactic he had employed against Xelbree. Opening a small side vent in the left exhaust, he sent a gush of fire into the housing of Obitoki's right engine. Fuel in the lines caught fire and exploded, and Obitoki's racer dived nose first into the desert, sending a wide spray of grit everywhere.

Habba Kee flew into it just ahead of Anakin, low and tight to the ground. Momentarily blinded, he swerved the wrong way and caught a piece of one of Obitoki's engines where it jutted from the sand. Engines and Pod tangled and crashed in a wild explosion. Anakin followed Habba Kee into the smoke and grit, blinded as well. A piece of steaming metal flew at him out of the haze, careening off his right engine housing and barely missing his head. But the boy was seeing with more than his eyes, sensing with his mind, calm and steady within himself. He could feel the danger waiting, and he worked the thruster bars smoothly, sliding past the wreckage.

Then he was in the clear again and bearing down on Sebulba.

He caught the Dug as they screamed past the arena and under the finish arch for the start of the third and final lap.

In his mind, Anakin could see Qui-Gon and Jar Jar watching him; Kitster, standing in the crew pits, his friend cheering wildly, and R2-D2 and C-3PO, the former beeping, the latter nattering back at him in response; Padmé, her beautiful face framed with worry; and his mother, her eyes filled with terror. He could see them all, as if he were standing among them, standing outside himself, watching the race . . .

He blocked their faces away, banished the images from his thoughts, and focused everything on Sebulba.

They were speeding out of Arch Canyon when Sebulba decided to put an end to Anakin once and for all. The Dug knew where all the droid observation cams were situated. He knew the angles of placement and how to avoid giving himself away. Swinging his racer close to Anakin's, he opened the side vent on his exhaust and tried to scorch the boy's engine housing as he had done with Xelbree and Obitoki. But Anakin had fallen victim to that particular trick once before and was looking for it this time. He shifted just above the cutting flame and out of reach. When Sebulba tried to follow, Anakin dropped down again—but too far, momentarily losing control. His racer veered from the course right into a line of warning signs, sending them flying in all directions. Desperate to recover, he lifted the nose of his craft skyward, jammed his thruster bars forward, and accelerated. The Radon-Ulzers boomed, his racer gave a frightening lurch, and he leapfrogged right over Sebulba to take the lead.

Down through the first set of caves and past Tusken Turn the racers tore, Anakin leading, Sebulba right on his tail. At speeds too great for maintaining proper control, the antagonists banked and angled as if safety were of no importance at all.

And finally burst into the clear once more.

Again, Sebulba tried to regain the lead, pushing for an opening. Anakin held him off, but then one of the horizontal stabilizers on the left engine began to shudder violently. A momentary vision of Sebulba hammering on his stabilizer just before the start of the race flashed through Anakin's mind. He eased off on the thruster bars, jettisoned the stabilizer, and switched to an auxiliary mount. In the process, he was forced to give way. Sebulba raced past him to take command of the lead once more.

Time and space were running out on Anakin Skywalker. He shoved the thruster bars forward and went after the Dug. Sebulba saw him coming and fishtailed his Pod back and forth in front of the boy to keep him from passing. Over the courseway they sped, jockeying for position. Anakin tried everything he knew, but Sebulba was a seasoned veteran and was able to counter each attempt. Metta Drop flew past as the racers roared out of the dune hills and onto the final stretch of flats.

Finally Anakin shifted left, then right. But this time when Sebulba moved to block him, Anakin faked a third shift, drawing the Dug left again. The instant Sebulba began his blocking move, Anakin jerked his racer hard to the right and nosed in beside the Dug.

Down the flat, open final stretch of the course the Podracers tore, side by side, the arena stands and warding statuary beginning to take shape ahead. Sebulba screamed in frustration and deliberately swerved his Pod into Anakin's. Infuriated by the boy's dogged persistence, he slammed into him, once, twice. But on the third strike, their steering rods caught, locking them together. Anakin fought with his controls, trying to break free, but the Pods were hooked fast. Sebulba laughed, jamming his racer against the boy's in an effort to force him into the ground. Anakin whipped the thruster bars forward and back, trying to disengage from the tangle. The Radon-Ulzers strained with the effort, and the steering rods groaned and bent.

Finally Anakin's rod broke completely, snapping off both the armature and the main horizontal stabilizer. The boy's Pod jerked and spun at the ends of the Steelton cables, shimmying with such force that Anakin would have been thrown from the Pod if he had not been strapped down.

But it was much worse for Sebulba. When Anakin's steering arm snapped, the Dug's Pod shot forward as if catapulted, collapsing the towlines, sending the engines screaming out of control. One engine slammed into a piece of the ancient statuary and disintegrated in flames. Then the second went, ramming into the sand and exploding in a massive fireball. The towing cables broke free, and the Dug's Pod was sent skidding through the flaming wreckage of the engines, twisting and bumping violently along the desert floor to a smoking stop. Sebulba extricated himself in a shrieking fit, throwing pieces of his ruined Pod in all directions only to discover that his pants were on fire.

Anakin Skywalker flew overhead, the exhausts from the big Radon-Ulzers sending sand and grit into the Dug's face in a stinging spray. Hanging on to maintain control as he crossed the finish line, he became, at nine years of age, the youngest winner ever of the Boonta Eve race.

As the viewing platform he occupied with Shmi, Padmé, and Jar Jar slowly lowered, Qui-Gon watched the crowd surge toward Anakin's racer. The boy had brought the Pod to a skidding halt in the center of the raceway, shut down the Radon-Ulzers, and climbed out. Kitster had already reached him and was hugging him tightly, and R2-D2 and C-3PO were scuttling around them both. When the crowd converged moments later, they hoisted Anakin aloft and carried him away, chanting and shouting his name.

Qui-Gon exchanged a warm smile with Shmi, nodding his approval of the boy's performance. Anakin Skywalker was special indeed.

The viewing platform settled in place smoothly, and its occupants off-loaded onto the raceway in a rush. Allowing his companions to join the celebration, the Jedi Master turned back toward the stands. Ascending the stairways swiftly, he reached Watto's private box in minutes. A knot of aliens departed just in front of him, laughing and joking in several languages, counting fistfuls of currency and credits. Watto was staring out at the chanting crowd, hovering at the edge of the viewport, a dejected look on his wrinkled blue face.

The moment he caught sight of Qui-Gon, his dejection transformed, and he flew at the Jedi Master in undisguised fury.

"You! You swindled me!" He bounced in the air in front of Qui-Gon, shaking with rage. "You knew the boy was going to win! Somehow you knew it! I lost everything!"

Qui-Gon smiled benignly. "Whenever you gamble, my friend, eventually you'll lose. Today wasn't your day." The smile dropped away. "Bring the hyperdrive parts to the main hangar right away. I'll come by your shop later so you can release the boy."

The Toydarian shoved his snout against Qui-Gon's nose. "You can't have him! It wasn't a fair bet!"

Qui-Gon looked him up and down with a chilly stare. "Would you like to discuss it with the Hutts? I'm sure they would be happy to settle the matter."

Watto jerked as if stung, his beady eyes filled with hate. "No, no! I want no more of your tricks." He gestured emphatically. "Take the boy! Be gone!"

He wheeled away and flew out of the box, body hunched beneath madly beating wings. Qui-Gon watched him depart, then started down the stairs for the racetrack, his mind already turning to other things.

Had he not been so preoccupied with his plans for what lay ahead, he might have caught sight of the Sith probe droid trailing after.

Within an hour, the arena had emptied, the racers had been stored or hauled away for repairs, and the main hangar left almost deserted. A few pit droids were still engaged in salvaging pieces of wreckage from the race, coming and going in steady pursuit of their work. Anakin alone of the Pod pilots remained, checking over his damaged racer. He was dirty and ragged, his hair spiky and his face streaked with sweat and grime. His jacket was torn in several places, and there was blood on his clothing where he had slashed his arm on a jagged piece of metal during the battle with Sebulba.

Qui-Gon watched him thoughtfully, standing to one side with Padmé and Shmi as the boy, Jar Jar, R2-D2, and C-3PO moved busily over the Pod and engines. Could it be? he was wondering for what must have been the hundredth time, pondering the way the boy handled a Podracer, the maturity he exhibited, and the instincts he possessed. Was it possible?

He shelved his questions for another time. It would be up to the Council to decide. Abruptly, he left the women, walking over to the boy and kneeling beside him.

"You're a bit worse for wear, Annie," he said softly, placing his hands on the boy's shoulders and looking him in the eyes, "but you did well." Smiling reassuringly, he wiped a patch of dirt off the boy's face. "There, good as new."

He ruffled the boy's unruly hair and helped bind his injured arm. Shmi and Padmé joined them and were moved to give Anakin fresh hugs and kisses, checking him over carefully, touching his cheeks and forehead.

"Ah, gee . . . enough of this," the boy mumbled in embarrassment.

His mother smiled, shaking her head. "It's so wonderful, Annie—what you've done here. Do you know? You've brought hope to those who have none. I'm so very proud of you."

"We owe you everything," Padmé added quickly, giving him an intense, warm look.

Anakin blushed scarlet. "Just feeling this good is worth anything," he declared, smiling back.

Qui-Gon walked over to where the hyperdrive parts were loaded on an antigrav repulsorsled harnessed to a pair of eopies. Watto had made delivery as promised, though not without considerable grumbling and a barrage of thinly veiled threats. Qui-Gon checked the container straps, glanced out into the midday heat, and walked back to the others.

"Padmé, Jar Jar, let's go," he ordered abruptly. "We've got to get these parts back to the ship."

The group moved over to the eopies, laughing and talking. Padmé hugged and kissed Anakin again, then climbed onto one of the eopies behind Qui-Gon, taking hold of his waist. Jar Jar swung onto the second animal and promptly slid off the other side, collapsing in a heap. R2-D2 beeped encouragingly as the Gungan tried again, this time managing to keep his seat. Good-byes and thank-yous were exchanged, but it was an awkward moment for Anakin. He looked as if he wanted to say something to Padmé, moving up beside her momentarily, staring up at her expectantly. But all he could manage was a sad, confused look.

Slowly, the eopies began to move off, Anakin and his mother standing with C-3PO, waving after.

"I'll return the eopies by midday," Qui-Gon promised, calling over his shoulder.

Padmé did not look back at all.

Qui-Gon Jinn and company rode out of Mos Espa into the Tatooine desert, R2-D2 leading the way, rolling along in front of the eopies and sled at a steady pace. The suns were rising quickly to a midday position in the sky, and the heat rose off the sand in waves. But the journey back to the Queen's transport was accomplished swiftly and without incident.

Obi-Wan was waiting for them, appearing down the rampway as soon as they neared, his youthful face intense. "I was getting worried," he announced without preamble.

Qui-Gon dismounted, then helped Padmé down. "Start getting this hyperdrive generator installed," he ordered. "I'm going back. I have some unfinished business."

"Business?" his protégé echoed, arching one eyebrow.

"I won't be long."

Obi-Wan studied him a moment, then sighed. "Why do I sense we've picked up another stray?"

Qui-Gon took his arm and moved him away from the others. "It's the boy who's responsible for getting us these parts." He paused. "The boy whose blood sample you ran the midi-chlorian test on last night."

Obi-Wan gave him a hard, steady look, then turned away.

On a rise overlooking the spacecraft, hidden in the glare of the suns and the ripple of the dunes, the Sith probe droid hung motionless for a final transmission, then quickly sped away.

Anakin walked home with his mother and C-3PO, still wrapped in the euphoria of his victory, but wrestling as well with his sadness over the departure of Padmé. He hadn't thought about what would happen to her if he won the Boonta Eve, that it would mean Qui-Gon would secure the hyperdrive generator he needed to make their transport functional. So when she bent to kiss and hug him good-bye, it was the first time he had given the matter any serious thought since her arrival. He was stunned, caught in a mix of emotions, and all of a sudden he wanted to tell her to stay. But he couldn't bring himself to speak the words, knowing how foolish they would sound, realizing she couldn't do so in any case.

So he stood there like a droid without its vocoder, watching her ride away behind Qui-Gon, thinking it might well be the last time he would ever see her, and wondering how he was going to live with himself if it was.

Unable to sit still once he had walked his mother to their home, he placed C-3PO back in his bedroom, deactivated him, and went out again. Qui-Gon had told him he was relieved of any work today at Watto's, so he pretty much could do what he wanted until the Jedi returned. He gave no thought to what would happen then, wandering down toward Mos Espa Way, waving as his name was shouted out from every quarter on his journey, basking in the glow of his success. He still couldn't quite believe it, and yet it felt as if he had always known he would win this race. Kitster appeared, then Amee and Wald, and soon he was surrounded by a dozen others.

He was just approaching the connector to Mos Espa Way when a Rodian youngster, bigger than himself, blocked his way. Anakin had cheated, the Rodian sneered. He couldn't have won the Boonta Eve any other way. No slave could win anything.

Anakin was on top of him so fast the bigger being barely had time to put up his arms in defense before he was on the ground. Anakin was hitting him as hard and fast as he could, not thinking about anything but how angry he was, not even aware that the source of his anger had nothing to do with his victim and everything to do with losing Padmé.

Then Qui-Gon, returned by now with the eopies, was looming over him. He pulled Anakin away, separating the two fighters, and demanded to know what this was all about. Somewhat sheepishly, but still angry, Anakin told him. Qui-Gon studied him carefully, disappointment registering on his broad features. He fixed the young Rodian with his gaze and asked him if he still believed Anakin had cheated. The youngster, glowering at Anakin, said he did.

Qui-Gon put his hand on Anakin's shoulder and steered him away from the crowd, not saying anything until they were out of hearing.

"You know, Annie," he said then, his deep voice thoughtful, "fighting didn't change his opinion. The opinions of others, whether you agree with them or not, are something you have to learn to tolerate."

He walked the boy back toward his home, counseling him quietly about the way life worked, hand resting on his shoulder in a way that made Anakin feel comforted. As they neared the boy's home, the Jedi reached beneath his poncho and produced a leather pouch filled with credits.

"These are yours," he announced. "I sold the Pod." He pursed his lips. "To a particularly surly and rather insistent Dug."

Anakin accepted the bag, grinning broadly, the fight and its cause forgotten.

He ran up the steps to his door and burst through, Qui-Gon following silently. "Mom, Mom!" he cried out as she appeared to greet him. "Guess what! Qui-Gon sold the Pod! Look at all the money we have!"

He produced the leather pouch and dropped it into her hands, enjoying the startled look on her face. "Oh, my goodness!"

she breathed softly, staring down at the bulging pouch. "Annie, that's wonderful!"

Her eyes lifted quickly to meet Qui-Gon's. The Jedi stepped forward, holding her gaze.

"Annie has been freed," he said.

The boy's eyes went wide. "What?"

Qui-Gon glanced down at him. "You are no longer a slave."

Shmi Skywalker stared at the Jedi in disbelief, her worn face rigid, her eyes mirroring her shock and disbelief.

"Mom? Did you hear that, Mom?" Anakin let out a whoop and jumped as high as he could manage. It wasn't possible! But he knew it was true, knew that it really was!

He managed to collect himself. "Was that part of the prize, or what?" he asked, grinning.

Qui-Gon grinned back. "Let's just say Watto learned an important lesson about gambling."

Shmi Skywalker was shaking her head, still stunned by the news, still working it through. But the sight of Anakin's face made everything come clear for her in an instant. She reached out to him and pressed him to her.

"Now you can make your dreams come true, Annie," she whispered, her face radiant as she touched his cheek. "You're free."

She released him and turned to Qui-Gon, her eyes bright and expectant. "Will you take him with you? Is he to become a Jedi?"

Anakin beamed at the suggestion, wheeling quickly on Qui-Gon, waiting for his answer.

The Jedi Master hesitated. "Our meeting was not a coincidence. Nothing happens by accident. You are strong with the Force, Annie, but you may not be accepted by the Council."

Anakin heard what he wanted to hear, blocking away everything else, seeing the possibilities that had fueled his hopes and dreams for so long come alive in a single moment.

"A Jedi!" he gasped. "You mean I get to go with you in your starship and everything!"

And be with Padmé again! The thought struck him like a thunderbolt, wrapping him in such expectancy that it was all he could do to listen to what the Jedi Master said next.

Qui-Gon knelt before the boy, his face somber. "Anakin, training to be a Jedi will not be easy. It will be a challenge. And if you succeed, it will be a hard life."

Anakin shook his head quickly. "But it's what I want! It's what I've always dreamed about!" He looked quickly to his mother. "Can I go, Mom?"

But Qui-Gon drew him back with a touch. "This path has been placed before you, Annie. The choice to take it must be yours alone."

The man and the boy stared at each other. A mix of emotions roiled through Anakin, threatening to sweep him away, but at their forefront was the happiness he felt at finding the thing he wanted most in all the world within reach—to be a Jedi, to journey down the space lanes of the galaxy.

He glanced quickly at his mother, at her worn, accepting face, seeing in her eyes that in this, as in all things, she wanted what was best for him.

His gaze returned to Qui-Gon. "I want to go," he said.

"Then pack your things," the Jedi Master advised. "We haven't much time."

"Yippee!" the boy shouted, jumping up and down, anxious already to be on his way. He rushed to his mother and hugged her as hard as he could manage, then broke away for his bedroom.

He was almost to the doorway when he realized he had

forgotten something. A chill swept through him as he wheeled back to Qui-Gon. "What about Mom?" he asked hurriedly, eyes darting from one to the other. "Is she free, too? You're coming, aren't you, Mom?"

Qui-Gon and his mother exchanged a worried glance, and he knew the answer before the Jedi spoke the words. "I tried to free your mother, Annie, but Watto wouldn't have it. Slaves give status and lend prestige to their owners here on Tatooine."

The boy felt his chest and throat tighten. "But the money from selling . . ."

Qui-Gon shook his head. "It's not nearly enough."

There was a hushed silence, and then Shmi Skywalker came to her son and sat down in a chair next to him, taking both of his hands in hers and drawing him close. Her eyes were steady as she looked into his.

"Annie, my place is here," she said quietly. "My future is here. It is time for you to let go . . . to let go of me. I cannot go with you."

The boy swallowed hard. "I want to stay with you, then. I don't want things to change."

She gave him an encouraging smile, her brow knitting. "You can't stop change any more than you can stop the suns from setting. Listen to your feelings, Annie. You know what's right."

Anakin Skywalker took a long, slow breath and dropped his gaze, his head lowering. Everything was coming apart inside, all the happiness melting away, all the expectancy fading. But then he felt his mother's hands tighten over his own, and in her touch he found the strength he needed to do what he knew he must.

Nevertheless, his eyes were brimming as he lifted his gaze once more. "I'm going to miss you so much, Mom," he whispered.

His mother nodded. "I love you, Annie." She released his hands. "Now, hurry."

Anakin gave her a quick, hard hug, and raced from the room, tears streaking his face.

Once within his own room, Anakin stood staring about in sudden bewilderment. He was leaving, and he did not know when he would be coming back. He had never been anywhere but here, never known anyone but the people of Mos Espa and those who came to trade with them. He had dreamed about other worlds and other lives, about becoming a pilot of a main-line ship, and about becoming a Jedi. But the impact of what it actually meant to be standing at the threshold of an embarkation to the life he had so often wished for was overwhelming.

He found himself thinking of the old spacer, telling him that he wouldn't be surprised at all if Anakin Skywalker became something more than a slave. He had wanted that more than anything, had hoped with all his heart for it to happen.

But he had never, ever considered the possibility he would have to leave his mother behind.

He wiped the tears from his eyes, fighting back new ones, hearing his mother's and Qui-Gon's voices from the other room.

"Thank you," his mother was saying softly.

"I will watch after him. You have my word." The Jedi's deep voice was warm and reassuring. "Will you be all right?"

Anakin couldn't hear her reply. But then she said, "He was in my life for such a short time . . ."

She trailed off, distracted. Anakin forced himself to quit listening, and he began pulling clothes out and stuffing them into a backpack. He didn't have much, and it didn't take him long. He looked about for anything of importance he might have missed, and his eyes settled on C-3PO, sitting motionless on the workbench. He walked over to the protocol droid and switched him on. C-3PO cocked his head and looked at the boy blankly.

"Well, Threepio, I'm leaving," Anakin said solemnly. "I'm free. I'm going away, in a starship . . ."

He didn't know what else to say. The droid cocked his head. "Well, Master Anakin, you are my maker, and I wish you well. Although I'd like it better if I were a little less naked."

The boy sighed and nodded. "I'm sorry I wasn't able to finish you, Threepio—to give you coverings and all. I'm going to miss working on you. You've been a great pal. I'll make sure Mom doesn't sell you or anything. Bye!"

He snatched up his backpack and rushed from the room, hearing C-3PO call after him plaintively, "Sell me?"

He said good-bye to his mother, braver now, more determined, and walked out the door with Qui-Gon, his course of action settled. He had gotten barely a dozen meters from his home when Kitster, who had trailed them back from the fight, came rushing up to him.

"Where are you going, Annie?" his friend asked doubtfully.

Anakin took a deep breath. "I've been freed, Kitster. I'm going away with Qui-Gon. On a spaceship."

Kitster's eyes went wide, and his mouth opened in a silent exclamation. Anakin fished in his pockets and came out with a handful of credits, which he shoved at his friend. "Here. These are for you."

Kitster's dark face looked down at the credits, then back up at Anakin. "Do you have to go, Annie? Do you have to? Can't you stay? Annie, you're a hero!"

Anakin swallowed hard. "I . . ." He glanced past Kitster to his mother, still standing in the doorway looking after him, then down to where Qui-Gon was waiting. He shook his head. "I can't."

Kitster nodded. "Well."

"Well," Anakin repeated, looking at him.

"Thanks for everything, Annie," the other boy said. There were tears in his eyes as he accepted the credits. "You're my best friend."

Anakin bit his lip. "I won't forget."

He hugged Kitster impulsively, then broke away and raced toward Qui-Gon. But before he reached him, he glanced back one more time at his mother. Seeing her standing in the doorway brought him about. He stood there momentarily, undecided, conflicting emotions tearing at him. Then his already shaky resolve collapsed altogether, and he raced back to her. By the time he reached her, he was crying freely.

"I can't do it, Mom," he whispered, clinging to her. "I just can't!"

He was shaking, wracked with sobs, disintegrating inside so quickly that all he could think about was holding on to her. Shmi let him do so for a moment, comforting him with her warmth, then backed him away.

She knelt before him, her worn face solemn. "Annie, remember when you climbed that dune in order to chase the banthas away so they wouldn't be shot? You were only five. Remember how you collapsed several times in the heat, exhausted, thinking you couldn't do it, that it was too hard?"

Anakin nodded, his face streaked with tears.

Shmi held his gaze. "This is one of those times when you

have to do something you don't think you can do. But I know how strong you are, Annie. I know you can do this."

The boy swallowed his tears, thinking she was wrong, he was not strong at all, but knowing, too, she had decided he must go, even if he found it hard, even if he resisted.

"Will I ever see you again?" he asked in desperation, giving voice to the worst of his fears.

"What does your heart tell you?" she asked quietly.

Anakin shook his head doubtfully. "I don't know. Yes, I guess."

His mother nodded. "Then it will happen, Annie."

Anakin took a deep breath to steady himself. He had stopped crying now, and he wiped the dampness of his tears from his face.

"I will become a Jedi," he declared in a small voice. "And I will come back and free you, Mom. I promise."

"No matter where you are, my love will be with you," Shmi told him, her kind face bent close to his. "Now be brave, and don't look back."

"I love you, Mom," Anakin said.

She hugged him one final time, then turned him around so he was facing away from her. "Don't look back, Annie," she whispered.

She gave him a small push, and he strode determinedly away, shouldering his pack, keeping his eyes fixed on a point well past where Qui-Gon stood waiting. He walked toward that point without slowing, marching right past the Jedi Master, fighting back the tears that threatened to come yet again. It took only a few minutes, and his mother and his home were behind him.

They went to Watto's shop first, where the Toydarian had completed the forms necessary to assure Anakin's freedom. The

transmitter that bound Anakin to his life of slavery was deactivated permanently. It would be removed surgically at a later date.
Watto was still grumbling about the unfairness of things as they
left him and went back out into the street.

From there, at Anakin's urging, they walked to Jira's fruit
stand a short distance away. Anakin, much recovered from the
trauma of leaving his mother, marched up to the old woman and
put a handful of credits into her frail hands.

"I've been freed, Jira," he told her, a determined set to his
jaw. "I'm going away. Use these for that cooling unit I promised
you. Otherwise, I'll worry."

Jira looked at the credits in disbelief. She shook her white
head. "Can I give you a hug?" she asked him softly. She reached
out for him, drawing him against her thin body, her eyes closing
as she held him. "I'll miss you, Annie," she said, releasing him.
"There isn't a kinder boy in the galaxy. You be careful."

He left her in a rush, racing after Qui-Gon, who was already
moving away, anxious to get going. They walked in silence down
a series of side streets, the boy's eyes taking in familiar sights he
would not soon see again, remembering his life here, saying
good-bye.

He was lost in his own thoughts when Qui-Gon swung
about with such swiftness it caught the boy completely by surprise. Down swept the Jedi's lightsaber in a brilliant arc, cutting
through the shadows between two buildings, clashing momentarily with something made of metal that shattered in the wake of
the weapon's passing.

Qui-Gon clicked off the lightsaber and knelt to inspect
a cluster of metal parts still sparking and fizzing in the sand.
The acrid smell of ozone and burning insulation hung in the dry
air.

"What is it?" the boy asked, peering over his shoulder.

Qui-Gon rose. "Probe droid. Very unusual. Not like anything I've seen before." He glanced about worriedly, eyes sharp and bright as he cast up and down the street.

"Come on, Annie," he ordered, and they moved quickly away.

Qui-Gon Jinn took the boy out of Mos Espa swiftly, hurrying through the crowded streets to the less populated outskirts. All the while, his eyes and mind were searching, the former the landscape of Tatooine, the latter the landscape of the Force. His instincts had alerted him to the presence of the probe droid tracking them, and his Jedi training in the ways of the Force warned him now of something far more dangerous. He could feel a shifting in the balance of things that suggested an intrusion on the harmony that the Force required, a dark weight descending like a massive stone.

Once out on the desert, in the open, he picked up the pace. The Queen's transport came into view, a dark shape just ahead, a haven of safety. He heard Anakin call out to him, the boy working hard to keep up, but beginning to fall behind.

Glancing over his shoulder to give his response and offer encouragement, he caught sight of the speeder and its dark-cloaked rider bearing down on them.

"Drop, Anakin!" he shouted, wheeling about.

The boy threw himself facedown, flattening against the sand as the speeder whipped overhead, barely missing him as it bore down on Qui-Gon. The Jedi Master already had his lightsaber out, the blade activated, the weapon held before him in two hands. The speeder came at him, a saddle-shaped vehicle with no weapons in evidence, made to rely on quickness and maneuverability rather than firepower. It was like nothing the Jedi had ever seen, but vaguely reminiscent of something dead and gone.

Its rider rode out of the glare of the suns and was revealed. Bold markings of red and black covered a demonic face in strange, jagged patterns beneath a crown of stunted horns encircling its head. Man-shaped and humanoid, his slitted eyes and hooked teeth were nevertheless feral and predatory, and his howl was a hunter's challenge to his prey.

The primal scream had barely sounded before he was on top of Qui-Gon, wheeling the speeder aside deftly at the last moment, closing off its thruster, and leaping from the seat, all in one swift movement. He carried a lightsaber of another make, and the weapon was cutting at the Jedi Master even before the attacker's feet had touched the ground. Qui-Gon, surprised by the other's quickness and ferocity, barely blocked the blow with his own weapon, the blades sliding apart with a harsh rasp. The attacker spun away in a whirl of dark clothing, then attacked anew, lightsaber slashing at his intended prey, face alight with a killing frenzy that promised no quarter.

Anakin was back on his feet, staring at them, clearly unable to decide what he should do. Fighting to hold his ground, Qui-Gon caught sight of him out of the corner of his eye.

"Annie! Get out of here!" he cried out.

His attacker closed with him again, forcing him back, striking at him from every angle. Even without knowing anything else, Qui-Gon knew this man was trained in the fighting arts of a Jedi, a skilled and dangerous adversary. Worse, he was younger, quicker, and stronger than Qui-Gon, and he was gaining ground rapidly. The Jedi Master blocked him again and again, but could not find an opening that would provide any chance of escape.

"Annie!" he screamed again, seeing the boy immobilized. "Get to the ship! Tell them to take off! Go, go!"

Hammering at the demonic-faced attacker with renewed determination, Qui-Gon Jinn saw the boy at last begin to run.

In a rush of emotion dominated by fear and doubt, Anakin Skywalker raced past the combatants for the Naboo spacecraft. It sat not three hundred meters away, metal skin gleaming dully in the afternoon sunlight. Its loading ramp was down, but there was no sign of its occupants. Anakin ran faster, sweat streaking his body. He could feel his heart hammering in his chest as he reached the ramp and bounded onto the ship.

Just inside the hatchway, he found Padmé and a dark-skinned man in uniform coming toward him. When Padmé caught sight of him, her eyes went wide.

"Qui-Gon's in trouble!" the boy blurted out, gasping for breath. "He says to take off! Now!"

The man stared, eyes questioning and suspicious. "Who are you?" he demanded.

But Padmé was already moving, seizing Anakin by the arm, pulling him toward the front of the spacecraft. "He's a friend," she answered, leading the way forward. "Hurry, Captain."

They rushed down the hallway into the cockpit, Anakin trying to tell the girl what had happened, his words tumbling over one another, his face flushed and anxious. Padmé moved him along in a no-nonsense way, nodding her understanding, telling him to hurry, taking charge of everything.

When they reached the cockpit, they found two more men at work checking out the craft's control panel. They turned at the approach of Anakin and his companions. One wore a pilot's insignia on the breast of his jacket. The second, Anakin was quite certain from the cut of his hair and the look of his clothing, was another Jedi.

"Qui-Gon is in trouble," Padmé announced quickly.

"He says to take off," Anakin added in support.

The Jedi was on his feet at once. He was much younger than Qui-Gon, his face smooth, his eyes intense, his hair cut short save for a single braided pigtail that fell over his right shoulder. "Where is he?" he demanded. Then, without waiting for an answer, he wheeled back to the viewport and began scanning the empty flats.

"I don't see anything," the pilot said, peering over his shoulder.

"Over there!" The sharp eyes of the Jedi caught sight of movement just at the corner of the port. "Get us into the air and over there! Now! Fly low!"

The man called Ric threw himself into the pilot's seat, while the others, Anakin included, scrambled to find seats. The big repulsorlifts kicked in with a low growl, the rampway sealed, and the sleek transport rose and wheeled smoothly about.

"There," the Jedi breathed, pointing.

They could see Qui-Gon Jinn now, engaged in battle with the dark-garbed, demonic figure. The combatants surged back and forth across the flats, lightsabers flashing brightly with each blow struck, sand and grit swirling in all directions. Qui-Gon's long hair streamed out behind him in sharp contrast to the smooth horned head of his adversary. The pilot Ric took the spacecraft toward them quickly, skimming the ground barely higher than a speeder bike, coming in from behind the attacker. Anakin held his breath as they closed on the fighters. Ric's hand slid over the control that would lower the ramp, easing it forward carefully.

"Stand by," he ordered, freezing them all in place as he swung the ship about.

The combatants disappeared in a fresh swirl of sand and the glare of Tatooine's twin suns. All eyes shifted quickly to the viewscreens, searching desperately.

Then Qui-Gon appeared, leaping onto the lowered rampway of the transport, gaining purchase, one hand grasping a strut for support. Ric hissed in approval and fought to hold the spacecraft steady. But the horned attacker was already in pursuit, racing out of the haze and leaping onto the ramp as the ship began to rise. Balanced precariously against the sway of the ship, eyes flaring in rage, he fought to keep his footing.

Qui-Gon attacked at once, rushing the other man, closing with him at the edge of the ramp. They were twenty meters into the air by now, the pilot holding the spacecraft steady as he saw the combatants come to grips yet again, afraid to go higher while Qui-Gon was exposed. The Jedi Master and his adversary filled the viewscreen commanding the rampway entrance, faces tight with determination and streaked with sweat.

"Qui-Gon," Anakin heard the second Jedi say quietly, desperately, watching the battle for just a moment more, then tearing his eyes away from the viewscreen and racing down the open corridor.

On the screen, Anakin watched Qui-Gon Jinn step back,

level his lightsaber, and swing a powerful, two-handed blow at his attacker. The horned man blocked it, but only barely, and in the process lost his balance completely. The blow's force swept him away, clear of the ramp and off into space. He dropped back toward the desert floor, landed in a crouch, and rose instantly to his feet. But the chase was over. He stood watching in frustration, yellow eyes aflame, as the ramp to the Queen's transport closed and the spacecraft rocketed away.

Qui-Gon had barely managed to scramble up the rampway and into the interior of the ship before the hatch sealed and the Nubian began to accelerate. He lay on the cool metal floor of the entry, his clothing dusty and damp with his sweat, his body bruised and battered. He breathed deeply, waiting for his pounding heart to quiet. He had barely escaped with his life, and the thought was worrisome. His opponent was strong and had tested him severely. He was getting old, he decided, and he did not like the feeling.

Obi-Wan and Anakin rushed down the hallway to help him to his feet, and it was hard to tell which of them looked the more worried. It made him smile in spite of himself.

The boy spoke first. "Are you all right?" he asked, his young face mirroring his concern.

Qui-Gon nodded, brushing himself off. "I think so. That was a surprise I won't soon forget."

"What sort of creature was it?" Obi-Wan pressed, brow furrowed darkly. He wants to go back and pick up where I left off, Qui-Gon thought.

The Jedi Master shook his head. "I'm not sure. Whoever or whatever he was, he was trained in the Jedi arts. My guess is he was after the Queen."

"Do you think he'll follow us?" Anakin asked quickly.

"We'll be safe enough once we're in hyperspace," Qui-Gon replied, sidestepping the question. "But I have no doubt he knows our destination. If he found us once, he can find us again."

The boy's brow furrowed. "What are we going to do about it?"

At this point, Obi-Wan turned to stare at the boy, giving him a look that demanded in no uncertain terms, What do you mean, "we"? The boy caught the look and stared back at him, expressionless.

"We will be patient," Qui-Gon advised, straightening himself, drawing their attention back to him. "Anakin Skywalker, meet Obi-Wan Kenobi."

The boy beamed. "Pleased to meet you. Wow! You're a Jedi Knight, too, aren't you?"

The younger Jedi looked from the boy to Qui-Gon and rolled his eyes in despair.

From the entry, they made their way back down the hall to the cockpit, where Ric Olié was at work preparing the ship for the jump to hyperspace. Qui-Gon introduced Anakin to each of those present, then moved to the console to stand next to Ric.

"Ready," the pilot announced over his shoulder, one eyebrow cocked expectantly.

Qui-Gon nodded. "Let's hope the hyperdrive works and Watto doesn't get the last laugh."

Standing in a group behind Ric, the company watched silently as he fitted his hands to the controls and engaged the hyperdrive. There was a quick, sharp whine, and the stars that filled the viewport turned from silver pinpricks to long streamers as the ship streaked smoothly into hyperspace, leaving Tatooine behind.

*   *   *

Night lay over the planet of Naboo, but the silence of Theed exceeded even that normally experienced by those anticipating sleep. In the ornately appointed throne room that had once been the sole province of Queen Amidala, a strange collection of creatures gathered to witness the sentencing of Governor Sio Bibble. Trade Federation Viceroy Nute Gunray had convened the assembled, which consisted of Rune Haako and several other Neimoidians, the governor and a handful of officials in the Queen's service, and a vast array of battle droids armed with blasters to keep the Naboo prisoners in line.

The Neimoidian was seated in a mechno-chair, a robotic walker that bore him from one part of the room to another, metal legs moving in response to a simple touch of his fingers. It carried him to Sio Bibble and the Naboo officials now, jointed armatures working in careful precision, allowing him to remain relaxed and comfortable as he took note of the fear in the eyes of the officials backing Bibble.

The governor was having none of it, however. Steadfast even now, he faced Gunray with anger and determination, his white head level, his eyes challenging. The Neimoidian glared at him; Sio Bibble was becoming a source of irritation.

"When are you going to give up this pointless strike?" he snapped at the governor, leaning forward slightly to emphasize his displeasure.

"I will give up the strike, Viceroy, when the Queen—"

"Your Queen is lost; your people are starving!"

Bibble stiffened. "The Naboo will not be intimidated, not even at the cost of innocent lives—"

"Perhaps you should worry more about yourself, Governor!" Gunray cut him off sharply. "The odds are good that you are going to die much sooner than your people!" He was shaking with rage, and all at once his patience was exhausted. "Enough of this!" he exploded. "Take him away!"

The battle droids moved quickly, surrounding Sio Bibble, separating him from his colleagues.

"This invasion will gain you nothing!" the governor called back over his shoulder as he was dragged out. "We are a democracy! The people have decided, Viceroy! They will not live in tyranny . . ."

The rest of what he said was lost as he disappeared through the doorway into the hall beyond. The Naboo officials filed out after him, silent and dejected.

The Neimoidian stared after them momentarily, then turned his attention to OOM-9 as the commander of his battle droids approached, metal face blank, voice devoid of inflection.

"My troops are in position to begin searching the swamps for the rumored underwater villages," OOM-9 reported. "They will not stay hidden for long."

Nute Gunray nodded and dismissed him with a wave of his hand. He thought nothing of these savages who occupied the swamps. They would be crushed in short order. For all intents and purposes, the planet was in his control.

He leaned back in the mechno-chair, a measure of calmness returning. All that remained was for the Sith Lords to bring him the Queen. Certainly they should have little difficulty in accomplishing that.

Nevertheless, he knew he wouldn't be happy until this business was over.

Aboard the Queen's transport, Anakin Skywalker sat shivering in a corner of the central chamber, trying to decide what he

should do to get warm. Everyone else was asleep, and he had
been asleep as well, but only for a short time, troubled by his
dreams. He came awake to the silence and could not make himself move, paralyzed by more than simply the cold.

Jar Jar slept to one side, stretched out in a chair, head back,
snoring loudly. Nothing kept the Gungan from sleeping. Or eating, for that matter. The boy smiled briefly. R2-D2 rested close
by, upright and mostly silent, his lights blinking softly.

Anakin stared into the darkness, willing himself to move, to
overcome his inertia. But his dreams haunted him still. He found
himself thinking of his mother and home, and everything closed
down inside. He missed her so much! He had thought it would
get better once he was away, but it hadn't. Everything reminded
him of her, and if he tried to close his eyes against those memo-
ries, he found her face waiting for him, suspended in the darkness
of his thoughts, anxious and worn.

Tears came to his eyes, unbidden. Maybe he had made a mistake by coming. Maybe he should go home. Except he couldn't
now. Maybe not ever again.

A slim figure entered the room, and Anakin watched the
light of a viewscreen illuminate Padmé's soft face. Standing as if
carved from stone, she clicked on a recording and stood watching the replay of Sio Bibble's plea to Queen Amidala to come
home, to save her people from starvation, to help them in their
time of need. She watched it all the way through, then shut it off
again and stood staring at nothing, her head bent.

What was she doing?

Suddenly she seemed to sense him watching, and turned
quickly toward where he crouched. Her beautiful face seemed
tired and careworn as she approached and knelt beside him. He
stiffened, trying desperately to stop from crying, but he couldn't

hide either the tears or his shivering, and was left huddled before her, revealed.

"Are you all right, Annie?" she asked him softly.

"It's very cold," he managed to whisper.

She smiled and removed her heavy overjacket, wrapping it around his shoulders and tucking it about him. "You're from a warm planet, Annie. Space is cold."

Anakin nodded, pulling the jacket tighter. He brushed at his eyes. "You seem sad," he said.

If she saw the irony in his observation, she did not say so. "The Queen is worried. Her people are suffering, dying. She must convince the Senate to intervene, or else . . ." She trailed off, unwilling to speak the words. "I'm not sure what will happen," she finished, her voice distant, her eyes sliding away from his to fix on something else.

"I'm not sure what's going to happen to me, either," he admitted worriedly. "I don't know if I'll ever see—"

He stopped, his throat tightening, the words fading away into silence. He took a deep breath, furrowed his brow, and reached into his pocket.

"Here," he said, "I made this for you. So you'd remember me. I carved it out of a japor snippet. Take it. It will bring you good fortune."

He handed her an intricately carved wooden pendant. She studied it a moment, face lowered in shadow, then slipped it around her neck.

"It's beautiful. But I don't need this to remember you." Her face lifted to his with a smile. "How could I forget my future husband?" She looked down at the pendant, fingering it thoughtfully. "Many things will change when we reach Coruscant, Annie. My caring for you will not be one of them."

The boy nodded, swallowing. "I know. And I won't stop caring for you, either. Only, I miss—"

His voice broke, and the tears sprang into his eyes once more.

"You miss your mother," the girl finished quietly.

Anakin nodded, wiping at his face, unable to speak a word as Padmé Naberrie drew him against her and held him close.

Even before an off-world traveler was close enough to understand why, he could tell that Coruscant was different from other planets. Seasoned veterans were always amazed at how strange the planet looked from space, casting not the softer blue and white shades of planets still verdant and unspoiled, but an odd silvery glow that suggested the reflection of sunlight off metal.

The impression was not misleading. The days in which Coruscant could be viewed in any sort of natural state were dead and gone. The capital city had expanded over the centuries, building by building, until it wrapped the entire planet. Forests, mountains, bodies of water, and natural formations had been covered over. The atmosphere was filtered through oxygen regulators and purified by scrubbers, and water was gathered and stored in massive artificial aquifers. Native animals, birds, plants, and fish could be found in the museums or the climate-controlled indoor preserves. As Anakin Skywalker could clearly see from the viewport of Queen Amidala's slowly descending transport, Coruscant had become a planet of skyscrapers, their gleaming metal towers stretching skyward in a forest of spear points, an army of frozen giants blanketing the horizon in every direction.

The boy stared at the city-planet in awe, searching for a break in the endless forest of buildings, finding none. He glanced at Ric Olié in the pilot's seat, and Ric smiled.

"Coruscant, capital of the Republic, an entire planet evolved into one city." He winked. "A nice place to visit, but I wouldn't want to live there."

"It's so huge!" the boy breathed softly.

They dropped into a landfall traffic lane and cruised slowly through the maze of buildings, sliding along the magnetic guidance lines that directed airborne vehicles. Ric explained how it worked to Anakin, who listened with half an ear, his attention still held captive by the vastness of the cityscape. In the background, the Jedi moved silently. Jar Jar crouched to one side, peering over the console through the viewport, clearly terrified by what he was seeing. Anakin knew the Gungan must long for the familiarity of his swamp home, just as the boy was thinking how much better he liked the desert.

The Queen's transport slowed now, edging its way out of the traffic lane, onto a landing dock that floated near a cluster of huge buildings. Anakin peered down doubtfully. They were several hundred stories up, hundreds and hundreds of meters in the air. He tore his gaze away, swallowing hard.

The ship docked with a soft bump on the landing platform, its antigrav clamps locking in place. The Queen was waiting in the main corridor with her retinue of handmaidens, guards, and Captain Panaka. She nodded at Qui-Gon, indicating that he should lead the way. Giving Padmé a quick smile, Anakin followed close on the heels of the Jedi Master as he moved to the hatchway.

The hatch slid open, the loading ramp lowered, and the Jedi Knights, Anakin Skywalker, and Jar Jar Binks exited into the sunlight of Coruscant. The boy spent the first few minutes concentrating on not being overwhelmed, which became even more difficult once he was outside the ship. He kept his eyes on the rampway and Qui-Gon, not allowing himself to look around at first for fear he might walk right off into space.

Two men clothed in robes of office of the Republic Senate stood at the end of the ramp, flanked by a contingent of Republic guards. The Jedi approached the pair and bowed formally in greeting. Anakin and Jar Jar were quick to do the same, though only Anakin knew who they were bowing to and why.

Now Queen Amidala appeared, dressed in her black and gold robes with the feathered headpiece lending height and flow to her movements as she descended the ramp. Her handmaidens surrounded her, wrapped in their cloaks of crimson, faces barely visible in the shadows of their drawn hoods. Captain Panaka and his complement of Naboo guards escorted them.

Amidala stopped before the two men who waited, eyes shifting to the man with the kindly face and anxious eyes. Senator Palpatine, the Queen's emissary to the Republic Senate, bowed in welcome, hands clasped in the folds of his blue-green robes.

"It is a great relief to see you alive and well, Your Majesty," he offered with a smile, straightening once more. "May I present Supreme Chancellor Valorum."

Valorum was a tall, silver-haired man of indeterminate age, neither young nor old in appearance, but something of each, his bearing and voice strong, but his face and startling blue eyes tired and worried.

"Welcome, Your Highness," he said, a faint smile working its way onto his stern features. "It is an honor to finally meet you in person. I must relay to you how distressed everyone is over the current situation on Naboo. I have called for a special session of the Senate so that you may present your request for relief."

The Queen held his gaze without moving even a fraction of a centimeter, tall and regal in her robes of office, white-painted face as still and cool as ice. "I am grateful for your concern, Chancellor," she said quietly.

Out of the corner of his eye, Anakin recognized Padmé staring out at him from beneath her concealing hood. When he turned toward her, she gave him a wink, and he felt himself blush.

Palpatine had moved to the Queen's side and was indicating an air shuttle that was awaiting them. "There is a question of procedure, but I feel confident we can overcome it," he was saying, guiding her along the rampway, her handmaidens, Captain Panaka, and the Naboo guards in tow.

Anakin started to follow, Jar Jar at his side, then stopped as he saw that the Jedi were still standing with Supreme Chancellor Valorum. Anakin glanced back questioningly at Qui-Gon, not certain where he was supposed to go. The Queen and her retinue slowed in response, and Amidala motioned for Anakin and the Gungan to join them. Anakin looked again at Qui-Gon, who nodded wordlessly.

Moving into the air shuttle with the Queen, Anakin and Jar Jar settled quietly into place in the very back seat. Senator Palpatine glanced over his shoulder at them from the front, a look of skepticism crossing his face before he turned away again.

"Me not feelen too good 'bout being here, Annie," the Gungan whispered doubtfully.

Anakin nodded and tightened his mouth determinedly.

They flew only a short distance to another cluster of buildings and another loading dock, this one clearly meant for shuttle-
craft. There, they disembarked and were escorted by Palpatine to
his quarters, a portion of which had been made ready for the
Queen and her entourage. Anakin and Jar Jar were given a room
and a chance to clean up and were left alone. After a time, they
were collected by one of the handmaidens—not Padmé, Anakin
noted with disappointment—and escorted to a waiting room situated outside what appeared to be Palpatine's office.

"Wait here," the handmaiden instructed, and disappeared
back down the hallway.

The doors to the senator's office were open, and the boy and
the Gungan could see inside clearly. The Queen was present,
dressed now in a gown of purple velvet, which was wrapped
about her slim form in layers, the sleeves long and full, hanging
gracefully from her slender arms. A fan-shaped crown with ornate beadwork and tassels rested upon her head. She was sitting
in a chair, listening as Palpatine spoke to her. Her handmaidens
stood to one side, crimson robes and hoods drawn close about
them. Anakin did not think either was Padmé. He wondered if
he should try to find her instead of waiting here, but he did not
know where to look.

The conversation within seemed decidedly one-sided, Senator Palpatine gesturing animatedly as he stalked the room, the
Queen as still as stone. Anakin wished he could hear what was
being said. He glanced at Jar Jar, and he could tell from the Gungan's restless eyes he was thinking the same thing.

When Captain Panaka walked past them and entered the
room beyond, screening them from view for just a moment,
Anakin rose impulsively. Motioning for Jar Jar to stay where

he was, putting a finger to his lips in warning, he moved to one side of the doorway, pressing close. Through the crack between the open door and the jamb, he could just make out the voices of Palpatine and the Queen, muffled and indistinct.

Palpatine had stopped moving and was standing before the Queen, shaking his head. "The Republic is not what it once was. The Senate is full of greedy, squabbling delegates who are only looking out for themselves and their home systems. There is no interest in the common good—no civility, only politics." He sighed wearily. "It's disgusting. I must be frank, Your Majesty. There is little chance the Senate will act on the invasion."

Amidala was silent a moment. "Chancellor Valorum seems to think there is hope."

"If I may say so, Your Majesty," the senator replied, his voice kind, but sad, "the chancellor has little real power. He is mired in baseless accusations of corruption. A manufactured scandal surrounds him. The bureaucrats are in charge now."

The Queen rose, standing tall and fixed before him. "What options do we have, Senator?"

Palpatine seemed to think on the matter for a moment. "Our best choice would be to push for the election of a stronger supreme chancellor—one who could take control of the bureaucrats, enforce the laws, and give us justice." He brushed back his thick hair, worrying his forehead with steepled fingers. "You could call for a vote of no confidence in Chancellor Valorum."

Amidala did not seem convinced. "Valorum has been our strongest supporter. Is there no other way?"

Palpatine stood before her. "Our only other choice would be to submit the matter to the courts—"

"There is no time for that," the Queen interrupted quickly, a hint of anger in her voice. "The courts take even longer to decide things than the Senate." She shifted purposefully, an edge sharpening her words further. "Our people are dying—more and more each day. We must do something quickly. We must stop the Trade Federation before this gets any worse."

Palpatine gave Amidala a stern look. "To be realistic about the matter, Your Highness, I believe we are going to have to accept Trade Federation control as an accomplished fact—for the time being, at least."

The Queen shook her head slowly. "That is something I cannot do, Senator."

They faced each other in the silence that followed, eyes locked, and Anakin Skywalker, hiding behind the door without, found himself wondering suddenly what had become of Qui-Gon Jinn.

Unlike other buildings in the vast sprawl of Coruscant, the Jedi Temple stood alone. A colossal pyramid with multiple spires rising skyward from its flat top, it sat apart from everything at the end of a broad promenade linking it with bulkier, sharper-edged towers in which solitude and mediation were less likely to be found. Within the Temple were housed the Jedi Knights and their students, the whole of the order engaged in contemplation and study of the Force, in codification of its dictates and mastery of its disciplines, and in training to serve the greater good it embodied.

The Jedi Council room dominated a central portion of the complex. The Council itself was in session, its doors closed, its proceedings hidden from the eyes and ears of all but fourteen people. Twelve of them—some human, some nonhuman—

comprised the Council, a diverse and seasoned group who had gravitated to the order from both ends of the galaxy. The final two Jedi, who were guests of the Council this afternoon, were Qui-Gon Jinn and Obi-Wan Kenobi.

The seats of the twelve Council members formed a circle facing inward to where Qui-Gon and Obi-Wan stood, the former relating the events of the past few weeks, the latter a step behind his Master, listening attentively. The room was circular and domed, supported by graceful pillars spaced between broad windows open to the city and the light. The shape of the room and the Council seating reflected the Jedi belief in the equality of and interconnection between all things. In the world of the Jedi, the balance of life within the Force was the pathway to understanding and peace.

Qui-Gon studied the faces of his listeners as he spoke, each of them familiar to him. Most were Jedi Masters like himself, among them Yoda and Mace Windu, seniors in rank among those seated. They were more compliant in the ways of the Jedi order than he had ever been or would probably ever be.

He stood apart in the mosaic circle that formed a speaker's platform for those who addressed the Council, his tall, broad form and deep voice commanding the attention of those gathered, his blue eyes fixing them each in turn, constantly searching for a reaction to his words. They watched him carefully—stately Ki-Adi-Mundi, young and beautiful Adi Gallia, slender Depa Billaba, crested and marble-faced Even Piell, and all the others, each different and unique in appearance, each with something vital to offer as a representative of the Council.

Qui-Gon brought his eyes back to Mace Windu and Yoda, the ones he must convince, the ones most respected and powerful of those who sat in judgment.

"My conclusion," he finished quietly, his story completed, "is that the one who attacked me on Tatooine is a Sith Lord."

The silence that followed was palpable. Then there was a stirring of brown robes, a shifting of bodies and limbs. Glances were exchanged and murmurs of disbelief quickly voiced.

"A Sith Lord?" Mace Windu repeated with a growl, leaning forward. He was a strong, dark-skinned man with a shaved head and penetrating eyes, smooth-faced despite his years.

"Impossible!" Ki-Adi-Mundi snapped irritably, not bothering to hide his dismay at the suggestion. "The Sith have been gone for a millennium!"

Yoda shifted only slightly in his chair, a small and wizened presence in the company of much larger beings, his eyes gone to slits like a contented sand panther's, his whiskery wrinkled face turned toward Qui-Gon's thoughtfully.

"Threatened, the Republic is, if the Sith are involved," he observed in his soft, gravelly voice.

The others began to mutter anew among themselves. Qui-Gon said nothing, waiting them out. They had believed the Sith destroyed. They had believed them consumed by their own lust for power. He could feel Obi-Wan shift uncomfortably at his shoulder, having trouble maintaining his silence.

Mace Windu leaned back heavily, his strong brow furrowing. "This is difficult to accept, Qui-Gon. I do not understand how the Sith could have returned without us knowing."

"Hard to see, the dark side is," Yoda said with a small snort. "Discover who this assassin is, we must."

"Perhaps he will reveal himself again," Ki-Adi-Mundi suggested with a nod to Qui-Gon.

"Yes," Mace Windu agreed. "This attack was with purpose,

that much is clear. The Queen is his target. Since he failed once, he may try again."

Yoda lifted one skinny arm, pointing at Qui-Gon. "With this Naboo Queen, you must stay, Qui-Gon. Protect her, you must."

The others murmured their approval, evidencing the confidence they felt in the Jedi Master's abilities. Still Qui-Gon said nothing.

"We shall use all our resources to unravel this mystery and discover the identity of your attacker," Mace Windu advised. One hand lifted in dismissal. "May the Force be with you, Qui-Gon Jinn."

"May the Force be with you," Yoda echoed.

Obi-Wan turned to leave. He stopped when Qui-Gon did not follow, but instead remained standing before the Council. Obi-Wan held his breath, knowing what was coming.

Yoda cocked his head questioningly. "More to say, have you, Qui-Gon Jinn?"

"With your permission, my Master," the Jedi replied, gaze steady. "I have encountered a vergence in the Force."

Yoda's eyes widened slightly. "A vergence, you say?"

"Located around a person?" Mace Windu asked quickly.

Qui-Gon nodded. "A boy. His cells have the highest concentration of midi-chlorians I have ever seen in a life-form." He paused. "It is possible he was conceived by midi-chlorians."

There was a shocked silence this time. Qui-Gon Jinn was suggesting the impossible, that the boy was conceived not by human contact, but by the essence of all life, by the connectors to the Force itself, the midi-chlorians. Comprising collective consciousness and intelligence, the midi-chlorians formed the link between everything living and the Force.

But there was more that troubled the Jedi Council. There

was a prophecy, so old its origins had long since been lost, that a chosen one would appear, imbued with an abundance of midichlorians, a being strong with the Force and destined to alter it forever.

It was Mace Windu who gave voice to the Council's thoughts. "You refer to the prophecy," he said quietly. "Of the one who will bring balance to the Force. You believe it is this boy."

Qui-Gon hesitated. "I don't presume—"

"But you do!" Yoda snapped challengingly. "Revealed, your opinion is, Qui-Gon!"

The Jedi Master took a deep breath. "I request the boy be tested."

Again, there was silence as the members of the Council exchanged glances, communicating without words.

Eyes shifted back to Qui-Gon. "To be trained as a Jedi, you request for him?" Yoda asked softly.

"Finding him was the will of the Force." Qui-Gon pressed ahead recklessly. "I have no doubt of it. There is too much happening here for it to be anything else."

Mace Windu held up one hand, bringing the debate to a close. "Bring him before us, then."

Yoda nodded somberly, eyes closing. "Tested, he will be."

"It is time to be going, Your Majesty," Senator Palpatine advised, moving to gather up a pile of data cards from his desk.

Queen Amidala rose, and Anakin hurried back to his seat beside Jar Jar, giving the Gungan another warning glance for good measure. Jar Jar looked hurt.

"Me not gonna tell dem," he protested.

A moment later Palpatine ushered the Queen and her handmaidens from his office and into the antechamber where the boy and the Gungan sat waiting. The senator went by them without a glance and was out the door immediately.

Queen Amidala slowed just a fraction as she passed Anakin.

"Why don't you come with us," the handmaiden Rabé said without looking at him, her voice a whisper. "This time you won't have to listen from behind a door."

Anakin and Jar Jar exchanged a startled, chagrined look, then rose and followed after.

While the others waited without, Queen Amidala, accompanied by her handmaidens, retreated to her chambers long enough to change into yet another ensemble, this one clearly meant to emphasize her status as leader of the Naboo. She emerged wearing a broad-shouldered cloak of crimson velvet trimmed with gold lace and a crown of woven cloth horns and tassels with a center plate of hammered gold. The gown and headdress lent both size and majesty, and she walked past a wondering Anakin and Jar Jar as if come down out of the clouds to mix with mortals, all cool grace and extraordinary beauty, aloof and untouchable.

Eirtaé and Rabé, the handmaidens who had accompanied her earlier, were present again, and they trailed the Queen in a silent glide, wrapped in their crimson hooded robes. Again Anakin looked for Padmé and did not find her.

"Please lead the way," Amidala requested of Palpatine, beckoning the boy, the Gungan, and Captain Panaka to accompany them.

They walked from Palpatine's quarters down a series of corridors that connected to other chambers and, eventually, to other buildings. The halls were empty of almost everyone, save for a scattering of Republic guards, and the company proceeded unchallenged. Anakin glanced around in awe at the tall ceilings and high windows, at the forest of buildings visible without, imagining what it would be like to live in a place like Coruscant.

When they reached the Senate chamber, he had cause to wonder anew.

The chamber had the look of an arena, circular and massive, with doors opening off exterior rampways at various levels above the main floor. At the center of the chamber a tall, slender column supported the supreme chancellor's platform, a broad, semienclosed area that allowed Valorum, who was already present, to sit or stand as he chose in the company of his vice chair and staff. All around the smooth interior walls of the arena, Senate boxes jutted from hangar bays off entry doors, some fixed in place while their senators conferred with staff and visitors, others floating just off their moorings. When a senator requested permission to speak and was recognized by the chair, his box would float to the center of the arena, close to the supreme chancellor's podium, where it remained until the speech was concluded.

Anakin picked up on all this in a matter of seconds, trailing the Queen and Palpatine to the entry doors opening onto the Naboo Senate box, which sat waiting at its docking. Banners and curtains hung from the rounded ceiling in brilliant streamers, and indirect lighting glowed softly from every corner, brightening the rotunda's cavernous interior. Droids bustled along the exterior rampways, carrying messages from one delegation to the next, the movement of their metal bodies giving the chamber the look of a complex piece of machinery.

"If the Federation moves to defer the motion, Your Majesty," Senator Palpatine was saying to the Queen, his head bent close, his voice low and insistent, "I beg of you to ask for a resolution to end this session and call for the election of a new supreme chancellor."

Amidala did not look at him, continuing to advance toward the Naboo box. "I wish I had your confidence in this proposal, Senator," she replied quietly.

"You must force a new election for supreme chancellor," Palpatine pressed. "I promise you there are many who will support us. It is our best chance." He glanced toward the podium and Valorum. "Our only chance."

A murmur had risen from the assembled as they caught sight of Amidala standing at the entry to the Naboo box, robes of office flowing out behind her, head erect, face calm. If she heard the change in tenor of the level of conversation around her, she gave no sign. Her eyes shifted momentarily to Palpatine.

"You truly believe Chancellor Valorum will not bring our motion to a vote?" she asked quietly.

Palpatine shook his head, his high brow furrowing. "He is distracted. He is afraid. He will be of no help."

Rabé handed a small metal viewscreen to Anakin and Jar Jar and motioned for them to wait where they were. Stepping into the Senate box with Palpatine, Amidala was joined by her hand-maidens and Panaka. Anakin was disappointed at not being included, but grateful when he discovered that the viewscreen Rabé had provided allowed him to see and hear what was happening in the Naboo box.

"She's going to ask the Senate for help, Jar Jar," he whispered, leaning over excitedly. "What do you think?"

The Gungan wrinkled up his billed mouth and shook his

floppy-eared head. "Me think dis bombad, Annie. Too many peoples to be agreeing on da one thing."

The Naboo box detached from its docking and floated a short distance toward the supreme chancellor's podium, waiting for permission to advance all the way. Palpatine, Amidala, and the rest of the occupants were seated now, facing forward.

Valorum nodded his short-cropped white head in the direction of Palpatine. "The chair recognizes the senator from the sovereign system of Naboo."

The Naboo box glided to the center of the arena, and Palpatine rose to his feet, taking in the assemblage with a slow sweeping gaze that drew all eyes toward his.

"Supreme Chancellor, delegates of the Senate," his voice boomed, quieting the chamber. "A tragedy has occurred on my homeworld of Naboo. We have become caught up in a dispute, one of which you are all well aware. It began with a taxation of trade routes and has evolved into an oppressive and lawless occupation of a peaceful world. The Trade Federation bears responsibility for this injustice and must be made to answer . . ."

A second box was rushing forward by now, this one bearing the markings of the Trade Federation and occupied by the Federation's senator, Lott Dod, and a handful of trade barons in attendance.

"This is outrageous!" the Trade Federation senator thundered, gesturing toward the podium and Valorum. A lean, wizened Neimoidian, he loomed out of the low-railed box like a willowy tree. "I object to Senator Palpatine's ridiculous assertions and ask that he be silenced at once!"

Valorum's white head swiveled briefly in Lott Dod's direction and one hand lifted. "The chair does not recognize the senator from the Trade Federation at this time." The supreme chancellor's voice was soft, but steady. "Return to your station."

Lott Dod looked as if he might say something more, but then he lowered himself back into his seat as his box slowly retreated.

"To state our allegations in full," Palpatine continued, "I present Queen Amidala, the recently elected ruler of the Naboo, to speak on our behalf."

He stepped aside, and Amidala rose to a light scattering of applause. Moving to the front of the box, she faced Valorum. "Honorable representatives of the Republic, distinguished delegates, and Supreme Chancellor Valorum. I come to you under the gravest of circumstances. In repudiation and violation of the laws of the Republic, the Naboo have been invaded and subjugated by force by droid armies of the Trade Federation—"

Lott Dod was on his feet again, voice raised angrily. "I object! This is nonsense! Where is the proof?" He did not wait for recognition as he turned to the chamber at large. "I recommend a commission be sent to Naboo to ascertain the truth of these allegations."

Valorum shook his head. "Overruled."

Lott Dod sighed heavily and threw up his hands as if with that single word his life had become hopeless. "Your Honor, you cannot allow us to be condemned without granting our request for an impartial observation. It is against all the rules of procedure!"

He scanned the chamber for help, and there was a murmur of agreement from the delegates. A third box glided forward to join those of Naboo and the Trade Federation. The chair recognized Aks Moe, the senator from the planet of Malastare.

Stocky and slow moving, his three eyestalks waving gently, Aks Moe put the thick, heavy pads of his hands on his hips. "The senator from Malastare concurs with the honorable delegate from the Trade Federation." His voice was thick and gnarly. "A commission, once requested, must be appointed, where there is a dispute of the sort we have encountered here. It is the law."

Valorum hesitated. "The point is . . ."

He trailed off uncertainly, left the sentence unfinished, and turned to confer with his vice chair, identified on the printed register as Mas Amedda. Amedda was of a species Anakin had never encountered, human in form, but with a head swollen by a pillow of cushioning tissue narrowing into a pair of tentacles that drooped over either shoulder and feelers that jutted from above the forehead. Together with their aides, the chair and vice chair engaged in a hurried discussion. Anakin and Jar Jar exchanged worried glances as Palpatine's voice reached them through the handheld viewscreen's tiny speaker.

"Enter the bureaucrats, the true rulers of the Republic, and on the payroll of the Trade Federation, I might add," he was whispering to the Queen. Anakin could see their heads bent close. Palpatine's tone was heavy. "This is where Chancellor Valorum's strength will disappear."

Valorum had moved back to the podium, a worn look on his face. "The point is conceded. Section 523A takes precedence here." He nodded in the direction of the Naboo box. "Queen Amidala of the Naboo, will you defer your motion in order to allow a Senate commission to explore the validity of your accusations?"

Anakin could see the Queen stiffen in surprise, and when she spoke, her voice was edged with anger and determination.

"I will not defer," she declared, eyes locked on Valorum. "I have come before you to resolve this attack on Naboo sovereignty now. I was not elected Queen to watch my people suffer and die while you discuss this invasion in committee. If the chancellor is not capable of action, I suggest new leadership is needed." She paused. "I move for a vote of no confidence in the supreme chancellor."

Voices rose immediately in response, some in support, some in protest. Senators and spectators alike came to their feet, loud mutterings quickly building to shouts that echoed through the cavernous chamber. Valorum stood speechless at the podium, stunned and disbelieving. He stared at Amidala, his face etched in sudden shock as the impact of her words registered. Amidala faced him boldly, waiting.

Mas Amedda moved in front of Valorum, taking charge of the podium. "Order!" he bellowed, his strange head swelling. "We shall have order!"

The assembly quieted then, and the delegates reseated themselves, responding to Amedda's command. Anakin noted that the Trade Federation box had maneuvered into position close beside the Naboo box. Lott Dod exchanged a quick glance with Palpatine, but neither spoke.

A new box floated to the center of the chamber, and the vice chair recognized Edcel Bar Gan, the senator from Roona.

"Roona seconds the motion for a vote of no confidence in Chancellor Valorum," Bar Gan intoned in a sibilant voice.

Mas Amedda did not look pleased. "The motion has been seconded."

He turned now to Valorum, speaking quickly to him, keeping his voice low and his words hidden behind his hand. Valorum looked at him uncomprehendingly, eyes distant and lost.

"There must be no delays," Aks Moe of Malastare declared

in a loud voice, drawing Mas Amedda's attention back to him. "The motion is on the floor and must be voted on at once."

Lott Dod was back on his feet. "I move the motion be sent to the procedures committee for further study—"

The Republic Senate erupted anew, chanting loudly, "Vote now! Vote now!" Mas Amedda was deep in discussion with Supreme Chancellor Valorum, hands on his shoulders as if to bring him back from wherever he'd gone by sheer force of determination.

"You see, Your Majesty, the tide is with us," Anakin heard Palpatine announce quietly to the Queen. The boy's eyes dropped to the viewscreen. "Valorum will be voted out, I assure you, and they will elect a new chancellor, a strong chancellor, one who will not let our tragedy be ignored . . ."

Mas Amedda was back at the podium, addressing the chamber. "The supreme chancellor requests a recess."

Shouts rose from the delegates, echoing across the chamber in waves as Valorum stared at Senator Palpatine and Queen Amidala, and even from where he stood watching now at the entry doors to the Naboo box, Anakin Skywalker could discern the look of betrayal registered on the supreme chancellor's anguished face.

Less than an hour later, Anakin burst through the open doors of the Queen's antechamber in search of Padmé and found himself face-to-face with Amidala instead. The Queen was standing alone in the center of the room, her eyes directed toward him, her robed form radiant and solitary.

"Excuse me," Anakin said quickly. "Your Majesty."

She nodded silently, white face smooth and perfect.

"I was looking for Padmé," he continued, standing rooted in place just inside the doorway, undecided on whether to stay or go. He glanced around doubtfully. "Qui-Gon says he will take me before the Jedi Council. I wanted Padmé to know."

A small smile flitted across the Queen's painted lips. "Padmé isn't here, Anakin. I sent her on an errand."

"Oh," he said quietly.

"But I will give her your message."

The boy grinned. "Maybe I will become a Jedi Knight!" he exclaimed, unable to contain his excitement.

Amidala nodded. "Maybe you will."

"I think Padmé would like that."

"I think she would, too."

Anakin backed away. "I didn't mean to . . ." He searched for the word and couldn't find it.

"Good luck, Anakin," the Queen said softly. "Do well."

He wheeled away with a broad smile and was out the door.

The day passed quickly for Qui-Gon Jinn and Obi-Wan Kenobi, and sunset found them standing together on a balcony outside the Jedi Temple overlooking Coruscant. Neither had said anything to the other for some time. They had collected Anakin Skywalker from Senator Palpatine's quarters following his return from the Republic Senate and brought him before the Council for examination. Now they were awaiting a decision.

As far as Obi-Wan was concerned, it was a foregone conclusion. The young Jedi was frustrated and embarrassed for his Master, who had clearly overstepped his bounds once again. Qui-Gon had been right in his suspicion that the boy was possessed of an inordinately high midi-chlorian count. Obi-Wan had run the test himself. But that alone was not enough to demonstrate Anakin was the chosen one. If there even was such a one, which Obi-Wan seriously doubted. There were hundreds of these old prophecies and legends, handed down through the centuries as a part of Jedi lore. In any case, Qui-Gon was relying on instinct once again, and instinct was useful only if born of the Force and not of emotion. Qui-Gon was insistent on championing the causes of underdogs, of empathizing with creatures he found in some peculiar, inscrutable way he alone could comprehend significant in the scheme of things.

Obi-Wan studied his mentor surreptitiously. Why did he insist on pursuing these hopeless causes? The Council might find the boy possessed of more midi-chlorians than normal, but they would never accept him for Jedi training. The rules were clear and established, and the reasons supporting them were proven and unassailable. Training for the order after more than a year of life was doomed to fail. At nine years of age, Anakin Skywalker was simply too old.

But Qui-Gon would not let it go. He would brace the Council once again, and the result would be the same as it had been on so many other occasions: Qui-Gon would be denied and his stature as a Jedi Master would fall a little further.

Obi-Wan moved to where the older Jedi stood staring out at the endless horizon of skyscrapers. He stood close to him, silent for a moment longer before speaking.

"The boy will not pass the Council's tests, Master," he said softly, "and you know it. He is far too old."

Qui-Gon kept his gaze directed toward the sunset. "Anakin will become a Jedi, I promise you."

Obi-Wan sighed wearily. "Don't defy the Council, Master. Not again."

The older man seemed to go very still, perhaps even to stop breathing, before he turned to his protégé. "I will do what I must, Obi-Wan. Would you have me be any other way?"

"Master, you could be sitting on the Council by now if you would just follow the code. You deserve to be sitting on the Council." Obi-Wan's frustration surfaced in a burst of momentary anger. His eyes sought the other's and held them. "They will not go along with you this time."

Qui-Gon Jinn studied him a moment, then smiled. "You still have much to learn, my young Padawan."

Obi-Wan bit off his reply and looked away, thinking to himself that Qui-Gon was right, but that maybe this time he should consider taking his own advice.

Inside, Anakin Skywalker faced the Jedi Council, standing in the same place Qui-Gon Jinn had stood some hours earlier. He was nervous at first, brought into the chamber by Qui-Gon, then left alone with the twelve members of the Council. Standing in the mosaic circle and ringed by the silent assemblage, awestruck and uncertain of what was expected of him, he felt vulnerable and exposed. The eyes of the Jedi were distant as they viewed him, but he sensed they were looking not past him, but inside.

They began to question him then, without preliminary introductions or explanations, without expending any effort at all to make him feel comfortable or welcome. He knew some of them by name, for Qui-Gon had described a few, and he was quick to put faces to names. They questioned him at great length, testing memory and knowledge, seeking insights at which he could only guess. They knew of his existence as a slave. They knew of his background on Tatooine, of his mother and his friends, of his Podracing, of Watto, of everything factual and past, of the order of his life.

Now Mace Windu was looking at a screen the boy could not see, and Anakin was giving names to images that flashed across its liquid surface. Images appeared in Anakin's mind with such speed he was reminded of the strange blur of desert and mountains whipping past his cockpit during a Podrace.

"A bantha. A hyperdrive. A proton blaster." The images whizzed through his mind as he named them off. "A Republic cruiser. A Rodian cup. A Hutt speeder."

The screen went blank, and Mace looked up at the boy.

"Good, good, young one," the wizened alien called Yoda praised. The sleepy eyes fixed on him, intent behind their lids. "How feel you?"

"Cold, sir," Anakin confessed.

"Afraid, are you?"

The boy shook his head. "No, sir."

"Afraid to give up your life?" the dark one called Mace Windu asked, leaning forward slightly.

"I don't think so," he answered, then hesitated. Something about the answer didn't feel right.

Yoda blinked and his long ears cocked forward. "See through you, we can," he said quietly.

"Be mindful of your feelings," Mace Windu said.

The old one called Ki-Adi-Mundi stroked his beard. "Your thoughts dwell on your mother."

Anakin felt his stomach lurch at the mention of her. He bit his lip. "I miss her."

Yoda exchanged glances with several others on the Council. "Afraid to lose her, I think."

Anakin flushed. "What's that got to do with anything?" he asked defensively.

Yoda's sleepy eyes fixed on him. "Everything. To the dark side, fear leads. To anger and to hate. To suffering."

"I am not afraid!" the boy snapped irritably, anxious to leave this discussion and move on.

Yoda did not seem to hear him. "The deepest commitment, a Jedi must have. The most serious mind. Much fear in you, I sense, young one."

Anakin took a deep breath and let it out slowly. When he spoke, his voice was calm again. "I am not afraid."

Yoda studied him a moment. "Then continue, we will," he said softly, and the examination resumed.

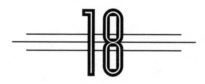

Jar Jar Binks of the Gungans and Queen Amidala of the Naboo stood together at a window that ran floor to ceiling in the Queen's chambers, looking out at the gleaming spires of Coruscant. An odd pairing at best, the Queen regal and composed, the Gungan awkward and jittery, they kept company in silence and watched the sunset color the sky a brilliant gold that reflected here and there off the flat metal and glass surfaces of the city in sudden, blinding explosions of light.

They had returned from the Republic Senate some hours ago, Jar Jar, Anakin, the Queen, and her handmaidens. They had come back principally because there seemed to be nothing else they could do to change the course of events regarding the future of Naboo. Senator Palpatine had stayed behind to politick with his colleagues over the selection of a new supreme chancellor, and Captain Panaka had remained with him, asked by the Queen to bring her news when there was any to offer. None had been forthcoming as yet. Now Anakin was gone as well, taken by

Qui-Gon to the Jedi Temple where he was to meet with the Council, and no one had seen Padmé in some time.

So Jar Jar had rattled around in Palpatine's quarters rather like a stray kaadu until Amidala had taken pity on him and invited him to sit with her. She had gone into seclusion on her return, changing out of her Senate robes into a less imposing gold-trimmed black gown that emphasized how slender and small she really was. She wore an inverted, crescent-shaped crown with a beaded gold medallion arced down over her smooth fore-head, but even so she stood several centimeters shorter than the Gungan.

She was clearly in pain, her eyes so sad and distant that it made Jar Jar want to comfort her. If it had been Annie or Padmé, he might have reached over and patted her on the head, but he was not about to try that with the Queen. There were no guards, but her handmaidens, Eirtaé and Rabé, cloaked in their crimson hooded robes and forever watchful, stood in waiting near the door, and he was certain there were guards somewhere close as well. He was careless of many things, oblivious to others, and in general given over to enjoying life in a haphazard way, but he was no fool.

Finally, though, he could ignore the situation no longer. He shuffled his feet and cleared his throat, drawing the Queen's at-tention. She turned, her white-painted face with red dots on each cheek and a red slash in the center of her lower lip doll-like and expressionless.

"Me wonder sometimes why da Guds invent pain," he of-fered sympathetically.

Amidala's cool gaze was steady and clear. "To motivate us, I imagine."

"Yous think yous people gonna die?" he asked, working his billed mouth around the bitter words as if he could taste them.

The Queen considered the question and shook her head slowly. "I don't know, Jar Jar."

"Gungans gonna get pasted, too, eh?"

"I hope not."

Jar Jar straightened, and a fierce pride brightened his eyes. "Gungans no die without a fight. We warriors! We gotta grand army!"

"An army?" she repeated, a hint of surprise in her soft voice.

"A grand army! Lotta Gungans. Dey come from all over. Dat why no swamp beings give us trubble. Too many Gungans. Gotta big energy shields, too. Nutten get through. Gotta energy balls, fly outta slings and splat electricity and goo. Bombad stuff. Gungans no ever give up to maccaneks or anyone!"

He paused, shrugged uncomfortably. "Dat why Naboo no like us, mebbe."

She was studying him closely now, her detached gaze replaced by something more intense, as if she were turning an unexpected thought over in her mind. She was preparing to speak to that thought, he believed, when Senator Palpatine and Captain Panaka strode through the doorway in a rush.

"Your Highness," Captain Panaka greeted, barely able to contain his excitement as both men bowed quickly and straightened. "Senator Palpatine has been nominated to succeed Valorum as supreme chancellor!"

Palpatine's smile was contained and deferential, and his voice carefully modulated as he spoke. "A surprise, to be sure, but a welcome one. I promise, Your Majesty, if I am elected, I will restore democracy to the Republic. I will put an end to the corruption that has plagued the Senate. The Trade Federation will lose its influence over the bureaucrats, and our people will be freed from the tyranny of this unlawful and onerous invasion—"

"Who else has been nominated?" Amidala asked abruptly, cutting him short.

"Bail Antilles of Alderaan and Aks Moe of Malastare," Panaka told her, avoiding Palpatine's eyes.

The senator was quick to recover from the unexpected interruption of his speech. "Your Majesty, I feel confident that our situation will generate strong support for us when the voting takes place tomorrow." He paused meaningfully. "I will be chancellor, I promise you."

The Queen did not look impressed. She moved past Jar Jar to the window and stared out at the lights of the city as they brightened with the fading of the sunset. "I fear by the time you have taken control of the bureaucrats, Senator, there will be nothing left of our cities, our people, or our way of life to salvage."

Palpatine looked taken aback. "I understand your concern, Your Majesty. Unfortunately, the Federation has seized possession of our planet. It will be nearly impossible to immediately dislodge them."

"Perhaps." Amidala turned from the window to face him. Her eyes were bright with anger and determination. "With the Senate in transition, there is nothing more I can do here." She walked to where he stood with Panaka. "Senator, this is your arena. I must return now to mine. I have decided to go back to Naboo. My place is with my people."

"Go back!" Palpatine was aghast, his pale face stricken. Panaka looked quickly from one to the other. "But, Your Majesty, be realistic! You will be in great danger! They will force you to sign the treaty!"

The Queen was calm and composed. "I will sign no treaty.

My fate will be no different from that of my people." She turned to Panaka. "Captain!"

Panaka snapped to attention. "Yes, Your Highness?"

"Ready my ship."

Palpatine stepped forward quickly to intercept her. "Please, Your Majesty. Stay here, where it is safe."

Amidala's voice was edged with iron. "No place is safe, if the Senate doesn't condemn this invasion. It is clear to me now that the Republic no longer functions." Her eyes locked on his. "If you win the election, Senator, I know you will do everything possible to stop the Federation. I pray you will find a way to restore sanity and compassion to the Republic."

She moved past him in a smooth, gliding motion and was out the door, her handmaidens and Panaka at her heels. Jar Jar Binks followed, shuffling after as unobtrusively as he could manage, glancing just once at Palpatine in passing.

He was surprised to catch the barest glimpse of a smile on the senator's shrewd face.

In the Temple of the Jedi, Qui-Gon Jinn, Obi-Wan Kenobi, and Anakin Skywalker stood before the Council of twelve. Clustered together at the center of the speaker's platform, they faced the circle of chairs in which the members of the Council were seated, and awaited their decision on the boy. Outside, the light was pale and wan as twilight replaced sunset, and night began its slow descent across the city.

"Finished, we are, with our examination of the boy," Yoda advised in his guttural, whispery voice. His eyes were lidded and sleepy, his pointed ears pricked forward. "Correct, you were, Qui-Gon."

Mace Windu nodded his concurrence, his dark, smooth face expressionless in the dim light. "His cells contain a very high concentration of midi-chlorians." There was emphasis on the word *very* as he spoke.

"The Force is strong in him," Ki-Adi-Mundi agreed.

Qui-Gon felt a rush of satisfaction on hearing the words, a vindication of his insistence on freeing the boy from his life on Tatooine and bringing him here. "He is to be trained, then," he declared in triumph.

There was an uncomfortable silence as the Council members looked from one to the other.

"No," Mace Windu said quietly. "He will not be trained."

Anakin's face crumpled, and there were tears in his eyes as he glanced quickly at Qui-Gon.

"No?" the Jedi Master repeated in disbelief, shocked almost speechless. He tried hard to ignore the I-told-you-so look on Obi-Wan's young face.

Mace Windu nodded, dark eyes steady. "He is too old. There is already too much anger in him."

Qui-Gon was incensed, but he held himself in check. This decision made no sense. It could not be allowed to stand. "He *is* the chosen one," he insisted vehemently. "You must see it!"

Yoda cocked his round head contemplatively. "Clouded, this boy's future is. Masked by his youth."

Qui-Gon searched the faces of the other members of the Jedi Council, but found no help. He straightened and nodded his acceptance of their decision. "Very well. I will train him then. I take Anakin Skywalker as my Padawan apprentice."

Out of the corner of his eye, he saw Obi-Wan stiffen in shock. He saw, as well, the sudden flicker of hope that crossed

Anakin's face. He did not respond to either, keeping his gaze directed toward the Council.

"An apprentice, you already have, Qui-Gon," Yoda pointed out sharply. "Impossible, to take on a second."

"We forbid it," Mace Windu advised darkly.

"Obi-Wan is ready," Qui-Gon declared.

"I am!" his protégé agreed heatedly, trying unsuccessfully to mask his surprise and disappointment in his mentor's unexpected decision. "I am ready to face the trials!"

Yoda's sleepy eyes shifted. "Ready so early, are you? What know you of ready?"

Qui-Gon and Obi-Wan exchanged quick, hard looks, and the measure of their newfound antagonism was palpable. The breach in their relationship was widening so quickly it could no longer be mapped.

Qui-Gon took a deep breath and turned back to the Council. "Obi-Wan is headstrong, and he has much to learn still about the living Force, but he is capable. There is little more he will learn from me."

Yoda shook his wizened face. "Our own counsel we will keep on who is ready, Qui-Gon. More to learn, he has."

"Now is not the time for this," Mace Windu stated with finality. "The Senate will vote tomorrow for a new supreme chancellor. Queen Amidala returns home, we are advised, which will put pressure on the Federation and could widen the confrontation. Those responsible will be quick to act on these new events."

"Drawn out of hiding, her attackers will be," Yoda whispered.

"Events are moving too fast for distractions such as this," Ki-Adi-Mundi added.

Mace Windu took a quick look about at the others sitting on the Council, then turned once more to Qui-Gon. "Go with the Queen to Naboo and discover the identity of this dark warrior who attacked you, be it Sith or otherwise. That is the clue we need to unravel this mystery."

Yoda's nod was slow and brooked no argument. "Decided later, young Skywalker's fate will be."

Qui-Gon took a deep breath, filled with frustration and disappointment at the unexpected turn of events. Anakin would not be trained, even though he had offered to take the boy as his Padawan. Worse, he had offended Obi-Wan, not intentionally perhaps, but deeply nevertheless. The rift was not permanent, but it would take time for the younger man's pride to heal—time they could not afford.

He bowed his acquiescence to the Council. "I brought Anakin here; he must stay in my charge. He has nowhere else to go."

Mace Windu nodded. "He is your ward, Qui-Gon. We do not dispute that."

"But train him not!" Yoda admonished sharply. "Take him with you, but train him not!"

The words stung, the force behind them unmistakable. Qui-Gon flinched inwardly, but said nothing.

"Protect the Queen," Mace Windu added. "But do not intercede if it comes to war until we have the Senate's approval."

There was a long silence as the members of the Council regarded Qui-Gon Jinn gravely. He stood there, trying to think of something more to say, some other argument to offer. Outside, the last of the twilight faded into darkness, and the lights of the city began to blink on like watchful eyes.

"May the Force be with you," Yoda said finally, signaling to the Jedi Master that the audience was over.

The Jedi and the boy, having been made aware of Amidala's imminent departure for Naboo, went directly to the landing platform where the Queen's transport was anchored to await her arrival. The shuttle ride over was marked by a strained silence between the Jedi and a discomfort in the boy he could not dispel. He looked down at his feet most of the time, wishing he could think of a way to stop Qui-Gon and Obi-Wan from being angry at each other.

When they disembarked from the shuttle at the landing platform, R2-D2 was already bustling about. The little droid beeped at Anakin cheerfully, then wandered over to the edge of the rampway to look down at the traffic. In doing so, he leaned out too far and tumbled over. Anakin gasped, but a second later the astromech droid reappeared, boosted back onto the rampway by his onboard jets. On hearing R2-D2's ensuing flurry of chirps and whistles, the boy smiled in spite of himself.

At the head of the loading ramp, Qui-Gon Jinn and Obi-Wan Kenobi were engaged in a heated discussion. Wind whipped down the canyons of the city's towering buildings, hiding their words from the boy. Carefully, he edged closer so that he could listen in.

"It is not disrespect, Master!" Obi-Wan was saying vehemently. "It is the truth!"

"From your point of view, perhaps." Qui-Gon's face was hard and tight with anger.

The younger Jedi's voice dropped a notch. "The boy is dangerous. They all sense it. Why can't you?"

"His fate is uncertain, but he is not dangerous," Qui-Gon corrected sharply. "The Council will decide Anakin's future. That should be enough for you." He turned away dismissively. "Now get on board!"

Obi-Wan wheeled away and stalked up the ramp into the ship. R2-D2 followed, still whistling happily. Qui-Gon turned to Anakin, and the boy walked up to him.

"Master Qui-Gon," he said uncomfortably, riddled with doubt and guilt over what was happening, "I don't want to be a problem."

Qui-Gon placed a reassuring hand on his shoulder. "You won't be, Annie." He glanced toward the ship, then knelt before the boy. "I'm not allowed to train you, so I want you to watch me instead and be mindful of what you see. Always remember, your focus determines your reality." He paused, eyes locked on Anakin. "Stay close to me, and you will be safe."

The boy nodded his understanding. "Can I ask you something?" The Jedi Master nodded. "What are midi-chlorians?"

Wind whipped at Qui-Gon's long hair, blowing strands of it across his strong face. "Midi-chlorians are microscopic life-forms that reside within the cells of all living things and communicate with the Force."

"They live inside of me?" the boy asked.

"In your cells." Qui-Gon paused. "We are symbionts with the midi-chlorians."

"Symbi-what?"

"Symbionts. Life-forms living together for mutual advantage. Without the midi-chlorians, life could not exist, and we would have no knowledge of the Force. Our midi-chlorians continually speak to us, Annie, telling us the will of the Force."

"They do?"

Qui-Gon cocked one eyebrow. "When you learn to quiet your mind, you will hear them speaking to you."

Anakin thought about it a moment, then frowned. "I don't understand."

Qui-Gon smiled, and his eyes were warm and secretive. "With time and training, Annie, you will."

A pair of shuttles eased up to the loading dock, and Queen Amidala, her handmaidens, Captain Panaka, and an escort of officers and guards disembarked. Last off the second shuttle was Jar Jar Binks. Amidala was wearing a purple velvet travel cloak that draped her body in soft folds and a gold-rimmed cowl that framed her smooth white face like a cameo portrait.

Qui-Gon rose and stood waiting beside Anakin as the Queen and her handmaidens approached.

"Your Highness," Qui-Gon greeted with a deferential inclination of his head. "It will be our pleasure to continue to serve and protect you."

Amidala nodded. "I welcome your help. Senator Palpatine fears the Federation means to destroy me."

"I promise you, we will not let that happen," the Jedi Master advised solemnly.

The Queen turned and with her handmaidens followed Panaka and the Naboo guards and officers into the transport.

Jar Jar hurried over and enveloped Anakin in a huge hug. "Weesa goen home, Annie!" he exclaimed with a grin, and Anakin Skywalker hugged him back.

Moments later they were all aboard, and the sleek transport had lifted off, leaving Coruscant behind.

*   *   *

It was night in the Naboo capital city of Theed, the streets empty and silent save for the occasional passing of battle-droid patrols and the whisper of the wind. In the Queen's throne room, Nute Gunray and Rune Haako stood attentively before a hologram of Darth Sidious. The hologram filled the space at one end of the room, rising up before them menacingly.

The dark-cloaked figure at its center gestured. "The Queen is on her way to you," the Sith Lord intoned softly. "When she arrives, force her to sign the treaty."

There was a momentary pause as the Neimoidians exchanged worried looks. "Yes, my lord," Nute Gunray agreed reluctantly.

"Viceroy, is the planet secure?" The dark figure in the hologram shimmered with movement.

"Yes, my lord." Gunray was on firmer ground here. "We have taken the last pockets of resistance, consisting of mostly primitive life-forms. We are now in complete control."

The faceless speaker nodded. "Good. I will see to it that in the Senate things stay as they are. I am sending Darth Maul to join you. He will deal with the Jedi."

"Yes, my lord." The words were a litany.

The hologram and Darth Sidious faded away. The Neimoidians stood where they were, frozen in place.

"A Sith Lord, here with us?" Rune Haako whispered in disbelief, and this time Nute Gunray had nothing to say at all.

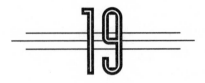

Aboard the Queen's transport, coming out of hyperspace and approaching the Naboo star system, Qui-Gon Jinn paused on his way to a meeting with the Queen to study Anakin Skywalker.

The boy stood at the pilot's console next to Ric Olié. The Naboo pilot was bent forward over the controls, pointing each one out in turn and explaining its function. Anakin was absorbing the information with astonishing quickness, brow furrowed, eyes intense, concentration total.

"And that one?" The boy pointed.

"The forward stabilizer." Ric Olié glanced up at him expectantly, waiting.

"And those control the pitch?" Anakin indicated a bank of levers by the pilot's right hand.

Ric Olié's weathered face broke into a grin. "You catch on pretty quick."

As quick as anyone he had ever encountered, Qui-Gon Jinn thought. That was the reason Anakin was so special. It gave evidence of his high midi-chlorian count. It suggested anew that he was the chosen one.

The Jedi Master sighed. Why could the Council not accept that this was so? Why were they so afraid of taking a chance on the boy, when the signs were so clear?

Qui-Gon found himself frustrated all over again. He understood their thinking. It was bad that Anakin was so old, but not fatal to his chances. What troubled them was not his age, but the conflict they sensed within him. Anakin was wrestling with his parentage, with his separation from his mother, his friends, and his home. Especially his mother. He was old enough to appreciate what might happen, and the result was an uncertainty that worked within him like a caged animal seeking to break free. The Jedi Council knew that it could not tame that uncertainty from without, that it could be mastered only from within. They believed Anakin Skywalker too old for this, his thinking and his beliefs too settled to be safely reshaped. He was vulnerable to his inner conflict, and the dark side would be quick to take advantage of this.

Qui-Gon shook his head, staring over at the boy from the back of the cockpit. Yes, there were risks in accepting him as an apprentice. But few things of worth were accomplished in life without risk. The Jedi order was founded on strict adherence to established procedures in the raising and educating of young Jedi, but there were exceptions to all things, even this. That the Jedi Council was refusing even to consider that this was an instance in which an exception should be made was intolerable.

Still, he must keep faith, he knew. He must believe. The decision not to train Anakin would be reconsidered on their return and reversed. If the Council did not embrace the boy's training as a Jedi voluntarily, then it would be up to Qui-Gon to find a way to make it do so.

He turned away then and walked from the cabin to the passageways beyond and descended one level to the Queen's chambers. The others she had called together for this meeting were already present when he arrived. Obi-Wan gave him a brief, neutral nod of recognition, standing next to a glowering Captain Panaka. Jar Jar Binks hugged the wall to one side, apparently trying to disappear into it. Amidala sat on her shipboard throne on a raised dais set against one wall, two of her handmaidens, Rabé and Eirtaé, flanking her. Her white-painted face was composed and her gaze cool as it met his own, but there was fire in the words she spoke next.

"When we land on Naboo," she advised the Jedi Master after he had bowed and taken up a position next to Panaka, "it is my intention to act on this invasion at once. My people have suffered enough."

Panaka could barely contain himself, his dark face tight with anger. "When we *land*, Your Highness, the Trade Federation will arrest you and force you to sign their treaty!"

Qui-Gon nodded thoughtfully, curious as to the Queen's thinking. "I agree. I'm not sure what you hope to accomplish by this."

Amidala might have been carved from stone. "The Naboo are going to take back what is ours."

"There are only twelve of us!" Panaka snapped, unable to keep silent. "Your Highness," he added belatedly. "We have no army!"

Her eyes shifted to Qui-Gon. "The Jedi cannot fight a war for you, Your Highness," he advised. "We can only protect you."

She let her gaze drift from them to settle on Jar Jar. The Gungan was studying his toes. "Jar Jar Binks!" she called.

Jar Jar, clearly caught off guard, stiffened. "Me, Your Highness?"

"Yes," Amidala of the Naboo affirmed. "I have need of your help."

Deep in the Naboo swamps, at the edge of the lake that bored downward to the Gungan capital city of Otoh Gunga, the fugitives from the Queen's transport were grouped at the water's edge, waiting for the return of Jar Jar Binks. Amidala and her handmaidens, the Jedi Knights, Captain Panaka, Anakin, R2-D2, Ric Olié and several other pilots, and a handful of Naboo guards clustered uneasily in the misty silence. It was safe to say that even now no one but the Queen knew exactly what it was she was attempting to do. All she had been willing to reveal to those in a position to inquire was that she wished to make contact with the Gungan people and Jar Jar would be her emissary. She had insisted on landing in the swamp, even after both Panaka and the Jedi had advised against it.

A single battleship orbited the planet, all that remained of the Trade Federation blockade. Housed within was the control station responsible for directing the droid army that occupied Naboo. When Panaka wondered aloud at the absence of the other battleships, Qui-Gon pointed out rather dryly that you don't need a blockade once you control the port.

Anakin, standing apart from the others with R2-D2, studied the group surreptitiously. Jar Jar had been gone a long time, and everyone but the Queen was growing restless. She stood wrapped in her soft robes, silent and implacable in the midst of her handmaidens. Padmé, Eirtaé, and Rabé had changed from their crimson hooded cloaks into more functional trousers, tunics, boots, and long-waisted overcoats, and there were blasters strapped to their waists. The boy had never seen Padmé like this, and he found himself wondering how good a fighter she was.

As if realizing he was thinking of her, Padmé broke away from the others and came over to him.

"How are you, Annie?" she asked quietly, her kind eyes locking on his.

He shrugged. "Okay. I've missed you."

"It's good to see you again. I'm sorry I haven't had a chance to talk with you before, but I've been very busy."

They hadn't spoken more than a few words to each other since leaving Tatooine, and Anakin hadn't even seen Padmé since their departure from Coruscant. It had bothered him, but he'd kept it to himself.

"I didn't—I—" he stuttered, looking down at his boots. "They decided not to make me a Jedi."

He recounted the story for her, detailing the events surrounding his appearance before the Jedi Council. Padmé listened intently, then touched his cheek with her cool fingers. "They can change their minds, Annie. Don't give up hope."

She bent close then. "I have something to tell you. The Queen has made a painful, difficult decision—a decision that will change everything for the Naboo. We are a peaceful people, and we do not believe in war. But sometimes there is no choice. Either you adapt or you die. The Queen understands this. She has decided to take an aggressive posture with the Trade Federation army. The Naboo are going to fight to regain their freedom."

"Will there be a battle?" he asked quickly, trying unsuccessfully to hide his excitement.

She nodded. "I'm afraid so."

"Will you be involved?" he pressed.

She smiled sadly. "Annie, I don't have a choice."

* * *

Qui-Gon and Obi-Wan stood together some distance away. The Jedi still weren't speaking to each other, or only barely so. Their words on the journey out from Coruscant had been reserved almost exclusively for others. The hard feelings caused by Qui-Gon's bid to train Anakin did not soften. The boy had tried to talk to Obi-Wan once aboard the Queen's ship, just to say he was sorry this had happened, but the younger Jedi had brushed him off.

Now, though, Obi-Wan was beginning to feel uncomfortable with the situation. He had been close with Qui-Gon for too long to let a momentary disagreement put an end to twenty-odd years of friendship. Qui-Gon was like a father to him, the only father he knew. He was angry that the Jedi Master would dismiss him so abruptly in favor of the boy, but he realized, too, the depth of Qui-Gon's passion when he believed in something. Training this boy to be a Jedi was a cause Qui-Gon championed as he had championed no other in Obi-Wan's memory. He did not do so to slight his protégé. He did so because he believed in the boy's destiny.

Obi-Wan understood. Who could say? Perhaps this time Qui-Gon was right. Perhaps Anakin Skywalker's training was a cause worth fighting for.

"I've been thinking," Qui-Gon announced suddenly, keeping his voice low, his eyes directed toward the others. "We are treading on dangerous ground. If the Queen intends to fight a war, we cannot become involved. Not even in her efforts to persuade the Gungans to join with the Naboo against the Federation, if that is what she intends by coming here. The Jedi have no authority to take sides."

"But we do have authority to protect the Queen," Obi-Wan pointed out.

Qui-Gon's eyes shifted to find his. "It is a fine line we walk, then."

"Master," Obi-Wan said, facing him now. "I behaved badly on Coruscant, and I am embarrassed. I meant no disrespect to you. I do not wish to be difficult in the matter of the boy."

"Nor have you been," the older Jedi replied, a faint smile appearing. "You have been honest with me. Honesty is never wrong. I did not lie when I told the Council you were ready. You are. I have taught you all I can. You will be a great Jedi, my young Padawan. You will make me proud."

They gripped hands impulsively, and as quickly as that the breach that had opened between them was closed.

Moments later, a dark shape broke the surface of the water with a splash, and Jar Jar Binks climbed from the lake, shaking water from his amphibious skin onto the assembled. Long ears dripping, billed mouth shedding water like a duck's, he shook his head worriedly.

"'Tis nobody dere! Deys all gone!" His eyestalks swiveled. "Some kinda fight, deys have. Maccaneks, mebbe. Very bombad. Otoh Gunga empty. All Gungans gone. All gone."

"Do you think they have been taken to the camps?" Panaka asked quickly, glancing around at the group.

"More likely they were wiped out," Obi-Wan offered in disgust.

But Jar Jar shook his head. "Me no think so. Gungans too smart. Go into hiding. When dey in trubble, go to sacred place. Maccaneks no find dem dere."

Qui-Gon stepped forward. "Sacred place?" he repeated. "Can you take us there, Jar Jar?"

The Gungan sighed heavily, as if to say "Here we go again," and beckoned for them to follow.

They traversed the swamp for some time, first skirting the lake, then plunging deep into a forest of massive trees and tall grasses, following a water-screened pathway that connected a series of knolls. Somewhere in the distance, Trade Federation STAPs buzzed and whined as a search for the transport fugitives commenced in earnest. Jar Jar glanced about apprehensively as he picked his way through the mire, but did not slow.

Finally, they emerged in a clearing of marshy grasses and stands of trees with roots tangled so thickly they formed what appeared to be an impassable hedge. Jar Jar stopped, sniffed the air speculatively, and nodded. "Dissen it."

He lifted his head and made a strange chittering noise though his billed mouth, the sound echoing eerily in the silence. The group waited, eyes searching the misty gloom.

Suddenly Captain Tarpals and a scouting party of Gungans riding kaadu emerged from the haze, electropoles and energy spears held at the ready.

"Heydey ho, Cap'n Tarpals," Jar Jar greeted cheerfully.

"Binks!" the Gungan leader exclaimed in disbelief. "Notta gain!"

Jar Jar shrugged nonchalantly. "We come ta see da Boss!"

Tarpals rolled his eyes. "Ouch time, Binks. Ouch time for alla yous, mebbe."

Herding them together, Gungans on kaadu providing a perimeter escort on all sides, Tarpals led them deeper into the swamp. The canopy formed by the limbs of the trees became so thick that the sky and the sun almost disappeared. Bits and pieces of statuary began to surface, crumbling stone facades and plinths sinking in the mire. Vines snaked their way across the broken remains, dropping down from limbs that twisted and wound together in vast wooden nets.

Pushing through a high stand of saw grass, they arrived in a clearing filled with Gungan refugees—men, women, and children of all ages and descriptions, huddled together on a broad, dry rise, many with their possessions gathered around them. Tarpals led the company past the refugees to where the ruins of what had once been a grand temple were being slowly reclaimed by the swamp. Platforms and stairs were all that remained intact, the columns and ceilings having long ago collapsed and broken apart. The massive heads and limbs of stone statues poked out of the mire, fingers clutching weapons and eyes staring sightlessly into space.

At the far end of the ruins, Boss Nass appeared, lumbering out of shadows with several more of the Gungan council to stand atop a stone head partially submerged in the water. Amidala and her retinue approached to within hailing distance over a network of causeways and islands.

"Jar Jar Binks, whadda yous doen back?" Boss Nass rumbled angrily. "Yous suppose ta take dese outlanders and no come back! Yous pay good dis time!" The fleshy head swiveled. "Who yous bring here ta da Gungan sacred place?"

The Queen stepped forward at once, white face lifting. "I am Amidala, Queen of the Naboo."

"Naboo!" Boss Nass thundered. "No like da Naboo! Yous bring da maccaneks! Dey bust up our homes! Dey drive us all out!" A heavy arm lifted, pointing at the Queen. "Yous all bombad! Yous all die, mebbe!"

Anakin noticed suddenly that they were completely surrounded by Gungans, some on kaadu, some on foot, all with
electropoles, energy spears, and some sort of throwing device.
Captain Panaka and the Naboo guards were looking around nervously, hands straying toward their blasters. The Jedi flanked the
Queen and her handmaidens, but their arms hung loose at their
sides.

"We wish to form an alliance with you," Amidala tried again.

"We no form nutten wit da Naboo!" Boss Nass roared
angrily.

Abruptly Padmé detached herself from the others and stepped
in front of the Queen. "You did well, Sabé. But I will have to do
this myself," she said quietly, and turned to face Boss Nass.

"Who dis?" the head Gungan snapped.

Standing next to Anakin, R2-D2 beeped softly in recognition. The droid had figured it out first.

Padmé straightened. "I am Queen Amidala," she announced
in a loud, clear voice. "Sabé serves from time to time as my decoy, my loyal bodyguard. I am sorry for my deception, but given
the circumstances, I am sure you can understand." She turned to
the Jedi, her eyes shifting momentarily to find Anakin. "Gentle-
men, I apologize for misleading you."

Her eyes returned quickly to Boss Nass, who was frowning
suspiciously, clearly not understanding any of what was happening. "Although our people do not always agree, Your Honor,"
she continued, her voice softening, "we have always lived in
peace. Until now. The Trade Federation, with its tanks and its
'maccaneks,' has destroyed all that we have worked so hard to
build. The Gungans are in hiding, and the Naboo have been im-
prisoned in camps. If we do not act quickly, all that we value will
be lost forever."

She stretched out her hands. "I ask you to help us, Your Honor." She paused. "No, I beg you to help us."

She dropped abruptly to one knee in front of the astonished leader of the Gungans. There was an audible gasp of surprise from the Naboo. "We are your humble servants, Your Honor," Padmé said so that all could hear. "Our fate is in your hands. Please help us."

She motioned, and one by one, her handmaidens, Panaka, and the Naboo pilots and guards dropped to their knees beside her. Anakin and the Jedi were the last to join them. Out of the corner of his eye, Anakin saw Jar Jar standing virtually alone in their midst, staring around in wonderment and shock.

For a moment, no one said anything. Then a slow, deep rumble of laughter rose out of the throat of Boss Nass. "Ho, ho, ho! Me like dis! Dis good! Yous no think yous greater den da Gungans!"

The head Gungan came forward, reaching out with one hand. "Yous stand, Queen Amidoll. Yous talk wit me, okay? Mebbe we gonna be friends after all!"

The senior Sith Lord appeared in a shimmer of robes and shadows as his protégé and the Neimoidians walked slowly down the corridor leading from the throne room back to the plaza.

"We have sent out patrols," Nute Gunray said, concluding his report to the ominous figure in the projection. "We have already located their starship in the swamp. It won't be long until we have them in hand, my lord."

Darth Sidious was silent. For a moment Nute Gunray was afraid he hadn't been heard. "This is an unexpected move for the Queen," the Sith Lord said at last, his voice so low it could barely be heard. "It is too aggressive. Lord Maul, be mindful."

"Yes, Master," the other Sith growled softly, yellow eyes gleaming.

"Be patient," Darth Sidious purred, head lowered in cowled shadows, hands folded into black robes. "Let them make the first move."

In silence, Darth Maul and the Neimoidians continued on as the hologram slowly faded away.

Boss Nass was as mercurial as he was large, and his change of attitude toward the Naboo was dramatic. Once he decided that the Queen did not consider herself his superior, that she was in fact quite sincere in her plea for Gungan help, he was quick to come around. The fact that his dislike of the battle droids was every bit as strong as hers didn't hurt matters, of course. Perhaps he had been hasty in his belief that the "maccaneks" wouldn't find the Gungans in the swamps. Otoh Gunga had been attacked at daybreak two days earlier and its inhabitants driven from their homes. Boss Nass was not about to sit still for that. If a plan could be put together to drive the invaders out, the Gungan army would do its part to help.

He took Amidala and her companions out of the swamp to the edge of the grass plains that ran south to the Naboo capital city of Theed. Any attack would be mounted from here, and the Queen had come to the Gungans with a very specific plan of attack in mind.

The first step in that plan involved sending Captain Panaka on a reconnaissance of the city.

As they stood looking out from the misty confines of the swamp toward the open grasslands, waiting for Panaka's return, Boss Nass trundled up to Jar Jar.

"Yous doen grand, Jar Jar Binks!" he rumbled, wrapping a meaty arm around the slender Gungan's shoulders. "Yous bring da Naboo and da Gungan together! Tis very brave thing."

Jar Jar shuffled his feet and looked embarrassed. "Ah, yous no go sayen dat. Tis nutten."

"No, yous grand warrior!" Boss Nass declared, squeezing the air out of his compatriot with a massive hug.

"No, no, no," the other persisted bashfully.

"So," Boss Nass concluded brightly, "we make yous bombad general in da Gungan army!"

"What?" Jar Jar exclaimed in dismay. "General? Me? No, no, no!" he gasped, and his eyes rolled up, his tongue fell out, and he fainted dead away.

Padmé was in conference with the Jedi and the Gungan generals, to whose number Jar Jar Binks had just been added, so Anakin, at loose ends, had wandered over to keep company with the Gungan sentries who were keeping lookout for Panaka. The Gungans patrolled the swamp perimeter on kaadu and kept watch through macrobinoculars from treetops and the remains of ancient statuary, making certain Federation scouting parties didn't come up on them unexpectedly. Anakin stood at the base of a temple column, still trying to come to terms with Padmé's revelation. Everyone had been surprised, of course, but no one more than he. He wasn't sure how he felt about her now, knowing she wasn't just a girl, but a Queen. He had declared he would marry her someday, believing it so, but how could someone who had been a slave all his life marry a Queen? He wanted to talk to her, but there wasn't any opportunity for that here.

He supposed things wouldn't be the same after this, but he

wished they could. He liked her as much now as he had before, and to tell the truth he didn't care if she was a Queen or not.

He glanced over at the girl and the Jedi Knights and thought how different things were here than they had been on Tatooine. Nothing had worked out the way he had hoped for any of them, and it remained to be seen if leaving his mother and home to come with them was a good idea after all.

The Gungan lookout standing atop a piece of statuary above him gave a grunt. "Dey comen," he called down, peering out into the grasslands through his macrobinoculars.

Anakin gave a yell in response and raced over to Padmé, the Jedi, and the Gungan generals. "They're back!" he shouted.

Everyone turned to watch a squad of four speeders skim over the flats and pull to a stop in the concealing shadow of the swamp. Captain Panaka and several dozen Naboo soldiers, officers, and starfighter pilots jumped down. Panaka made his way directly to the Queen.

"I think we got through without being detected, Your Highness," he advised quickly, brushing the dust from his clothing.

"What is the situation?" she asked as the others crowded close to them.

Panaka shook his head. "Most of our people are in the detention camps. A few hundred officers and guards have formed an underground movement to resist the invasion. I've brought as many of the leaders as I could find."

"Good." Padmé nodded appreciatively toward Boss Nass. "The Gungans have a larger army than we imagined."

"Very, very bombad!" the Gungan chief rumbled.

Panaka exhaled wearily. "You'll need it. The Federation army is much larger than we thought, too. And stronger." He gave the

Queen a considering look. "In my opinion, this isn't a battle we can win, Your Highness."

Standing at the edge of the circle, Jar Jar Binks looked down at Anakin and rolled his eyes despairingly.

But Padmé was undeterred. "I don't intend to win it, Captain. The battle is a diversion. We need the Gungans to draw the droid army away from Theed, so we can infiltrate the palace and capture the Neimoidian viceroy. The Trade Federation cannot function without its head. Neimoidians don't think for themselves. Without the viceroy to command them, they will cease to be a threat."

She waited for them to consider her plan, eyes fixing automatically on Qui-Gon Jinn. "What do you think, Master Jedi?" she asked.

"It is a well-conceived plan," Qui-Gon acknowledged. "It appears to be your best possible move, Your Highness, although there is great risk. Even with the droid army in the field, the viceroy will be well guarded. And many of the Gungans may be killed."

Boss Nass snorted derisively. "They bombad guns no get through our shields! We ready to fight!"

Jar Jar gave Anakin another eye roll, but this time Boss Nass saw him do so and gave his new general a hard warning look.

Padmé was thinking. "We could reduce the Gungan casualties by securing the main hangar and sending our pilots to knock out their orbiting control ship. Without the control ship to signal them, the droid army can't function at all."

Everyone nodded in agreement. "But if the viceroy should escape, Your Highness," Obi-Wan pointed out darkly, "he will return with another droid army, and you'll be no better off than you are now. Whatever else happens, you must capture him."

"Indeed, we must," Padmé agreed. "Everything depends on

it. Cut off the head, and the serpent dies. Without the viceroy, the Trade Federation collapses."

They moved on to other matters then, beginning a detailed discussion of battle tactics and command responsibilities. Anakin stood listening for a moment, then eased his way close to Qui-Gon and tugged on his sleeve.

"What about me?" he asked quietly.

The Jedi Master put a hand on the boy's head and smiled. "You stay close to me, Annie, do as I say, and you'll be safe."

Keeping safe wasn't quite what the boy had in mind, but he let the matter drop, satisfied that as long as he was close to Qui-Gon, he wouldn't be far from the action.

In the Theed palace throne room, Darth Sidious loomed in hologram form before Darth Maul, Battle Droid Commander OOM-9, and the Neimoidians. Smooth and silky, his voice oozed through the shadowy ether.

"Our young Queen surprises me," he whispered thought-fully, hidden within his dark robes. "She is more foolish than I thought."

"We are sending all available troops to meet this army of hers," Nute Gunray offered quickly. "It appears to be assembling at the edge of the swamp. Primitives, my lord—nothing better. We do not expect much resistance."

"I am increasing security at all Naboo detention camps," OOM-9 intoned.

Darth Maul glared at nothing, then shook his horned head. "I feel there is more to this than what we know, my Master. The two Jedi may be using the Queen for their own purposes."

"The Jedi cannot become involved," Darth Sidious soothed, hands spreading in a placating motion. "They can only protect the Queen. Even Qui-Gon Jinn cannot break that covenant. This will work to our advantage."

Darth Maul snorted, anxious to get on with it.

"I have your approval to proceed, then, my lord?" Nute Gunray asked hesitantly, avoiding the younger Sith's mad eyes.

"Proceed," Darth Sidious ordered softly. "Wipe them out, Viceroy. All of them."

By midday, with the sun overhead in a cloudless sky and the wind died away to nothing, the grasslands lying south of Theed between the Naboo capital city and the Gungan swamp lay empty and still. Heat rose off the grasslands in a soft shimmer, and it was so quiet that from a hundred meters away the chirp of birds and the buzz of insects could be heard as if they were settled close by.

Then the Trade Federation army's bubble-nosed transports and armor-wrapped tanks roared onto the rolling meadows, skimming the tall grasses in gleaming waves of bright metal.

It was quiet in the swamps as well, the perpetual twilight hushed and expectant beneath the vast canopy of limbs and vines, the surface of the mire as smooth and unbroken as glass, the reeds and rushes motionless in the windless air. Here and there a water bug jumped soundlessly from place to place, stirring puddles to life in the wake of its passing, bending blades of grass like springboards. Birds swooped and banked in bright flashes of color, darting from limb to limb. Small animals crept from cover to drink and feed, eyes bright, noses twitching, senses alert.

Then the Gungan army surfaced in a rippling of murky water and a stream of bubbles, lop-eared heads popping up like corks, first one, then another, and finally hundreds and eventually thousands.

Both on the plain and in the swamp, the small animals raced back into hiding, the birds took wing, and the insects went to ground.

Astride their kaadu, the Gungans rode from their concealment with armor strapped to their amphibious bodies and weapons held at the ready. They carried long-hafted energy spears and metal-handled ball slings for long-distance fighting and energy shields for close combat. The kaadu shook themselves as they reached dry ground, shedding the swamp water from their smooth skins, eyes picking out the solid patches of ground as their riders urged them on. Numbers swelling as they reached the fringes of the swamp, the Gungans began to form up in ranks of riders that stretched away as far as the eye could see.

As the first wave rode clear, the swamp boiled anew with the appearance of fambaa—huge, four-legged lizards with long necks and tails and massive, scaly bodies. The fambaa bore shield generators atop their broad backs, machines that when linked would activate a force field to protect the Gungan soldiers against Trade Federation weaponry. The fambaa lumbered heavily beneath their loads, necks craning from side to side as their drivers prodded them impatiently.

Jar Jar Binks rode with them at the head of his new command, wondering what it was he was supposed to do. Mostly, he believed, he was supposed to stay out of the way. Certainly the other generals and even his own subordinate officers had made it clear that this was what they preferred. Boss Nass might think it clever to make him a general in the Gungan army, but the career officers found it less amusing. General Ceel, who was commander-in-chief, grunted sourly at Jar Jar, on being informed of his new position, and told him to set a good example for his people and die well.

Jar Jar had responded to all this by keeping a low profile until the march out of the swamp began, and then he had assumed his required position at the head of his command. He had gotten barely a hundred meters after emerging from concealment when he had fallen off his kaadu. No one had bothered to stop to help him climb back on, and so now he was riding somewhere in the middle of his troops.

"Tis very bombad," he kept whispering to himself as he rode with the others through the marshy haze.

Slowly, steadily, the Gungan army cleared the tangle of the swamps and moved out onto the open grasslands where the Trade Federation army was already waiting.

Anakin Skywalker hunkered down in the shadows of a building directly across from the main hangar of the Naboo starfleet in the city of Theed. It was quiet here as well, the bulk of the battle droids dispatched to the field to deal with the Gungan army, the remainder scattered throughout the city in patrols and on perimeter watch. Nevertheless, tanks crowded the plaza fronting the hangar complex, and a strong contingent of battle droids warded the Naboo fleet. Seizing control of the starfighters was not going to be easy.

Anakin glanced over at those with him. Padmé, dressed as a handmaiden, crouched with Eirtaé beside the Jedi, waiting for Captain Panaka's command to get into position on the other side of the square. Sabé, the decoy Queen, and her handmaidens wore battle dress, loose-fitting and durable, with blasters strapped to their sides. R2-D2 blinked silently from behind them in the company of twenty-odd Naboo officers, guards, and pilots, all armed and ready. It seemed to the boy like a pathetically small number of fighters to carry the day, but it was all they had.

At least Qui-Gon and Obi-Wan were talking again. They had begun doing so on the journey in from the swamps, a few words here, a few there, exchanging comments guardedly, testing the waters. Anakin had listened carefully, more attuned to the nuances of their conversation than others could be, hearing in the inflection of their voices more than simply the words spoken. After a time, when the words had healed enough of the breach that they felt comfortable again, there were smiles, brief and almost sad, but clear in their purpose. The Jedi were old friends and their relationship that of father and son. They did not want to toss it all away over a single disagreement. Anakin was thankful for that—especially since the disagreement in question was over him.

Padmé had spoken to him as well, joining him for a few moments as they approached the city through the forests east, her smile banishing all his doubts and fears in a moment's time.

"I'm sorry I couldn't tell you sooner," she said, apologizing for hiding her identity. "I know it was a surprise."

"It's okay," he said, shrugging bravely.

"I guess knowing I'm a Queen makes you feel differently about me, doesn't it?" she asked.

"I guess, but that's okay. Just so you still like me. Because I still like you." He looked over at her hopefully.

"Of course, Annie. Telling you who I really am doesn't mean

my feelings for you have changed. I was the same person before, whether you knew the truth about me or not."

He thought about it a moment. "I suppose." He brightened. "So I guess my feelings for you shouldn't be any different now either."

She moved away, smiling broadly back at him, and just at that moment he felt ten meters tall.

So now he was at peace with himself about the Jedi and Padmé, but was beset with new concerns. What if something happened to them during the fight ahead? What if they were hurt or even . . . He couldn't bring himself to finish the thought. Nothing bad would happen to them, that was all. He wouldn't let it. He glanced at them, kneeling in silence at the edge of the plaza, and promised himself he would keep them safe no matter what. That would be his job. His mouth tightened with determination as he made his pledge.

"Once we get inside, Annie, you find a safe place to hide until this is over," Qui-Gon advised suddenly, bending close, almost as if he could read the boy's mind.

"Sure," Anakin promised.

"And stay there," the Jedi Master added firmly.

Across the way, Panaka and his contingent of fighters were in position now, placing the tanks and battle droids in a crossfire with Padmé's group. Padmé produced a small glow rod and flashed a coded signal to Panaka across the square.

All around Anakin, weapons slid free of holsters and fastenings, and safeties were released.

Then Panaka's fighters opened up on the battle droids, blasters shattering their metal bodies in a hail of laser fire. Other droids wheeled about in response and began exchanging fire, drawn toward the source of the conflict and away from Padmé's group.

Qui-Gon came to his feet. "Stay close," Qui-Gon whispered to him.

A moment later, the boy was running with the Jedi, Padmé, Eirtaé, R2-D2, and their Naboo contingent of soldiers and pilots toward the open door of the hangar.

Jar Jar sat tall astride his kaadu, having regained his composure and resumed his position at the head of his troop. The Gungan army was spread out all along the grasslands on either side of where he rode for as far as the eye could see. Birdlike, the kaadu picked their way through the tall grasses, heads dipping, Gungan riders swaying with the motion. The Gungans wore leather and metal headgear and body armor, with small, circular shields strapped at their hips and tri-plate energy packs for abetting the force field jutting like metal feathers from their saddle backs. The fambaa, bearing the shield generators, were spaced evenly down their lines to achieve maximum protection once the generators were activated. Like tanks, the massive lizards lumbered amidst the more nimble kaadu, and the grasslands shook with the weight of their passing.

At the head of the army rode General Ceel and his command unit, the flags of Otoh Gunga and the other Gungan cities borne in their wake at the end of long poles.

The army crested a rise, a great, rolling wave of dark bodies, and on a hand signal from General Ceel, drew to a halt.

Across a long, shallow depression, its position secure on the next ridge over, the Trade Federation army waited. Lines of STAPs and tanks formed the first rank, spread out over a distance of more than a kilometer, armor plating and weapons gleaming in the midday sun. Buttressing the smaller vehicles were the huge Federation transports, massive bodies hovering just off the ground, bulbous-nose gates closed and pointed forward toward the Gungans. Battle droids controlled tanks and STAPs, faceless and empty metal shells impervious to pain, devoid of emotion, and programmed to fight until destroyed.

Jar Jar Binks stared at the droid army in awe. There was not a living creature in sight, not one made of flesh and blood, not one that would react to the terrible roil of battle as the Gungans would. It made his skin crawl to think of what that meant.

The fambaa were in place now, and General Ceel activated the shield generators. The big turbines hummed to life, and a pulse of red light arced from a generator atop one fambaa to a dish atop the next, the beam widening and broadening as it grew in size to encompass the whole of the Gungan army until each soldier and kaadu was safely enfolded. The coloring of the protective light changed from red to gold, shimmering like a mirage on a desert. The effect was to make it appear as if the Gungan army was underwater, as if it had been swallowed in a bright, clear sea.

The Federation was quick to test the shield's effectiveness. On a signal from Droid Commander OOM-9, who in turn was responding to a command from the deep-space control center, the tanks opened fire, their laser cannons sending round after round into the covering. Searing beams hammered into the shield and shattered ineffectively against the liquid energy surface, unable to penetrate.

Within their protective covering, the Gungans waited patiently, weapons ready, trusting the strength of their shield.

Astride his kaadu, Jar Jar Binks flinched and squirmed fearfully, muttering various prayers to ward off the destruction he was certain would find him otherwise. Relentlessly, the Trade Federation cannons continued their attack, streamers of energy lancing from their barrel mounts, pounding at the covering. The flash and burn and explosion were blinding and deafening, but the Gungans held their ground.

Finally, the Trade Federation guns went still. Try as they might, they could not break through the Gungan energy shield. Within their protective canopy, the Gungans cheered and brandished their weapons triumphantly.

But now the tanks and STAPs withdrew, and the massive transports advanced to the fore. The rounded-nose doors opened, widening to reveal a cluster of racks mounted within. The racks rolled forward on long rails, revealing row after row of battle droids neatly folded up and suspended on hooks. When the racks were fully extended, they began to lower and separate outward, filling the open space in front of the transports with thousands of droids.

Positioned at the forefront of their army, General Ceel and his Gungan commanders exchanged worried looks.

Now the racks began to release the battle droids, who unfolded in unison into standing positions, arms and legs extended, bodies straight. Metal hands reached back over shoulders to pull free the blaster rifles with which each unit was equipped.

On command from OOM-9, the entire array of battle droids began to march toward the Gungan army, bright metal ranks filling the grasslands from horizon to horizon.

The Gungan shield wall was designed to deflect large, slow-moving objects of density and mass such as artillery vehicles and small, fast-moving objects generating extreme heat such as projectiles from weapons fire. But it would not deflect small, slow-moving droids—even massed together in such numbers as they were here. Jar Jar Binks began to wish he were somewhere else, thinking that as mighty as the Gungan army was, it was dwarfed by the metal machine that marched against it now.

But the Gungans had come prepared for battle, and they were not so deterred by the number of their enemies that they were ready to quit. All up and down their lines, Gungans activated their energy spears and straight-handled slings, arming them for the attack. At the foot of the rise on which they waited, the front ranks of the battle droids reached the perimeter of the energy field and began to pass through. The shield had no effect on them. Lifting their blasters to their shoulders, they began to fire.

Amid a wail of great, curved battle horns, the Gungans retaliated. A shower of spears rained down on the advancing droids, shafts and points exploding on impact, ripping metal limbs and torsos apart. Energy balls flung from the slings followed, inflicting further damage. Mortars dumped their loads in the center of the droid ranks, opening huge gaps in the attack. The battle droids reeled and slowed, then regained momentum and came on, hundreds more taking the place of those who had fallen, marching mindlessly through the protective shield and into the range of the Gungan weapons.

At the center of his command unit, General Ceel urged his warriors on, tightening his defensive lines in front of the fambaa and the shield generators to protect them from harm, knowing that if the force field came down, the Trade Federation's tanks would strike the Gungans as well.

Battle-droid ranks, metal parts reflecting sun and fire, and Gungan lines, orange-skinned and supple, closed to do battle.

Resisting the temptation to shut his eyes against what he

knew was coming, Jar Jar Binks kicked his heels into the flanks of his kaadu and charged ahead with the rest of his command.

In the relative seclusion of the Theed palace throne room, in a place they had believed safely removed from any real danger, Nute Gunray and Rune Haako stared at a giant viewscreen and its rapidly changing images of the battle taking place in the main hangar. The Jedi Knights were inside the complex, accompanied by Naboo soldiers and pilots, their lightsabers wreaking havoc on the battle droids who tried to stop them.

"How did they get into the city?" Rune Haako whispered in dismay.

Nute Gunray shook his head. "I don't know. I thought the battle was going to take place far from here." His eyes were wide and staring. "This is too close!"

They turned as one when Darth Maul stalked into the room, bearing a long-handled lightsaber. Yellow eyes gleamed out of the Sith's red and black tattooed face, and his dark cloak billowed out behind him.

Nute Gunray and Rune Haako backed away instinctively, neither of them wanting to get in the way. "Lord Maul," Gunray greeted, inclining his head briefly.

Darth Maul glanced at him disdainfully. "I told you there was more to this than was apparent!" His eyes had a wild, manic look to them. "The Jedi have come to Theed for a reason, Viceroy. They have a plan of their own for defeating us."

"A plan?" the Neimoidian asked worriedly.

"One that will fail, I assure you." The striped face glinted wickedly in the light. "I have waited a long time for this. I have trained for it endlessly. The Jedi will regret their decision to return here."

There was an edge to his rough voice that was frightening. The Sith was anxious for this confrontation, his body coiled and ready, his hands flexing about his weapon. The Neimoidians did not envy those he sought.

"Wait here until I return," he ordered abruptly, and swept past them.

"Where are you going?" Nute Gunray demanded frantically as the Sith Lord crossed toward the speeder docks.

"Where do you think I'm going, Viceroy?" the other sneered. "I'm going to the main hangar to rid you of the Jedi once and for all."

Anakin Skywalker rushed through the open doors of the main hangar after the Jedi and Padmé, with R2-D2 and the rest of the Naboo freedom fighters on their heels. Battle droids turned to confront them, but lightsabers and blasters cut apart the foremost before the others even knew what was happening. The droids rallied in response, summoning help from without, but Panaka and his men had those in the plaza already occupied, and for a moment the Jedi and the Naboo were in control.

Mindful of Qui-Gon's admonition, Anakin ducked beneath the fuselage of the closest starfighter, laser bolts searing the air around him in brilliant bursts of fire.

"Get to your ships!" Padmé shouted at her pilots, leading the contingent of Naboo soldiers under her command in pursuit of the retreating battle droids.

Ducking and crouching, she fired her blaster with quick, precise moves, bringing down droid after droid, her charges finding their targets with unerring accuracy. The Jedi fought just ahead of her, blocking droid laser fire with their lightsabers, striking down those unfortunate enough to cross their path. But it was Padmé on whom Anakin's eyes were riveted, for not only had he never seen this side of her, he hadn't even known it existed. She moved with the skill and training of a seasoned fighter, no longer seeming in any way a young girl, becoming instead a deadly combatant.

He thought suddenly of his dream of Padmé leading an army in another time and place, and suddenly the dream didn't seem so impossible.

Pilots from the attacking force and R2 units freed from storage in the hangar lockers moved quickly to board the Naboo fighters, scattering swiftly through the hail of blaster fire. Clambering aboard their starships, pilots in the cockpits, R2 units in their sockets, they switched on their control panels and ignited their engines. A roar of power filled the massive hangar, drowning out the sound of laser fire, building to an ear-shattering crescendo. One by one, the fighters began to levitate and shift into position for takeoff.

A Naboo pilot rushed past Anakin and climbed into the fighter he was crouched behind. "Better get out of here, kid!" she called down from the cockpit. "Find yourself a new hiding place! You're about to lose this one!"

Anakin darted away in a low crouch, droid blaster fire crisscrossing the air above him, centering on the departing ships. The fighter he had abandoned began to lift off, wheeling toward the open hangar doors. Other ships were already speeding away into the blue, engines booming.

As the Jedi and the Naboo fighters continued to push the droid hangar watch steadily back, Anakin searched hastily for a new hiding place. Then he heard R2-D2 whistle at him from another fighter close at hand, the little droid already ensconced in his socket, domed head rotating, control lights flashing. The boy raced across the hangar floor littered with the shattered bodies of battle droids, laser fire whizzing all about him, and jumped into the cockpit with a gasp of relief.

Peering out from the safety of his bolt-hole, he watched the last pair of Naboo fighters rocket out of the hangar. The first got free, but the second was hit by tank fire and knocked sideways so that it pinwheeled into the ground and exploded in a ball of flame. Anakin winced and crouched lower.

Now Panaka, Sabé, and the Naboo soldiers who had been engaged in combat outside the hangar burst through the doors as well, firing as they came. Caught in a crossfire, the remaining battle droids were quickly overwhelmed and destroyed. There was a hurried conference between the Jedi, Padmé, and Panaka, and then the entire Naboo fighting force began to move toward an exit in the hangar that took them directly past Anakin's hiding place.

"Hey, where are you going?" the boy asked, popping his head out of the cockpit as they passed.

"Annie, you stay there!" Qui-Gon ordered, motioning him back down. His long hair was wild and his face intense. "Stay right where you are!"

The boy ignored him, standing up instead. "No, I want to go with you and Padmé!"

"Stay in that cockpit!" Qui-Gon snapped in a tone of voice that brooked no argument.

Anakin froze, undecided, as the contingent hurried past him toward the exit door, weapons at the ready. He did not want to be left behind. He had no intention of letting Qui-Gon and Padmé go on without him, especially since he could do nothing to help them if he was stuck here in this empty hangar.

He was still wrestling with the matter when the entire group slowed in front of the exit door. A dark-cloaked figure stepped through the opening to confront them. Anakin's breath caught in his throat. It was the Sith Lord who had attacked them on the Tatooine desert, a dangerous adversary, Qui-Gon had advised the boy later, an enemy of the Jedi Knights. He stepped out of the shadows like a large sand panther, his red and black tattooed face a terrifying mask, his yellow eyes bright with anticipation and rage.

Blocking the way out, he stood waiting for the Jedi and their charges, a long-handled lightsaber held before him. Captain Panaka and his fighters backed away at once. Then, on command from Qui-Gon, Padmé and her handmaidens gave ground as well, though less quickly and with more obvious reluctance.

Qui-Gon Jinn and Obi-Wan Kenobi stood alone in the Sith Lord's path. Together, they removed their capes and ignited their lightsabers. Their horned antagonist stripped away his cloak as well, then lifted the long-handled lightsaber he bore as if offering it for inspection. Gleaming blade fire jutted from both ends of the handle, revealing a deadly, dual-blade weapon. A smile crossed the bearer's feral face as he swung the weapon before him in an idle, casual gesture, beckoning the Jedi ahead.

Spreading out to either side, Qui-Gon and Obi-Wan slowly advanced to meet him.

On the plains south of Theed, the battle between the Trade Federation and the Gungan armies was fully joined. Gungans and battle droids were locked in close combat, a tangle of amphibious bodies and metal shells. The shield generators still held the Trade Federation tanks at bay. Only the droids had broken through, but there were many more of them than there were of the Gungans, and General Ceel had committed all his reserves to the struggle.

Jar Jar Binks fought at the center of the maelstrom, wielding a broken energy spear as a club, wheeling and stumbling this way and that, careening wildly. Caught up in the wiring of a battle droid he had decapitated, he could not manage to free himself from the debris, and so was dragging the headless torso after him. The droid, still operating on autopilot despite the loss of its head, was firing its blaster continuously as Jar Jar whipped it this way and that, finding droid targets more often than Gungans, cutting a swath through their faltering ranks.

"Tis bombad! Tis bombad!" The Gungan shouted out the refrain over and over as he swung his shattered spear and fought to get free of his headless companion.

When at last he broke away and was able to smash the remains of the droid into the ground, he was left standing in a wide open space that everyone on both sides was trying desperately to avoid. For a terrifying moment, Jar Jar literally did not know which way to turn.

Then a cry went up from the Gungans closest. "Jar Jar Binks! Jar Jar Binks!"

"Who, me?" the befuddled Gungan gasped.

Inspired troops rallied around him and pressed ahead once more, sweeping him along in a wild and unexpected counterattack.

But the Trade Federation, unlike the Gungans, had other weapons left to call upon. OOM-9, responding to orders from the orbiting battleship command station, unleashed a battalion of destroyer droids from the transports. Down long rampways they wheeled, across the grasslands, over the bodies of shattered battle droids, and through the Gungan energy shield. Transforming into battle mode, they began to advance through the carnage, twin blasters firing in steady cadence. Gungans and kaadu went down in broken heaps, but other Gungans moved quickly to fill the gaps in their lines, slowing the destroyer droids, fighting to hold their ground.

Back and forth the battle raged, the outcome undecided.

Anakin Skywalker had made a promise to himself that he would protect Qui-Gon Jinn and Padmé Naberrie from harm, that he would see to it somehow that nothing bad happened to them. He knew when he made the promise how hard it was going to be to keep. Somewhere in the back of his mind where he would admit such things privately, he knew how foolish it was even to make such a commitment. But he was young and brave at heart, and he had lived his life pretty much on his own terms because to live it any other way would have broken him long ago. It hadn't been easy doing so, especially as a slave. He had survived mostly because he had been able to find small victories in difficult situations and because he had always believed that one day he would find a way to overcome the circumstances of his birth.

His belief in himself had been rewarded. His life had been changed forever by his victory just days earlier in the Boonta Eve Podrace on Tatooine.

It was not so strange then that he should decide he could somehow affect the lives of a Jedi Knight and a Naboo Queen as well, even if he did not know precisely how. He was not afraid to accept such responsibility. He was not daunted by the challenge his decision presented.

But now his resolve was put to the test.

Qui-Gon and Obi-Wan closed with the Sith Lord in a clash of lightsabers that produced the shriek of diamond-edged saw blades cutting through metal. Wheeling across the center of the hangar, the combatants lunged and parried, attack and counter-attack carried out in a fierce, no-holds-barred, no-quarter-given struggle. The Sith Lord was supple and quick, and he worked his way between the Jedi with confidence and ease, whipping his two-ended lightsaber back and forth between them, more than holding his own against their efforts to bring him down. He was skilled, Anakin saw—more skilled, perhaps, than the men he faced. And he was confident in a way that was disturbing. He would not be overcome easily.

But Padmé and the Naboo faced a more dangerous situation still. At the far end of the hangar, from off the plaza, a cluster of three destroyer droids wheeled through the doorway and began to unfold, assuming battle stance. R2-D2 saw them first and beeped a warning to the boy. Anakin tore his gaze away from the Jedi and the Sith Lord. The destroyer droids had transformed and were already moving forward, laser guns firing into the Naboo. Several soldiers went down, and Sabé was stung by a glancing blow that knocked her backward into the arms of Panaka. Padmé and her companions resisted determinedly, but already they were falling back to find cover.

"We've got to help, Artoo," the boy declared, standing up in the cockpit with the intention of doing something, anything, casting about futilely for a weapon.

But R2-D2 was way ahead of him. The little droid had plugged himself into the starfighter's computer system, lights blinking across his control panel as he triggered the big engines. Everything roared to life at once, startling Anakin, who fell back in the pilot's seat in surprise.

Slowly, the ship began to levitate, wheeling out of its mooring space.

"Great work, Artoo!" Anakin shouted excitedly, reaching at once for the steering bars. "Now, let's see . . ."

He wheeled the fighter about so that it was facing toward the combatants. His eyes scanned the control panel desperately, searching for the weapons systems. He knew something of fighters from salvaging wrecks, but nothing of Naboo fighters in particular or of weapons systems in general. Most of what he knew was about guidance systems and engines, and most of that about Pods, speeders, and aging transports.

"Which one, which one?" he muttered, his fingers passing over buttons and levers and switches, undecided.

He lifted his eyes momentarily. One of the Naboo soldiers went down in a crumpled heap, his helmet and blaster flying away in a clatter of metal. Laser charges burned the metal girders and walls about the defenders as the destroyer droids continued their relentless attack on Padmé's dwindling force.

In desperation, Anakin threw a bank of switches set into a red panel. The fighter began to shake violently, a reaction to a shift in the stabilizers.

"Uh-oh, wrong ones," the boy breathed, throwing the switches back into place. His gaze roamed to a bank of four dark buttons recessed deep into finger holes and circled in green. "Maybe these . . ."

He pressed down on the buttons. Instantly, the nose lasers fired, their charges ripping into the battle droids. Three went down, charred and smoking scrap.

"Yeah! Droid blasters!" he shouted gleefully, and behind him, R2-D2 beeped his approval.

The remaining destroyer droids wheeled toward him,

spreading out across the hangar floor to present a more difficult target. Behind them, Padmé, her handmaidens, Panaka, and the remainder of the Naboo soldiers were racing for the door that led back toward the palace. Anakin watched over the rim of the cockpit as they disappeared safely out the door. "Good luck," he whispered.

The destroyer droids were advancing on him now, their blasters firing, charges exploding all around him, shaking the fighter's slim frame. Anakin had a momentary glimpse of the Sith Lord driving the Jedi across the hangar and through an opening into a room beyond, pressing them backward relentlessly, pursuing them with a fury that was terrifying.

Then they disappeared from view as well, and the boy was alone with his attackers.

A laser blast struck the nose of his craft and knocked the ship sideways. The boy tightened his grip on the steering. He fired his own lasers in retaliation, but the destroyer droids had moved too far to either side to be affected, and his charges missed everything but the hangar walls.

He dropped below the rim of the cockpit once more, eyes searching the control panel anew. "Shields up," he hissed, forcing himself to concentrate as laser blasts streaked all around. "Always on the right side! Shields are always on the right!"

He flipped several likely switches, and the afterburner ignited with a rumble. He pushed another, then one more. The steering handle fought itself free of his grip, and the fighter wheeled about and streaked out through the hangar doors, lifting swiftly away.

The cockpit hood slid smoothly into place, locking about the boy. "Artoo, what's happening?" he screamed. R2-D2's nervous beeps and whistles sounded through the intercom speakers. "Yes, I know I pushed something!" the boy answered. "No, I'm not doing anything!" He caught his breath as the beeps continued, and read R2's words on his cockpit display. "It's on automatic pilot? Well, try to override it!"

The sleek yellow fighter had left the Naboo atmosphere and was entering deep space, leaving the planet behind, a green and blue jewel receding into the black.

Ahead, a series of small, silver dots appeared, growing steadily larger. Other ships.

"Artoo, where are we going?" Anakin gasped, still trying to decipher the control panel.

The comm system squawked, and suddenly he was h the voices of Ric Olié and the Naboo pilots who had tak ahead of him.

"This is Bravo Leader." Ric's leathery voice broke thr the static. "Bravo Two, intercept enemy fighters. Bravo Tl make your run on the transmitter station."

"Copy, Bravo Leader," the response came back.

Anakin could see them now, the silver dots taking on rec nizable shape, transforming into Naboo starfighters, spread against the blackness, approaching the larger, blockier form the Federation battleship.

"Enemy fighters straight ahead," Ric Olié warned suddenl on the comm.

At the same moment, R2-D2 beeped hurriedly at Anakin. The boy felt his stomach lurch as he read the display. "What do you mean, the autopilot is searching for the other ships? What other ships?" His eyes shifted to the Naboo fighters ahead. "Not those?"

R2-D2 whistled a quick confirmation. Anakin collapsed in his seat. "The autopilot is taking us up there, with them? Into battle?" His mind raced. "Well, get us off autopilot, Artoo!"

The astromech droid beeped and whistled some more. "There is no manual override!" Anakin shouted in despair. "Or at least not any I can find! You'll have to rewire or something! Artoo, hurry!"

He stared helplessly through the cockpit glass as his fighter streaked directly toward the heart of the Trade Federation swarm, wondering what in the world he was going to do to save himself now.

Qui-Gon Jinn was one of the most able swordsmen in the Jedi order. The Jedi Master he had trained under had considered him one of the best the Master had taught in his more than four hundred years in the order. Qui-Gon had fought in conflicts all across the galaxy in the span of his life and against odds so great that many others would not have stood a chance. He had survived battles that had tested his skill and resolve in every conceivable way.

But on this day, he had met his match. The Sith Lord he battled with Obi-Wan was more than his equal in weapons training, and he had the advantage of being younger and stronger. Qui-Gon was nearing sixty; his youth was behind him and his strength was beginning to diminish. His edge now, to the extent that he had one, came from his long experience and intuitive grasp of how an adversary might employ a lightsaber against him.

Obi-Wan brought youth and stamina to the combat, but he had fought in only a few contests and was not battle hardened. Together, they were able to hold their own against the Sith Lord, but their efforts at attack, at assuming the offensive against this dangerous adversary, were woefully inadequate.

Darth Maul was a warrior in his prime, never to be any better, his powers at their apex. In addition, he was driven by his messianic hatred for and disdain of the Jedi Knights, the enemies of the Sith for millennia. He had worked and trained all his life for this moment, for a chance to meet a Jedi Knight in combat. It was an added bonus that he was able to engage two. He had no fear for himself, no doubt that he would win. He was focused in a way that Qui-Gon recognized at once—a Jedi's focus, mindful of the present, locked in on what was needed in the here and now. Qui-Gon saw it in his mad eyes and in the set of his red and black tattooed features. The Sith Lord was a living example of what the Jedi Master was always telling Obi-Wan about how best to hear the will of the Force.

The three combatants fought their way across the hangar floor, lightsabers flashing, bringing to bear every skill they had acquired over the years. The Jedi Knights tried continually to press the attack, and indeed, the Sith Lord was moving away from the Naboo and the starfighters and back toward the hangar's far wall. But Qui-Gon recognized that while it might seem as if the Jedi were driving him before them, it was the Sith Lord who was controlling the struggle. Wheeling and spinning, leaping and somersaulting with astonishing ease, their enemy was taking them with him, drawing them on to a place of his own choosing. His agility and dexterity allowed him to keep them both at bay, constantly attacking while at the same time effectively blunting their counterattacks, relentlessly searching for an opening in their defense.

Qui-Gon pressed hard in the beginning, sensing how dangerous this man was, wanting to put an end to the combat quickly. Long hair flying out behind him, he attacked with ferocity and determination. Obi-Wan came with him, following his lead. They had fought together before, and they knew each other's moves. Qui-Gon had trained Obi-Wan, and while the younger Jedi was not yet his equal, he believed that one day Obi-Wan would be better than he had ever been.

So they challenged the Sith Lord quickly, and just as quickly discovered that their best efforts were not good enough to achieve an early resolution. They settled into a pattern then, working as a team against their enemy, waiting for an opening. But the Sith Lord was too smart to give them one, and so the battle had gone on.

They fought their way out of the main hangar through an entry that led into a power station. Catwalks and overhangs crisscrossed a pit in which a tandem of generators that served the starship complex was housed. The room was cavernous and filled with the noise of heavy machinery. Ambient light filtered away in clouds of steam and layers of shadows. The Jedi and the Sith Lord battled onto one of the catwalks suspended above the generators, and the metal frame rang with the thudding of their boots and the clash of their lightsabers.

Alone in the power station, hidden from the rest of Theed and its occupants, they intensified their struggle.

The Sith Lord leapt from the bridge on which they fought to the one above, strange face shining with the heat of the battle and his own peculiar joy. The Jedi followed, one coming up in front of him, one behind, so that they had him pinned between them. Down the length of the catwalk they fought, lightsabers flashing, sparks flying from the metal railing of the walk as they smashed against it.

Then Darth Maul caught Obi-Wan off balance and with a

powerful kick knocked the Jedi completely over the railing. Taking advantage of the Sith Lord's assault on Obi-Wan, Qui-Gon forced Darth Maul over the railing as well. Down the Sith Lord tumbled, landing hard on a catwalk several levels below Obi-Wan. The force of the fall or perhaps the unexpectedness of it left him visibly stunned, and Qui-Gon leapt down after him, sensing a chance to put an end to things. But the Sith Lord struggled back to his feet quickly and raced away, taking the battle in a new direction.

By the time Obi-Wan had recovered, Qui-Gon was in pursuit of Darth Maul, following him down the catwalk toward a small door at the far end of the power station. The Jedi Master went swiftly, legs and arms pumping, lightsaber flashing. He was worn and battered by now, close to exhaustion, but the Sith Lord was on the defensive at last, and he did not want to give him a chance to regroup.

"Qui-Gon!" Obi-Wan called after him, trying to catch up, but the Jedi Master did not slow.

One after the other, the three antagonists passed through the small door into a corridor beyond. They were moving quickly in their frenzied chase and were into the corridor before they realized what it was. Lasers ricocheted off buffer struts, pulsing in long bursts of crisscrossing brilliance that segmented the corridor at five points. The lasers had just begun to kick in when the Sith Lord and the Jedi Knights rushed through the entry. Darth Maul, in the lead, got farthest down the corridor and found himself trapped between walls four and five. Qui-Gon, in close pursuit, was caught only one wall away. Obi-Wan, who was farthest away in the chase, did not get past even the first wall.

Shocked into immobility by the buzz and flash of the lasers, the antagonists froze where they were, casting about for an escape, finding none. Qui-Gon took a quick measure of their location. They were in the service corridor for the melting pit, the disposal unit of the power station's residue. The service corridor was armed with lasers against unauthorized intrusion. There would be a shutoff switch somewhere at both ends of the passage, but it was too late to look for it now.

The Jedi Knights stared down the laser-riddled corridor at the Sith Lord, who gave them a wicked grin. Don't worry, they could read in his dark countenance, you won't have long to wait for me.

Qui-Gon exchanged a meaningful glance with Obi-Wan, then dropped into a guarded crouch to meditate and wait.

Padmé Naberrie, Queen of the Naboo, along with her handmaidens and Captain Panaka and his soldiers, followed the passageways that led out of the main hangar through the city and back to the palace. It was a running battle fought building by building, corridor by corridor, against the battle droids who had been left behind to garrison Theed. They encountered the droids both singly and in entire squads, and there was nothing for it each time but to fight their way clear without becoming entangled in a full-fledged engagement.

As a consequence, they avoided a direct route in favor of one less likely to necessitate contact with the droids. At first they had no choice but to make straight for the palace, fleeing the battle in the main hangar, hoping that speed and surprise would carry them through. When that failed, Panaka began to take a more cautious approach. They used underground tunnels, hidden passageways, and connecting skywalks that avoided the patrols scouring the streets and plazas. When they were discovered, they fought their way clear as quickly as possible and went to ground, all the while continuing steadily on.

In the end, they reached the palace much more quickly than Padmé had dared to hope, entering from a skywalk bridging to a watchtower, then making their way along the palace halls toward the throne room.

They were in the midst of this endeavor when an entire patrol of battle droids rounded a corner of the passage ahead of them and opened fire. Padmé and her followers pressed back into the alcoves and doorways of the hall, firing their own weapons in response, searching for a way out. More battle droids were appearing, and alarms were sounding throughout the palace.

"Captain!" Padmé shouted at Panaka above the din of weapons fire. "We don't have time for this!"

Panaka's sweat-streaked face glanced about hurriedly. "Let's try outside!" he shouted back.

Turning his blaster on a tall window, he blew out the frame and transparisteel. While her handmaidens and the bulk of the Naboo soldiers provided covering fire, the Queen and Panaka, together with half a dozen guards, broke from cover and climbed swiftly out the shattered window.

But now Padmé and her defenders found themselves trapped on a broad ledge six stories above a thundering waterfall and catchment that fed into a series of connecting ponds dotting the palace grounds. Pressed against the stone wall, the Queen cast about furiously for an escape route. Panaka shouted at his men to use their ascension guns, motioning toward a ledge four stories farther up on the building. The Naboo pulled the grapple-line units from their belts, fitted them to the barrels of their blasters, pointed them skyward, and fired. Slender cables uncoiled like striking snakes, the steel-clawed ends embedding themselves in the stone.

Swiftly Padmé and the other Naboo activated the ascension mechanism and were towed up the wall.

From behind, in the hallway where her handmaidens and the rest of the Naboo soldiers still held the battle droids at bay, the firing grew more intense. Padmé ignored the sounds, forcing herself to continue ahead.

When they were on the ledge above, they cast away the cables, and Panaka used his blaster on a window to open a way back into the building. Transparisteel and permacrete shards lay everywhere as they climbed through once more, finding themselves in yet another hallway. They were close to the throne room now; it lay only another story up and several corridors back. Padmé felt a fierce exultation. She would have the Neimoidian viceroy as her prisoner yet!

But the thought was no sooner completed than a pair of destroyer droids wheeled around one end of the hallway, swiftly transforming into battle mode. Mere seconds later, a second pair appeared at the other end, weapons held at the ready.

In a hollow, mechanical monotone, the foremost of the droids ordered them to throw down their weapons.

Padmé hesitated. There was no possibility for an escape unless they went back out the window, and if they did that, they would be trapped on the ledge and rendered helpless. They could try to fight their way free, but while they stood a reasonable chance against battle droids, they were seriously overmatched by their more powerful cousins.

In the wake of this chilling assessment, an inspired thought occurred to her, a solution that might give them the victory they sought in spite of their situation. She straightened, held out her arms in surrender, and tossed aside her blaster.

"Throw down your weapons," she ordered Captain Panaka and his soldiers. "They win this round."

Panaka blanched. "But, Your Majesty, we can't—"

"Captain," Padmé interrupted, her eyes locking with his. "I said to throw down your weapons."

Panaka gave her a look that suggested he clearly thought she had lost her mind. Then he dropped his blaster to the floor and motioned for his men to do the same.

The destroyer droids skittered forward to take them prisoner. But before they reached the Naboo, Padmé was able to complete a quick transmission on her comlink.

"Have faith, Captain," she urged a bewildered Panaka, her voice cool and collected as she slipped the comlink out of sight again.

Things were not going well for the Gungan army. Like the Naboo, the Gungans were no match for the destroyer droids. Slowly, but surely, they were being pushed back, unable to stand against the relentless Trade Federation attack. Here and there along their beleaguered lines, cracks were beginning to appear in their defense.

Jar Jar Binks was at the heart of one of those points.

For a time, his had been one of the strongest positions, his soldiers rallied by what they mistakenly believed to be his unrivaled bravery, turning a rout into a counterattack. But the counterattack had extended itself too far, and with the appearance of the destroyer droids, it collapsed completely. Now Jar Jar and his comrades were in flight, falling back to where the rest of the army crouched in the shadow of the failing generator shield, desperately trying to find a way to regroup.

Jar Jar, his kaadu long since lost, was running for his life. Desperate to increase the distance between himself and the pursuing destroyer droids, he caught up with a fleeing wagon filled with dozens of the energy balls used by the Gungan catapults. Grabbing hold of the wagon gate, he tried to haul himself into the bed, the wagon jouncing and creaking over the uneven ground. But in his effort to save himself, he unwittingly released the latch on the gate, causing it to flop open. Energy balls released out the back in a wild tumble, bouncing and rolling backward in a swarm. Jar Jar danced out of the way, scrambling to avoid being struck. He was successful in this, but the less nimble destroyer droids on his heels were not. Energy balls smashed into them, exploding on contact, and droid after droid went up in a rain of fire and shattered metal.

"Tis good!" Jar Jar howled in glee, watching the Federation droids wheeling this way and that in an effort to escape the carpet of energy balls rolling into them.

Elsewhere, however, the battle was taking a turn for the worse. Destroyer droids had broken through the Gungan lines fronting the shield generators, and were firing their weapons into the machines over and over. The fambaa on which the generators rode shuddered and dropped to their knees, the generators smoking and sparking. Abruptly, the force field began to waver and fade. OOM-9, watching it all through electrobinoculars, was quick to report back to the Neimoidian command. Federation tanks were ordered forward at once, their guns firing anew.

When General Ceel saw the shield generators lose power, he realized the battle was lost. The Gungans had done all they could for the Queen of the Naboo. Turning to his staff, he signaled for a retreat. The battle horns sounded the call, wailing out across the grasslands, and the entire Gungan army began to fall back.

Jar Jar had gained control of a new mount and was riding madly for the safety of the swamp. Fleeing in the midst of pursuing droids and tanks, he had his kaadu blown out from under him and was thrown sideways onto the back of a nearby tank's gun turret. Hanging on for dear life, he rode the enemy vehicle across the plains as the battle raged on all about him. The droids inside the tank quickly became aware of his presence, and the driver tried to throw him off by swiveling the turret gun from side to side. But Jar Jar had a death grip on the barrel, hugging it tightly to him, and refused to be dislodged.

"Hep me! Hep me!" he screamed out.

Captain Tarpals astride a kaadu worked his way alongside the tank, yelling at Jar Jar to jump. Laser fire ricocheted off the tank, barely missing Jar Jar as he struggled to overcome his fear and break free of his precarious perch. Hatches were beginning to open and droid heads to appear. His eyes widened as he saw weapons being lifted and brought to bear.

He jumped then, flinging himself clear of the tank, landing awkwardly behind the Gungan who had stayed to save him. The kaadu, burdened by two riders, lurched wildly, then righted itself and swerved quickly away.

Explosions mushroomed all around them, sending gouts of dirt skyward, and Jar Jar Binks, arms wrapped around the other rider, eyes closed in terror against the chaos taking place all around him, was pretty sure that this was the end.

Anakin Skywalker, meanwhile, was caught up in the midst of a dogfight between Naboo and Federation starfighters. Still struggling to get off autopilot, he had avoided engagement with

the enemy mostly because his craft was flying in an erratic, evasive manner that took it out of combat range every time it got
too close for comfort. Fighters were exploding all around him,
some so close he could see the pieces as they flew past his canopy.

"Whoo, boy, this is tense!" he breathed as he tried switch after switch on the control panel, the fighter dipping and yawing in
response to his unwelcome interference with its operation.

But he was learning the control panel, too, his trial-and-error
exploration yielding knowledge of what various switches, buttons, and levers did. The downside to all this was that the firing
triggers to the laser guns had locked, and try as he might, he
could not find a way to break them free.

He glanced up from his search at a loud beep from R2-D2 to
find a pair of Federation fighters approaching him head-on.

"Artoo, Artoo, get us off—!"

The astromech droid overrode the rest of what he was going
to say with a series of frantic whistles.

"I've got control?" Anakin exclaimed in shock.

He seized the steering, flipped on the power feeds, and
jammed the thruster bars left. To his surprise and everlasting
gratitude, the fighter banked sharply in response, and they shot
past the fighters and rode into a new swarm of combatants.

"Yes! I've got control!" Anakin was ecstatic. "You did it,
Artoo!"

The astromech droid beeped at him through the intercom, a
short, abrupt exchange.

Anakin's eyebrows shot up as he read the display. "Go back
to Naboo? Forget it! Qui-Gon told me to stay in this cockpit,
and that's what I'm gonna do! Now, hang on!"

His enthusiasm overrode his good sense, and he whipped his
fighter toward the center of the battle. All of his flying instincts

kicked in, and he was back in the Podraces on Tatooine, a part of his ship, locked in on the intoxicating challenge of winning. Forgotten was his promise to look after Qui-Gon and Padmé; they were too far away for him to think about them now. All that mattered was that he had found his way into space, taken command of a starfighter, and been given a chance to live his dream.

An enemy fighter drifted into his sights ahead. "Sit tight, Artoo," he warned. "I'm gonna blast this guy."

He brought his ship into firing position behind the Trade Federation craft, remembering belatedly that the triggers to his laser guns were locked. Frantically, he searched for the release.

"Which one, Artoo?" he shouted into his helmet. "How do I fire this thing?"

R2-D2 beeped wildly.

"Which one? This one?"

He punched the button the astromech droid had indicated, but instead of releasing the firing mechanism, it accelerated the fighter right past the enemy ship.

"Whoa!" Anakin gasped in dismay.

Now the Trade Federation fighter was on his tail, maneuvering into firing position against him. Anakin yanked hard on the steering, shooting past the massive Federation battleship, screaming out into the void in a series of evasive actions.

"That wasn't the release!" the boy screamed into his intercom. "That was the overdrive!"

R2-D2 whistled a sheepish reply. The enemy fighter was behind them again and closing. Anakin banked his ship hard to the right and brought it back toward the blockade and the swarming fighters. Wrenching the stabilizers in opposite directions, he began to spin his fighter like a top. R2-D2 shrieked in despair.

"I know we're in trouble!" Anakin shrieked back. "Just hang on! The way out of this mess is the way we got into it!"

He streaked toward the control station, taking the enemy fighter with him. Laser blasts ripped past him, barely missing. He waited a second longer, until he was so close to the battleship that the emblem of the Trade Federation painted on the bridge work loomed like a wall, then engaged the reverse thrusters and banked right again.

His fighter nearly stalled, dropping away like a stone for a heart-wrenching moment before stabilizing. The enemy fighter, on the other hand, had no time to respond to the maneuver and rocketed past him into the side of the battleship, exploding in a shower of fire and metal parts.

Reengaging the forward thrusters, Anakin wheeled the ship about, searching for new enemies. Through his canopy, he could see a handful of Naboo starfighters engaged in attacking the Trade Federation flagship.

Ric Olié's voice came over the intercom. "Bravo Three! Go for the central bridge!"

"Copy, Bravo Leader," came the response.

A squad of four fighters plummeted toward the battleship, lasers firing, but the big ship's deflector shields turned the attack aside effortlessly. Two of the fighters were hit by cannon fire and exploded into ash. The remaining two broke off the attack.

"Their shields are too strong!" one of the surviving pilots shouted angrily. "We'll never get through!"

Anakin, in the meantime, was under attack once more. Another Federation fighter had found him and was giving chase. The boy jammed the thruster bars forward and sped down the hull of the flagship, twisting and turning through its channels and around its tangle of protrusions, laser fire ricocheting past in a constant stream.

"I know this isn't Podracing!" Anakin snapped at R2-D2, as the astromech droid beeped reprovingly at him.

But in his heart, it felt as if it were. A fierce glee rushed through him as he whipped the Naboo fighter along the length of the battleship. The speed and the quickness of the battle fed into him in a rush of adrenaline. He would not have been anywhere else for the world!

But this time his luck ran out. As he neared the ship's tail, a laser blast struck his fighter a solid blow, knocking it into a stomach-lurching spin. R2-D2 screamed anew, and Anakin fought desperately to regain control.

"Great gobs of bantha poodoo!" the boy hissed, fighting to stabilize his stricken craft.

He was hurtling directly toward the hull, and he pulled back on the thruster bars, cutting power and drifting into a long slide. He regained control too late to turn back, and pointed the ship toward a giant opening at the battleship's center. Cannon fire whipped all about him as the droids controlling the flagship's guns tried to bring him down, but he was past them in a microsecond, rocketing into the battleship's cavernous main hangar. Reverse thrusters on full power, dodging transports, tanks, fighters, and stacks of supplies, he struggled to keep his fighter airborne as he looked for a place to land.

R2-D2 was beeping wildly. "I'm trying to stop!" Anakin shouted in reply. "Whoa! Whoa! I'm trying!"

The Naboo fighter struck the decking and bounced, reverse thrusters powering up in an effort to brake the craft. A bulkhead loomed ahead, blocking the way. Anakin brought the fighter down on the decking with a bone-jarring thud and held it there, skidding down the rampway in a screech of metal. The fighter slowed and did a half turn and came to an unsteady halt. The power drive stalled and then failed completely.

R2-D2 whistled in relief.

"All right, all right!" Anakin gasped, nodding to himself. "We're down. Let's get the engines started again and get out of here!"

He ducked down to adjust the feeders to the fuel lines, checking the control panel indicators worriedly. "Lights are all red, Artoo. Everything's overheated."

He was working on the coolants when R2-D2 beeped suddenly in warning. The boy popped his head over the edge of the cockpit and looked out into the hangar. "Oh, oh," he muttered softly.

Dozens of battle droids were approaching across the hangar floor, weapons raised menacingly. Their only escape route was blocked.

Obi-Wan Kenobi prowled the front end of the service corridor to the melting pit like a caged animal. He was furious at himself for getting trapped so far from Qui-Gon and furious with Qui-Gon for letting this happen by rushing ahead instead of waiting for him. But he was worried, too. He could admit it to himself, privately, if only just. They should have won this battle long ago. Against any other opponent, they would have. But the Sith Lord was battle trained and seasoned well beyond anyone they had ever encountered before. He had matched them blow for blow, and they weren't any closer to winning this fight now than they had been in the beginning.

Obi-Wan stared down the length of the corridor, measuring the distance he would have to travel to reach Qui-Gon and his antagonist when the lasers paused. He had caught a glimpse of them deactivating while rushing to catch up with Qui-Gon, then of reactivating again in a matter of seconds. He would have to be quick. Very quick. He did not want the Master facing this tattooed madman alone.

Down the way, pinned between two walls of laser beams, Qui-Gon Jinn knelt in meditation, facing toward the Sith Lord and the melting pit, his head lowered over his lightsaber. He was gathering himself for a final assault, bringing himself in tune with the Force. Obi-Wan did not like the weariness he saw in the slump of the older man's shoulders, in the bow of his back. He was the best swordsman Obi-Wan had ever seen, but he was growing old.

Beyond, the Sith Lord worked at binding up his wounds, a series of burns and slashes marked by charred tears in his dark clothing. He was backed to the edge of the chamber beyond, keeping a close watch on Qui-Gon, his red and black face intense, his yellow eyes glinting in the half light. His lightsaber rested on the floor before him. He saw Obi-Wan staring and smiled in open derision.

At that instant, the laser beams warding the service corridor went off.

Obi-Wan sprinted ahead, launching himself down the narrow passageway, lightsaber raised. Qui-Gon was on his feet as well, his own weapon flashing. He catapulted through the opening that led into the melting pit and closed with the Sith Lord, forcing him back, out of the passageway completely. Obi-Wan put on a new burst of speed, howling out at the antagonists ahead, as if by the sound of his voice he could bring them back to him.

Then he heard the buzz of the capacitors kicking in once more, cycling to reactivate the lasers. He threw himself ahead, still too far from the corridor's end. He cleared all the gates but the last, and the lasers crisscrossed before him in a deadly wall, bringing him to an abrupt stop just short of where he needed to be.

Lightsaber clutched in both hands, he stood watching help-lessly as Qui-Gon Jinn and Darth Maul battled on the narrow ledge that encircled the melting pit. A stream of electrons was all that separated him from the combatants, but it might as well have been a wall of permacrete three meters thick. Desperately he cast about for a triggering device that might shut the system down, but he had no better luck here than he'd had at the other end. He could only watch and wait and pray that Qui-Gon could hold on.

It appeared that the Jedi Master would. He had found a fresh reserve of strength during his meditation, and now he was at-tacking with a ferocity that seemed to have the Sith Lord stymied. With quick, hard strokes of his lightsaber, he bored into his adversary, deliberately engaging in close-quarters combat, refusing to let the other bring his double-bladed weapon to bear. He drove Darth Maul backward about the rim of the over-hang, keeping the Sith Lord constantly on the defensive, press-ing in on him steadily. Qui-Gon Jinn might no longer be young, but he was still powerful. Darth Maul's ragged face took on a frenzied look, and the glitter of his strange eyes brightened with uncertainty.

Good, Master, Obi-Wan thought, urging him on voice-lessly, anticipating Qui-Gon's sword strokes as if they were his own.

Then Darth Maul back-flipped across the melting pit, giving himself some space in which to recover, gaining just enough time to assume a new battle stance. Qui-Gon was on him in an instant, covering the distance separating them in a rush, hammering into the Sith Lord anew. But he was beginning to weary now from carrying the battle alone. His strokes were not so vigorous as be-fore, his face bathed with sweat and taut with fatigue.

Slowly, Darth Maul began to edge his way back into the fight, becoming the aggressor once more.

Hurry! Obi-Wan hissed soundlessly, willing the lasers to pause and the gates to come down.

Stroke for stroke, Qui-Gon and Darth Maul battled about the rim of the melting pit, locked in a combat that seemed endless and forever and could be won by neither.

Then the Sith Lord parried a downstroke, whirled swiftly to the right, and with his back to the Jedi Master, made a blind, reverse lunge. Too late, Qui-Gon recognized the danger. The blade of the Sith Lord's lightsaber caught him directly in the midsection, its brilliant length burning through clothing and flesh and bone.

Obi-Wan thought he heard the Jedi Master scream, then realized it was himself, calling his friend's name in despair. Qui-Gon made no sound as the blade entered him, stiffening with the impact, then taking a small step back as it was withdrawn. He stood motionless for an instant, fighting against the shock of the killing blow. Then his eyes clouded, his arms lowered, and a great weariness settled over his proud features. He dropped to his knees, and his lightsaber clattered to the stone floor.

He was slumped forward and motionless when the lasers abruptly went off again, and Obi-Wan Kenobi, seething with rage, rushed to his rescue.

Nute Gunray stood with Rune Haako and four members of the Trade Federation Occupation Council as Captain Panaka, one of the Queen's handmaidens, and the six Naboo soldiers who had fought to protect them were marched into the Theed palace throne room by a squad of ten battle droids. The viceroy recognized Panaka at once, but he was unclear as to the identity of the handmaiden who accompanied him. He was looking for the Queen, and while this handmaiden bore a certain resemblance to her . . .

He caught himself in surprise. It *was* the Queen, without her makeup and ornate robes, stripped of her symbols of office. She looked even younger than she had in ceremonial garb, but her eyes and that cool gaze were unmistakable.

He glanced at Rune Haako and saw the same confusion mirrored in his associate's face.

"Your Highness," he greeted as she was led up to him.

"Viceroy," she replied, confirming his conclusion as to her identity.

That settled, he swiftly assumed the pose of a captor confronting his captive. "Your little insurrection is at an end, Your Highness. The rabble army you sent against us south of the city has been crushed. The Jedi are being dealt with elsewhere. And you are my captive."

"Am I?" she asked quietly.

The way she spoke the words was unnerving. There was something challenging in the way she said them, as if she were daring him to disagree. Even Panaka turned to look at her.

"Yes, you are." He pressed ahead, wondering suddenly if he had missed something. His face lifted. "It is time for you to put an end to the pointless debate you instigated in the Republic Senate. Sign the treaty now."

There was a commotion outside the doorway leading into the throne room, the sound of blasters and the shattering of metal, and all at once Queen Amidala was standing in the anteway beyond, a clutch of battle droids collapsed on the floor and a handful of Naboo soldiers warding their Queen against the appearance of more.

"I will not be signing any treaty, Viceroy!" she called out to him, already beginning to move away. "You've lost!"

For a moment Nute Gunray was so stunned he could not make himself move. A second Queen? But this was the real one, dressed in her robes of office, wearing her white face paint, speaking to him in that imperious voice he had come to recognize so well.

He wheeled toward the battle droids holding Panaka and the false Queen at bay. "You six! After her!" He gestured in the direction of the disappearing Amidala. "Bring her to me! The real one, this time—not some decoy!"

The droids he had indicated rushed from the room in pursuit of the Queen and her guards, leaving the Neimoidians and the four remaining droids with their Naboo captives.

Gunray wheeled on the handmaiden. "Your Queen will not get away with this!" he snapped, enraged at having been deceived.

The handmaiden seemed to lose all her bravado, turning away from him with her head lowered in defeat, moving slowly toward the Queen's throne and slumping dejectedly into it. Nute Gunray dismissed her almost at once, turning his attention to the other Naboo, anxious to have them taken away to the camps.

But in the next instant the handmaiden was back on her feet, any sign of dejection or weariness banished, a blaster in either hand, pulled from a hidden compartment in the arm of the throne. Tossing one of the blasters to Captain Panaka, she began firing the second into the depleted squad of battle droids. The droids were caught completely by surprise, their attention fixed on the Naboo guards, and the handmaiden and Panaka dispatched them in a flurry of shots that left the throne room ringing with the sound of weapons fire.

Shouting instructions to the Naboo, the handmaiden—if that's who she really was, because by now Nute Gunray was beginning to think otherwise—moved to the throne room doors, triggering the locks. The doors swung shut, the bolts engaged, and the girl smashed the locking mechanism with the butt of her weapon.

She turned then to the Neimoidians, who were huddled together in confusion at the center of the room, eyes darting this way and that in a futile search for help. All the battle droids lay shattered on the floor, and the Naboo had seized their blasters.

The handmaiden walked up to Gunray. "Let's start again, Viceroy," she said coolly.

"Your Highness," he replied, tight-lipped, realizing the truth too late.

She nodded. "This is the end of your occupation."

He stood his ground. "Don't be absurd. There are too few of you. It won't be long before hundreds of destroyer droids break in here to rescue us."

Even before he finished, there was the sound of heavy wheels in the anteway, then of metal bodies unfolding. The viceroy permitted himself a satisfied smile. "You see, Your Highness? Rescue is already at hand."

The Queen gave him a hard look. "Before they make it through that door, we will have negotiated a new treaty, Viceroy. And you will have signed it."

Free at last of the laser wall, Obi-Wan Kenobi charged out of the service tunnel and into the chamber that housed the melting pit. Abandoning any pretense of observing even the slightest caution, he barreled into Darth Maul with such fury that he almost knocked both of them off the ledge and into the abyss. He struck at the Sith Lord with his lightsaber as if his own safety meant nothing, lost in a red haze of rage and frustration, consumed by his grief for Qui-Gon and his failure to prevent his friend's fall.

The Sith Lord was borne backward by the Jedi Knight's initial rush, caught off guard by the other's wild assault, and pressed all the way back to the far wall of the melting pit. There he struggled to keep the young Jedi at bay, trying to open enough space between them to defend himself. Lightsabers scraped and grated against each other, and the chamber echoed with their fury. Lunging and twisting, Darth Maul regained the offensive and counterattacked, using both ends of his lightsaber in an effort to cut Obi-Wan's legs out from under him. But Obi-Wan, while not so experienced as Qui-Gon, was quicker. Anticipating each blow, he was able to elude his antagonist's efforts to bring him down.

The struggle took them around the edge of the melting pit and into the nooks and alcoves beyond, into shadowed recesses and around smoky pillars and pipe housings. Twice, Obi-Wan went down, losing his footing on the smooth flooring of the melting pit's rim. Once, Darth Maul hammered at him with such determination that he scorched the young Jedi's tunic, shoulder to waist, and it was only by countering with an upthrust counterstrike to the other's midsection and by rolling quickly away and back to his feet that Obi-Wan was able to escape.

They fought their way back toward the laser-riddled service passage, past Qui-Gon's still form, and into a tangle of vent tubes and circuit housings. Steam burst from ruptured pipes, and the air was filled with the acrid smell of scorched wiring. Darth Maul began to use his command of the Force to fling heavy objects at Obi-Wan, trying to throw him off balance, to disable him, to disrupt the flow of his attack. Obi-Wan responded in kind, and the air was filled with deadly missiles. Lightsabers flicked right and left to ward off the objects, and the clash of errant metal careening off stone walls formed an eerie shriek in the gloom.

The battle wore on, and for a time it was fought evenly. But Darth Maul was the stronger of the two and was driven by a frenzy that surpassed even the frantic determination that fueled Obi-Wan. Eventually, the Sith Lord began to wear the young Jedi down. Bit by bit, he pressed him back, carrying the attack to him, looking to catch him off guard. Obi-Wan could sense his body weakening, and his fear of what it would mean if he, too, were to fall, began to grow.

Never! he swore furiously.

Qui-Gon's words came back to him. *Don't center on your fears. Concentrate on the here and now.* He struggled to do so, to contain the emotions warring within and bearing him down. *Be mindful of the living Force, my young Padawan. Be strong.*

Sensing his opportunity slipping away from him and his strength waning, Obi-Wan mounted a final assault. He rushed the Sith Lord with a series of side blows designed to bring the two-bladed lightsaber horizontal. Then he feinted an attack to his enemy's left and brought his own lightsaber over and down with such force that he severed the other's weapon.

Crying out in fury, he cut triumphantly at the Sith Lord's horned head, a killing blow.

And missed completely.

Darth Maul, anticipating the maneuver, had stepped smoothly away. Discarding the lesser half of his severed weapon, he counterattacked swiftly, striking at Obi-Wan with enough force that he knocked the young Jedi sideways and off balance. Quickly he struck him again, harder still, and this time Obi-Wan lost his footing completely and tumbled over the edge of the pit, his lightsaber flying from his hand. For an instant, he was falling, tumbling away into the dark. He reached out in desperation and caught hold of a metal rung just below the lip of the pit.

There he hung, helpless, staring up at a triumphant Darth Maul.

When Anakin Skywalker got a look at the number of battle droids surrounding his starfighter, he ducked back out of sight again at once. If it had been at all possible, he would have vanished into the ship's fuselage and willed them both right through the hangar floor to a safer haven.

"This is not good," he told himself softly.

Sweat beaded on his forehead as he tried to decide what to do. He was just a boy, but he had experience with being in tight places and a cool head when it came to dealing with trouble. Find a way out of this! he admonished himself.

A quick glance at the main and sublevel control panels revealed that all the indicator lights were still red. No help there.

"Artoo," he whispered. "The systems are still overheated. Can you do something?"

Footsteps approached, and a metallic droid voice demanded, "Where is your pilot?"

R2-D2 beeped bravely in reply.

"You are the pilot?"

The astromech droid whistled affirmatively.

There was a confused pause. "Show me your identification," the battle droid commanded, reverting to rote.

Anakin could hear the sound of switches clicking and circuits kicking in. R2-D2 was still trying to save them. Good old Artoo. The astromech droid beeped softly at Anakin, and the boy saw the systems lights change abruptly from red to green.

"Yes, Artoo!" he hissed in relief. "We're up and running!"

He threw the ignition switches, and the fighter's engines roared to life. Swiftly, he leapt from hiding and took his place in the pilot's seat, hands reaching for the steering.

The droid commander saw him now and brought up his weapon. "Leave the cockpit immediately or we will disable your craft!"

"Not if I can help it!" the boy threw back, reaching for the deflectors. "Shields up!"

Hauling back on the steering, he released the antigrav lifts. The starfighter rose from the hangar floor, throwing off the droid commander, sending him sprawling in a crumpled heap. The droids under his command began firing their blasters, the laser beams ricocheting off the fighter's deflectors, angling away in a tangle of bright streamers.

R2-D2 beeped wildly. "The gun locks are off!" Anakin exclaimed with a joyful shout. "Now we'll show them!"

He punched in the firing buttons and held them down, rotating the fighter clockwise above the hangar floor. Laser beams rocketed in a pinwheel pattern, scything into the unprotected battle droids, disabling them before they could even think to flee. Anakin was howling with glee, caught up in the exhilaration of finding himself back in control. Lasers firing, he swept the hangar floor clean of droids, watching those still distant rush for cover, watching ships and supplies fly apart as the deadly beams cut through them.

Then something moved at the end of a long corridor, no

more than a shadow, and deep inside, his instincts kicked into high gear, shrieking at him in a frenzy of need. He didn't know if what he was seeing was a weapon or a machine or something else, and it didn't matter. He was back in the Podraces, locked in battle with Sebulba, and he could see what no one else could, what was hidden from all others. He reacted without thinking, responding to a voice that spoke to him alone, that whispered always of the future while warding him in the present.

Acting of its own accord, faster than thought, his hand left the laser firing buttons and threw a double-hinged switch to the right. Instantly, a pair of torpedoes sped down the corridor in the direction of the shadow. The torpedoes whipped past the battle droids, supply stacks, transports, and everything else, and disappeared through a broad vent.

The boy groaned. "Darn! Missed everything!"

Giving the matter no further thought, he swung the fighter about swiftly and threw the thruster bars forward. The power drive kicked in with a ferocious roar, and the starfighter shot across the hangar deck, scattered droids in every direction, and catapulted back out into space, cannon fire from the battleship chasing after it in a stream of deadly white fire.

Darth Maul walked slowly to the edge of the melting pit, tattooed face bathed in sweat, eyes wild and bright with joy. The battle was finished. The last Jedi was about to be dispatched. He smiled and shifted the remnant of his shattered lightsaber from one hand to the other, savoring the moment.

Eyes fixed on the Sith Lord, Obi-Wan Kenobi went deep inside himself, connecting with the Force he had worked so hard to understand. Calming himself, stilling the trembling of his heart, and banishing his anger and fear, he called upon the last of his reserves. With clarity of purpose and strength of heart, he launched himself away from the side of the pit and catapulted back toward its lip. Imbued with the power of the Force, he cleared the rim easily, somersaulting behind the Sith Lord in a single smooth, powerful motion. Even as he landed, he was drawing Qui-Gon Jinn's fallen lightsaber to his outstretched hand.

Darth Maul whirled to confront him, shock and rage twisting his red and black face. But before he could act to save himself, Qui-Gon's lightsaber slashed through his chest, burning him with killing fire. The stricken Sith Lord howled in pain and disbelief.

Then Obi-Wan turned, thumbed his saber off, and watched his dying enemy tumble away into the pit.

"Whoa, this is way better than Podracing!" Anakin Skywalker shouted at R2-D2, grinning broadly as he zigzagged his Naboo fighter back and forth to throw the gunners off.

The astromech droid was beeping and chirping as if he had fried all his circuits, but the boy refused to listen, rolling and banking the starfighter wildly, angling back toward Naboo and away from the control station.

Then a shocked voice came over the intercom from another of the fighters. "Bravo Leader, what's happening to the control ship?"

In the next instant, a flash of pulsing light swept past him. He glanced over his shoulder and saw the battleship he had escaped wracked by a series of explosions. Huge chunks tore away from the core, hurtling into space.

"It's blowing up from the inside!" the voice on the intercom exclaimed.

"Wasn't us, Bravo Two," Ric Olié replied quickly. "We never hit it."

The battleship continued to break apart, the explosions tearing through it, shattering it, engulfing it, and finally consuming it altogether in a brilliant ball of light.

Debris flew past the canopy of Anakin's fighter, and the light of the explosions faded to black.

"Look!" Bravo Two broke the sudden silence anew. "That's one of ours! Outta the main hold! Must've been him!"

Anakin cringed. He had hoped he might get back to the planet unseen, avoid having to explain to Qui-Gon what he was doing up here. There was no chance of that now.

R2-D2 beeped reprovingly at him. "I know, I know," he muttered wearily, and wondered just how much trouble he had gotten himself into this time.

Blaster shots hammered into the door of the throne room in the palace at Theed. Captain Panaka and the Naboo soldiers spread out to either side in a defensive stance, preparing a crossfire for the droids. Nute Gunray wanted to move out of range, but the Queen was still facing him, her blaster leveled at his midsection, and he did not care to risk provoking her into a hasty action. So he stood there with the others of the Trade Council, frozen in place.

Then abruptly, everything went still. All sound of weapons fire and droid movement beyond the battered throne room doors ceased.

Captain Panaka looked at the Queen, his dark face uncertain. "What's going on?" he asked worriedly.

Amidala, her weapon pointed at Nute Gunray, shook her head. "Try communications. Activate the viewscreens."

Her head of security moved quickly to do so. All eyes were on him as he slowly brought the outer screens into focus.

On the Naboo grasslands, the Gungan army had been over-run. Some of the Gungans had escaped back into the swamp on their kaadu, and some had fled into the hills west. All were being chased by battle droids on STAPs and by Trade Federation tanks. There was not much hope that they would remain free for long.

Most of the Gungans had already been taken prisoner, Jar Jar Binks among them. He stood now in a group of Gungan officers that included General Ceel. All around them, their fellow Gun-gans were being herded away by Trade Federation droids.

"Dis very bombad," Jar Jar ventured disconsolately.

General Ceel nodded, equally forlorn. "Me hope dis worken for da Queen."

Jar Jar sighed. And Annie, Quiggon, Obi-One, Artoo, and all the rest. He wondered what had happened to them. Had they been captured, too? He thought suddenly of Boss Nass. Da Boss wasn't gonna like this one bit. Jar Jar hoped he wasn't going to get the blame, but he couldn't quite rule out the possibility.

Suddenly, all the droids started shaking violently. Some be-gan to run around in circles, others to dip and sway as if their gears had snapped and their circuits shorted out. Tanks skidded to a halt and STAPs crashed. All activity came to a complete stop.

Jar Jar and General Ceel exchanged a confused look. The droid army had locked up. For as far as the eye could see, it stood frozen in place.

Gungan prisoners stared at the motionless droids. Finally, at General Ceel's urging, Jar Jar edged out of the containment circle and touched one of his metal captors. The droid tipped over and lay lifeless on the grass.

"Dis loony," Jar Jar whispered, and wondered what in the world was going on.

Obi-Wan did not pause to consider what it had cost him to win his victory over Darth Maul, but rushed immediately to Qui-Gon. Kneeling at the Jedi Master's side, he lifted his head and shoulders and cradled him gently in his arms.

"Master!" he breathed in a whisper.

Qui-Gon's eyes opened. "Too late, my young Padawan."

"No!" Obi-Wan shook his head violently in denial.

"Now you must be ready, whether the Council thinks you so or not. You must be the teacher." The strong face twisted in pain, but the dark eyes were steady. "Obi-Wan. Promise me you will train the boy."

Obi-Wan nodded instantly, agreeing without thinking, willing to say or do anything that would ease the other's pain, desperate to save him. "Yes, Master."

Qui-Gon's breathing quickened. "He is the chosen one, Obi-Wan. He will bring balance to the Force. Train him well."

His eyes locked on Obi-Wan's and lost focus. His breathing stopped. The strength and the life went out of him.

"Master," Obi-Wan Kenobi repeated softly, still holding him, bringing him closer now, hugging the lifeless body against his chest, and crying softly. "Master."

Three days later, Obi-Wan Kenobi stood in a small room of the Theed temple in which the deaths of heroes were mourned and their lives celebrated. Qui-Gon Jinn's body lay in state on a bier in the plaza just outside, awaiting cremation. Already the citizenry and officials of the Naboo and the Gungan peoples were gathering to honor the Jedi Master.

Much had changed in the lives of those who had fought in the struggle for Naboo sovereignty. With the collapse of the droid army, the Trade Federation's control over Naboo had been broken. All of the ground transports, tanks, STAPs, and weapons and supplies were in the hands of the Republic. Viceroy Nute Gunray, his lieutenant, Rune Haako, and the remainder of the Neimoidian occupation council had been shipped as prisoners to Coruscant to await trial. Senator Palpatine had been elected as supreme chancellor of the Republic, and he had promised swift action in the dispensing of justice to the captives.

Queen Amidala had outfoxed the Neimoidians one final time by pretending to surrender so she could gain safe access to the viceroy before he had time to flee. She had communicated to Sabé to break away from the struggle taking place several floors below and to use the service passages to reach the Queen's chambers and then make her appearance before the viceroy. It was a calculated risk, and Sabé might not have been able to get there in time. Had she not, Amidala would have triggered the secret compartment release and fought for her freedom in any case. She was young, but she was not without courage or daring. She had shown intelligence and insight from the beginning of the time the Jedi had come to assist her. Obi-Wan thought she would make a very good Queen.

But it was a nine-year-old boy who had saved them all. Even without knowing exactly what he was doing, Anakin Skywalker had flown a starfighter into the teeth of the Federation defense, penetrated their shields, landed in the belly of the Neimoidian flagship, torpedoed the ship's reactor, and set off a chain reaction of explosions that destroyed the control station. It was the destruction of the central transmitter that had caused the droid army to freeze in place, their communications effectively short-circuited. Anakin claimed not to have attacked with any sort of plan in mind or fired his starfighter's torpedoes with any expectation of hitting the reactor. But after hearing the boy's tale and questioning him thoroughly, Obi-Wan believed Anakin was guided by something more than the thinking of ordinary men. That extraordinarily high midi-chlorian count gave the boy a connection to the Force that even Jedi Masters on the order of Yoda might never achieve. Qui-Gon, he now believed, had been right. Anakin Skywalker was the chosen one.

He paced the room, dressed in fresh clothing for the funeral, soft, loose-fitting, sand-colored Jedi Knight garb, Qui-Gon's lightsaber, now his own, hanging from his belt. The Jedi Council had come to Naboo for the funeral and to speak again with Anakin. They were doing so now, close by, making a final assessment based on what had transpired since their last session with the boy. Obi-Wan thought the outcome of their deliberations must be a foregone conclusion. He could not imagine now that it wouldn't be.

He stopped his pacing and stared momentarily at nothing, thinking of Qui-Gon Jinn, his Master, his teacher, his friend. He had failed Qui-Gon in life. But he would carry on his work now, honoring him in death by fulfilling his promise to train the boy, no matter what.

Listen to me, he thought, smiling ruefully. I sound like him.

The door opened, and Yoda appeared. He entered the room in a slow shuffle, leaning on his walking stick, his wizened face sleepy-eyed and contemplative.

"Master Yoda," Obi-Wan greeted, hurrying forward to meet him, bowing deferentially.

The Jedi Master nodded. "Confer on you the level of Jedi Knight, the Council does. Decided about the boy, the Council is, Obi-Wan," he advised solemnly.

"He is to be trained?"

The big ears cocked forward, and the lids to those sleepy eyes widened. "So impatient, you are. So sure of what has been decided?"

Obi-Wan bit his tongue and kept his silence, waiting dutifully on the other. Yoda studied him carefully. "A great warrior, was Qui-Gon Jinn," he gargled softly, his strange voice sad. "But so much more he could have been, if not so fast he had run. More slowly, you must proceed, Obi-Wan."

Obi-Wan stood his ground. "He understood what the rest of us did not about the boy."

But Yoda shook his head. "Be not so quick to judge. Not everything, is understanding. Not all at once, is it revealed. Years, it takes, to become a Jedi Knight. Years more, to become one with the Force."

He moved over to a place where the fading light shone in through a window, soft and golden. Sunset approached, the appointed time for their farewell to Qui-Gon.

Yoda's gaze was distant when he spoke. "Decided, the Council is," he repeated. "Trained, the boy shall be."

Obi-Wan felt a surge of relief and joy flood through him, and a grateful smile escaped him.

Yoda saw the smile. "Pleased, you are? So certain this is right?" The wrinkled face tightened. "Clouded, this boy's future remains, Obi-Wan. A mistake to train him, it is."

"But the Council—"

"Yes, decided." The sleepy eyes lifted. "Disagree with that decision, I must."

There was a long silence as the two faced each other, listening to the sounds of the funeral preparations taking place without. Obi-Wan did not know what to say. Clearly the Council had decided against the advice of Yoda. That in itself was unusual. That the Jedi Master chose to make a point of it here emphasized the extent of his concerns about Anakin Skywalker.

Obi-Wan spoke carefully. "I will take this boy as my Padawan, Master. I will train him in the best way I can. But I will bear in mind what you have told me here. I will go carefully. I will heed your warnings. I will keep close watch over his progress."

Yoda studied him a moment, then nodded. "Your promise, then, remember well, young Jedi," he said softly. "Sufficient, it is, if you do."

Obi-Wan bowed in acknowledgment. "I will remember."
Together, they went out into a blaze of light.

The funeral pyre was lit, the fire building steadily around
the body of Qui-Gon Jinn, the flames slowly beginning to en-
velop and consume him. Those who had been chosen to honor
him encircled the pyre. Queen Amidala stood with her handmaidens, Supreme Chancellor Palpatine, Governor Sio Bibble,
Captain Panaka, and an honor guard of one hundred Naboo soldiers. Boss Nass, Jar Jar Binks, and twenty Gungan warriors
stood across from them. Linking them together were the members of the Jedi Council, including Yoda and Mace Windu. Another clutch of Jedi Knights, those who had known Qui-Gon
longest and best, completed the circle.

Anakin Skywalker stood with Obi-Wan, his young face intense as he fought to hold back his tears.

A long, sustained drum roll traced the passage of the flames
as they reduced Qui-Gon to spirit and ash. When the fire had
taken him away, a flight of snowy doves was released into a crimson sunset. The birds rose in a flutter of wings and a splash of
pale brilliance, winging swiftly away.

Obi-Wan found himself remembering. For his entire life, he
had studied under the Jedi, and Qui-Gon Jinn, in particular.
Now Qui-Gon was gone, and Obi-Wan had passed out of an old
life and into a new. Now he was a Jedi Knight, not a Padawan.
Everything that had gone before was behind a door that had
closed on him forever. It was hard to accept, and at the same
time, it gave him an odd sense of release.

He looked down at Anakin. The boy was staring at the ashes
of the funeral bier, crying softly.

He put his hand on one slim shoulder. "He is one with the Force, Anakin. You must let him go."

The boy shook his head. "I miss him."

Obi-Wan nodded. "I miss him, too. And I will remember him always. But he is gone."

Anakin wiped the tears from his face. "What will happen to me now?"

The hand tightened on the boy's shoulder. "I will train you, just as Qui-Gon would have done," Obi-Wan Kenobi said softly. "I am your new Master, Anakin. You will study with me, and you will become a Jedi Knight, I promise you."

The boy straightened, a barely perceptible act. Obi-Wan nodded to himself. Somewhere, he thought, Qui-Gon Jinn would be smiling.

Across the way, Mace Windu stood with Yoda, his strong dark face contemplative as he watched Obi-Wan put his hand on Anakin Skywalker's shoulder.

"One life ends and a new one begins in the Jedi order," he murmured, almost to himself.

Yoda hunched forward, leaning on his gnarled staff, and shook his head. "Not so sure of this one as of Qui-Gon, do I feel. Troubled, he is. Wrapped in shadows and difficult choices."

Mace Windu nodded. He knew Yoda's feelings on the matter, but the Council had made its decision. "Obi-Wan will do a good job with him," he said, shifting the subject. "Qui-Gon was right. He is ready."

They knew of what the young Padawan had done to save himself from the Sith Lord in the melting pit after Qui-Gon had been struck down. It took an act of extraordinary courage and strength of will. Only a Jedi Knight fully in tune with the

Force could have saved himself against such an adversary. Obi-Wan Kenobi had proved himself beyond everyone's expectations that day.

"Ready this time, he was," Yoda acknowledged grudgingly. "Ready to train the boy, he may not be."

"Defeating a Sith Lord in combat is a strong test of his readiness for anything," the Council leader pressed. His eyes stayed with Obi-Wan and Anakin. "There is no doubt. The one who tested him was a Sith."

Yoda's sleepy eyes blinked. "Always two there are. No more, no less. A master and an apprentice."

Mace Windu nodded. "Then which one was destroyed, do you think—the master or the apprentice?"

They looked at each other now, but neither could provide an answer to the question.

That night Darth Sidious stood alone on a balcony overlooking the city, a shadowy figure amid the multitude of twinkling lights, his visage dark and angry as he contemplated the loss of his apprentice. Years of training had gone into the preparation of Darth Maul as a Sith Lord. He had been more than the equal of the Jedi Knights he had faced and should have been able to defeat them easily. It was bad luck and chance that had led to his death, a combination that even the power of the dark side could not always overcome.

Not in the short run, at least.

His brow furrowed. It would be necessary to replace Darth Maul. He would need to train another apprentice. Such a one would not be easy to find.

Darth Sidious walked to the railing and put his hands on the cool metal. One thing was certain. Those responsible for killing Darth Maul would be held accountable. Those who had opposed him would not be forgotten. All would be made to pay.

His eyes glittered. Still, he had gotten what he wanted most from this business. Even the loss of Darth Maul was worth that. He would bide his time. He would wait for his chance. He would lay the groundwork for what was needed.

A smile played across his thin lips. A day of reckoning would come about soon enough.

There was a grand parade the following day to publicly recognize the newfound alliance of the Naboo and Gungan peoples, to celebrate their hard-fought victory over the Trade Federation invaders, and to honor those who had fought to secure the planet's freedom. Crowds lined the streets of Theed as columns of Gungan warriors astride kaadu and Naboo soldiers aboard speeders rode through the city to the sounds of cheering and singing. Fambaa lumbered down the avenues, draped in rich silks and embroidered harnesses, heads weaving from side to side on long necks. Here and there, a captured Federation tank hovered amidst the marchers, Naboo and Gungan flags flying from cannons and hatchways. Jar Jar Binks and General Ceel led the Gungans, both riding their kaadu, Jar Jar managing to stay aboard this time for the entire parade, though he looked to those in attendance to be having a bit of trouble doing so.

Captain Panaka and the Queen's own guards stood at the top of the stone steps in the central plaza, watching the parade approach. Panaka's uniform was creased, metal insignia on his epaulets gleaming, proud and strong.

Anakin Skywalker stood with Obi-Wan Kenobi near the

Queen. He was feeling out of place and embarrassed. He thought the parade wonderful, and he appreciated being honored with the others, but his mind was elsewhere.

It was with Qui-Gon, gone back into the Force.

It was with Padmé, who had barely spoken to him since he had been accepted for training by the Jedi Council.

It was with his home, to which he might never return.

It was with his mother, whom he wished could see him now.

He wore the clothing of a Jedi Padawan, his hair cut short in the Padawan style, a student in training to become a Knight of the order. He had achieved all that he had hoped in coming with Qui-Gon to Coruscant and beyond. He should have been happy and satisfied, and he was. But his happiness and satisfaction were clouded by the sadness he could not banish at losing Qui-Gon and his mother both. They were lost to him in different ways, to be sure, but they were gone out of his life. Qui-Gon had provided the stability he required to leave his mother behind. With the Jedi Master's death, Anakin was left adrift. There was no one who could give him the grounding that Qui-Gon had provided—not Obi-Wan, not even Padmé. One day, perhaps. One day, each of them would play a part in his life that would change him forever. He could sense that. But for now, when it mattered most, he felt all alone.

So he smiled, but he was sick in spirit and lost in his heart.

Perhaps sensing his discomfort, Obi-Wan reached over to put a reassuring hand on his shoulder. "It's the beginning of a new life for you, Anakin," he ventured.

The boy smiled back dutifully, but said nothing.

Obi-Wan looked off at the crowds in front of them. "Qui-Gon always disdained celebrations. But he understood the need for them, as well. I wonder what he would have made of this one."

Anakin shrugged.

The Jedi smiled. "He would have been proud to see you a part of it."

The boy looked at him. "Do you think so?"

"I do. Your mother would be proud of you as well."

Anakin's mouth tightened, and he looked away. "I wish she was here. I miss her."

The Jedi's hand tightened on his shoulder. "One day you will see her again. But when you do, you will be a Jedi Knight."

The parade wound through the central plaza to where the Queen and her guests viewed the procession. She stood with her handmaidens, Governor Sio Bibble, Supreme Chancellor Palpatine, Boss Nass of the Gungans, and the twelve members of the Jedi Council. R2-D2 occupied a space just below the handmaidens and next to Anakin and Obi-Wan, domed head swiveling from side to side, lights blinking as his sensors took everything in.

R2 beeped at the boy, and Anakin touched the little droid's shell gently.

Boss Nass stepped forward and held the Globe of Peace high over his head. "Dis grand party!" an exuberant Jar Jar shouted above the noise of cheering and clapping. "Gungans and Naboo, dey be friends forever, hey?"

His enthusiasm made Anakin smile in spite of himself. The Gungan was dancing up and down, long ears flapping, gangly limbs twisting this way and that as he mounted the steps. Jar Jar would never let the bad things in life get him down, the boy thought. Maybe there was a lesson to be learned in that.

"We bombad heroes, Annie!" Jar Jar laughed, lifting his arms over his head and showing all his teeth.

The boy laughed. He guessed maybe they were.

On the broad avenue below, in a long, colorful ribbon of life, the parade that had carried them to this place and time continued on.

ABOUT THE AUTHOR

A writer since high school, TERRY BROOKS published his first novel, *The Sword of Shannara*, in 1977. It became the first work of fiction ever to appear on the *New York Times* Trade Paperback Bestseller List, where it remained for more than five months. He has published fourteen consecutive bestselling novels since.

The author was a practicing attorney for many years but now writes full-time. He lives with his wife, Judine, in the Pacific Northwest and Hawaii.

ABOUT THE TYPE

This book was set in Galliard, a typeface designed by Matthew Carter for the Merganthaler Linotype Company in 1978. Galliard is based on the sixteenth-century typefaces of Robert Granjon.